A LONELY PLACE OF DYING

DI ROB MARSHALL
BOOK THREE

ED JAMES

OTHER BOOKS BY ED JAMES

DI ROB MARSHALL SCOTTISH BORDERS MYSTERIES

Ed's first new police procedural series in six years, focusing on DI Rob Marshall, a criminal profiler turned detective. London-based, an old case brings him back home to the Scottish Borders and the dark past he fled as a teenager.

1. THE TURNING OF OUR BONES
2. WHERE THE BODIES LIE
3. A LONELY PLACE OF DYING
4. A SHADOW ON THE DOOR (31st October 2023)

Also available is FALSE START, a prequel novella starring DS Rakesh Siyal, is available to buy on Amazon or for **free** to subscribers of Ed's newsletter – sign up at https://geni.us/EJLCFS

POLICE SCOTLAND

Precinct novels featuring detectives covering Edinburgh and its surrounding counties, and further across Scotland: Scott Cullen, a rookie eager to climb the career ladder; Craig Hunter, an ex-squaddie struggling with PTSD; Brian Bain, the centre of his own universe and bane of everyone else's. Previously published as SCOTT CULLEN MYSTERIES, CRAIG HUNTER POLICE THRILLERS and CULLEN & BAIN SERIES.

1. DEAD IN THE WATER
2. GHOST IN THE MACHINE
3. DEVIL IN THE DETAIL

4. FIRE IN THE BLOOD
5. STAB IN THE DARK
6. COPS & ROBBERS
7. LIARS & THIEVES
8. COWBOYS & INDIANS
9. THE MISSING
10. THE HUNTED
11. HEROES & VILLAINS
12. THE BLACK ISLE
13. THE COLD TRUTH
14. THE DEAD END

DS VICKY DODDS SERIES

Gritty crime novels set in Dundee and Tayside, featuring a DS juggling being a cop and a single mother.

1. BLOOD & GUTS
2. TOOTH & CLAW
3. FLESH & BLOOD
4. SKIN & BONE
5. GUILT TRIP

DI SIMON FENCHURCH SERIES

Set in East London, will Fenchurch ever find what happened to his daughter, missing for the last ten years?

1. THE HOPE THAT KILLS
2. WORTH KILLING FOR
3. WHAT DOESN'T KILL YOU
4. IN FOR THE KILL
5. KILL WITH KINDNESS

6. KILL THE MESSENGER
7. DEAD MAN'S SHOES
8. A HILL TO DIE ON
9. THE LAST THING TO DIE

Other Books

Other crime novels, with Lost Cause set in Scotland and Senseless set in southern England, and the other three set in Seattle, Washington.

- LOST CAUSE
- SENSELESS
- TELL ME LIES
- GONE IN SECONDS
- BEFORE SHE WAKES

CHAPTER ONE

The Stagehall Arms might as well not exist.

A Sixties block that should've been condemned in the Seventies but was somehow still trading. The owners didn't seem to want to attract any customers – the single light above the door didn't cut away at the darkness. Windows painted over. No sign outside. Rooms above the bar, but you'd have to be desperate to even consider drinking downstairs let alone sleeping upstairs. A decent walk from the main road through Stow, that nothing-y village somewhere between Edinburgh and Galashiels, and not far from the reopened train station, but it wasn't going to attract anyone from further afield.

Chunk sat in the cold van, waiting. Freezing his nuts off. He was always the one who waited. He preferred it that way – there are those who plan and those who do. Not that he minded the doing, but planning was where he excelled.

Didn't even have the radio on in case some old sod complained. The nearby houses were also dark. Down past the health centre and the primary school, a gang of lads played on the all-weather pitches – tonight's forecast was going to challenge that intention.

He tooted on his vape pen and got a nice burn of hash. Good stuff. Kept him mellow. Level. And he needed to be mellow and level.

He opened the door and stepped out into the cold night air. Aye, the magnetic GoMobile signs were good. Made it seem like they were installing a phone mast. They'd slip them off later and the police would be away looking for someone else entirely.

The pub's front door opened and a big man walked out. Hat and gloves. Big black coat that barely covered his belly. Narrow eyes scanning the area. He approached Chunk, making eye contact, then breaking it. Crossed the road, then walked around the van and got in the passenger side. 'He's still inside.'

Chunk hopped back in the driver's side. 'Cool.' He waited for the fat git to shut the door.

Baseball didn't. He just grabbed his bat and cradled it like a child with his blanket. 'Boy's gone radge. Shouting the odds at the barman. Won't be long— Aha.'

The door burst open and a man spiralled out onto the street. Stood right in the middle of the road, shouting and pointing back at the pub, his voice echoing off the nearby houses.

Baseball laughed. 'Bit early for that on a Wednesday, eh?'

'Burns Night.'

'Eh?'

'Tonight's Burns Night, you tube.'

'Is it? Doubt the Bard would be proud of that prick.'

Their target turned his back on the bar, then trudged on along the cold street. He stopped and shouted back at the pub. Curtains twitched over the road.

Chunk waited for them to settle again, then put the van in gear and drove off, following him.

Baseball kept the door open all the way, only widening it as they passed, trapping their target between the van and a wall.

He turned to face the van. 'What the fu—'

Baseball jabbed his bat in his face.

Caught the bugger right on the nose, and he stumbled back against the railings.

Baseball hopped out and tore open the side door, the metal rumbling as it slid.

Absolutely Baltic out there. Chunk reached over and shut the passenger door. He didn't need to do anything. Just had to sit there.

Baseball helped their target into the back, then slid the door shut. A thump on the wall behind Chunk. Then another.

Off we go.

Chunk slipped it into gear and drove off through the village. Not a panicked escape, but a leisurely drive. The kind that said, 'Nothing to see here, officer. Just fixing a phone mast.' Not that there would be any cops about at this hour.

Still, you didn't want to raise any suspicion.

Chunk stopped at the crossroads where a new bookshop was opening and took a toot on his vape stick. A bookshop? In this day and age? *Here?* The village was moving upmarket, that's for sure. The Stagehall Arms would soon follow, doing food and wine rather than beer and violence.

The A7 was empty so he lumbered over, past the post office and the café, then around the bend and up the steep incline, which the van wasn't too keen on. He hoped Baseball was okay with the angle of the ascent, and also the lack of speed. If he wasn't, he'd tell him.

Chunk passed the national speed limit sign at the end of Stow and took it to an easy forty as he headed up into the darkness, just his headlights lighting the frosted grass and stone walls hiding trees on both sides. The drum roll of a cattle grid, then he was following the bends, keeping to the exact middle of what passed for a lane. At least there were two here, unlike some of the roads nearby.

Really exposed up here – during the day you could see for miles to the hills in the distance. Now, though, Chunk managed to pick out some lights, but he couldn't even see Lauder up ahead.

A sign warned:

YOUNG LAMBS ON THE ROAD

Chunk just saw old sheep, huddled together on the other side. Must be freezing for the poor buggers. He saw the spot on the right, so he slowed and steered the van into the car park. He grabbed his head torch from the door pocket and it slotted onto his bonce. He left the engine running and got out into the freezing air.

He slid the side door open and Baseball was sitting there, cross-legged like some violent Buddha. His eyes flashed open. 'Alright?'

Their target lay on the wooden floor, hands and wrists tied together, mouth taped up.

Chunk reached for his ankles. 'Bagsy this end.'

'Mug.' Baseball grabbed his hands, then slid out of the van. Reached behind to slide the back door shut and almost dropped the target. 'How far is it?'

'Couple hundred metres.' Chunk reached up to switch on his head torch, making the purple heather glow red. Much less peripheral illumination and it didn't kill his night vision. Thing wouldn't be visible from four metres away, let alone all the way over to the road. 'Come on, then.' He set off, keeping a tight grip on their target's feet. 'What did you do to him?'

Baseball was stomping between the gorse and heather ahead. 'What do you mean?'

'He's out of it.'

'Just hit him with the bat.'

'That's it?'

'Saying I'm a liar?'

'No. Just maybe a bit less hard next time, eh?' Chunk spotted it, a little hollow surrounded by some big stones. Not far now. There. He let go and their target tumbled into the middle, landing face down on the heather. Chunk hopped in and turned him over so he was at least staring up at the stars. Checked the ankle and wrist bonds were tight enough.

Baseball was already walking back, relying on his phone torch.

Chunk made eye contact with the target. Didn't know the guy's name. Hoped he never learnt it. He gave him a shrug, which was the only thing he could offer, then turned and walked back to the van.

'Chunk.' Baseball's voice was a sharp call. His phone was off. 'Down!'

A car was hurtling along the road, fast enough to catch the police's attention. Fast enough to *be* the police.

Chunk turned off his head torch and ducked low.

The headlights swept over them, but the taxi drove on, its signage glowing in the night.

Big Man Taxis

Chunk waited for the red lights to recede. Took ages. Freezing and he didn't even have gloves on. Or a hat. Brassic.

The lights disappeared, leaving the swishing of the car's tyres on the gritted tarmac.

'Let's go.' Baseball's voice was lost in the darkness.

Chunk switched his torch back on and sped on towards the van. And its warmth. He opened the driver door and got in.

Just as the snow started to fall.

CHAPTER TWO

Rory Tait checked his watch. Eight o'clock, on the dot. And no sign of her. Hands gripped the steering wheel, though he wasn't going anywhere – the car was dark and silent, the engine off. The warm air still lingered, flavoured with the fresh fragrance tree – smelled like a new computer, that sweet piney scent you got from new electronics. Gorgeous. But like his mother warned him, it was probably carcino—

What was the word?

Carcinogenetic? Aye, the scent was probably carcinogenetic. But fuck it. He soaked it up all the same.

The park was all lit up, little cones of light focused on the benches dotted along the path at the side heading towards the playground. The fire station next door was cast in darkness. Snowflakes flashed in the lights, flurrying down to the ground. And it was lying. Always did in Gala – as soon as the snow was forecast, that was it. Expect delays. Disruptions. Massive ones. You'd think the town would be used to it, but nope. Every time.

Getting brutal now, actually. Could barely see the path or

the grass in those little bulbs of light, just the carpet of too-white snow.

Still no sign of her.

Aye, this was a mistake.

He should get back home. Leave her for another time. But it'd been such a long, slow build up and taken so much effort. And he might never get another chance. If he walked away now, she might change her mind.

He was gripping the steering wheel like he was strangling someone, so he let go. Just sat there, trapped by his indecision.

No – there she was!

Walking through the park, hood up, arms wrapped around her thin body. Jeans tucked into boots. Not exactly dressed for the snow. The offer of a lift in a warm car would be *very* welcome in this weather.

Was it her, though?

He got out his mobile and unlocked it. Opened straight to her Schoolbook profile. The photo he'd analysed so many times. Her bright eyes, her blonde hair, her school uniform.

She was perfect, unblemished like the snow.

He looked up again and tried to cross-reference the profile image with the figure trudging through the snow towards him.

She stopped three benches in and swept snow off the seat with a gloved hand, then perched on the metal, leaning forward, hands stuffed into her coat pockets. Breath misting in the air. Shivering.

The bench he'd suggested. Far enough from either entrance. He could watch her from over here and suss out the surroundings.

Aye, it was her.

Tait sat there for a few minutes. Watching, soaking in her innocence. Imagining things he shouldn't but couldn't help.

She swept her gaze across the park. Her head tilting

through the full angle, the sleeping cars like minute markers on a clock. She was looking for him. Getting fed up, maybe. Her hope diminishing.

He looked at her Schoolbook account again on his phone and felt a trickle of sweat running down his back. He checked the messages again:

See you there, honey xxx

That generation were obsessed with their text messages. To them, a full stop was like a punch in the mouth. Rory Tait remembered getting his first moby twenty-five years ago.

He read the message again and his mouth went dry at that word.

Honey.

He'd got inside her mind. She wanted him as much as he wanted her.

He reached into his pocket and touched the tube of lube, just in case. Then the knife, also just in case. And the Viagra pill – not that he needed it usually, but he didn't want to leave anything to chance. At his age and in his condition, it was a crapshoot, so he wanted to cut the odds. He picked up the bright-blue Tango Ice Blast he'd had to drive to the Spar for, up in deepest, darkest Langlee. He parked next to the bloody cinema – guess what they did in there? And the vape cartridges, the ones her mum wouldn't buy her – the reason for their meeting.

He took a glug of ice-cold water and set the water bottle back down.

Decision time.

Now or never.

Well. Now or another time.

But that queasy feeling returned – there might not be a

better time. She was here now, she was a fly in his web, but might not be that way forever. Anything could happen. He had her *now*. Forget about tomorrow or next week.

Now.

Fuck it.

He opened the door and got out onto the frozen street, then nudged it shut again. Could barely hear the cars on the main road. He tucked his hands into his pockets and walked over to the park entrance, his feet crunching on the brittle snow, the sound deadened.

He stopped in the entrance, in the darkness between two streetlights, and watched the snow falling. It was like he was in a film, meeting his beautiful girlfriend. Nervous and desperate.

He set off across the park, his hungry gaze focusing on her. Not far away now. He had to keep tearing his gaze away.

Didn't want her to see that hunger.

Didn't want her to feel like she had any power in this.

This wasn't her decision to make.

Didn't even look at her as he sat next to her, his heart like a thundering drum solo. 'Hey, Kelly.' He lay the vape cartridges down on the bench between them, then the Tango Ice Blast. 'How you doing?'

'I'm good.'

Her voice was different to what he'd expected. Deeper, without the softness of youth. Like she was putting it on.

He looked around and an adult woman sat there.

His gut squirmed. He reached for the cartridges.

She grabbed his hand. Tight. Firm. Squeezing. 'Rory John Tait, my name is Detective Sergeant Jolene Archer and I'm arresting you for child groom—'

Two big men appeared at the entrance.

Cops.

Fuck.

He wrestled his hand free and shot to his feet, then ran off through the snow, back towards the entrance and his car.

Something cut into his ankle.

He went down, spinning and rolling through the virgin snow.

He pushed up to his hands and knees. Something thumped his arse and he fell forward again. He reached out for the bench, touching the freezing metal, then rolled over.

She was standing over him. 'You sick bastard.' She kicked his balls and he squealed.

The big men were coming towards him. They must've seen that! The other two entrances were swarming now with cops. Someone must've seen it!

Tait raised his hands in the air. 'This isn't what you think it is!'

'It's precisely what I think it is.' Jolene had her cuffs out, reaching out to his wrist. 'You were going to—'

He jerked to the side and lashed out with his fist.

She danced back, then pushed forward, locking her leg into the back of his knee and pushing him flat down again.

His cheek touched the snow, pressing into the hard ground below.

The cuff wrapped around his wrist.

Fuck.

CHAPTER THREE

D I Rob Marshall sat back in the chair and yawned, closing his eyes. He didn't try to hide it, just let it all come out. Let it rasp, overtake his whole body, then it finished with an 'uhhh'. He opened his eyes again, licked his lips and looked across the table at Rory Tait.

Greasy dark hair slicked back, but silver roots exposed. Lines on his forehead like someone had scraped grout from between them. Tait wouldn't look at either Marshall or DS Rakesh Siyal. Hadn't even laid his eyes on his lawyer.

The guy was fucked.

And he knew it.

Marshall leaned forward. 'Sorry if it feels like I'm not enjoying this, but I really am. It's not often we catch someone like you in the act like that. Especially in the snow. You were either brave or stupid. Maybe both.'

Tait narrowed his eyes at him. Brown irises, but yellowy whites scarred with red. He'd done a lot of living in thirty-eight years.

Marshall waited for something. Anything. But he didn't get

it. So he folded his arms. 'Here's how it'll play out, Rory. Within minutes of this interview ending, you'll be charged with indecent communication with a child and attempted groo—'

'What?' Tait cracked his elbow off the table. Looked like it hurt too. '*Indecent* communication?'

'We've got all the messages between yourself and the child in question.'

'Indecent? I didn't say *anything* indecent and that woman was no child!'

Marshall gave him a few seconds of stony face. 'Oh, Rory, there were plenty of messages.'

'No!' Tait thumped the table. 'Check my phone!'

'We have, Rory. Online and on your device. Why do you think you—'

'There's nothing on there!'

Marshall laughed. 'Look, just because you delete a message on *your* app, doesn't mean it's deleted from the other user's phone. And it *certainly* doesn't delete it from the server. Police Scotland has priority access to Schoolbook for cases such as this. Grooming children.'

Tait's Adam's apple bobbed up and down. Swallowing down his guilt. 'I never sent anything!'

'You did.' Marshall nudged Siyal on the arm. 'Show him.'

Siyal slid a photo across the table, face straight. 'This is your penis.'

'No! It's not!' Tait didn't even look at it. 'This is utter bullshit!'

'You sent it to Kelly-Jane on Saturday night at one thirteen.'

'That's not my cock!'

'If it's not, then you've got access to a stash of photos of the same penis.' Siyal pushed another five pages across the table. 'They've all got the same mark on the left side.' He paused. 'I imagine that's actually on the right. Must've cut it somehow.

Masturbating, probably.' Another five sheets of the same member. 'Anyway. That's where our general warrant here comes into play.' He tapped the stack of paperwork. 'Allows us to take a picture of yours for comparison's sake. I'm betting they match perfectly. When you're in court, there's going to be a lot of discussion of your phallus. Photos of your plonker will go to every juror.'

'Fuck.' Tait slumped forward. 'Fuck.' He stank of sweat and second-hand booze. Twitching. Slicking back his hair. Staring into space.

Marshall let him stew in his filth for a minute, then cleared his throat. 'Going back to my previous statement, before I was so rudely interrupted. After you've been charged with that offence and a few others, you'll spend the night in the cells here, then you'll be shipped off to Selkirk to plead in the morning.' He raised his finger. 'You won't have to show your ding-dong in court at this juncture.'

Tait covered his eyes with his hand, slowly shaking his head.

'You'll be at His Majesty's Pleasure as a child molester. A convicted child molester.'

'I'm not! Christ!'

'We could sit around and talk about paedophiles, hebephiles, whatever. Get really technical about which flavour of nonce you are. Bottom line, though, is most people don't discriminate like that. Kelly's thirteen. She's legally a child. Because let's be honest, not even a jury of other child molesters would believe you were there innocently or that you hadn't sent her those unsolicited photos of your wanger. The evidence is super-tight. You're a child molester who was picked up for chatting up a thirteen-year-old girl online and for sending her photos of your John Thomas. Presumably you were drunk, but that's no defence. When you woke up, you probably had a visit from the Onion Man and—'

'The Onion Man?'

'Aye, the wee fella who sits on the edge of your bed after a night on the sauce and whispers into your ears about all the shameful things you did. He made you realise what you'd done, so you deleted the photos from your account. Thought you'd solved the problem. But it wasn't just once, was it? We've got photos of Wee Rory standing to attention on Thursday night, Friday *and* Saturday.'

Tait was digging the heels of his hands into his eye sockets.

'Thing you need to focus on, Rory, is that Kelly-Jane didn't know what to do with that message on Thursday. You obviously didn't notice any difference in her messages on Friday. What happened was she spoke to her mum and showed her the photo of your willy. And her mum, bless her, didn't hesitate in calling us. Since Friday morning, my colleague here—' Marshall patted Siyal's arm. '—has had control of Kelly-Jane's Schoolbook account. You were chatting to him, not Kelly-Jane. You declared your love to him. You sent him photos of your chopper. But you didn't know that, did you? Didn't even notice. Just focused on the desire for an underage girl to meet up. And you agreed to meet her in the park tonight with a Tango Ice Blast and the vape cartridges her mother wouldn't let her have.'

Tait sat back in the chair, glancing at his lawyer, but he was fixated on his legal pad. Tait slicked his hair back. Didn't say anything.

'Rory, we want to know what you were going to make her do in exchange for all of that.'

'No comment.'

'A kiss? A cuddle?'

'No comment.'

'Had you put something in the Ice Blast?'

'No comment.'

'We're getting it analysed by forensics. They'll find whatever compound you put in there.'

'No comment.'

'Or do you prefer it to be consensual? Keep them straight and then you know it's love?'

'No comment.'

'Okay. So you're playing it that way. Right.' Marshall sighed. 'I imagine whatever you were planning has something to do with a knife, lubrication jelly and a Viagra pill. Would've thought an alpha male like yourself wouldn't need medical assistance and you'd be very keen to demonstrate your prowess via the—'

'No comment.'

'Was she the first?'

'What?'

'Was Kelly-Jane your first victim?'

'No comment.'

'Do you always go for pubescent females or are you open to other ages?'

'No comment.'

'Is she the youngest?'

'No comment.'

'Oh God, is she the *oldest*?'

'No!'

'What about boys?'

'Fuck off!'

'Rory, I notice you're not denying any of this. Would you like to deny it?'

'No comment.'

'You don't want to offer an explanation, maybe go through how this is all some sort of mistake?'

'No comment.'

'Come on, I'd love to hear it. And you know, not mentioning it now could harm your defence, such as it is.'

'No comment.'

'If that's how you're going to play it, then we'll just have to charge you and prosecute you. Good thing for society at large is it means you'll be on the Sex Offender's Register for life. Means that any time something happens in this area of that sordid nature like, say, a child going missing or someone being raped, then you'll be spoken to. And people will know you're on the register. They'll know you tried to abduct a thirteen-year-old girl after you sent photos of your penis to—'

'I wasn't going to abduct her. Just wanted to speak to her.'

That actually seemed like the truth. Tait wasn't the sharpest operator, but he wasn't a caveman who clonked his victim on the head and carried them off. No, he was a case of arrested development – years of repressed sexuality trapped in amber, swallowed down by booze and pills. Not that it excused anything, but it helped Marshall crawl into the cesspit of his mind and see where he could be manipulated.

So Marshall sat back, arms folded. 'Just a nice wee chat, aye?'

'That's all I wanted. Just to see if it was genuine.'

'Genuine?'

'Aye. I was never going to go through with anything. Just wanted to warn her off. Tell her about the evils of meeting men online.'

'Fortunately, Rory, the law doesn't care what you were going to do, or not do. No, the law's pretty clear you can't invite a child to do those things for any reason, and you *certainly* can't show up like you did, with the knife, the lube, and the Viagra.'

Siyal cleared his throat. 'And the Tango Ice Blast.'

Marshall kicked the bottom of Siyal's chair, then cracked his knuckles. 'Rory, I've got a request to make.'

Tait looked up at him, mouth hanging open, eyes full of hope. 'What?'

'Rory, you're a drug dealer.' Marshall raised his finger again. 'Don't try denying it, please. We've got six separate witness statements that'll convict you on that score, over and above your child sex stuff. And drug offences are in an interesting place. They're going tough on them just now. But we both know, Rory, that you're low level in your organisation. A street dealer. How you sell from your flat on Scott Street. But if you were to give us some information on your supplier...?'

Tait's eyebrows shot up. 'I'll get off with it?'

Marshall laughed, arching back to bellow up at the ceiling. A performance, sure, but when he looked back at Tait, it seemed to have worked. 'Don't be daft.' He wiped a hand over his mouth. 'The procurator fiscal doesn't offer deals to child abusers. Especially for a locked-in conviction like this. This is a solid charge, one that'll help our statistics. And when we're finished digging into your messages, I bet we'll discover Kelly-Jane wasn't the only one you've been sending photos of your willy to.' He left a long pause, watching Tait sweating in the hot room. 'Rory, the best you can hope for is a lower sentence on the drug charges, with a placement recommendation that takes you to a better spot.'

'A placement recommendation?'

'One thing you're going to have to accept, Rory, is you'll be spending a lot of time at the pleasure of our new king. If you help us, we can get you into a prison that's closer to a Premier Inn than a Mad Max sequel. But it's only closer, okay? You won't feel like you're in a hotel, but you won't be in Barlinnie.'

Tait flinched at the name. Not that it was that bad these

days – still, hard-won reputations had a habit of persisting. 'Where are you talking?'

Marshall shrugged. 'Somewhere like Inverness, maybe.'

Siyal scowled. 'Oh, God no. I wouldn't go there. Far too many nonces...'

Marshall fixed him with a raised eyebrow. 'Sure?'

Siyal laughed. 'Oh, aye. Quite right. Mr Tait here would fit right in there.'

Marshall nodded along with it. 'Suppose we could suggest HMP Grampian up in sunny Peterhead.'

'Oh, it's new enough. Still got that fresh-paint smell and not too many child sex offenders have been killed there. Yet.'

Marshall scratched his chin. 'Addiewell would be an option, right?'

Siyal stroked his chin. 'Privately run and chances are nobody who Mr Tait knows will be there. More importantly, the chances anyone there knows him will be even slimmer.' He left a pause. 'And it's in West Lothian. Close enough to home that your family can visit you. Your wife and your daughter, for instance.' He frowned. 'Remind me how old she is, again?'

'You...' Tait swallowed something down. 'So I'd be able to go to one of those places?'

Marshall raised his hands. 'Depends on what you give us.'

Siyal scratched at the stubble on his chin. 'I mean, if it was me, I'd cooperate the hell out of this. I know I'm screwed, but the recommendation of getting one of those places... I could rest easy at night. Serve my sentence and get out again. Otherwise, I'd be risking one of the other prisons. I'm sure they're all great. Lots of friends to make. Chance to read books and do a ton of exercise. And you get to have sex three times a day, whether you want it or not.'

'Fuck you.' Tait banged both fists off the table. 'Fuck the pair of you. I'm not saying anything.'

Marshall smiled. 'So you're not going to play nice?'

'No.'

'Even though you've sent dick pics to a girl the same age as your daughter? Even though you tried to pick her up?'

'Fuck you.'

Tait wasn't going to bite. Just sat there, scratching at the table. No amount of twisting and turning would get him to open up. Not tonight, anyway.

'Well, Rakesh, can't say we didn't try. I'll give you one last chance in the morning, Rory. But you better wear your best court suit. Actually, it'll probably be Friday now, so you'll have the pleasure of spending the day meeting the great and good of Gala as they come and go.' Marshall took his time getting to his feet. 'Come on, Sergeant, let's get home. I've got a lovely new memory-foam mattress that's like sleeping on a giant marshmallow.'

Siyal opened the door and led them out into the corridor, then pushed it shut. 'Think he'll bite?'

Marshall shook his head. 'Someone like that, he'll be looked after inside.'

'Even if he's a nonce?'

'Even so. He'll deny it all forever, say we framed him, no matter how strong the evidence is. Trouble is, whoever's running the show for him would normally promise to look after his wife and kid while he's rotting away, and when he gets back out, he certainly won't be dealing again but he'll get some shitty work to do. Driving a lorry full of heroin from the Channel, maybe. He'll be expendable but he'll know he'll get looked after because he's already been looked after. Trouble is, he's a child molester, so it's possible he'll be cut free. And if he blabs, he won't live to testify.'

Siyal stared into space, shaking his head.

'Rakesh, I know this isn't exactly why you got into the

police, but it's another evil bastard off the street. That's very positive.'

The obs suite door opened and Jolene stepped out. 'Did well in there, Rob.' She patted Siyal on the arm. 'You too, Shunty.'

'You're the one who did brilliantly, Jolene.' Marshall smiled at her. 'You caught him.'

'Shunty did most of that. Who knew you could sound so much like a thirteen-year-old girl, Rakesh?'

Siyal shrugged. 'I watch a lot of anime.'

A shiver ran up her arms, goosebumps pockmarking her flesh. '*Freezing.* Going to get in the shower for like an hour.' She skittered off along the corridor. 'See you tomorrow.'

The obs suite door opened again and Pringle stepped out, clutching a white mug that read 'I wish this was gin'. 'You've left your effing mug!' He looked Marshall up and down. 'Oh. She's gone.' He handed the mug to Siyal. 'Make sure you clean that and put it in our special cupboard, would you? And thank you, Rob. I know you're up to your earballs in the Devil's earwax, but you stepped up to the all-you-can-eat buffet plate here.'

Marshall tried smiling through it all. 'This is DI Elliot's investigation, so I feel a bit odd picking it up. Shame she isn't here to see the results of her work.'

'We can't all go to strategic meetings up in Edinburgh, can we?' Pringle barked out a loud laugh. Tait and his solicitor would've heard it in the interview room. 'Anyway, it's time to learn the subtle art of delemagation, Rob. This is a chance to build up the skills of my team, vis-à-vis doing the things I don't enjoy like attending meetings.'

Marshall wondered which meetings would be coming his way in the ancient art of 'delemagation'. 'All the same, sir, it's—'

'Robert, the cold truth is Andi actually wants in on those meetings, so she can have it. Beside, this is a bread-and-butter case. Open and shut. A dirty nonce chatting up a child. You did the doings, didn't you? Supervised her team as well as your own. A teenaged lassie isn't being abused right now. And nobody expected her target to start chatting up a thirteen-year-old on Schoolbook, so we had no choice but to jump.'

Marshall was just glad he hadn't been delemagated to sit in on those meetings, which were as far from active policing as you could get. 'How do you want to play it now?'

Pringle clicked his tongue a few times, then laughed at some stray thought. 'We let him stew in his own juices until he's nice and tender. Mr Tait will soon appreciate that life inside as a sex offender isn't going to be all roses and champagne. Perhaps he'll reconsider our offer when his bumhole is large enough to stick twenty vape cartridges up.' Another laugh. 'Until then, we've got one less subhuman piece of shite to contend with. He's not going to be stealing any oxygen on the outside.' He whistled again. 'Thing is, the drug gangs we think he's involved with are pretty brutal. Gala's not that big a town, but it's getting worse and worse. Not just locals anymore – an Albanian mob were using a florist in St Boswells to smuggle drugs in. While we shut that down and the brewery in Selkirk, it's *still* coming in. One less arsehole on the street is a result we can be proud of.' He clapped Marshall on the arm. 'You can get off home, but don't do anyone I wouldn't do! Not that it leaves a lot!' He smacked Siyal's arm. 'This is your result as much as Andi's, though. You've been working your tight wee nuts off.'

'Thank you, sir.' Siyal raised his eyebrows, then checked his watch. 'I'm supposed to be heading to a Burns supper tonight.'

'That'll be tough for a vegan.' Pringle smirked at Marshall. 'How do you know someone's a vegan?' He paused nowhere near long enough. 'They tell you!' He laughed again. 'Supposed to be at one myself.'

Siyal frowned at him. 'Aren't you doing Dry January?'

'I am, but my take is the twenty-fifth is a free pass. Nobody in Scotland is dry on Robbie Burns day.' Pringle winced. 'Like I say, the worst part will be getting some decent food. Veganuary is a worse nightmare.'

Siyal smiled at him. 'How's that going?'

'I'd say your meal plans have been useful and saved my life this month, but I tried one and it felt like I was eating cardboard. And not the tasty kind!'

'What are you eating?'

'Chips.'

'Chips?'

'Aye.'

Siyal laughed. 'You're just eating chips all month?'

'Aye. They're vegan.'

Siyal's lips twisted up. 'Are you doing them at home?'

'God, no. Get them from McDonalds or the chipper.'

'Those are cooked in animal fat.'

'Oh, for crying out loud!' Pringle wrapped his arms around his torso. 'I'll have to go back to your cardboard meal plans! Thing is, Shunty, your people aren't good at that sort of thing.'

Siyal's eyes bulged. 'My people? You mean Indian?'

'God no! Glaswegian! You weegies could burn water, and you're stubborn enough to stick with it.' He clapped Siyal's arm with less velocity than a moment ago. 'Get yourselves home.' He strolled off along the corridor. 'I'll arrange for Tait to be charged in the morning. Let him marinate overnight.'

'Cheers.' Marshall watched him go. 'He gets worse, doesn't he?'

'Not my words, *sir*.' Siyal rubbed at his neck. 'Listen, I've been meaning to speak to you, Rob.'

'Oh?'

'I don't fancy you, if that's what you're wondering.'

Marshall hadn't. 'What's up?'

'It's just that... Like... I've been in the job a year and I need to know how I'm doing.'

'Thing is, Rakesh, I think you're doing fine but Elliot's your line manager. She doesn't give a shit what Doctor Donkey here thinks, so you'll have to discuss it with her.'

Siyal nodded, then walked off, shoulders slumped.

CHAPTER FOUR

'H-h-h-h-h-help.'

The snow swallows up the sound. Maybe I didn't even make it. I'm so cold. My lips must be blue. Another shiver erupts, sailing up from my stomach, up my chest and makes my teeth clatter together. I can still taste blood. Those fuckers hit me with a baseball bat. Jesus.

I try to speak again, but another shudder rattles through me. I'm lying on heather. Rough and scratchy. That's all I know.

'Help.'

I definitely heard that.

Definitely.

Shit.

Can anyone hear me?

What's that?

A light. A few hundred metres away, ghosting through the darkness. Two lights, in fact. A car? A car! The sound's softened by the snow, but it's crunching towards me.

I try to move my arms again, but my wrists are locked

together. Same with my ankles. At least if I can get my hands free, I can stand. Right? Then I can just hop over to the road. Can't be far. But it's... It's too tight. Whoever did this, they knew what they were doing.

The car passes in a blur of red, along with my hope.

It's a few hundred metres away. Not far. Not far at all.

I need to get up again. Get to my feet. But there's nothing to... No way to...

So cold. I feel it deep in my bones now. Another shuddering shiver rides up the whole length of my body.

Maybe I can just roll over there. I try that. One full turn. And I roll back the way.

Shit, I'm in some kind of hollow, like a golf bunker. But there isn't a golf course around for miles. Is it that one down by Gala? Torwoodlee, I think? No, the road's too far from that.

Actually. You know what? The air isn't *that* cold. The ground is. And the snow. But the air? It's not bad.

I'm not shivering anymore, so I give it another go at rolling. Almost, almost, almost.

No.

I tip back into the hollow. Facing up at the sky.

The falling snow looks so beautiful. Tumbling down in giant chunks, like parachutes. I stick my tongue out and taste the gorgeous, fresh flakes.

I'm warm now.

It's glorious.

Fucking glorious.

You know what? I want a flying saucer to come down and take me up. There must be tons of them flying around, everywhere. Using the darkness as cover, when there's nobody watching for them. Like in that film, where it was dancing around in the clouds.

Nah, I'll just keep going on this mortal coil. Wait this out.

I'm okay. It might be cold, but I'm not. Not anymore. I'll be able to wait this out until first light. If someone's using that road in the middle of the night, then hopefully more will use it in the morning.

They'll see me. Even if I just sit up.

I'll be fine.

I'll be more than fine!

And I'll find who did this to me. Catch them, turn the tables and do the same to them. Like that other film. The Korean one with the octopus.

Because nobody does this to me and gets away with it.

Or maybe dying won't be too bad. If this is it, I've had a good life. Good enough, anyway, to avoid going to the other place. I'll get to meet my maker. Have a nice chat with him. Reflect on the mortal life and the eternal life I'll now have.

But will I go there? Will I really? I go to church every Sunday. I say a prayer before bed. I've... I've been good.

I know I've been a bit naughty at times, but who hasn't?

Surely St Peter will see me as someone who has at least tried to do the right thing. And that's got to count.

I'll go to Heaven. I know I will.

Just shut my eyes now. Rest them. They'll need to be working well to take in the Almighty. Or I'll need to be refreshed for the morning when I track down the first cars.

I try to get up again and actually manage it this time. Thank God. I'll walk home now. Thing is, Mummy will be really cross with me. I've skinned my knee. It doesn't hurt, but I know I've ripped my trousers. She's going to kill me! The pain in my knee doesn't stop me from running, though. I'm running faster and faster and I'm so warm and toasty and the sun's in the sky and I'm climbing towards it and its rays are wrapping all around me like Mummy's cuddle and—

CHAPTER FIVE

Forget about snow piling up at the side of the road.

Here, it covered both carriageways. The bus Marshall followed along the road to Clovenfords cut ruts into the fresh powder.

He hoped the distance he was keeping was safe enough.

Working in London for so long – and in Durham – meant Marshall had forgotten all about winter in the Borders. It might be southern Scotland, but it was high enough above sea level to fit snugly into the Highlands. Which meant some years the snow lasted for months until spring thawed it all out. He hoped this wasn't one of them.

Bloody chucking it down now, giant flakes drifting until the bus's wake sucked them in.

Round that last bend and they were in Clovenfords. One of those blink-and-you'll-miss-it villages, stretched out on both sides like pizza dough, climbing up the hills it was wedged between.

The bus pulled in opposite the hotel, which looked warm

and inviting, but Marshall shot right past it then left towards home.

Their estate was covered in a thick crust of snow. All the houses seemed to look out on each other, giving no privacy.

He pulled up in front of the garage and the tiny flat he called home. It didn't feel like a home. Still, he didn't have to be here long, just a year or two until his sister and niece were settled, then he'd decide where to live his life.

The lights were on in the flat, and he could just about make out Zlatan's soft shape and sharp eyes looking down at him. Wondering why Marshall was stupid enough to go out in the snow.

Some of us have to work for a living, sonny.

The house itself was dark, just a light on in the back casting a glow across the snowy garden. Hard to make out the shape of it in the blackness, and he hadn't lived here long enough to etch it into his brain.

Marshall got out and scurried across the snow and took it slowly climbing the spiral stairs leading up to his door. His hands were freezing and he struggled to get the key in the lock, like some drunk on a Saturday night. He managed to get it open and the heat wafted out. Something snaked around his ankles.

'MERWM!' Curt enough to show how hungry Zlatan was.

Marshall dumped his laptop bag and kicked off his shoes, already soaking from the melting snow. 'Okay, sonny, just let me get myself straight.' He took off his coat and hung it by the door.

His tiny little place would be fine for a weekend's break in the Tweed Valley, but spending a year or two here...

Bollocks – either he'd left the bedroom door open, or Zlatan had forced it again to lie on his bed all day. Fair play to the lad – at least the bed still looked made from this morning.

The other door was shut, thankfully. He didn't want the big guy getting into the staircase that led down to the main house's kitchen.

He filled the kettle in the sink and set it to boil. Too late for a coffee, but a decaf tea would be fine.

Zlatan hauled his way up the cat climbing post in the window, back to where he'd been earlier. 'Meow!' He set off across the counter, rammed with the microwave, fridge and an air fryer Marshall still didn't quite trust.

He went over to the fridge and found tonight's dinner. Own-brand microwave lasagne. At least it wasn't the value range. He put it into the microwave and started it. Then tipped out some biscuits into Zlatan's bowl.

Cat ate better than him, that was for sure.

Marshall sat on the sofa, the only furniture he'd bought for the place. The only furniture he'd been allowed to buy. Or had space to fit it in. Glad he hadn't been the one getting it up those stairs.

He should put something on Netflix, but he couldn't be bothered. He reached over to the coffee table and lit the candle, dowsing the flat in a sweet vanilla scent. Place seemed like a home when it smelled nice.

His phone rang.

One day, he'd be able to shut that thing off when he left the station. But that wasn't today.

DI Andrea Elliot calling...

He still needed to update that contact card, didn't he? He answered it and sat forward in his chair. 'Evening, Andrea, to what do—'

'You arrested him, didn't you?'

Tait.

Right.

More territorial pissings from her. Either Jolene or her husband on the front desk at Melrose was the leaker.

'We did. It was a case of "speak now or forever hold your peace." Pringle supported my call to arrest and charge.'

'Congratulations.' She silently fumed down the line. 'These bloody meetings, Marshall. I can feel brain cells dying in that room. It's worse for you than drinking five bottles of voddy and smoking eighty a day in a room made of asbestos. What did you charge him with?'

'Usual. Leaving another interview until the morning. Why?'

'Just wouldn't mind having been there to see it.'

'You're more than welcome to take over.'

'I'll have a word with Pringle then.' Elliot sighed. 'Sweet dreams, Dr Donkey.' Click and she was gone.

Aye, that was going to help Marshall's shoddy sleep pattern no end.

He didn't give a shit about office politics but it gave several shits about him.

The microwave pinged and he hauled himself to his feet.

'JUST SHUT THE FUCK UP!'

The shout came from below. Even in the flat above the garage, he could still hear his sister and niece going at it hammer and tongs.

Just not usually this loud.

Marshall walked over to the inner door and unlocked it. He stepped out into the staircase and climbed down, emphasising each step.

Thea was in the kitchen at the bottom, squatting in front of the freezer. 'Well, I won't wait up!' She turned around to face him. Almost the same height as him but about a third of his weight. Her lopsided blonde bob showed she had an AirPod in one ear. 'Uncle Robert.'

'You can just call me Rob, you know?'

'Feels weird.'

'Right.' He smiled at her. 'Where's your mother?'

'She's out.'

'Again?'

'I know. Said she had a date after work. Straight out.' Thea nibbled at her thumbnail. 'Bit worried about it.'

'Why?'

'Just... Her dating again after what happened with Dad... It's a bit soon, don't you think?'

'Listen, I've known my sister all of our life and she doesn't take any sh— *nonsense* from anyone. She'll be fine.'

'Take your word for it.' She held up the tub of ice cream. 'Want some?'

'Got my tea in the microwave just now.'

'Okay, but do you want some ice cream, Uncle Robert?'

He smiled at her. 'Fine. I'll have some.'

Thea got out a couple of bowls and softened the tub in the microwave.

Marshall took in the kitchen – the yellow units needed a bit of refreshing, but only if you went up close to them. The table was far too big for the room but Jen was far too proud to leave it at their old place.

Thea scooped some ice cream out into the bowls. 'You could bring your Pot Noodle down and eat somewhere a bit more civilised than up there.'

Marshall took the bowl. 'Thanks.'

'Though "civilised" is stretching it when Mum's in a strop.' Thea sat on the bench. 'Which is all the time.'

The truth was, Marshall liked the family dynamic. Spending time with them, even when Jen was annoying, made him feel that little bit centred. And eating a meal with them avoided some rubbish from the microwave upstairs.

He smiled at her. 'Spoon?'

'Crap!' She slapped a hand to her forehead.

Marshall got them one each out of the drawer and had to pull the bench out on his side so he could get in. 'Who were you shouting at on the phone?'

'You heard that?'

'I think your granny in Melrose heard it.'

'My granny in Dumfries too.' She spooned the melting ice cream. 'It was Dad.'

'Right. What's up with your dad?'

'What's not?' She splatted the spoon flat against the ice cream. 'He's a selfish narcissist.'

'That's a tautology.'

She looked up. 'Eh?'

'All narcissists are selfish, so you don't—'

'Right. Smart arse.'

Marshall took a mouthful of his ice cream and let the salty caramel melt on his tongue. He tried to switch off the psychologist part of his brain – something that usually took wine or gin.

'It's good that you're speaking to him.'

'Is it?'

'Of course.'

'Thing is... I was supposed to go there tonight, right, but he's pulled out. Again. He's seeing another floozy. I mean, I know I shouldn't use that word, but...' She swallowed down a big mouthful of ice cream without tasting it. 'We never really got along but he is still my dad so I do want to see him. But when he doesn't want to see me? I mean... Jesus. I thought I was being disloyal to Mum, but it's not exactly hard to choose sides here, is it? Mum does everything for me and I'm *so* grateful for it. But Dad... He's...' Her head slumped forward over her bowl.

'Thea, me and your mother never really knew our dad. He buggered off when we were pretty young. Haven't seen him since. Not trying to say count your blessings, but it sounds like you're giving your old man a fair crack of the whip, which is all you can do. What does your mum—'

The landline blasted out loud enough to drown out his thoughts, let alone his words.

Marshall squinted at the phone handset resting on the sideboard.

Mum calling...

'Gran's the only one who uses that thing.' Thea grabbed her bowl and got up. 'See you later.'

'Aren't you going to get that?'

'I've got homework to do.' She sashayed out of the room and popped in the other AirPod.

Marshall dropped his spoon into the bowl with a rattle and walked over to pick up the phone. 'Hi, Mum.'

'Robert? Is that you?'

'No, Mum, it's Uncle Ian.'

'Cheeky sod. Is your sister in?'

'No, she's out tonight.'

'Right, right. Well, I was just checking to see if you're going to be able to make it?'

'Make what?'

'It's Grumpy's birthday tomorrow night.'

Their paternal grandfather. A mad old coot who was still clinging on in his nineties. And who did not give a single shit. Marshall loved him for it.

'I'll make sure we all make it.'

'That's brilliant, Robert. Thank you.' Click and she was gone.

Typical Mum...

Marshall picked up his bowl and ate the rest of his ice cream, watching the snow falling outside.

How could none of them know what happened to Dad?

'Dad' was stretching it.

That Nirvana song about trying to have a father but instead had a dad. Kurt Cobain had it the wrong way around. All their father had done was provide sperm that happened to be in the right place to fertilise two eggs at the same time.

Wherever he was, Marshall hoped their father was happy.

Maybe he should talk to Thea more about her dad before her irritation became full-blown daddy issues.

Hell, he should talk to her father. Sort him out – make him see what he was doing to his daughter.

His mobile buzzed in his pocket:

Motion detected!

He tapped the notification and a video filled the screen.

Someone was lurking on the exterior stairs. Hood up, thick coat on.

Marshall dumped his bowl in the sink and went over to the door.

Jen wouldn't let him install cameras that covered the whole house – and he'd listened to her – but there was no way he was going to leave his own entrance exposed like that.

He went out into the freezing cold and spotted footsteps leading over from the road. The metal resonated.

Definitely someone lurking out there.

Shite – was it an associate of Rory Tait?

Marshall crept over in his socks and started up the stairs.

Didn't have his baton with him or his pepper spray. Just his fists – they'd have to do.

He clambered up slowly, his feet freezing, fists balled.

Someone lurched out and kissed him full on the lips.

Kirsten stood there, wide-eyed and smirking. Her natural hair colour was back, the dark brown sucking in the light. 'You look like you've seen a ghost.'

'It's been a few weeks and...' His heart was still thumping from the threat. But it did that flipping over thing he still got every time he saw her. 'You could've texted me rather than just showing up.'

She laughed. 'Why, is your wife inside?'

'She's out at her book club with Megan, Claire, Sarah and Sarah.'

Kirsten rolled her eyes. 'All the Sarahs, eh?'

'I would've come and picked you up, that's all. Maybe treated you to dinner.' Marshall opened the door for the second time that night and went in. 'What brings you here?'

'Had a meeting about the refit at Gala. Basically, I'm going to have to sort stuff out as it's gone to shit since I moved back to Edinburgh. Sally's not exactly cutting the mustard.'

Marshall slid off his sticky, cold socks and walked through to the bedroom and tipped them into his washing basket. 'And Sally won't—'

Kirsten grabbed him and kissed him deeply.

CHAPTER SIX

A wall of white noise hit Marshall and he opened his eyes.

The clock read half past six. But the alarm hadn't gone off yet. Huh.

The door opened and light burst out of the bathroom, silhouetting Kirsten. She padded over to the bed and jumped on top of Marshall. 'Hey you.'

'Morning.' Marshall couldn't stop himself from yawning. 'How did you sleep?'

'This mattress, Rob. I want to marry it.'

'I thought you weren't the marrying kind of girl.'

'Well, I am now. Wow.' She flopped down and lay next to him, wrapping her legs around him. 'How did *you* sleep?'

'Like a log.' Another yawn grabbed hold of him. 'With a chainsaw in it.'

'That bad?'

'Lot going on in my head, Kirst.'

She fanned out her hair. 'You can talk to me.'

'It's... Just... Picking up Elliot's slack while she fannies about in meetings up in Edinburgh.'

'Tell me about it. The other reason I'm down here.'

'Eh? Those are drugs meetings, aren't they?'

'Drug investigations still need forensics. And Elliot is causing absolute bloody havoc with her complaints. Asking for the moon on a bloody stick. And getting it with two sticks, even.'

'So you're avoiding her?' He smiled. 'Mature.'

She play-punched his arm. 'Watch it, buster.'

'I'm half serious. But it is Elliot, so I'll let you off.'

'You know she put in a formal complaint about Sally, right?'

'No?'

'Elliot thinks she's a drunk. Which she might be.' Kirsten buried her head in the pillow. 'I hate managing people. It's just... Constant stress.'

'Aren't you getting any support for that side of things?'

'From James Anderson? Aye, right. He's not exactly hands on.'

'Okay. Never met the guy. Do you want my advice?'

'I'll take anything, Rob. I'm desperate.'

'Okay. "Sally, you've got two options. First, you get help for your addiction and we're all sorted. Second, I'll performance manage you out of the door." She either admits she has a problem, or if there isn't one in her mind then she's just shite at her job and you can boot her out.'

'That's cold.'

'Been a line manager for ten years.' Marshall shrugged. 'You're dealing with the bad, mad and sad triangle. Bad is that she's inept at her job, so you add training. Mad is she's a disgruntled employee, so you add discipline.'

'And sad?'

'There's some other noise in her life or just general interference, so you add therapy.'

'Don't get paid enough for this shite, Rob. Rather just help catch the bad guys.'

'You and me both.' He leaned over and kissed her on the mouth. 'I really like you being here, Kirst.'

'I like being here.' She put a finger to his lips. 'But let's just take it a step at a time, okay?'

'That's what we're doing, isn't it?'

'Felt like you were getting a bit too lovey-dovey.'

Marshall swallowed something down. Felt like he was doing a lot of that. 'I'm not going to change who I am.'

'I know. And I'm not either. Look, the reason I haven't seen you for two weeks is... Well, you were staying at mine every night or I was staying here for, like, two weeks.'

'That's okay, isn't it?'

'Is it?' She shook her head, hair scraping against her pillow. 'I just don't know, Rob. I just don't know.'

That same impasse. They were both stubborn sods.

Marshall reached over and stroked her arm. 'Okay, we've both got work today, but how about getting something to eat tonight. Go down to the hotel. The food in there's really good. Good beer and wine too.'

She smiled. 'Let's do that.'

Marshall's mobile blasted out.

He groaned as he rolled over. 'A phone call at this time is *never* good.' He grabbed it off the charging mat and checked the display, hoping it was about being in a car accident that wasn't his fault.

DCI James Pringle calling...

Aye, scratch that hope.

Marshall lay down and answered. 'Morning, sir. What's up?'

'Got a suspicious death taking the high road between Stow and Lauder. Need your arse up there, tout suite.'

CHAPTER SEVEN

Marshall stepped off the bottom rung of the staircase and his welly crunched into crisp snow. He felt the cold through the sole. 'Sorry, but there'll be wellies in your size at the station.' He hurried across the dark drive towards his car.

Kirsten came to a crunching halt next to him. 'Yeah, your roller skate isn't going to cut it.'

Marshall's car might've been great on the streets of London, but it wasn't cut out for a Borders winter. And it was covered in about a foot of snow.

Unlike Jen's SUV...

Some pheasant and cat prints dotted the garden. He peered into the house. No sign of anyone inside. Thea would be getting up soon, but Jen would usually have a pot of coffee on the go by now.

'Hey, you two.'

Marshall swung around.

Jen was hopping down from her VW Tiguan. 'Good to see

you.' She crunched over and wrapped her arms around Kirsten. 'What's up?'

'Called out to a case, Jen.' Marshall frowned at her. 'Where have you been?'

'Me? Just been to get some bacon and rolls from the shop in Gala.'

Marshall didn't mention the lack of human prints in the snow – her love life and her daddy issues were none of his business. Until it was. 'Would I be able to—'

'You look like you've had some bedroom action.' Kirsten was smiling at Jen. 'Right?'

Jen deflected it back with a sly wink. 'You two can talk.'

'Least we're open about it.'

'Aye, to me.' Jen yawned into her fist. 'Anyway. Bacon rolls?'

'Not today, thanks.' Marshall pointed at the car. 'Jen, I need to get up to the Stow-Lauder road. Any chance I can borrow your car?'

Jen raised her eyebrows and rolled her tongue across her teeth. 'Rob, I've got a four-by-four because nurses need to get to work whatever the weather.' She prodded a finger into his chest. 'Like cops do. Your roller skate here isn't going to cut it, is it?'

Marshall swallowed down the anger about his choice of car. 'Jen. Please. I'm desperate.'

She sighed. 'You can take it, but on one condition.'

'Deal.'

'You didn't ask what the condition is.'

'Jen!'

'Right.' Jen held up her mobile. 'Got a text. School's closed today, so I need you to drop Thea at Mum's on—'

'I can't do that!'

'Come on, Rob. I'm doing you a massive—'

'I'll do it.' Kirsten crunched across the snow. 'Jen, you drive Rob up, then I'll take Thea over to Melrose.'

CHAPTER EIGHT

Jen drove along the Stow-Lauder road, the long ridge running between the villages. Still dark, with no sign of the sun rising, just the occasional flash of sheep huddled together on the moorland. Lights twinkled on the hills in the distance.

She pulled in at the start of the convoy of police cars, pretty far away from the centre of the action. 'Here.'

'Thank you for dropping me off.'

'Don't mention it.' Jen sighed. 'See you later.'

Marshall opened the door and got out of Jen's car into the freezing cold, gripping his bag and wrapping his jacket extra tight. Didn't help any.

Jen shot off along the road, going way too fast.

Aye, he was going to pay for that.

Marshall stepped through the virgin snow towards a groove cut through it, the result of scores of feet trampling across to the crime scene.

The CSI tent was glowing in the morning gloom, flapping in the stiff breeze up here. A few hundred metres from the road.

Marshall trudged on across the snow towards it. Hard going and so bloody cold. His phone torch wasn't cutting it, but the one thing a pool car would be good for was all the crap in the boot, including a military flashlight that would light up the moon. What he wouldn't give for one just now. A packet of Refreshers or half a Mars bar.

He stopped outside and took the log from the crime scene manager. 'How're ye?' A big guy, with thick stubble and a thicker Dublin accent.

Marshall didn't recognise him – he needed to remedy that, couldn't be a DI who didn't know at least three personal things about each member of the wider team.

Then it clicked.

Marshall smiled at him. 'Liam, right?'

'PC Liam Warner at your service, sir.' He nodded slowly, his eyes glowing. 'Glad you remember me, sir.'

'We worked on a case three months ago, right? Down near Hawick. I try to remember everyone I've worked with.'

'Oh, right. Yeah, sure. That's a good way to be, sir. Some of them here, they don't act the same way.'

The police tape was flapping in the wind, but the movement didn't seem to be raising the temperature any.

'That's something that needs to be remedied then.' Marshall smiled at him and handed the clipboard back, then stepped through. Not far to the inner locus, with a much bigger operation securing the scene.

Someone was glowering at him, half in a suit. DS Jolene Archer. 'Boss?'

'Morning, Jolene.' Marshall grabbed one from the stack and stepped into the trousers. Easier said than done with size thirteen wellies on, which were covered in snow. 'Absolutely perishing up here.'

'I've still not got warm from last night.'

'Last night?' Marshall frowned. Then he got it. 'Ah, right. Tait.'

She nodded. 'Heard they charged him with seven counts.'

'Good.'

She was still scowling. 'Who was that who dropped you off?'

'Oh, nobody.' Marshall swallowed. 'My sister's car.'

'Ah, okay.'

Spies everywhere...

'Did you get the pool car?'

'The Land Rover, yeah. Don't really know how to drive it but it seems fine.'

'Good.' Marshall finished doing up the zip. 'What have we got here, then?'

'Body in the snow, Rob.' Jolene snapped her goggles to her forehead and secured her mask on her chin. Already speckled with snow.

Marshall attached his goggles and mask to his head. Bastard things never fitted him properly. He took in a deep breath. 'Let's see then.'

Jolene signed them in and entered the tent first.

A few people in there, one of them whistling like a drunk uncle. Pringle. He winked at Marshall and gave a drunk uncle's camera-shutter click. 'Time was, a murder down these parts would be a once-in-a-decade thing...'

Marshall ignored the five or six others in there and squatted next to the body, just as a camera flashed.

A woman lying face down, the snow covering her clothes and much of the heather. Her head was buried in the stuff – it hadn't melted from her body heat, though those arc lights would do the job soon enough. She wore a little black dress. No sign of her shoes. Or a coat.

Pringle snorted. 'Okay, Sally, are you happy to lift her out?'

A crouching figure looked up. 'Sure thing. Trev? Jay?'

Two big lumps knelt down at either end of the body, while the photographer aimed his camera. They lifted and flipped her over onto her back.

Marshall got a better look at her. Pale face, but blood on her nose and lips. Raven hair, shoulder length.

'Oh, shit!' Sally stepped into the hollow and bent down.

A second body lay there, no longer underneath her. A man. Jeans, T-shirt and a thin jacket. Adidas trainers. Not exactly dressed for the elements either. His nose was flattened like pastry and spattered with tomato ketchup.

'Let's have a look at this guy, then.' South African accent. Meaning Dr Belu Owusu. She stood there, but her eyes were flashing all over the corpse.

Marshall looked at both of the bodies, some aspect of his training forcing him to focus on the aggregate, on similarities and differences, rather than treating them as individuals. The main thing he noticed was both were bound at the ankles and wrists.

'My god. It's like they've been dumped and left here.' Owusu voiced his thoughts. 'Give me a second, guys.'

Marshall watched her go about her work. 'Have they frozen to death or did they die first?'

'That's what I'll find out.'

Marshall felt that throbbing in his skull. Questions were piling up here and he needed to answer some. He focused on Sally as she checked through the male victim. 'Any ID? Wallet, purse?'

'Can't see anything, sorry.' She took her gloved hands away from the male's pockets. 'He looks so peaceful. Almost like he's smiling. Despite the broken nose.'

She was right – whoever he was, he was very well preserved and definitely had a smile filling his face.

Marshall got out his phone and took a photo. Looked pretty good, nowhere near bad enough to worry about a complaint when he showed it to anyone. He reached over to snap one of the woman.

'You don't need to do that, Rob.' Owusu pointed at the body. 'I know her. Dr Louisa Baird. She's an oncologist at Borders General.'

'Okay.' Marshall nodded at Jolene. 'We need to get out there and speak to people. But we also need to identify the second victim.'

'On it, Rob.' She left the tent.

'Gadzooks.' Pringle got to his feet with a few clicks and followed her out of the tent.

Marshall didn't feel like he had much choice but to do likewise. Outside, he tore off his goggles, thick with steam, and the mask, letting him breathe in the fresh, cold air again. Jolene was crunching across the dark snow towards the hub of activity by the cars.

'Dr Marshall, there's obviously a connection here. But... what?' Pringle put a hand to his chin.

'Let's focus on identifying him first, sir.'

'Drugs.'

Marshall savoured the cold on his face. 'You think this is drug-related?'

'Yes, I do. Yes, I do do do.' Pringle was already unzipping his suit. 'We have a problem with drugs down here in the sticks, you know. If one was to get too deep in debt by, say, getting high on your own supply, then you very swiftly become...' He whistled and dragged a finger across his throat. 'Persona non grata. Gangs often beat the crap out of people and drop them in the wilds, then let them walk back to town. Next time they do it, it'll be that bit further out. They usually get the message after that. And if they don't...'

Marshall could see it, but he could also see a hundred other explanations. 'I want us to keep an open mind on this lot, sir. Could be any number of explanations.'

'But it's clear someone killed them, right?'

'Very. Who found them?'

Pringle let his suit hang free and cupped his hands around his mouth. 'Shunty!'

A snowy figure wandered over, wrapped up in several layers. A fragment of Siyal's face poked out of his hood. 'What's up, sir?'

'Where's the boy who found them?'

'What about him?' Siyal frowned. 'Wait. *Them?* I thought it was a woman not a non-binary—'

'No, Shunty. Plural them. It's a woman. Female oncologist at Borders General. But she was lying on top of a man.'

'Oh.' Siyal's frown deepened. 'Just finished speaking to the man who found them.' He thumbed behind him. 'Jim Thompson. Lives in Clovenfords. Just driving through to catch a train from Berwick to London, which he was never going to.' His lips twisted together. 'Wonder if I should speak to the train company and get his ticket refunded.'

Pringle laughed. 'Shunty, give him the crime number and let him do the working.'

'But he's helping us, sir. And I have offered him a lift to Berwick.'

'You *what?*' Pringle shut his eyes. 'Come on.' He grabbed Siyal's sleeve and led him away. 'Let's see if he recognises the victims.'

Marshall was going to follow them, but Jolene was waving at him, just by the long row of cars, so he trudged over to her. Heavy going and it felt like it was getting worse, despite the clear conditions. Must've been the cold wind drifting it. 'What's up?'

'The guy who manages the site has just turned up.'

'What site? It's a sheep farm.'

She pointed south. 'See them?'

The sky was starting to lighten to a brash purple and the whole landscape was a white Christmas, just a month late. The range of hills was like a wedding cake, the snow all smoothed out by the wind. Three wind turbines stood there like giant statues, their blades moving in the breeze. A fourth was just half a central nacelle with no sign of any ... on a plane it'd be a propeller, but here... He had no idea. Work was going on nearby, presumably the base for a fifth. A large area was fenced off – this was going to be a sizeable operation when it was finished.

'Okay, I see now. He's managing a wind farm.'

'Aye. An active installation. Remember the stramash in the papers about it. This is a notoriously difficult area to get planning for that kind of thing. Low-fly area here and tons of NIMBYs around.' She set off towards the road and a man leaning against a Range Rover. 'Mr Talbot?'

'That's me, aye.' Tall guy, dressed for the weather in at least three layers, so hard to tell how big he was. A thick scarf covered his throat. Green bobble hat. Arms folded, the fingers of his thick gloves flexing. He lifted his hat and showed silvery hair, spiked like it was the Nineties. A long cut on his temple, fresh but scabbed over. His dark eyes stared at her, then followed her gaze up to his forehead. He pulled the hat down. 'Got into an argument with a rotor blade.' Right, that was it – a rotor. 'The blade won.' He laughed, then waved a hand at the turbines. 'Still, the beautiful beast spinning away is quite the thing now, eh?'

If Marshall had to place his accent, he'd guess at a low G postcode – inner Glasgow. 'You're not local, right?'

'Govan born and bred, aye. Much nicer now, though, eh no?

Commute down here on a Monday morning and stay in a cara-van.' Another wave towards the work site. 'Too cold right now, so I'm in the Stagehall Arms in Stow. Not great but it's cheap enough and mostly warm.'

Marshall gave Talbot a smile. 'Doing a good job by the looks of it.'

'Tell that to the boss, eh?' Talbot chuckled. 'Do these all over Scotland. Did another one on the hills to the south a few years back. One turbine there supplies all the electricity in Stow. Another does most of Gala and all the money from it goes to the community here. This new lot is next-generation and will do most of the central Borders and southern Midlothian once it's all up and running.'

Marshall raised his eyebrows. 'That seems adventurous.'

'Not really. Hardly any people live there but this lot are absolute monsters. I won't bore you with the technical details, but they generate a lot. Halfway through, but. Should've finished in October, but we've had to delay it into winter because of issues with the Chinese manufacturing. Bit of covid shutting down the factory, then a royal pain in getting all the parts here within six months, but. Tell you, we should be building them in this country, but hey ho, who am I? Just some numpty from Govan who installs the buggers. Getting double the money for this one, so not a bad thing, but being out in this weather... Ten times wouldn't be enough. Total nightmare, but the landowner won't listen.'

'That'll be Blainslieshaw Mains, aye?' Pringle had appeared from somewhere, rubbing his hands together and smiling at him.

Talbot took a step back from him and kept them both equally distant. 'That's right. Napier Rattray.'

Marshall felt that little tickle at the back of his neck. 'I know his son from school.'

Pringle screwed up his face. 'You were at school with Balfour Rattray?'

'Aye.' Marshall could see this being another Pringle rabbit hole, so he focused on Talbot. 'How many people have you got working here?'

'Sixteen. We going to get out today?'

Marshall waved at the snow. 'You're going to work in this?'

'Time and tide waits for no man, and all that.' Talbot shifted his gaze between them. 'Mate, if we're not working, I need to get on the phone and tell the team. Then explain to the boss.' His eyes settled on Marshall. 'So?'

'Not my call.' Marshall gestured to Pringle. 'Sir?'

'Aye, just so long as you keep speaking to my guys.' Pringle waved over at the site. 'Do you have any security cameras over there?'

'Just got them inside to make sure the tools don't go walkies.'

'We'd still appreciate access to it.'

'Not a problem. And thank you.' Talbot walked off and took out his mobile. Then eased off his gloves with his teeth.

Jolene had her phone out. 'I'll get on top of that, sir.' She walked off, calling someone.

Pringle was watching Talbot talking on the phone. 'What's your thinky here, Doctor Donkey?'

Marshall shrugged. 'He's a guy who works here, right? Doesn't know anything.'

'Okay, but I was asking you about...' Pringle sighed. 'Young man, you're going to have to explain why the offspring of a landowner is going to a comprehensive school with you.'

'What's that supposed to mean?'

'Well, you didn't come from money.'

'I was raised by a single mother, if that's what you mean. There's no stigma attached now, sir.' Marshall felt the blood tickling his veins. The trick to dealing with Pringle was to just wind him up and keep winding him up until he found some new shiny. 'Truth is, Napier tried to avoid all pretension by sending his son to a comprehensive. Remember him coming in to talk at an assembly once. "Being nobility should mean acting nobly and not acting like a knob." Got a big laugh from the kids, but not from the teachers. Truth is, Balf had been expelled from Edinburgh Academy and St Mary's in Melrose, so he didn't really have a choice.'

'That's *an* explanation, I suppose.'

A car pulled up not far away from them. DC Jim McIntyre was behind the wheel, practically filling the driver's side.

Kirsten got out of the passenger door. She jogged over to them. 'Morning, gents.'

Pringle looked her up and down. 'To what do we owe the pleasure?'

'I'm going to muck in and make sure we avoid any more complaints.'

'A-well-ah, well-ah, well-ah.' Pringle smiled. 'I appreciate it.'

'Thankfully caught Jim McIntyre at the station.' Kirsten stomped her wellies. 'Gather Shunty isn't permitted to drive in this weather...'

Pringle laughed. 'Not after last time, no. Or the time before.'

'McIntyre says Shunty insists he delegated driving to McIntyre. Quoting you, Sir Pringle.'

'Cheeky beggar.'

'See you later.' Kirsten set off towards the tent. 'I'll get the body shifted to Borders General.'

'Good having some competence on the case...' Pringle leaned in close. 'You're in charge here, okay? I'm happy to PUFO.'

Pick up, fuck off.

Aye, Marshall didn't need to be told twice. 'Will do what I can, sir.'

'I know you're used to tracking serial offenders and this is obviously another serial—'

'No, sir. This technically isn't a serial killer. It's barely a spree killer.' Marshall tried to slow down. Stop winding him up. Just deal in facts. 'No, it is a spree. Two in close proximity in the same location. But I can't profile that. This case has two bodies and no leads...'

Pringle clapped his arm. 'You'll have to do the shoe leather work most cops have done on the way up.'

'Are you—'

'Jim!' Dr Owusu emerged from the crime scene tent and Pringle practically skipped across the snow to meet her.

Marshall followed, trying not to shake his head.

'—probably died of exposure.' Owusu took off her gloves and dumped them in the discard pile, already overflowing and covered in snow. 'Both of them were stiff. Body temperatures are very low.'

'So they froze to death?'

'Heart failure from hypothermia.' She raised a finger. 'Which needs to be confirmed.'

Pringle nodded along with it. 'They say freezing to death is one of the more peaceful deaths. Almost euphoric.'

Owusu smiled at him. 'Once you get past the bitter cold part at the start and the shivering stops, they say you feel warm, almost intoxicated as the brain begins its slow temperature drop.' She dumped her suit onto the discard. 'Now, I know what you two are going to ask and yes, they were dumped at different times.'

Pringle tilted his head to the side. 'Go on?'

'I'd estimate her time of death at three a.m., give or take.

Need to do a full post-mortem to check, obviously. For him, it's hard to say because of proximity to her.'

'But he was earlier than her?'

'I'd say three to four hours earlier, plus or minus two.'

Pringle frowned. 'So she was dumped on top of him after he was already dead?'

Marshall couldn't even consider that. Dying on top of a freezing corpse. Your last moments being the heat sucked out of you by a dead body. 'Were they killed by the same person?'

'Not my call, but I'd say it's the same MO. Left there, wrists and ankles bound. And someone knew there was a body already there. So yeah, I'd suggest this is intentional.' Owusu smiled at them both. 'Off the record, of course. Now, I'll get on with the post-mortem as soon as the bodies arrive, okay? I've cleared my calendar.'

'Thank you. I'll get DS Siyal to focus on identifying the victim.' Marshall looked at Owusu. 'You said you knew the victim?'

'Just professionally. There's a channel from oncology to pathology when things don't go to plan. But I do know Louisa's husband.'

CHAPTER NINE

J olene managed to find a space at the back of some shops. She let the engine die but didn't speak. The car didn't sound too healthy and smelled a lot worse. Still, it was a four-by-four so they'd got down to Gala reasonably easily.

'Well done getting the good pool car.'

She smiled at Marshall. 'Cheers.'

The sun was almost up now, but still hid behind the hills east of Galashiels. Not many people out on Overhaugh Street, a narrow lane jammed between the town's two main shopping roads: Channel Street, with its former chain stores gradually being replaced by smaller concerns, and Bank Street, with its boutiques, gelato parlours and vegan cafés. All this one had was a nightclub, a grim pub, a takeaway and three law offices.

Marshall leaned forward to tie up his shoelaces. He wouldn't need those wellies here, thankfully. Getting the buggers off inside the car hadn't been easy, though. 'You okay to lead in here?'

'I've done my time in the trenches, Rob.' She opened the driver door and let the cold air in.

Marshall got out onto the street. 'Are you implying I haven't?'

'Not you. You've been a DI for longer than I've been a cop.'

She meant Siyal, then. That old chestnut was still roasting on an open fire...

Jolene crossed the road and entered the office of Baird & Cruikshank. The signage swayed in the breeze, the maroon-and-white colours of the town's rugby club. Rugby and the law usually went hand in hand, especially in these parts.

The door was stiff and needed a good nudge. Marshall stepped into the reception area, cramped and dark, with decor a few decades too old.

Jolene was over by the desk. She turned around and beckoned for Marshall to follow her through a door, which led to a maze of corridors. No sign of any staff, just the sounds of people talking, somewhere. Eerie as hell.

Jolene rapped on a door marked with:

Hugo Baird
Partner

'Come!' A deep voice, but less a shout and more loud speaking.

Jolene opened the door and stepped into a square box.

Hugo Baird was on his feet, hand outstretched, big grin on his face. Tall and broad with a thick head of hair streaked through with grey. His face was beetroot red. 'Hi there.' His gaze was like an eagle's, shifting back and forth between them, like he was trying to figure out who was the easier prey. 'How can I help?'

Marshall had expected the office to face the back of the

shops on Channel Street, but somehow it looked out onto a garden, with walls on all sides. Three sets of tables and chairs out there for lunch in the warmer months or smoking in the colder ones. Right now, it looked like snow men and snow women were using the tables for their annual meeting.

'Police, sir.' Jolene held out her warrant card. 'DS Jolene Archer. DI Rob Marshall. Need a word about an important matter.'

Hugo let out a deep and resonant sigh. 'Listen, I'm far too busy with work, so can you come back later? Or can I put you in touch with a colleague?'

'Sir, we need to have a word. The sort that might be better done with you sitting down.'

Hugo tilted his head to the side. 'What do you mean?'

He wasn't going to sit, was he?

Jolene looked at Marshall and he gave a nod. She fixed Hugo with a soft look. 'Sir, I'm afraid we found a body this morning, which we believe belongs to your wife.'

Hugo just stood there, frozen like a rock. 'I...' His forehead flickered. 'What?'

'We believe she died during the night, sir.'

Hugo collapsed back into his chair and rolled back until it hit the cabinet. 'You're sure it's her?'

'A colleague was able to identify her.'

Hugo stared into space for a few seconds. 'Well. I know what you're thinking.' He stared at Marshall. The grieving widower was gone, replaced by a patter-merchant lawyer. Gleaming eyes, and not from tears. 'I'm twice her age. More than that, still. Lou's thirty-two. I'm sixty-five next month. Spent too much of my life building up this business and not enough building my private life. Then I met her. Whirlwind romance, married and I was a dad within a year. The boy's four. He's in the kindergarten at St Mary's. Big boy's school next year. We live in Lauder. South end of the village. Lot of our neighbours commute to Edinburgh by car or on the train from Stow. But we both work locally. Of course, it's different since the pandemic. Most businesses are remote a good chunk of the week.'

Marshall cleared his throat and waited until he got eye contact. 'Did you know of anyone your wife might've had issues with?'

'Issues? God no.'

'What about at work?'

'We don't talk about work. Hers or mine. But I know what you're asking and all I can say is Lou's a pillar of the community. I mean, who can get angry with an oncologist? Sure, she's lost patients to cancer but she's the kindest woman in the world and always looked after them, often to the detriment of her own wellbeing. She does runs and walks for a couple of charities she's involved with.'

'What about her family?'

'Mother lives locally. Father passed away a long time ago.' Hugo laughed. 'I know what you're thinking – he'd be about my age!'

Jolene smiled. 'I wasn't thinking that, sir. It must be a horrible shock.'

'It is, it is.' Hugo got up and walked over to the window. 'Lou's very family focused. We spend a lot of time with her cousins and my nieces and nephews. Do a lot of walking in the hills. Fair amount of nice dining locally, trips into Edinburgh. Weekends are always full. Make sure when I close that door on a Friday, I don't have to open it again until Monday morning. The boy plays mini rugby. Take him swimming, too. All the usual stuff.' He stared hard at them. 'Lou's just well loved.' His voice was close to breaking, but he still didn't cry.

Marshall stood there, listening to it all. Processing it or trying to. 'Did you report her missing?'

Hugo shifted his focus to the signed rugby shirt in the cabinet. 'I didn't know she was.'

'Do you mind me asking why?'

'Of course not.' But his jaw was clenched tight. 'While I was rolling up my sleeves to get on with work, Lou was at a function last night. We're up against it this month, lots of things needing done by April and this is the crunch time. I worked until midnight then went straight to bed. Up at six to drop the boy off at kindergarten. Snowed, didn't it, but I battled in here to get the work done. I'm blessed with a diligent staff, who share my passion for the law.'

Jolene was struggling to hide her scowl. 'You didn't notice your wife hadn't come home?'

'We sleep in separate rooms and she was on a later shift today. Lou's a horrendous snorer and I'm a very light sleeper.'

Jolene was frowning. 'I take it your son wasn't home alone last night?'

'God no. We have a live-in nanny. Or an au pair, I think you're supposed to call them now.'

Bingo.

Wouldn't be the first man in his position to 'trade the lady wife in for a new model' as the rugby club banter would go.

'What's her name?'

'Becky. Becky Ferguson.'

Jolene scribbled it down, then looked back up.

'She's a gap year student. Comes from Forres, up in the Highlands. Not great but she's getting there. Off to St Andrews in the summer. Mine and Lou's rooms are either side of the boy's and hers is opposite, so at least one of us will hear him crying in the night. But it's her job to get the little monster up and ready in the morning. I drive him to school, come rain or shine.' He laughed. 'Or snow.'

Jolene flashed a smile. 'Do you know where your wife's function was last night?'

'I don't.' Hugo walked back over with agility then grabbed his desk phone. 'Alison, can you consult my wife's itinerary for yesterday, please?' He stood there, smiling, listening. 'Thanks.' He put the phone down again. 'Lou was at a Burns supper last night.'

'Did she drive there?'

'I don't know.'

Marshall shook his head. 'How can you not know?'

'It's fairly common, Inspector. She won't know my movements day-to-day. But her car wasn't there this morning.'

'Sir, this is about your wife not coming home. How can you—'

'Look, I have a pressing appointment waiting in reception. They've been getting increasingly unhappy, so we need to park this matter for now.'

CHAPTER TEN

DI Andrea Elliot strolled through the bustling corridors of St Leonards police station.

Weird being back to her old stomping ground in Edinburgh.

She stopped outside the meeting room door and took a deep breath. The cold, sterile walls echoed her feelings – she knew she needed to keep numb to this, and not rise to whatever bullshit the drugs squad threw at her.

There, centred again.

She knocked on the door and entered the cramped, windowless meeting room, the hum of fluorescents above combined with the scent of stale coffee and old paperwork.

The tables were arranged in a square and the three detectives from the drugs squad looked up from their laptops, their faces etched with the marks of the gritty world they navigated daily. Two of them looked back down again.

DCI Ryan Gashkori, though, acknowledged her arrival with a curt nod. A man who had weathered many storms throughout his long career, but who bore the scars on his face, a roadmap of creases and lines. Those piercing blue eyes held a steely determination and daft cheekiness, but the dark skin surrounding them hinted at countless sleepless nights. He held out a stubby hand and seemed to rise up to be closer to Elliot's height. 'Just you today, eh?'

'Just me.' Elliot shook it. 'Pringle couldn't be arsed.'

'You didn't think to bring anyone else?'

'Unlike you, Ryan, I don't need back up and can handle myself.'

'Aye, good one.' Gashkori sat back down again and checked his watch. 'Thought the Golden Child would be coming too?'

'That's better than his last nickname. And drugs aren't his particular strong point, what with the number of times he's buggered up a strategic investigation. And those long months seconded to your team... No, Scott's in Tenerife. Or Lanzarote. Can't remember which.'

'Can't beat a bit of winter sun. What about that new pet of Pringle's? Marshall, is it?'

'He's holding the fort down there.'

'Not like you've got many crimes there. Bit of shoplifting, noncing and arson, right?'

'I wish.'

'Have a seat, then, Andi. Coffee's on the way.'

Elliot smiled as she sat. Felt like she was in an interview. Whether it was for a job or a police one, she hadn't made her mind up.

Gashkori shut his laptop lid and cleared his throat loud enough for his lackeys to look up. 'Alright, let's get started, then. How did you feel yesterday's session went?'

'As well as I expected.'

'The queen of the back-handed compliment. Did we get to where you needed to?'

'I got what I needed out of it. Upping the surveillance on the harbour at Eyemouth should help.'

'Excellent.' Gashkori leaned back in his chair and stuffed his hands into his pockets. Only took a few seconds for the keys to start jingling. 'Now we've got yesterday's crap out of the way, let's focus on the dish of the day. Gary Hislop.'

Elliot winced. Just the name had a physical reaction with her. 'That wasn't on the agenda.'

'No. I chatted with my super afterwards and she feels we need to move on this.'

Bloody hell.

She sighed. 'Your meeting, Ryan.'

'Brass want us to circle the wagons and agree a strategy across us in Drugs and you lot in the murder squad. For our part, we've been tracking him for years, monitoring him for months. We believe Hislop's the key to cracking open a larger operation. A sinister one with tentacles all over the country. But we think the heroin flooding Scotland just now centres around him.'

Elliot frowned. 'Ryan, I understand your concerns, but we don't have enough to nail this guy.' She was keeping her voice measured but firm. 'All you really have are rumours and innuendo. We need something solid, something irrefutable. We can't risk tipping him off after a half-baked investigation.'

Gashkori bristled, his jaw clenching. 'Andi, our view is we can't sit on our hands any longer. There's a bloody epidemic out there and this guy's at the centre of it. We need to press ahead, now.'

'That your view or are you getting leaned on from above?'

'Leaned on?'

'Aye. We both know how this is all about politics. With a capital P. If it was just the office variety, you wouldn't be getting me to traipse up here, would you?'

'Can't deny it. UK election coming up in the next eighteen months, probably. Want to tighten this all down.'

'Still, you've got to agree that going after Hislop now would be a mistake.'

'Elliot's right.' The detective to Gashkori's left. Older guy, dressed in the standard uniform of a well-worn suit and a tie dotted with various stains. 'I'm not saying we *shouldn't* move on Hislop, but we need to be sure we have enough evidence to make it stick.'

'See why I don't need anyone else with me, Ryan? Your lads are making my point for me.' She grinned at him and let it settle for a few seconds. 'He's right, though. If we move too soon and with a flimsy premise, we could spook Hislop, and he'll disappear. Or worse, he starts chasing our lot. Remember what happened in Glasgow last year. Tried to go after the big dog and ended up getting bitten. Big Cal Taylor's still in hospital.'

Gashkori slammed his fist on the table. 'We've got to do something!'

'Agreed. But arresting him now? We need a major lead to act. Some irrefutable evidence. Have you got anything?'

'No... But every day we wait, more people die.'

'I know that. You know that. But we haven't even got enough to bring him in for questioning. If he comes in, he'll be out within the hour. And nobody enjoys looking stupid.'

'But if we got him on the record, that could be the break we needed.'

'That's a gamble, pure and simple. The Americans would call it a Hail Mary pass. We do need to get him in, but I'm insisting on a more cautious approach.'

Gashkori laughed. 'You're insisting are you?'

'Advocating. Respectfully.' She brushed her hair back. 'Look, Ryan, I get it. You lot have been watching Hislop for ages. And you're itching to take action. You're frustrated and you want to make a dent in the drug trade ravaging our communities. But if we go off half-cocked, we risk jeopardising the whole thing.'

'Okay.' Gashkori slipped off his jacket and hung it on the back of his chair, then started rolling up his shirt sleeves to reveal the hairiest arms Elliot had ever seen. 'Here's what we'll do. You and me, in a room for a week. We'll look through all the evidence. All the stuff you've got, those assaults and abductions. All the stuff we've got, those dealer interviews and surveillance logs. And we'll prepare a case to take to our superintendents. They'll make the final call. We all want the same thing here; we just need to figure out the best way to get it done.'

Elliot shifted her focus between them. She knew she had one on her side. Gashkori would never go against his own proposal. Leaving another one who could go either way. A draw or a victory – not bad odds for an away game. He looked young enough to be persuaded of the folly of his boss's ways. 'Fine.' She picked up her chair and carried it around to sit next to Gashkori. 'Show me your moves, Ryan.'

He laughed. 'You're getting as bad as that boss of yours.'

'Nobody's that bad...'

Her phone chimed in her pocket. Then again. She got it out to check it.

Pringle calling...

'Speak of the devil and he shall whistle nonsense in your ear.' She got up and walked over to the door to answer it. 'Morning, sir, I'm just with Ryan Gashkori.'

'Thanks for taking that one off me, Andi. I believe in you!'

That was new. 'Okay, thanks.'

'Trouble is, I need you to turn around, bright eyes, because your help is required down here with a double murder.'

CHAPTER ELEVEN

'Park this matter for now.' Marshall couldn't get the words out of his head by any other means, so speaking them might work. 'How can—'

But Jolene was already out of the car.

Marshall made sure Jolene had stuck the 'Official Police Business' sign in the windscreen and followed her out into the biting cold. Wouldn't be the first time she'd forgotten and he'd rather avoid dealing with the council over parking again.

Borders General Hospital was unusually quiet, just two desperate patients sucking on cigarettes in the shelter, though there was more snow inside than out. Poor sods watched them walk past towards the building, whose layers of sandstone and pink breeze blocks made it look like a different sort of cake than the surrounding hills.

Marshall entered the building and spotted the path to Oncology, marked out by a green arrow pointing deep into the hospital. 'What's your take on Hugo Baird?'

'He's a creepy, red-faced old perv.' Jolene stopped at the bottom of the stairs and winced. 'Sorry, I don't mean that.'

'Look, it's okay to express your feelings like that. If nobody said something that everyone thought, then we'd get into trouble. Why is he creepy?'

'He's literally old enough to be her dad.' She smirked. 'Round this way, he might even be her dad.'

'That's a bit harsh.'

'Okay, down in Hawick, maybe.' She started up the stairs, skipping up two at a time. 'It's called a joke, Rob.'

Marshall followed at a slower pace but was relieved to not lose any breath as he climbed.

Jolene held the door for him. 'Seeing as how we're being honest, what's your take on him?'

'Not knowing where his wife was last night is a red flag to me. I can get not wanting to see her body, but throwing himself into his work like that...'

'So he's clearly a workaholic. Someone who can't switch off, whose life is based on that office and that business he's built up.' She glanced over as they walked. 'Do you think he's a suspect?'

'He's on the list, for certain. I think their marriage doesn't quite stack up. And that's just from an initial chat.'

'Not to mention the live-in nanny old enough to be his granddaughter...'

Something Marshall agreed with. 'That and them sleeping in separate rooms.'

She stopped, hands on hips. 'I do that.'

'What?'

'Our son sleeps with us most nights and it winds my husband up something rotten. He works shifts as a fireman in Hawick. Sleep's precious to him. So we switched to him sleeping in wee Joe's room and him in with me.'

'Listen, I'm sorry if—'

'I get it, Rob. You're judging people.'

'No, it's... I don't know.'

'What gets me is how he couldn't really explain it. With us, it's temporary. When Joe's older, he'll be back in his bed and it'll be back to normal. I hope. And there's something we need to dig into here.' Her mobile blasted out and she checked the display. 'Better take this.' Before Marshall could complain, she marched off back the way they'd come.

Aye, he'd put his foot right in a big pile of steaming shite there...

He walked through to the oncology ward and smiled at the receptionist, a middle-aged woman with a kind face but frantic energy fizzing in her fingers dancing across the keyboard. 'Police. We called ahead to—'

'Marshall and Archer? Sounds like a TV show.' She laughed. 'You wanted time with Dr Fairfax.' She sat back and brushed a hand through her hair. 'His office is just through there on the right. Hasn't got a patient until eleven.'

'Thank you.' Marshall looked back the way.

Jolene stormed in, clutching her phone.

Marshall set off down the corridor and found the door. He didn't knock yet. 'Who was that?'

'Elliot. She's junked her meetings and is working the case. She's just arrived at the crime scene and wanted my take on things.'

'Having her experience and connections will be useful.' Marshall hoped it would work out that way. The alternative was she'd be pissing on his chips at every opportunity. Probably a forlorn hope, but hope was important. 'Any update?'

'Said it's hard going up at the wind farm. She's searching for more bodies, but they've not found any.'

'I wasn't expecting them to.'

'Right.'

'Have they IDed the male victim?'

'Nope. Not a lot of places to go door-to-door up there. Both villages either end are getting a good going over. She said Pringle's doing a press release and a TV pitch. Think that might work?'

'Decent chance of it, aye.' Marshall knocked on the door. No way was Pringle going to get a result on that.

The door opened and a thin man stood there. Grey trousers, turquoise shirtsleeves rolled up to his elbows, orange and lime tie. Late thirties but stinking of second-hand cigarettes and deodorant. Typical doctor – do what they say, not what they do... 'Kenneth Fairfax.' He held out a hand. No eye contact. 'DI Marshall, is it?'

'Aye, and this is DS Archer. We need a word about Dr Louisa Baird.'

'In you come, in you come.' Fairfax held the door while they entered, then leaned back against it. 'What's she done?'

'I'm afraid her body was found this morning.'

'Oh.' Fairfax walked over to his desk and sat down. 'I see. Listen, I've got a lot of cases on just now, so—' Something shifted in him and he collapsed back in his chair. 'Oh my. I can't believe it. Oh my. She...' He shook his head. 'Louisa was one of the best. I... I'm sorry. You must think I was cold and indifferent just there, but the truth is I see death every single day. They walk in here months before they die and those cases it's inevitable. People who've left it too late, or some idiot told them to use alternative medicine instead of the real stuff. You know, medicine. An alternative to stuff that works. But when it's a colleague, it's...' He huffed out a deep breath. 'It's hard to take. What happened to her?'

'We're trying to figure that out, sir. She was found up on the road between Stow and Lauder. We believe she froze to death.'

'Oh my. Was it...' Fairfax swallowed. 'Was it suicide?'

71

'We don't believe so, no.' Marshall wanted to keep as many of the details back. 'Why do you ask?'

'Being an oncologist is one of those professions with a high suicide rate, like vets or soldiers. Like I said, you deal with death every day. Even worse, you have to deal with *hope*. People say it's a battle for the patient against cancer and they win or lose that fight, but really it's a battle between the consultant and the patient's body. She totally got that and she was incredibly supportive of her patients.'

And they still didn't know who her partner in dying was. 'Do you think it's possible she could've killed herself?'

'No, but... You never know what's going on inside someone's head, do you? Sometimes they can be bright and breezy and the next thing, they're... I'm sure I don't have to spell it out for you.'

Marshall nodded in sympathy. 'The reason we're here, sir, is to get an overview of her life. Develop an idea of anyone who'd want to harm her. Anyone who disagreed with her.'

'Louisa was an exemplary doctor. Extremely compassionate and entirely focused on her patients' wellbeing, without harming her own mental health. Some may say she was young and idealistic, but that idealism didn't seem to be fading any, especially not with motherhood. She was one of the good ones and I was proud to have her on my team.'

'When did you last see her?'

'Yesterday at five. I had to rush down to Accident and Emergency to meet with a poor soul who collapsed in the waiting area. Stage four testicular cancer, which had spread to his lungs and stomach.'

Marshall felt a spear of revulsion at that. No hope in that case. 'We gather she was at an event last night?'

'Sorry, I've no idea. We didn't have that kind of relationship.'

'Was she friendly with anyone here?'

'Oh, yes. It's me who's the curmudgeon. Best to keep a professional distance in this field. But Louisa... She was loved by all. Especially— Well, I better not go there.'

'What was that?'

Fairfax gave a polite smile. 'Nothing.'

Marshall folded his arms. 'Sir, your colleague is on her way to the morgue downstairs. If there's something that can help us find her killer, then...'

'Okay. There was an HR issue last summer.'

Jolene looked over at Marshall, then at Fairfax. 'Can you give us some more details, please?'

'I don't know if I should go into it or not...'

'Please.'

'No. It was closed off. I need to respect the confidentiality of both parties.'

Interesting...

Marshall got out his phone and showed him the photo of the male victim. 'Was it him?'

Fairfax squinted at it, then looked away from them. 'I'm not at liberty to say.'

'Was it him?'

Fairfax shook his head. 'No, I don't recognise that man. Is he dead?'

'He was found underneath her body. He probably died first.'

'Oh my.'

'Sir, we really need a name.'

Fairfax finally made eye contact. 'No, you really need a warrant.'

CHAPTER TWELVE

Marshall descended the stairs after Jolene, much slower than her rapid pace. 'Our priority is finding this guy.'

She stopped at the bottom, waiting, her arms crossed over her shoulders. 'You want to get a warrant for that?'

'Cheeky sod.' Marshall smiled at her. 'I've got another way to get that information.'

She tilted her head to the side. 'Go on?'

'Give me five minutes.'

'What are you doing, Rob?'

'Nothing hooky.' Marshall set off along the corridor. 'My sister works here and she's a massive gossip. If anyone knows, she will.'

'Okay. Can I get you a coffee?'

'Please. I'll take it black, cheers.'

'Call me when you're done.' She headed towards the café at the front of the hospital.

Marshall pushed through the door to the A&E waiting area.

Pretty busy at this time of day. A big man sat there, crouching forward with a bloody nose dripping on the tiles. Whether someone had done that to him or he'd done it to himself wasn't immediately obvious.

The guy diagonally opposite, though... it was clear he hadn't done it to himself – a chisel was stuck into the top of his head and he was holding it in place, looking around the room for sympathy or understanding. Or maybe just the guy who'd done it to him.

Marshall cut between them and pushed through the double doors into the main treatment area. The receptionist didn't seem to notice him, as she was too busy dealing with a patient wearing a face mask.

Jen was standing in the middle of the area, hands on hips, dressed in her navy uniform, shaking her head at a male colleague in cornflower blue. She glanced over at Marshall, then did a double take. She patted her pal on the arm then strode over to him. 'Rob? What are you doing here?'

He gave a broad smile. 'Hi, Jen, thanks for the lift this morning.'

She grabbed his arm and dragged him into a treatment room. 'Don't mention it. We're a bit busy, though. Slips and falls like nobody's business.'

'I'm sorry, but I'll be quick.' Marshall let out a slow breath. 'So I need to—'

'—get a new car.' She had that intense look, like she wasn't going to let this one go. 'One that's suitable for where you live now, eh?'

'It's not that—'

'Your roller skate is a boy racer's dream and you're not a boy anymore.'

'Fine, I'll get myself something.'

'Great.' Though Jen didn't seem too convinced. 'See if you

haven't done anything about it by September? I'm dragging you kicking and screaming to a car dealership.'

'Fine.'

She drilled that hard stare into him for a few long seconds, then mercifully looked away. 'I want to have a chat with you about her, though.'

'About Kirsten?'

'Aye.'

'What about—' Marshall stopped himself with a splutter. 'Jen, this isn't the time.'

'No? When is?'

'I'm serious.'

'Thing is, she's staying over a lot.'

'In my flat, which I rent from you. And I'm staying at hers in Edinburgh occasionally too. What's the issue?'

'All the same, if this is—'

'I can move out, if you want.'

'I'm not saying that. I love having you there. Thea does too. I'm just...' Jen looked up at the ceiling and seemed to spot a few spiders crawling around up there, because her eyes shot all over the place. She looked back and sighed. 'What are your plans for her?'

'My plans?' Marshall laughed. 'You sound like Mum.'

'*Rob*. Is Kirsten marriage material?'

Jesus Christ...

Marshall fixed a hard stare on her – two could play at that game. 'Jen. First, you can piss off. Second, who were you with last night? Was *he* marriage material?'

She narrowed her eyes at him. 'Okay, I withdraw the question, officer.' Then she prodded him in the chest. 'And you can piss off too.'

'What's sauce for the goose is sauce for the gander, Jen. I

won't pry into your love life, so you don't pry into mine. Even though Kirsten's a friend of yours.'

Her lips twitched. 'Fine.' She looked away. 'So, darling brother, what brings you here?'

'The case is a double murder.'

'*Double?*'

'Two victims, found together. Both frozen to death.'

'Double suicide?'

'Nope. Wrists and ankles bound. A few hours apart.'

'Jesus. That's not what you expect around here.'

'No.' He held that stare. 'Both bodies are down in Dr Owusu's lair.'

Jen rolled her eyes at him. 'She *hates* it being called that.'

'Noted. Anyway. The female victim is Dr Louisa Baird.'

Jen's eyebrows shot up. 'Oh shit.'

'You knew her?'

'We've had to work together a fair bit, aye. Sometimes people show up in A&E and it turns out to be, like, stage four cancer. Several times a year. Had someone in that same boat last night. Absolutely brutal, Rob.' Jen let her hair go then swept a hand through it. 'Thing is, Louisa was always the one who came down to help out. She'd take over the case. She's great. *Was* great. One of the best in this place.'

'This one last night wasn't her, was it?'

'This what?'

'Case like that.'

'Oh, right. Aye. Almost forgot. I was on my way out of the door, but luckily Georgia could cover for me. No, it was Fairfax who came down, sadly.'

'Why sadly?'

'The guy's a robot. Just looks at you as if the patients are like car parts to him. No warmth, no emotion, no eye contact.

Probably good at some bits of his job, but he's shite at the people side of things.'

'Speaking of which, I gather there was an HR issue relating to her?'

'How the hell do you know that?'

'Dr Fairfax mentioned it. But didn't give us any detail on it.'

Jen retied her hair, then glowered at a spot on the wall. Then she shifted her focus to him. 'I'm a bit wary about talking about stuff like that.'

'Like what?'

'HR issues that are none of my business.' She snorted. 'Rob, this is my job, okay? It's nothing to do with you and I as brother and sister.'

'Come on. We're twins.'

'Whatever, Rob. It's... I just shouldn't. It's unprofessional.'

Marshall nodded just enough to soothe her a bit. 'But it was with a colleague of hers?'

That spot on the wall was getting a lot of attention. 'A colleague of mine. One of the young doctors here in A&E.' Jen bit her cheek. 'Obviously we're different line management streams, so it's not *technically* a colleague but someone I work reasonably close with, aye.'

'What happened?'

'Why?'

'Because Dr Baird's dead, Jen. Murdered. And there's someone else too. It's my job to find who killed them.' Marshall let the words sink in for a few seconds. 'Someone with an HR issue against him is someone I need to speak to. Surely you can see that, right?'

She looked away from the wall, head dipped low. 'Young lad called Ben Rougier. Not been here long.' She looked up at him. 'Word is he became a bit stalkerish.'

'Stalkerish how?'

'Wouldn't take no for an answer. Following her home. All of that.'

And Marshall wondered why he had to hear this from his sister and not the victim's husband.

CHAPTER THIRTEEN

The A&E doctors had two rooms for admin work, each with three desks in, both doors open. Only one was occupied, with a male doctor working at a desktop computer. The room smelled of boiled cabbage, though Marshall couldn't tell if he'd been eating any.

He gestured for Jolene to lead and sipped his coffee through the lid. Tasted a bit burnt but it wasn't too bad.

Jolene knocked on the door.

The doctor swung around. Heavy dark eyes, stubble that looked like pencil shading, hair like a boy band pop star. Face like a boy. 'How can I help?' Voice like a boy.

Jolene smiled at him. 'Looking for a Dr Rougier?'

'That's me.' His smooth forehead creased. 'What's up?'

Well, Rougier wasn't the male victim, at least. Looked nothing like him, in fact. A decade or two separated them.

'DS Jolene Archer.' She flipped out her warrant card. 'Need to ask you a few questions.'

'Can it wait?' Rougier got to his feet. 'It's just, I've got to get back to treating patients and—'

'I'm sure you can get a colleague to help.' Marshall smiled at him. 'We won't be here long.'

Rougier slumped back in his chair with a hefty sigh. He got out his phone and tapped a message, then put it away. 'I've paged the consultant.' He picked up a banana skin from his desk and dumped it into the bin next to him. 'So. How can I help?'

Jolene took the office chair next to him. 'DI Marshall and myself need to ask you a few questions about what happened between you and Dr Louisa Baird.'

Rougier frowned, then shifted his gaze between them. 'What?'

Jolene seemed to notice the defensiveness and leapt on it. 'We gather an HR issue was raised against you.' Kept her voice level and left it hanging there.

Rougier looked at Marshall, then back at Jolene. His nose wouldn't stop twitching. 'Who told you that?'

'That's not a denial.'

'No, but...' Rougier swallowed. 'It's... It's bullshit, quite frankly.'

'Okay.' Jolene raised her eyebrows. 'We'd love to know what's bullshit, Ben. Is that possible?'

'I don't know if I should tell you.'

'It'd help us a lot.'

Rougier leaned back in his chair and something in the mechanism seemed to crack. 'I mean, I don't know if I *can* tell you. Legally, I mean.'

'This is a police matter.'

Rougier drummed his fingers on the tabletop. 'Look, I thought we had a relationship. Me and Louisa. Louisa Baird.' He nibbled at his fingernails. 'But we didn't. Turns out there was nothing.'

'Why did you think there was something?'

Rougier was more interested in his fingernails than either of the detectives in the room. 'Because we kissed a couple of times.'

'You kissed?'

'Once at the Christmas party.'

'This Christmas?'

'No, last one. 2021. All of the doctors in the hospital were there. Well, the ones that didn't need to be on shift. And the ones who wanted to go to a party. Two weeks later, Omicron was sweeping everywhere and this place was... It was brutal.'

'You kissed.'

'Right. Dinner at that Italian in Gala. Then a few of us went to a club. She hit on me there. Right on the dance floor. That Madonna song was playing. "Like a Virgin". It was... It was wild.'

'Did anybody see you?'

'Don't think so. It was busy in there. Dark too.'

'You said you kissed a couple of times. At work?'

'No. She blanked me. Luckily we didn't have to deal with each other. But one Saturday, I was out with friends in Edinburgh and I bumped into her. Nice pub on Dundas Street, just around the corner from my flat. I offered to go back there. We did. We just kissed. She got a taxi home.'

'So why did she report you?'

His head dipped. 'Because I didn't take no for an answer.'

'Are you talking about sexual assault?'

'God no.' Rougier snorted. 'No... It's... I kept trying to woo her.'

Jolene's snort was less disgust and more humour. *Woo her?*

Rougier nodded. 'Woo her. You know, like in the movies.'

'I don't follow you. How were you trying to woo her?'

'Sending her stuff. Chocolates. Cards. Turned up in her office with flowers once.'

'You know she's married with a son, right?'

'Yeah, but it's a loveless marriage. I wanted to be with her. Fuck, I wanted to be dad to her kid.'

Jolene sat back in her seat. 'How old are you?'

'Twenty-seven.' He picked up a pen and twirled it around, then put it down on the table again. 'You think that's too young?'

'No.' Marshall thought that age was way too old for this kind of behaviour, even though Rougier looked about fifteen. Trouble with that generation is they didn't get the smack in the mouth for stupidity. No, they found all the other similarly stupid idiots online and formed gangs. They hated challenge and didn't see it as how you grew up or how you learnt. 'Did Dr Baird's husband find out?'

'Find out what? There was nothing. I sent her flowers and stuff. That's it.'

'You said you kissed her? She went back to your flat?'

'Well, yeah, we did, but... those were a few months before I started wooing her. But she found out it was me and came in here, shouting at me for it. I... I thought I... I went around to her house to have it out with her. That's when she reported me.'

'What happened?'

'Nothing. We sat with an HR manager. Agreed a few things. I said I'd stop speaking to her, even professionally. If a patient came in and had to go upstairs to Oncology, or came down here from there, then I'd get a colleague to deal with it. Same with her. And we both wouldn't talk about it.'

'Sounds stressful.'

'It was. I mean... Aye. It was. I won't be in this hospital forever, so I thought it was the easiest solution.'

Marshall moved around the office space so Rougier had to

pay attention to him. 'Ben, the reason we're asking you these questions is we found her body this morning.'

His eyes bulged. 'You... You what? You...' He gulped. Then covered his hand over his mouth. 'I...' He shut his eyes. 'Sorry.' He leaned over and was sick into the bin.

Marshall waited for him to recover, trying to ignore the sharp stink that overpowered the cabbage smell.

Rougier looked around at him, rubbing his lips. 'Sorry. I...' He grabbed a bottle of water and glugged it down. 'What happened?'

'We're trying to determine that. I need to know your movements last night.'

'What, you can't think I did it?'

Marshall shrugged. 'We need to eliminate everyone. Especially someone with an HR case against them for stalking the victim.'

'I didn't *stalk* her!'

'Okay. Look, I'm not going to argue with you on that score, but you certainly behaved inappropriately to a colleague.'

Rougier rubbed at his lips and took another drink. 'Last night, I got the train home then went to the gym. Same as every night. I live in Edinburgh. New Town. It's a friend's place from university. We share it. I want my own place but... It's expensive, right? And I hate the commute here, but it's only for another six months, then I'll be able to transfer to civilisation. Like, this morning I had to get the train in the pitch darkness then walk from the station through the snow to here. It's brutal.'

Jolene had her notebook out, splayed on her lap. 'Can anyone prove that?'

'There's CCTV at the gym? And both train stations will have it, right?'

'We'll dig into that, of course.' Jolene scratched out a note. 'What time was that?'

'Finished here at six.' He sighed. 'Ran to the station, I think. Just caught the train by seconds. Then I went straight to the gym.'

'Which one?'

'Edinburgh Uni.'

Jolene looked up at him. 'At the Pleasance, right?'

'That's right. You a fellow graduate?'

'Me? Aye. Not that it got me a good job.' Jolene smiled.

But the joke didn't land.

Marshall caught a whiff of second-hand sick, so took out his phone and held it out with the photo of the male victim showing. 'Do you recognise this man?'

Rougier's lips twisted up as he scanned the screen. Took a few good seconds at it. At least *he* was taking it seriously. 'I do.' He looked up at Marshall. 'Why?'

'Who is he?'

'I... Sorry, I don't know.'

'But you do recognise him?'

'Right.'

'Do you know where from?'

'Sorry, no. Must be a patient.' Rougier took the mobile and gave the photo a full examination. 'I do know him. Just... Just can't place him.' He clicked his fingers hard a few times. 'Got it. I triaged him the other night.' He pointed a few times now with both fingers. 'He was in a pub fight. Thursday, maybe? Can't be Friday as I wasn't on shift.'

Marshall held the phone up again. 'Definitely him?'

'Definitely.'

'You know who treated him?'

CHAPTER FOURTEEN

One thing Marshall knew about his sister was it was next to impossible to find her when he needed her – like trouble, she'd always find him. Never the other way around. He should've bought a lottery ticket after managing it so quickly earlier.

And here he was yet again, standing in the A&E treatment area he'd just vacated, and there was no sign of her.

He walked up to the nurses' station and tried to get noticed during the chaos. Nobody was staying still, instead walking around and being busy.

Jolene joined him. 'What's your assessment of Rougier?'

Marshall kept looking around the place, but all the nurses were doing a great job of ignoring him. Like standing at the bar on Hogmanay. Or at the bar anywhere. 'My take is he's a daft kid who watched too many Hollywood films. And not *Die Hard* rip-offs, either.' The joke didn't land with Jolene. 'He confused cute determination and resilience in a screenplay with gross inappropriateness in real life. I guess some people take the wrong messages from slushy romantic comedies.'

'One man's earnest determination against the odds is another's HR issue.'

'Too right.' Marshall stepped in the way of a passing nurse. 'Hi, I'm a police officer and I desperately need to speak to Jennifer Armstrong.'

'You mean Marshall, right?' Soft Northern Irish accent. She was tiny too.

'Sure, yes. Sorry. I forgot she was using her maiden name again.'

'I'll see if I can find her.' She squelched away on her crocs, leaving them alone again.

Jolene was looking him up and down. 'Don't even know your own sister's surname, eh?'

Marshall laughed it off. 'Hard to get used to again, that's all. Took me long enough to get it right the other way.'

'You're single, right?'

Marshall looked at her, frowning. 'What's that got to do with anything?'

'It's just... Nothing.'

'No, spill it.' Not least because Marshall hated to think people had been gossiping about him. Or worse, that they'd been gossiping about Kirsten.

'Okay. It's just, you seem like the sort to marry and have a family. You're strong and determined. And stable.' She pouted. 'Are you gay?'

Well, that was a good way of knowing the rumour mill hadn't been busy on his score.

Or his and Kirsten's.

'No, I'm not. And you know asking someone could result in an HR complaint for yourself.'

'What, asking if someone's gay?'

No sign of Jen or the nurse he'd sent to find her. 'It's their own business.'

'Right.'

'But if you must know, all that stuff? Marriage, kids, white picket fence... It's not something I've been able to think about, really. Too busy with my career.'

'The grass isn't greener on the other side.' Jolene dipped her head. 'More like some wee bastard's torched the adjacent field with petrol they've stolen from your tractor.'

He waited for her to look up. 'You don't fill a tractor with petrol.'

Another joke that didn't land.

He smiled at her. 'I thought things were okay?'

'There's okay and there's wishing to fuck you'd chosen better.' She sighed then covered it over with a laugh. 'Three glasses of yellow liquid all at the halfway mark. The optimist says his glass is half-full. The pessimist says his is half-empty. The police officer says, "that's piss, right?"' She waited for a laugh.

Marshall gave her one, but it sounded forced and fake. 'A pessimist is never disappointed. A police officer always is, despite never hoping for anything.'

'Very true.'

'Rob?' Jen charged over, her hair scraped back in an even tighter ponytail. 'What's up?' Her narrowed eyes showed she didn't want him to have spilled her confidence over Rougier.

'Can we do this somewhere?'

'All the rooms are busy.' Jen smiled at Jolene. 'Hey, how are you doing?' Then her gaze was back on her brother. 'Can we do this here?'

Marshall held out his mobile. 'Do you recognise this man?'

She took her time checking it, looking a bit flustered. 'Sure, but I don't know where from. Is he an actor or something?'

'A patient.' Marshall moved the phone over a bit in case the movement jogged her memory any. 'We gather he was in A&E for an injury incurred during an assault.'

Jen ushered them to the side to let a gurney past. The man with the chisel lay in the middle, his face pale. Her focus was devoted to him and not her brother.

Marshall stepped back into the way. 'Apparently you treated him, Jen. Pub fight on Thursday.'

'Oh God, *him*.' She rolled her eyes. 'Aye. A cop broke up a fight.'

'In the pub?'

She laughed, then pointed behind him. 'No, in the waiting area. This guy was shouting at someone. Both were three sheets to the wind. We got him through and triaged him. Can't think who was on call.'

'Rougier.'

'Makes sense.' Jen narrowed her eyes again. 'Deemed him to be okay, just needed a couple of stitches in his head wound. We were really busy, so muggins here had to do it. Cops were in here, making a nuisance. He was refusing to press charges, despite his head being cut open.'

'What about the other guy?'

'Cut to his temple. Pretty bad, but this guy was much worse.'

'Going to need his name.'

'Happy to oblige.' Jen sighed. 'Jonathan Doe.'

'Right, I see. Jen, it's important we can identify this guy.'

'Why?'

'Because he's dead. If it's related to this pub fight, then we need to—'

'Both of them gave details. I'll have to look through the paperwork to see what happened.'

'But you can't remember?'

'Nature of the beast, Rob. See so many people. Should see

me in Tesco. Half the people in there, I've treated or seen in here. It melts your brain. And it's been a bit busy in here. Both got stitched and off they went.'

Marshall could just see the lead slipping out of his fingers. So close to identifying the other victim and their potential on their killer.

Jen kept looking back in the direction of the gurney. Always onto the next patient.

Jolene was writing something in her notebook, but Marshall didn't really know what. 'How did he get here? Ambulance?'

Jen shook her head. 'Dropped off by someone.'

'Friend? Family? Taxi? Good Samaritan?'

'Don't know. Sorry. My job is to stick them back together again. I patched him up and he left.'

Jolene had her notebook out again. 'I'll be able to get hold of the CCTV for the front door here and track them down.'

'That'd be great.' Marshall focused on his sister. 'Tell me you at least know who the cop was?'

CHAPTER FIFTEEN

Marshall slammed the door and shot across the car park, leaving Jolene to weave between the squad cars. He pushed into the Gala nick's reception area and waved at the desk sergeant, then swiped through into the station's innards.

He stepped into the canteen, which was jumping like a pub at five on a Friday. That time where the day shift were taking their early lunches, the air filled with a cacophony of aromas, from burnt toast to pungent curry spices to some monster cooking smoked fish in a microwave.

The wee man at the till was eagerly looking at Marshall as though he could put his rudimentary barista skills to use.

Marshall spotted his prey sitting at the back of the room.

PC Liam Warner sat at a table with another four uniforms. They'd all finished their lunches, while he still had what looked like three quarters of his sandwiches left. That, or he was eating two lunches. Not so much holding court as giving a private lecture series to his colleagues.

Marshall took a seat at the empty table next to them.

'They're trying to call it Stow of Wedale rather than plain old Stow.' Warner took a bite of his sandwich and chewed, but it didn't seem to slow him any or put him off this theme. His Irish accent was a bit jarring here. 'Trying to make the place seem grander than it is. Same with Clovenfords. There's a campaign to revert back to the name of Whytbanklea or just Whytbank. Sure, it's much nicer. Cloven isn't exactly a nice word, is it? But that sort of thing causes havoc, doesn't it?' He finally seemed to notice Marshall and nodded at him. 'How're ye?'

'Remember me?'

Warner looked around his colleagues, then pointed at Marshall. 'Lads, this is DI Rob Marshall. This about you lot moving in here?'

'Moving in?'

'Sure. I'm on the committee to make sure it all goes smoothly. The MIT's offices are just about finished. Moving in April, right?'

'No, it's not about an office move, it's—'

'You'll be deputy SIO on those murders, right?'

'That's correct. Need a word about that.'

'Well, we're on our lunch break. So, if you need anything, I'll be another twenty minutes.'

Marshall shifted his smile to his colleagues. 'Lads and lasses, any chance you could give us a minute?'

'Easier if I come and sit next to you.' Warner shifted over to Marshall's table, bringing his sandwiches with him. Looked like peanut butter and some kind of sausage. With something green. Stank of vinegar too. 'What's up?'

'I won't take up too much of your lunch hour and you should get your sergeant to square it off with me, if he's arsey.'

'She, and she is.'

'Well, I'm ordering you to give me five minutes of your

lunch hour.' Marshall clocked Jolene at the coffee maker, ordering for both of them. He looked back at Warner. 'You moved up from Hawick to Gala, right?'

'Last month, yeah. Bit more happening up here. And I get the chance to sit on committees, like making you lot welcome here. Wouldn't mind a word about how I could become a detective.'

'Sure that can be arranged. But not now.'

'Sure. So. What's up?'

Marshall got out his mobile and showed him the photo of the victim. 'Do you recognise this man?'

'Who's he?'

'The murder victim you were guarding up on the high road from Stow this morning.'

'Oh, right. Him. Tell you, we had a load of journalists show up. Absolute night—'

'Do you recognise him?'

'Sure.' Warner took a bite of his weird sandwich and started chewing. 'Thursday night, me and Stish here.' He thumbed towards one of his mates. Marshall couldn't identify which one of the three was Stish. 'We were on back shift, right? Sitting at McDonald's on our break and we got a call. I had chicken McNuggets on the side of a Big Mac meal. Diet Coke to drink, no ice. Got receding gums, so I can't have anything colder than my brother's heart.' Another bite of his sandwich.

Marshall wanted to throttle him already. Or just get him to cut to the chase. Still, he didn't want to miss on any details that might prove salient, despite sitting through all this.

'We got called out to a pub fight at the Stagehall Arms in Stow. Did you hear how they're trying to rename it to Stow of Wedale?'

Marshall stifled his groan. 'Heard it somewhere, aye.'

'Daft, isn't it? Just leave things as they are, you know? It's

not like someone's going to end up there instead of Stow-on-
the-Wold, is it? Hundreds of miles away.' Another bite of his
sandwich and some slow chews. He got out his notebook.
'Anyway, me and Stish turn up at the pub. Bit of a grimy little
boozer, have to say. I wouldn't even drink tap water in there.
Not that I drink anymore, you know? One turns to eight and
before you know it, you're texting your exes.' He shook his
head. 'Always a lot to explain in the morning. Someone should
invent an app that lets you see all the drunken messages you
sent the night before. And unsend them. Anyway.' He looked at
his notebook again then at Marshall, his lips twisting. 'What
was the question?'

There was no fast forward button on this guy, was there?

Marshall tapped his phone's screen again. 'This guy?'

'Right, right. Where was I? That pub is grimy as hell, like.
Me and Stish get out of the car, stick our hats on. Get out our
batons. Make sure our cuffs and pepper sprays are accessible.
And we make our way over to the pub. And it's all kicking off in
there. Like in a western, you know? Well, not quite tables flying
everywhere and guns going off, but the bit before, you know?
About six of them were all gathered around the pool table. Real
Mexican stand-off. Then something happened and they start
going at it. Swoosh. This daft bastard here swung his pool cue
through the air and clobbered his mate on the forehead. Guy
went down like two tons of coal, you know? Place was deadly
silent and the other five loons clocked us. Thought that was it,
all over. So Stish goes to put him in cuffs and we think that's it.
Doing our bit to stabilise society and this particular community. But no.' He took another bite of his sandwich. Somehow
there was still half of it left. 'Just as Stish got the cue off him,
which took more than a little bit of physical persuasion from
yours truly.' He made some karate noises and chopped the air.
'I sorted him out. Sure you can imagine. Did a lot of judo and

karate at university. The two martial arts blend well together, you know? But as Stish was about to cuff him, your man here attacked him with the same cue.'

Marshall jumped in as he took another bite. 'He attacked Stish?'

'No. This guy here.' Warner tapped the screen. 'Your fella. He had blood pouring down his face from a cut but he still managed to lash out with the cue. Must've dropped it when I battered him!' He giggled, high and shrill. Seemed to go on forever. 'Guess who he hit?' He reached over and patted his nearest mate on the arm. 'Fell on your arse, Stish, eh?'

Stish rolled his eyes. 'Yeah, sure. So what?' Newcastle accent. Gaze as cold as a winter stroll along the promenade in Whitley Bay. 'Battered the attacker with the cue but caught me on the follow through.'

'Took him ages to get up!' More shrill giggling from Warner.

Marshall glared at him. 'Any chance you can give me the edited highlights here?'

'Sure, I'll—' Warner looked up at Jolene. 'Oh, hey you.'

'Here you go, Rob.' She sat down next to Marshall, pushing a coffee in front of him. 'Hi, Liam, still freaky eating I notice.'

Warner looked at his sandwich. 'Oh, come on. Didn't know peanut butter, jalapeño and chorizo on rye was that unusual until I came to Gala.' He pronounced the latter two ingredients in their native tongues. 'Just telling your boss here about how me and Stish were called out to—'

'*Constable.*' Marshall raised his eyebrows, trying to enforce some sternness. His voice had silenced quite a few nearby diners. 'She doesn't need to hear that story again.' And Marshall certainly didn't. 'Edited highlights. Please.'

'Where was I?' Warner stared deep into his sandwich box. 'Oh yeah, Stish fell on his arse. The guy who'd been cut, but who smashed the other fella in the face with the pool cue, left the pub.'

'You let him get away?'

'Right. I mean, he'd just twonked someone with a pool cue and his face was opened up, but I needed to help Stish to his feet and the other guy wasn't moving. And—'

'What happened?'

'We drove him to hospital.'

Marshall pointed at the mobile. 'Him?'

'No, the other guy. Your man's the one who left. We took him to A&E.' Warner picked up the second half of his second sandwich. 'Of course, his mate was already there, wasn't he?' He pointed at the phone. 'This guy. And me and Stish had to separate them in the waiting area in A&E.' He wrapped an arm around his own throat. 'Grabbed him like that and got him to settle down. Was going to charge him after he'd been treated, but he somehow got away.'

Probably when Warner was regaling a nurse or seven with the takedown but starting from the Big Bang and winding forward a millisecond at a time.

Whatever Warner's skills were, he'd be useless in court.

'Need a name.'

'Kyle Talbot was the one we drove.'

He worked on the estate, assembling the wind farm.

Marshall clocked Jolene's sigh. 'Sure about that?'

'Positive.'

'And the other guy?'

Warner scratched at his neck. 'I don't know off the top of my head.'

'Can you check?'

Warner put his sandwich down and got out his notebook. He started reading it like a child at their first Roald Dahl, going line by line.

Jolene rolled her eyes. 'Liam, hand me your notebook for Thursday's shift, please.' She took it and scratched a piece of something green off the page. 'I hope that's dried lettuce.' She started flicking through it. 'Here we go. Name's Justin Lorimer.'

Meant nothing to Marshall, but at least they now had something.

CHAPTER SIXTEEN

Marshall sat in the passenger seat, gripping his phone tight, pressed against his skull, the ringing tone burning in his ear.

Jolene weaved around the traffic on the A7, a dodgy road at the best of times but awful today in the snow and ice. This stretch cut around hills the Gala Water had gouged into a valley over the millennia. The tiny river twinkled in the middle of a field, separating two herds of cows, all puzzled by the snow but just getting on with it. A brick fireplace sat next to them, the only remnant of an old house.

And Marshall definitely wouldn't have overtaken that bus and certainly not there.

Up ahead, the village of Stow nestled on the river's banks, most of the buildings dusted white. The church spire at the near end and the three-storey manse, then the post-war houses climbing up the hill to the Lauder road, where the bodies had been found.

The call was finally answered. 'Doctor Donkey.' Elliot's

voice. Sounded like she was outside, with wind buffeting her speaker. 'Thought you'd never call me.'

'Andrea. Heard you were on the case.'

'Pringle called. Let me junk those meetings he'd foisted on me, so aye. I'm on the case. How goes it?'

'We think we've identified the male victim.'

'You think?'

'Name's Justin Lorimer. Uniform in Gala took him to A&E last Thursday. Can you get the street teams asking around for him?'

'I'll get them focusing on what your last slave died of too.'

'Ha. Ha.'

'On it. But you and I need to have a wee chinwag with Pringle, vis-à-vis who's doing what.'

'Sure thing. Just trying to get on with the job, Andrea. Not easy when you're one DI with a big team.'

'Now we can share all that glory, Marshall.' She sniffed. 'Who is Lorimer?'

'All we know is he's dead and was in a pub fight with Kyle Talbot last Thursday.'

'And who's Talbot?'

'Works on the wind farm. We spoke to him first thing.'

'Right, right. Shunty was havering about someone. Is this the idiot who's staying in that grotty boozer in Stow?'

'That's where he's staying, aye.'

'We'll speak to him again, then.'

Jolene entered Stow itself, a long village lining the main road between Edinburgh and Carlisle. A twenty limit for miles. A sign read:

Wedale House
Putting the "you" in boutique

She was muttering under her breath, 'That doesn't work in the slightest...'

Marshall faced away from her. 'What are you doing now, Andrea?'

But Elliot had already gone. Typical.

Jolene took the left at the junction and headed towards the train station. A brown sign pointed to the Stagehall Arms, like it was some kind of national monument and not a grim boozer. She pulled up outside a rundown home a few doors down. The house was a grey post-war building, probably prefabricated in the age of rationing and only intended for habitation for a decade or so, yet here it was almost eighty years later. Two cars sat outside – a silver Skoda saloon lurked behind a brute of a Toyota pick-up. 'Let's get this over with, then.' She got out first.

Marshall put his phone away and stepped out into the bracing cold. His face was roasting and he was glad of the cool.

Jolene stepped back from pressing the button. 'No sign of—'

The door clattered open and a frantic woman appeared. Mid-thirties, maybe. Dirty-blonde hair tied back in a ponytail. Trackie bottoms and an over-sized T-shirt advertising 'The Werewolf Chase', a fell running competition in the hills squeezing the village in. She looked between them. 'Listen, I'm kind of a bit—'

'Police.'

The word stopped her dead.

Jolene's warrant card made her forehead crease. 'Acting DS Jolene Archer.' She put the ID away. 'This is DI Rob Marshall. We're looking for Justin Lorimer.'

'So am I.' Hands on her hips. 'He's not come home. Again.'

'Can I take your—'

'I'm Rachel. Rachel Lorimer. His wife. What's he done now?'

'We should do this in—'

'You've found his body. Right?'

Jolene nodded slowly. 'I'm afraid so.'

'Jesus.' Rachel shook her head then looked away, tears flowing down her cheeks. 'What happened?'

'It was discovered up on the road to Lauder.'

'My God.' Rachel's hand slapped to her mouth. 'That was on the news. It's *him*?'

'We believe so.'

'When I heard it on the radio, I told myself, Rach, it's not him. It can't be him. He'll be back home soon. He always comes back, smiling wide. Because he loves me. Loves the kids. How the hell am I going to cope?' She brushed a hand across her face. 'Can I see him?'

CHAPTER SEVENTEEN

'Riddle me this, Shunty.' Elliot sat in the passenger seat, arms folded, the belt dangling free, watching a house in Darnick. Where Louisa Baird's mother lived – a humble Sixties bungalow, not too far from the ancient buildings in what passed for a village centre, almost surgically attached to Melrose, but far from the prettiest house in the area. Still, someone could live a life in there. Three cars were parked in the drive, with another couple on the street outside. Probably a few neighbours in there to comfort Louisa Baird's mother. 'A man grieving for his wife shouldn't be outside on the phone, should he?'

Hugo Baird stood under the eaves of the house, mobile clamped to his skull, staring into space. The snow hadn't started up again, but some flakes were blowing from the roof and the nearby trees.

'It is odd, aye.' Shunty was behind the wheel, drumming his fingers off it. Actually seemed to be able to keep good time, though there wasn't any music playing. The big lump slicked back his hair and looked around at her, his eyes like chunks of coal. 'What's the plan here?'

'Well, Dr Donkey and Jolene didn't make any inroads with this boy, so I want to give it a shot. Curious how he's left his office to come here, though.'

'Curious how?'

'Jolene told me he didn't want to leave.'

'So you're thinking that's a work call?'

'Let's find out, shall we?' Elliot didn't wait for his reply and got out into the bright morning. Almost chilly. She crunched over the road to the drive, though the snow was turning to slush and revealing buried plants. She smiled at Hugo as she passed.

He barely seemed to notice the fact that two police officers were coming to the door. Maybe he was heavily medicated. Or drunk. 'No, no. I think we should do that. I'll approve it, just... Just don't spend too long on it. The client funds are running low. Maybe chase them for more, yes.'

A work call.

Time and tide waited for no man, but surely his business partner would let him have a day off when his wife died?

The front door was open, but the glass inner door was closed. The facing door opened and a sprightly woman appeared. A bathroom, judging by the white noise rushing out of the house. She scowled at Elliot, then walked over and opened the door. 'Can I help? Are you friends of Louisa? Or Hugo's?'

'Neither. DI Andrea Elliot.' She held out her warrant card. 'This is DS Rakesh Siyal.' She put the ID away and offered her hand.

'Ailsa Johnstone.' She couldn't resist shaking it. 'Has something else happened?'

'No, just wondering if we could have a chat about your daughter.'

Ailsa scratched at her arm. 'Come in, come in.' She staggered through the hallway, then took a right turn.

Maybe they were all drunk.

Elliot let Shunty go first. 'You're good cop here, okay?' She followed him through into a kitchen. Tiled walls, appliances maybe ten years old, but a nice cosy feel to it. Open bottles of red and white wine on the counter. Voices came from two other rooms, a lounge and a dining room.

Ailsa pulled a tray of food out of the oven without an oven glove. Party food – prawn vol-au-vents, pakoras, mini pizzas. She started divvying them up into bowls all laden on a tray. 'There we go.'

Elliot stayed standing in the doorway. Best place to exert control over this situation. 'How are you bearing up?'

Ailsa squinted at her and seemed to consider the question for the first time. 'How do you think? I've lost my daughter!'

'It's okay to grieve.'

'What's that supposed to mean?'

'Just that you're focusing on entertaining your friends and relatives. Being the good host. It's okay to admit you're struggling with what's happened.'

Ailsa stared into the bowl of pakoras for a few seconds. Then shut her eyes and wiped a hand across them. 'I don't know what I did with the dipping sauce.'

Shunty pointed at the back door. 'It's over by the bin.'

'Right you are.' Ailsa walked over and picked up two little tubs of red sauce. She tipped them both into a soup bowl, then grabbed the tray and left the room.

'Displacement activity.' Shunty looked wistful. 'Recognise it from when my mum died.'

Elliot felt a stab in her gut. 'I'm sorry, I didn't know.'

'You never ask.'

True.

Very true.

'Any time you want to talk—'

The door rattled open again and Ailsa walked in, a fake smile plastered on her face. 'Now.' She smiled at them in turn. 'No top ups. Can I get either of you a drink?'

The way the air moved, Elliot could smell the second-hand booze mixing with her sweet perfume. Gin or vodka, probably.

'We're on duty.' Elliot thumbed behind her. 'We saw your son-in-law outside.'

Ailsa grimaced. 'It's a very difficult time for his business.'

'Must be hard, though. Having this ball of grief in the pit of your stomach and he's out there on the phone about business matters.'

'It is what it is.' Ailsa snorted. 'Now.' She crouched with an agility that belied her age and got two pizzas out of the fridge. She dumped them onto the counter and started tearing at the packaging. One was covered in a rainbow of vegetables, the other in beige meat. 'My daughter married well.' She chuckled. 'Even though Hugo's not far off my age.' Something seemed to catch in her throat.

Elliot gave her time and space, letting her put the pizzas into the hot oven. Then she waited for eye contact. 'I gather Louisa's father passed away?'

She stared into space, then she focused on Elliot. 'He was never really on the scene. I had to raise Louisa myself.'

Elliot spotted a parallel with Dr Donkey. Marshall and that twin sister of his were raised by a single mother. She hoped he was using that to get an insight into Louisa's psychology, but he was probably just fannying about with profiles instead of doing real police work.

'Louisa was a precocious child and a very difficult teenager.

Wasn't easy, I have to say. But she blossomed into an incredibly kind woman and...' She shut her eyes and seemed to lose herself to grief.

Experience taught Elliot to let it play out.

Experience Shunty didn't have. 'Can I ask about their nanny?'

Ailsa opened her eyes and shot him a glare. 'Their what?'

'Nanny. Au pair.'

'Right. Well, Becky's a lovely girl.' Ailsa pressed a few buttons on the oven, then walked over to a side door. 'Becky, can I have a hand through here?' She went over to the back door and slipped outside.

Shunty made to go after her.

Elliot pulled him back. 'Give her a minute, okay?'

A girl stepped through the side door. She was tall and was all stretched out like she was in the wrong screen mode, but this was real life and Elliot didn't have to wrestle with her dad's remote control to unwind what he'd done to his TV. Despite that, she was stunning. Shiny dark hair, baby blue eyes, but her naively applied makeup was smudged. Clearly been crying. And definitely a girl, rather than a woman. Eighteen, if a day.

Elliot hated her already.

Becky shifted her gaze between them, her forehead creasing. 'Where's Ailsa?'

Shunty took control. 'She's just stepped outside for a minute. Becky, isn't it?'

'What's happened? Is she okay?'

'She's just getting some air. Rakesh and I are police officers, Becky. I'm Andi.'

'Has something else happened?'

'No, Becky, it's okay. We're just here to ask a few more questions, that's all. I gather you stay with Hugo and Louisa?'

'That's right.' Becky bit her top lip. 'I'm on a gap year. Working to earn money for uni. I babysit their son during the day when they're at work. He's in the room opposite mine. And they give me the occasional night off to do stuff.' She looked at her shoes, flat-soled red things. 'Like last night.'

Elliot frowned. 'I thought they were both out?'

'Oh, yeah, they were. That's not what I meant. Mrs Baird invited me to that Burns supper. I'd been looking forward to it for ages.'

'But?'

'But Hugo put his foot down. Said he needed to work, so I did too.'

Shunty smiled at her. 'That must've been frustrating.'

'Tell me about it. Pissed off, to be honest. Kid was asleep by eight, but *he* wasn't home, so I just sat and watched some mindless shite on Netflix when I could've been dancing and having fun.'

Elliot gave a sympathetic smile, but really, when you make a deal with the devil, you've just got to count the money coming into your bank account until he comes calling for the debt. Lassie like Becky will have plenty of opportunities to dance and drink at university, not with some red-faced toffs at a farm. 'When did Mr Baird come home?'

'Be about midnight. Woke me up.'

Elliot struggled to keep her eyebrows down. That interesting. 'He work you up? Like physically?'

'No. When he opened the door. He's not a quiet man.'

'You get on with Mrs Baird, right?'

'Louisa… She's… She's great. I really liked Louisa. She was always super friendly, like a big sister.'

'And Hugo?'

'What about him?'

'How did you get on with him?'

'He's fine.' Her smile was polite and forced. Hopefully even Shunty could see that. 'Kind, polite, but firm.'

There was something the girl didn't like about him, though.

'Becky, can you elab—'

An almighty scream tore out from the living room, 'MUUU-UMMMMMMMYYYYY!'

'Crap, sorry.' Becky ran off.

Elliot watched her go, the light feet of youth scooting across the floor tiles. 'Saved by the screaming bairn.'

Siyal was following her path. 'You think there's something going on?'

'I mean, it's convenient timing, but she ran off to look after the crying kid when the questioning got a bit difficult.'

'I'm not sure that's what happened.' Shunty snorted. 'But do you think the boy sees her as his mother or—'

'Sorry about that.' Hugo marched into the kitchen, smiling like he was meeting up with some clients he hadn't seen for a few months. 'Had to take a work call.'

'Sorry to hear about that.'

'My partner is stressing about things. Kind of guy who sweats the small stuff. It's probably why we work together so well. Sometimes I skirt over some essential details. And sometimes I need to remind him of the bigger picture.'

'I know people like that.' Elliot's smile was a bit more conspiratorial than his, but she hoped it got through to him. 'Why did he call you today of all days?'

'Oh, I called him.'

What the hell?

That threw Elliot. Making calls the day his wife's body was found.

There was cold and there was...

That.

Shunty stepped in. 'Sir, does the name Rougier mean anything to you?'

'Rougier? No. Should it?'

'We understand a Dr Benjamin Rougier was the subject of an HR issue at your wife's hospital. She was the complainant.'

Hugo sighed. 'Well, Louisa certainly didn't mention it to me.'

'Why weren't you at the Burns supper last night?'

'Why should I? Complete waste of my time. Who wants to eat sheep entrails and common vegetables in homage to a long-dead mediocre poet who barely even rhymes? What's the point?'

Elliot choked a laugh in her throat. 'You know you could've just said it's not your scene and you've too much work on.'

'I've learned in my years on this planet that it pays not to lie. The unvarnished truth is something to cherish.'

'Okay, but it feels like somebody is lying here.'

'So why are you assuming it's me?'

'Because your wife's dead and you're sweating about work. Calling up your partner when your son's being looked after by your nanny.'

Hugo shut his eyes and seemed to think. Or feel. He seemed to shudder. 'Let me be perfectly clear.' He reopened his eyes and a fiery rage burned there. 'I've been a lawyer far longer than I've been a husband and a father. In my position, you don't have the luxury of grieving for days on end. I have responsibilities both to my clients and to my firm. I might only be a partner in a small firm, but people rely on me. The community depends on me. I have so much weight on my shoulders just now. So much pressure. And, as much as it troubles me to say, I can't save my wife now.'

Harsh, harsh words. No warmth or emotion in them.

Elliot fixed him with a hard stare. 'You can't save her, no, but you can help us find her killer.'

He met her glare for a few seconds, then seemed to rock back. 'Listen, the truth is our marriage was...' He rested against the hot oven. 'Loveless is the best way to describe it. A genuine marriage of convenience. I needed an heir, Lou wanted my money and a certain lifestyle even a doctor couldn't afford. It was a compromise, but I'd be lying if I said I didn't... have some affection for her. I was prepared to be the doting husband and father, but she wasn't prepared to be my wife. In reality, she died to me a while ago. Yet I'll still miss what we might've had.'

Elliot let the words rattle around the room, losing to the extractor fan and the hiss of the oven. That amount of honesty often came in packs of two, three, sometimes more. So she did what a good cop would and kept her mouth shut.

Now Louisa was gone, Hugo really missed her. The reality of the loss of something he'd already thought gone seemed to defeat him.

'Was it an open marriage?'

Bloody hell, Shunty couldn't keep his mouth shut, could he?

'An *open marriage?*' Hugo was turning purple. 'I don't appreciate you using a crass term like that.'

'I'm sorry, sir, I was using a euphemism to—'

'I get it. And no, ours wasn't an open marriage. If I'd got wind of her sleeping around, then I would've divorced her.'

'Did you ever cheat on her?'

'Excuse me?'

'Did you ever sleep with—'

'I know what it means, sonny. And no, I didn't.'

'See, it's interesting how you've got a nanny—'

'Ex*cuse* me?'

'Becky. We just spoke to her. Hard to not be tempted by a young girl like her.'

'I've never been so insulted in all my days!' Hugo looked like he was going to thump Shunty. But he was a lover, not a fighter, so he backed down. Maybe not a lover, but a businessman who preferred to do his fighting in law courts. 'Becky has been a lifesaver. Louisa realised pretty quickly she didn't want to be a mother, so she went back to work and we had an issue. Becky plugged a gap, so to speak. Eventually, my son will take over my share of the business when he's old enough, but I hope to still be working for years to come. I want him raised by the best. And Becky is highly regarded.'

The back door opened and Ailsa stormed back in. 'Oh my, the pizzas!' She raced over and opened the oven. 'They're buggered!' She took them out and placed them on a giant wooden chopping board. She was scowling at the oven. 'The bloody beeper didn't go off, did it?'

Shunty shook his head. 'I've been listening for it.'

'Ach, they'll be fine.' She looked at Hugo, then at Elliot. 'Why are you still here on a day like this?'

'MUUUUUUUMMMMMMMMMMMMYYYYYY!'

Hugo dipped his head. 'And now he's losing his shit too. I'll sort him out.' He left the room.

Ailsa watched him go, standing there, hands on hips. 'What have you been asking him?'

'A few questions. That's all.'

'I've never seen him like that. He's the most placid man but he looked like he was going to lamp you.'

'Ms Johnstone, we—'

'Please. Call me Ailsa.'

'Ailsa. We—'

'What on earth were you asking him?'

Elliot held her fiery gaze. 'Let me be clear. We're searching for your daughter's killer. Her husband might know something about what's happened. Directly or indirectly. So we need to ask some searching questions. It's either here or it's in a police station.'

'Yes, well. There's a time and a place.' Ailsa got out a pizza wheel and scored the first one. 'Bugger, I've done the meat one first. Ach, well.' She did the second. Then her head dipped and she sighed. 'I want to see my daughter's body.'

'She's already been identified by a colleague.'

'All the same, I want to see her.'

CHAPTER EIGHTEEN

Marshall held the door and let Jolene lead Rachel Lorimer into the pathology department's identification room. The place smelled of bleach, softened by fresh daffodils, though where they'd been sourced from at this time of year was anyone's guess.

Rachel had changed out of her leisurewear into more formal attire. Black slacks and a navy blouse. She couldn't look at either of them for longer than a glance.

Dr Owusu appeared through a side door. Marshall couldn't hear what she said, but she touched Rachel's arm, then guided her over to the gurney against the far wall.

Marshall stayed back, watching them through the glass, trying to get a better view of her watching the body on a gurney, hidden behind a screen. Looking for any reaction, anything unusual.

Poor woman was in shock. Not many worse things you could experience than the loss of a partner – Marshall knew that pain all too well. Hopefully for Rachel Lorimer, her grief would be briefer than his had been.

So many questions they still needed to answer – how many she'd be able to help with was their highest priority now.

The door clattered open and Elliot wandered in, one hand in her trouser pocket. 'In here, please.' She stopped dead and focused on Marshall. 'Sorry, I'll just be a second.' She nudged the door to and faced Marshall again. Her mousy fringe hung over her left eye and she tucked it behind her ear. 'Marshall, what are you doing here?'

'Mrs Lorimer's identifying the body.'

'Thought you'd be finished by now.'

'Aye, so did I.'

'Got to hand it to him.' She thumbed behind her. 'Shunty's managed to persuade Hugo Baird to come in. Given what Jo told us about him not identifying her, he thought that didn't make sense, so he insisted on getting Hugo to play ball.'

'Good effort.' Marshall looked through the window just in time for Rachel Lorimer to nod at Owusu. Jolene made eye contact with Marshall then led Rachel through the door at the other side, into the family interview rooms.

At least they'd avoid a log jam.

Owusu came out through the door. 'There you are, Andi. We're ready for you now in the other room.'

'Cool beans.' Elliot opened the door. 'In you come.'

Siyal led Hugo Baird in, then stopped and frowned at Marshall. 'Sir.'

Hugo looked at Marshall sternly, then followed Owusu over to the door. Seemed impatient to get back to his work once the trivial business of identifying his wife's body was out of the way.

A sprightly woman in her seventies entered the room, her tired gaze shifting between everyone in there. Dressed up like she was going out for the evening. She made a beeline for

Marshall. 'Ailsa Johnstone. I'm Louisa's mother.' She held out a hand. 'And you must be the mortician?'

'No, I'm DI Rob Marshall. I'm a colleague of DI Elliot.' He shook her hand. 'This is Dr Owusu, who is the pathologist. She'll take you through the process.'

'If you'll just follow me?' Owusu shot Marshall and Elliot daggers then led them into the room, with Siyal following.

Elliot had a coy grin on her face. 'See, people just can't help but see you as a doctor.'

'I have got a doctorate.' Marshall watched another body being identified, even though Owusu had already given a positive match.

Elliot stood next to him. 'The nanny's looking after Toby.'

'Hugo just called him "the boy".'

'That right?' Elliot's forehead creased. 'They're not far apart in age, are they?'

Siyal led Hugo and Ailsa out of the far door.

Marshall avoided going down that rabbit hole for fear it was mined. 'Did you mention Lorimer's name to them?'

'To both, aye. Neither recognised Lorimer or had even heard of him.' Elliot leaned back against a table. 'She said Louisa's father's not on the scene.'

'That's a bit of a euphemism.'

'Lot of death around today, Marshall. Sometimes you just let them get on with their euphemisms, you know?'

Marshall knew. Boy did he know. 'What about Rougier?'

'Bloody Shunty asked.' Elliot shook her head. 'Sometimes he's Mr Woke and sensitive, sometimes he's like a farmer with a shotgun. Anyway, Hugo denies even hearing the name.'

'So the HR issue never made it home?'

'If it did, he's denied it and lied to our faces. Nice wee trap to catch a fly in.' She nudged Marshall. 'Though I gather young Dr Rougier did.'

'Did what?'

'Make it home. To her house.'

'Aye. Allegedly. Turned up with flowers one day.'

The door clattered open.

Marshall and Elliot both swung around.

Pringle was staring at it, shaking his head. 'Thought she was going to get out the WD40 to fix that lousy asshole of a door.' He spun around to them. 'Ah, looky here! I'm such a lucky man to have my team laden before me. Nay, festooned before me!'

Jolene came through the side door. 'Rob, we got a positive ID.'

'I saw.' Marshall patted Pringle's arm. 'Back in a couple of minutes, sir.' He followed Jolene through into the long corridor he'd become familiar with in his time based up here.

Through the doors he saw that one family room had Siyal, Hugo Baird and Ailsa Johnstone, while the other just had Rachel Lorimer.

Marshall closed the door behind them and focused on Rachel. 'I'm truly sorry for your loss.'

'Find them.' Rachel was sitting on the sofa, a tissue scrunched up in her hand. 'Find the fucker who did this to Justin.'

'We'll do our best. And that's a promise.'

'Is that good enough, though?' Her eyes narrowed at him, then she looked away. Seemed to be good enough. For now.

Marshall sat in the armchair opposite. 'Need to ask you a few questions, if that's okay?'

'Like what?'

'Where did he work?'

'How's that going to help?'

'If he was a prison officer, say, then—'

'Right. I get it.' She clamped a hand to the side of her head. 'Justin was the estate manager at Blainslieshaw Mains farm.'

'I know the family. It's Napier Rattray who runs it, right?'

'Aye, but Justin's the main doer there.'

'Do you know where your husband was last night?'

'I don't. I was working. Kids were at my mother's. Slim pickings. Sat on the rank a few times. January's dead, isn't it?'

'You're a taxi driver?'

'Right. About to call it a night, when a fare came in. Airport transfer to Newcastle airport at half two. Planned on driving themselves but the roads were too bad. Even for an experienced driver like myself, it wasn't much fun in all that snow, but I got through it. Got back home at seven to collect the kids from Mum's then get them ready for school, which was bloody cancelled. And I heard the news on the radio as I was making some soup.'

'Your husband didn't come home last night?'

'His car's there, so I presumed he did, aye.'

That didn't stack up quite right for Marshall.

Sure, she had an alibi for the approximate time of death, but not noticing if he was home or not?

'Do you know where he was?'

'Nope.' She yawned into her fist. 'Sorry, I haven't slept since yesterday morning and even then...'

'Is your husband not coming home a common occurrence?'

'Not *uncommon*, but on a Wednesday? Friday, sure. Maybe a Saturday. But...' She huffed out a sigh and scratched out another tissue from the table.

'Does the name Louisa Baird mean anything to you?'

She shook her head. 'Should it?'

'Your husband's body was found next to hers.'

'Right.' She blew her nose. 'Never heard of her. Sorry.'

Marshall showed her a photo of Louisa, all red-faced after

running a marathon, but all he got was a shake of the head. He put his phone away. 'What about a Kyle Talbot?'

'Nope. Why, should I?'

'Did your husband mention being in a fight on Thursday?'

'News to me.' Her face twisted. 'Was it with this Talbot?'

Marshall nodded. 'He was taken to hospital.'

'Said he fell off his bike. Rides up to the farm some days for the exercise. Daft sod never wears a helmet.'

'Okay.' Marshall tapped Jolene on the arm. 'I've got a few things to check out but my colleague will be here until a family liaison officer is appointed.'

'Thank you.'

Marshall left the room and didn't know what to think. The only thing Louisa and Justin seemed to have in common was their spouses had literally no idea what happened in their lives.

Pringle and Elliot were in conference at the end of the corridor, just outside Owusu's room. Heads almost touching, voices low.

Marshall strode towards them, the sound making them break apart. 'She doesn't know Louisa Baird.'

Elliot winced. 'Same story as across the way. They've never heard of Justin Lorimer.'

'Disaster for Scotland...' Pringle whistled a tune Marshall didn't recognise. 'Okay, here's what I think we need to do. It's obvious these two victims are connected. Same dump site, same MO, same day but different time. Clearly been done by the same people. We don't know how this pair is connected and we need to know.' He looked at Marshall. 'Our priority is to trace the movements of both victims before they died. Got her at a Burns supper. Him?'

'Wife had no idea where he was. Suggested the pub.'

'Okay, so how about we split it up so Andi focuses on him and you focus on her, Rob?'

Marshall shrugged. 'Happy with that.'

Elliot shifted her gaze between them. 'Fine, Jim, but the problem is I'm playing catch up here.'

'One thing you're good at, Andi, is playing games.' Pringle click-winked. 'Start with the pub assault on Thursday night. That might explain a few things.'

'Me and Shunty will speak to Kyle Talbot about that.' Elliot stared at Pringle. 'He's the lad who lamped him one.' She frowned. 'Actually, can you lamp someone with a pool cue?'

Pringle scratched his head. 'Why is he of interest?'

'Because Dr Donkey here spoke to him, sir, and he didn't mention the incident, or identify the victim.'

Pringle looked at Marshall. 'Did you ask him?'

'True, we didn't. But still. I think it's a decent avenue.' Marshall leaned against the wall. 'I suggest we track down the Good Samaritan who dropped Lorimer at hospital. Could be a friend, family member, taxi driver. Unlikely he got the bus. Couldn't have walked. And someone picked him up from the hospital.'

Elliot arched her eyebrow. 'What about the wife?'

'Claims she didn't know about the fight. Said he told her he fell off his bike.'

'Okay, that's rocking.' Pringle smiled. 'A nice wee trap to catch some flies in.'

Elliot glowered at him. Probably for stealing her line. 'I don't get why we're focusing on this fight, though?'

Marshall folded his arms. 'I think there could be something in it. Maybe Talbot finished the job.'

'Seems unlikely.' She brushed her fringe out of her eyes. 'But I get it. We want to close off all the questions.' She took out her notebook and started flicking through the pages. 'What about her stalker?'

'Dr Rougier? Odd behaviour, that.' And Pringle would know. 'I want him eliminated.' He laughed. 'And not like that!'

Elliot smirked. 'I'll look into him too, see if I can get a better result than Dr Donkey did.'

Marshall tried to laugh it off. Trouble with nicknames was when they stuck – and that'd been with him for three months now. 'Jolene's team are working on Rougier's alibis.'

Elliot scribbled it down. 'I'll hook up with them.'

Owusu appeared out of a door and jabbed a finger at Pringle. 'Here, Jim!'

He trudged over to her like a naughty schoolboy. 'What's up?'

'Does this place look like Waverley station?'

'No?'

'Good. Because I don't expect to have queues of grieving people waiting to identify their loved ones!'

'Sorry.'

'I mean it.'

'I'll sort it out.'

'Good.' She looked around and noticed them. 'Andrea, I got your voicemail. The answer's yes. Lorimer just needed a couple of stitches in his head wound.'

'What caused it?'

'A blunt force of some kind.'

'So, consistent with getting battered in a pub fight?'

'Consistent, yes.' She looked back at Pringle. 'I mean it. Otherwise I'll have to start introducing a ticketing system for you.' She slipped off and let the door slam behind her.

Pringle stared at the door for a few seconds, then walked back over, whistling something tuneless but with a lot of trilling. 'Drug gangs.'

Elliot looked up at Pringle, eyebrow raised. 'You think it's drug gangs?'

'That's what I said, diddle I?' Pringle cackled. 'Usual MO. Dealer gets in debt to supplier, takes you out into countryside, kicks four or five bells of crap out of you and leaves you to walk home. Do it again, and it's seven bells and you're way further out.'

'What about the wrist and ankle bonds, though?'

Pringle shrugged. 'Had a few cases like that over the years.'

'Have we?'

'Must've done.'

'And did they involve oncologists and farm estate managers, or was it neds from Langlee?'

Pringle tapped his nose. 'Even oncologists snort coke.'

'But this one? Have you any evidence to suggest she did?'

'Just look into it.' Pringle got out his phone and glanced at the screen, whistled and put it away. 'Marshall, I want you to go down the road of considering a serial attacker.'

'Sir, we've been over this. It's not.'

Elliot got between them. 'Jim, are you only excited by sexy cases these days?'

'No!' Pringle glared at her. 'While DI Marshall is reluctant to consider it, I can certainly see the logic. Same MO, same location. Stands to reason it could be an escalation from a few people being abducted but not killed over the years.'

'Nothing else chimes, though.' Marshall shoved his hands deep in his pockets. 'They're from different social strata.'

'Ex-squeeze me?' Pringle did a mock shake of his head. 'Different what?'

'She's a doctor. He's a farm labourer. The shared victimology doesn't exist.'

Pringle clapped him on the arm. 'Rob, just see what you can come up with on that score.' He opened the door to

Owusu's lab. 'I'm going to attend the PM. See you later, alligator and crocodile.'

Elliot waited for the door to swing shut. 'Drug gangs... Next it'll be cattle-mutilating UFOs.' She looked at Marshall. 'What's your thinking?'

'He's the boss, so we have to humour him.'

'Fed up of that, though.' She scowled at the door. 'Heard you went to school with the landowner's son?'

'Balfour, aye.'

'That's not a conflict of interest, is it?'

'No, but it might become one. It'd be better if you did that strand.'

'Marshall, if I had to avoid people I know, I'd have to work in London or the bloody Highlands.' Elliot buggered off towards the family room. Timed it perfectly, two FLOs were there, ready to relieve Siyal and Jolene. 'Just get on with it.'

'Okay, I'll head up to the farm and see what Napier Rattray's got to say first.'

Elliot turned back to face Marshall. 'Didn't you hear?'

CHAPTER NINETEEN

Unlike the chaos down in A&E, the intensive therapy unit was as calm as Dr Owusu's pathology department in the hospital's basement. On the top floor and with something approaching a view, across the rooftops of Darnick and Melrose, hidden behind the trees, towards the sleepy hills behind Gattonside. Quite a distance to travel between here, A&E and Pathology, the departments that it would naturally connect to.

Jolene nudged the swing door open and disappeared through the curtain.

Marshall followed her into the ward.

Jolene was already by the desk, showing her credentials. 'We're looking for Napier Rattray?'

The receptionist smiled at her. 'He's in room five.' She pointed along the corridor. 'Down there, then next right.'

'Thanks.' Jolene tilted her head then led on. 'Odd to find a toff in a council hospital like this.'

Marshall followed her. 'He had some funny ideas.'

'It's not funny.'

'No, but it is for someone of his means, hence you mentioning it.'

'Suppose I see your point.' Jolene knocked on the door to room five, then twisted the handle.

A frail man lay flat on the bed, the sheet tucked up to his chest. Eyes closed. The metronomic inhale-exhale cycle of a respirator.

Marshall barely recognised him as the burly farmer who'd made the whole school laugh way back when. He'd seemed massive, with shovels for hands, but now it was like he'd wilted.

By the window, a woman was fussing over a vase of flowers. 'You'll never believe what happened in *Eastenders*, Napier.' She cut the stems and starting refilling the vase with new water. 'That young lad you hate came back.' She turned around. 'You'll never guess what— Oh my!' Her hand went to her chest and her mouth fell open. Luckily she had the presence of mind to not drop the vase. 'Can I help you?'

'DS Jolene Archer.' She held out her warrant card. 'This is DI Rob Marshall. We wanted to—'

'Rob Marshall... Now where do I know that name from?'

He gave her a reluctant smile. 'I was at school with Napier's son. For a while.'

'Ah, that'll explain it.' She thrust out a hand. 'I'm Rhona. Napier's wife.' She shook Marshall's first. 'Balfour's mother.'

Jolene shook the hand next.

Rhona looked at the body on the bed. 'I'm afraid you won't get much out of him today, though.'

Jolene jerked her head back. 'I'm sorry, has he died?'

'No, love, we're not quite at that point yet.' She went over and plumped up his pillows. 'He's been in a vegetative state after an accident on the farm.' She shook her head. 'Stupid old goat fell off a turbine in the high winds in October. Fixing a rotor blade. Stupid. Told him it was daft, but he's a stubborn sod. Almost four months he's been like this.'

'I'm very sorry to hear that.' Marshall didn't know where to stand, so just settled for staying where he was. 'Your husband visited our school once and gave a very interesting speech.'

She giggled. 'Ah yes, the "knob" heard around the world. He wasn't invited back after that.' She stopped fussing with the bedding. 'I want the machine to stay on. Napier's a fighter. Always has been. So I'm fighting for him. But I don't know if it's the right thing to do.'

Marshall held her gaze. 'I've been there.'

'Oh?'

'Long story, but... I've been there. I know how hard it is to make the decision to switch off the ventilator. In my case, it should've happened a long time before. But it wasn't my choice to make. Trouble is, there are plenty of other cases where people survive. So it's... Well. It's an impossible choice.'

'That's the thing, isn't it? Can I decide to end his life? Legally, yes. Morally? I'm not so sure. And so I cling to hope. And hope's a slippery devil.'

Marshall left space for a few seconds. 'I don't know if you heard, but there was a discovery on land owned by your estate. Two bodies.'

'Oh my. No, I hadn't heard. I've been too busy here. I like to freshen up his room once a week. New flowers, make sure the bedding is how he'd like it. Read to him from a book and the paper.'

'That's a good thing to do.' Marshall knew from personal experience how soothing it could be to cling to the hope that someone in a coma was listening to you. But he also knew how corrosive it was the longer it went on, way after all hope was dashed. 'We wanted to discuss a few matters relating to the estate.'

'Our number one son, Balfour, is running things now.' She nodded at Marshall. 'Sure you'll be friends with him on Schoolbook?'

'I'm not really a social media kind of guy.'

'You can tell me the truth, if you want. Balfour had his share of difficulties at school. I know all about them, believe you me.'

Marshall gave a tight, sympathetic smile. 'One of the victims was Justin Lorimer.'

'Justin? Oh no. That's... Oh no. I really liked him. Everyone did. Good boss for the workers, good employee. Helped my son take the strain with what happened to... to Napier here. Justin almost ran the farm singlehandedly... Had done for years. Oh and his dear wife and kids. Oh heavens, this is a tragedy. I'll have to arrange some means of support for them. A benefit, perhaps. I could host it, of course. Hell, I could just finance it myself. *Could* do? No, Rhona, don't be so crass! *Will* do. There, it's decided!'

'The other victim was Dr Louisa Baird.'

'Louisa?' Her mouth hung open. 'You're kidding me.'

'Do you know her?'

'She was my oncologist.'

Marshall felt his gut go – starting to build a connection between them. 'Oh, I didn't know.'

'It's okay. We didn't make a big deal of it and those who did know kept it to themselves at our request. I'm long in remission now. I get it checked every six months like clockwork. Yet another thing the NHS is good for nowadays.'

Jolene raised both eyebrows. 'You didn't go private?'

'My husband and I are strong believers in the NHS. And the local education system. Shopping locally. We don't drive Ferraris even though we could.'

'That's very noble of you.'

Rhona smiled. 'You know, my husband used to say, "just because you're from the nobility doesn't mean you have to be a knob." I mean, that's the joke he told at school, but it makes you think, doesn't it? A man should be defined by his actions, not his station in life.' She clicked her tongue a few times. 'Louisa was at my son's Burns supper last night.'

'Oh?'

'I was there only briefly. Had a few appointments to make. It was the bard's night, after all.'

'You're sure it was Dr Baird?'

'We spoke briefly. My next appointment is in a month or so. She wanted to know how I was doing. No complaints.'

'Is this an annual Burns supper?'

'No. But it was the first one Balf ran himself. It was in aid of an appeal for a cancer charity.'

Jolene smiled. 'Is your son working at the farm today?'

CHAPTER TWENTY

Even though she was the DI and Shunty was her subordinate, Elliot liked to drive. Because driving meant control. And she hated it when she wasn't in control. That, and Shunty didn't get his nickname by driving well.

This case had almost missed her, but like her old man would say – "what's for you won't go past you."

Better to be out in the community and solving murders than stuck in stuffy meeting rooms in St Leonards, trying to show the idiots in the drugs squad how to use both of their brain cells in the right order. And that was the world of the DCI – doing that all day, every day.

Be careful what you wish for...

She tore up the A7, heading away from Gala towards Edinburgh. Miserable day – those heavy black clouds were clearly going to dump another load of snow, she just knew it. 'Awful stuff.'

Shunty was staring at his phone. 'Huh?'

If he wouldn't cry to HR about it, she'd consider changing his nickname to Dafty.

Hmm...

Doctor Donkey and Dafty, his feeble-minded assistant. She should write children's books about them. Bound to make as much money as Charlie the bloody Seahorse or whatever her kids were after now.

She looked over at him. 'Snow, Shunty. Snow.'

'Is it?'

'Forget about your Christmas cards with robins and snowmen. Forget about your North American winters where it doesn't matter if you're in Fahrenheit or centigrade.' She had to slow as they approached Stow and pulled in to let a tractor overhanging its lane pass. 'Or Fahrenheit in summer, centigrade in winter like any sensible person would.'

Now he looked over. 'What?'

'Fahrenheit's human-scaled. You know it's hot when it's seventy. What the hell does twenty-three centigrade mean? Nothing.'

'And you switch in winter?'

'Aye. Switch when the clocks change. Celsius is all about water boiling and freezing. Sub-zero like today, you know you're in for it.'

'That sounds quite complex.'

'Switch when the clocks change, Shunty. Mark my words.' She had to pull up at the lights to let a woman cross the road with her two wee darlings. Probably heading back to school for the afternoon. Scratch that – the schools were all off. 'How's your flat going, Shunty?'

He looked over at her, frowning like the bullied kid at school suddenly getting a bit of positive attention that didn't involve abuse. 'My flat?'

'You stay in Gala, right?'

'Up Scott Street, aye.'

'Be easier for you when we shift from Melrose to Gala.'

'That still happening?'

'That's the plan, aye. Trouble is, that useless sod Kirsten and her gang of chumps keep setting fire to their lab. Answer me this, Shunty. Are they all drunks or is it just Sally?'

'You think Sally's a drunk?'

'Think? I know it, Shunty. Bit of a party girl.' Elliot pulled in opposite the Stagehall Arms and waved at the pub. 'Wouldn't be surprised to see her in there on a Wednesday at Mike Hogg's Karaoke Night.' She waited but didn't get anything back. 'Get it?'

'Get what?'

'Mike Hogg. Mic hog. Microphone hog.'

'Right.'

'Jesus Christ, Shunty. It's a joke. And a bloody funny one. Maybe I should send you up to those meetings in Edinburgh instead of me.'

'Can you trust me?'

'Nope.' She laughed. 'Right. Let's get on with this.'

'Shouldn't we be up at the wind farm speaking to Kyle Talbot?'

'Shunty, you still need to learn a few things. If you go in half-cocked, well, you've got half a cock. And everybody wants the full wanger, don't they?'

'That's not—'

'I know it's not PC. But my point is, Talbot stays here during the week, so we want to get the story straight first. Understand him and his movements. Garner as much background info as we can, then we can nail him for lying to Dr Donkey earlier. It's called being a cop, Shunty. This is basic stuff.' Elliot got out of the car into the cool air. Pleasant enough sensation on her cheeks but she wouldn't want to be tied up at the side of the road in it.

She crossed the road to the pub and pushed in through the doors like she was just going for a pint.

The place was busy with lunchtime trade. Six lads propping up the bar, all on their second pint judging by the empties. Red-faced, burping and laughing. The nearest one took a long look at them, then turned away and shuffled down the counter. Clearly clocked them as detectives.

Elliot walked up to the pumps. 'Don't worry, gents, we're not after you, unless you've been abducting and tying people up.' She nodded at the barman. 'Afternoon, Archie.'

'Andi. How you doing?' Archie was old school. Brown Fred Perry tucked into Levi 501s, both sharing the brunt of his eight-month-pregnant belly. The polo bore the eight-month-pregnant man boobs all on its own. Saggy, but his nipples were at attention. Not so much a silver fox as a grey walrus, with that elaborate moustache thing that started at his ears and traced a winding path down and back up. 'What can I get you, Andi?'

The workmen grabbed their pints and headed over to the pool table.

'Looking for someone who knows Justin Lorimer.' She said it loud enough for them to overhear but they weren't listening.

'You've found someone.' Archie picked up a glass and starting drying it with a dishtowel. 'Boy's a regular. In most nights for a pint or two after work. Occasionally for more.'

The pool balls rattled and rolled.

Elliot drummed her fingers on the bar top. 'One of those nights would be last Thursday, aye?'

'Might've been.'

'Might've been.' Elliot laughed. 'Never change, Archie, eh?'

He picked up another glass and started drying it now.

'Doubt I need to tell you, Andi, but there was a fight between two lads. Your colleagues were in to break it up.'

'Names?'

'Eh. Warner? Other was a Geordie, I think?'

'No, you daft sod. The punters knocking seven bells out of each other.'

'Oh, aye. Justin Lorimer and Kyle Talbot. Turfed them both out. Well, tried to. Pair of wankers were resisting. Barred them both.'

'Talbot stays here, though?'

'Aye, through the week. Hard to bar someone from the pub when you're serving him a cooked breakfast in the morning, eh? Still did it, mind.' Archie took another glass and set about drying it. 'Your boy Warner took Talbot to A&E to stitch him up. Lorimer had scarpered. Came in last night to apologise. Told him he was on his last warning.'

'So he was in last night?'

'For a bit, aye.'

'How long's a bit?'

'We were pretty busy, so I couldn't say. An hour, maybe?'

'An hour. Maybe.'

'He bought a round of three pints for him and his mates.'

'You let him back in after he'd hospitalised someone?' Shunty laughed. 'What would get an outright ban? Shooting someone?'

Archie put the glass and towel down. 'Definitely. Or stabbing.' He didn't think Shunty was joking. 'Or crapping your pants. Or grabbing a karaoke mic at Mike Hogg's. Or singing anything other than happy birthday. Or saying anything against our new king. Or pouring your own pint when my back's turned. Or pissing yourself where you're standing. Or ordering a cocktail when the bar's rammed. Or ordering a cocktail, full stop. Or wearing football colours, especially Celtic's. All of which have happened in the last month.'

Shunty laboriously scribbled down each entry. 'You've barred someone for ordering a cocktail?'

'Only because wee Sean wanted a vodka martini, shaken not stirred, to impress some lassie. I've got vodka and I've got ice, but I've no shaker, no olive garnish and no fucking vermouth. Got sick of telling the wee toe rag after each pint of vodka and lemonade. So I barred him.'

'A pint of vodka?'

'Five shots, topped up with ice and lemonade.'

This was going nowhere. Elliot thumped the bar top. 'Can we see the CCTV?'

Archie shifted his gaze back to her. 'Thought we had a deal, Andi.'

'Aye, we did. But the boy's been murdered.'

Archie's thick eyebrows met. 'Justin?'

She nodded.

'Christ.' Archie ran a hand across his lips. 'Fair dos, then.' He reached down behind the bar and hefted up a wee TV monitor, beige and wood-panelled, absolutely covered in stoor.

Elliot stepped back from it. 'Christ, Archie, that looks like it's been in service since the Eighties.'

'Seen more prime ministers than you can shake a stick at. Still works, like, and I'm not made of money.' He turned it around so they could all see the screen, then picked up a remote control and wound it back. Took a bit of clunking and whirring from another device Elliot couldn't see, but there it was.

Lorimer stood in the middle, shouting at Talbot over by the pool table. Both clutched pint glasses that looked like they were going to end up smashed against the other's head.

'Justin got a bit argie bargie about some lad leaving his pint pot on the edge of the table.' Archie pointed at Shunty. 'Add that to your list. That's a straight red.'

Onscreen, Lorimer picked up a pool cue and Elliot expected him to hit Talbot with it. But he got nothing for his shouting, just a rock face from Talbot. Then Archie the barman lumbered over and started arguing with him. Took ages and there was no sound. Eventually, Archie dragged Lorimer out of the picture.

Shunty was taking copious notes. 'You chucked Lorimer out?'

'Straight red.'

'He was only complaining, though.'

'Sorry, he was ranting about Thursday night's scuffle.'

'What? I thought this was Thursday?'

'This is last night. Said he was going to kill Talbot.'

Well, well, well.

Elliot pointed at the doors. 'You got anything outside here?'

'So much for our wee agreement...' Archie crouched down and pulled up another monitor, just as old but without all the wood on the side. He fiddled with the remote and it started playing a video taken from outside the pub.

The air was cold and misty, smearing the camera lens like someone had stuck Vaseline on it. Maybe they had.

Lorimer left the pub, then swung round and jabbed a finger at Archie in the doorway. He walked off with the limp of a drunk.

A van pulled up down the street from him. Seconds later it drove off and Elliot couldn't tell if it had taken him.

The mist made it hard to ID the vehicle. Looked like a work van, but hard to make out the signage.

Elliot smiled at Shunty. 'Come on, Sergeant. We're going to have that word with Kyle Talbot.'

CHAPTER TWENTY-ONE

arshall could pop home for lunch right now.

Not something he would've had to consider back in the days he was living in London, but he could see Jen's house from the steep road north through Clovenfords. He couldn't quite see Zlatan sitting watching the birds from atop his cat empire, but he knew he was there, making his little hunter's chirrups. Not that there were many birds left at this time of year, but those that were would be out scavenging in the light.

Marshall's stomach was rumbling – he'd have to pick something up and soon.

The village had a good amount of traffic going between Gala and Peebles, but this road heading north was much quieter. Today, the traffic was all bunched up, a column of five cars heading uphill. At least the road was gritted. And Marshall was driving a pool four-by-four. The only one.

The road weaved up around the last houses in the village then out into open country, a vista of white fields and hills.

Two old cottages sat on the corner – Marshall was the only one turning left at the end.

And he soon saw why.

Past a couple of garages and a sprawling new-build house, which must've taken a hefty brown envelope or two, the road was indistinguishable from the fields. The only demarcation was the dry-stone walls on both sides. Three cars were stuck in the snow. None seemed to have anyone in them, at least.

Must've been heading to the cottages and farmhouse perched on top of the hill but had to abandon their vehicles.

Marshall managed to get past the first two with ease. Then he started sliding across the road towards an ancient dry-stone dyke.

Jolene laughed. 'This must be how Shunty felt...'

'No laughing matter.' Marshall managed to right it and avoided the drainage ditch too. He shifted down to first then powered up the hill.

The field on the left was filled with horses, idly taking in the frozen chaos. On the right, a countless number of red hens filled a path cut through frosted grass. Seemed a bit perplexed by their world being thrown into disarray like this. Hopefully they'd have thawed water and food wherever they roosted for the night.

The car stopped.

Marshall hoofed it but the wheels just spun. 'Ah, shite.' He tried again but nothing was happening. Not even the rear wheels were helping. 'Bloody hell.'

Jolene looked up from her phone. 'What's up?'

'Stuck.' Another go, but all he was achieving was burning fuel. 'Have to slide back down.' Marshall put the car in neutral and let the brake go.

Nothing happened.

He put it in reverse and gunned the engine.

All he achieved was a spray of mucky snow out the back.

'Rob. Do you want me to give it a shot?'

Embarrassing, sure, but Marshall would rather get where they needed to than save face. 'On you go.' He got out into the cold and it felt a few degrees colder up at this elevation. The wind was up too.

Aye, the car was stuck – a mound of snow in front of the wheel and behind it. The view back the way was Meigle, the hulking mass looming over the village. A few more cars lurked over the crest of the hill.

'Where the hell does this road go, anyway?'

Jolene got in the car but didn't shut the door. 'Back road to Stow. Eventually. Goes past a massive farm and a reservoir. I think.'

'Christ, I've been here. Years ago. Big party in a field. Cops came and moved us on. Took *ages* to walk to Gala.' Marshall was back in his shoes, which were damp and cold already. 'Okay, you give it some welly. I'll push from behind.' He walked over and gripped the back of the car.

'Sure.' She floored it but all that happened was a fug of spent diesel and a smearing of sludge on Marshall's legs. 'Bloody hell.'

'Not so easy, eh?' Once she stopped fruitlessly revving, Marshall heard an engine somewhere nearby. 'Hold on a sec.' He passed the car and walked on up to the turning for the farm. Hard to see anything in amongst all the white, blinding at this time of day, even with a low winter sun.

Wait.

A Land Rover, pulling a Fiesta up the hill by a tow rope.

'Wait there.' Marshall crunched through the snow after it, going faster than a car for once.

The Land Rover stopped near the brow of the hill. The

thing looked older than Marshall and was just as sprayed with sludge.

A man hopped out. Dressed like a ski instructor with slimming gear on. No scarf, no hat, just a pair of thin gloves and narrow shades. He unhooked the Fiesta and turned around. Tilted his head to the side. 'Robert?'

Marshall squinted to try and make out his face.

Tidy beard. Small eyes, too far apart. Rough hair like a clown wig but brown instead of red or green.

'Robert sodding Marshall.' He charged down the hill like an elf leaping over the snow. He grabbed Marshall's hand and shook it. 'Bloody hell, mate. It's been years!'

Marshall still didn't recognise him.

Wait.

No.

'Balfour?'

'People call me Balf these days, but aye. It's me!' Balfour Rattray was still shaking Marshall's hand, vigorous and hard. 'It's been bloody years, Roberto. How the devil are you?' He stopped shaking but didn't let go. 'Also, what the hell are you doing here?'

'Coming to see you, as it happens.'

'Oh?'

'I'm a cop now, Balf.' Marshall managed to wrestle his hand free and scratched at his neck. 'Got into a bit of bother with the car, mind.'

'Say no more.' Balfour bounded back up to his Land Rover, then executed a U-turn where a three-point seemed the only option. And on snow too. He stopped by Marshall and reached over to let him in. 'Hop in.'

Marshall got in the passenger seat and strapped in. 'Thanks for this.'

'Least I can do for an old pal.' Balfour thundered down to

the junction, then took a left instead of right and reversed back towards Jolene and their waiting car. 'My guys are gritting the road down to the village this afternoon. Least I can do. But for now, it's just the road up past the reservoir that's clear, so I'd take that way home. Heard you were back in the area, Robert. What with all that... recent nastiness and everything, your name's been mentioned. Keep yourself to yourself, though, and quite right too. Hear you're staying down in the village?'

Marshall smiled. 'Nothing's sacred these days, eh?'

'Nope. You're going some to get that beast stuck in the snow.' Balfour hopped out of the van and started grinning at Jolene. 'You do this or was it him?'

'Him.'

Marshall joined them but kept a close eye on Balfour. Hard to trust someone who could be your best mate one minute then kick your arse the next.

Balfour bellowed with laughter.

Marshall joined them.

Balfour poked his head out of the window. 'You hadn't engaged four-wheel drive!'

Marshall stared up at the sky. 'Bloody hell.'

Jolene steered them up to the crossroads, fighting the wheel to correct and stop over-correcting, but she got there.

Balfour dug him in the ribs, like they were in a scrum on the rugby pitch at school. 'What do you drive?'

'BMW one series.'

'A roller skate!' Another dig in the ribs. 'Nice motor, don't get me wrong, but it's rear-wheel drive so useless on snow and ice.'

As much as Marshall wanted to be schooled on cars, he gave Balfour a wide smile. 'Got a case we need to talk to you about.'

'Come on, let's get you warmed up at mine. Follow me!'

CHAPTER TWENTY-TWO

'Like hell am I climbing that.' Elliot looked up into the coal-black clouds filling the middle of the sky and felt herself start to lean.

The wind turbine stretched up as far as she could see. Or it felt like it. Massive white thing. Just sitting there. Doing nothing, its rotor blades limp and useless. From a distance, they had a bit of grace to them, but up close...

Terrifying.

'I mean, we do have a choice.' Shunty stood there like a smug prick. Which he was. 'We could wait until his shift's over or come back.'

Elliot tried to move to get rid of the deep shiver that was forming. Sure, Kyle Talbot was up there, but it was *up there*. Miles up. She could see someone up there. Definitely heard something, a clattering or a clanging. Maybe hitting a spanner off metal or whatever the hell they did on the job.

'What kind of numpty goes up a wind turbine on a day like this?'

'Boss, are you scared of heights?'

'Am I hell.' Elliot stomped across the snow to the open door, tore it open and went inside.

The place was like a fridge, cramped and cold. Outside was bad enough but in here, she felt it chilling her marrow. Not so much a sardine tin as a matchbox. A staircase spiralled up, made of steel but a sort of transparent mesh.

Elliot sucked in a deep breath, gripped the railing and started up. Left, right, left, right.

Shunty was in lock step with her.

Left, right, left, right. Don't look down. 'You okay down there, Shunty?'

'Mmf fine, boss. Mmf you?'

Elliot turned around to look at him but caught sight of how far she'd already climbed. She steadied herself and kept on climbing. 'Are you *eating*?'

'Piece time.'

'Jesus wept.' She looked back down at him. Big mistake. The steel mesh flooring swam around like it wasn't even there.

She almost toppled over.

Steady!

She gripped the central pillar, her knuckles throbbing, shut her eyes and tried to centre herself.

'Mmf you okay, boss?'

Nothing to see here. All fine. She kept on going, eyes shut. 'Doing fine, Shunty.' Left, right, left, right. 'Doing just fine.'

'Mmmf. Mind if I ask you what the agreement is?'

'Agreement?'

'Back in the pub. Archie said, "So much for our agreement."'

'Daft sod.'

'Me or him?'

'I refuse to answer that on the grounds it might make you a smugger git than you already are.' Left, right, left, right. 'When

I first started, I was based in Lauder station. Used to be manned and everything. Walked the beat, got to know people. Broke up a big fight in that very boozer. Of course, Archie was a lot younger. Weren't we all... He gave me names and addresses, in exchange for keeping him out of it.'

'That's it?'

'That's it. Got to keep barmen and barwomen sweet, Shunty. When the punters are six pints deep and the lips are loosened, they're still sober as a puritan judge. And they listen. The better ones remember what they hear.' She looked up at the light coming out of a hole in the side. Hopefully Kyle Talbot was up there. 'What have you got in your sangers, Shunty?'

'Cheese and Marmite.'

'You're a barbarian.' Even colder now, but she was able to open her eyes again. Another couple of spirals to go and she'd be at the top.

Aye, and getting down was going to be so much fun.

She came out onto the— What was the big open flat bit at the top? A landing? She had no other word for it.

The hole the light came through was another door, open to the elements. And the primary one was wind, a freezing blast slicing in like an ice pick in the face.

Nothing to hold onto so she slowly made her way over. 'Hello?' She gripped the side of the door and peered outside. 'Hello?'

Oh my Christ in the name of hell.

Really far up here.

Really far.

DON'T LOOK DOWN.

DON'T.

LOOK.

DOWN.

Snow everywhere, all the way to the Tweed Valley and

past. The Eildons over by Melrose. The Cheviots down past Jedburgh.

Nothing to stop her just tumbling outside.

'Hello?' She checked over to the side, trying to not look down. 'Hello?'

A man was suspended on ropes attached to a rotor blade, bouncing away as he inspected something. The thing was at a sharp angle, rising up even further.

'Kyle?'

He looked over and raised his head. 'Aye?'

'Police!'

'Right.' Talbot pushed up onto the top of the blade, then let the ropes go. Untethered, he ran down the arm and stopped to lean against the wall just next to Elliot. And stayed there. 'Looking a bit green around the gills there.'

Elliot couldn't look at him. 'Some view up here, eh?'

'Cracking.' Talbot stared out across the landscape. 'Never tire of it.'

'What are you working on?'

'Fixing a rotor. This is the first one we put in. Always the way – they want the stairs in, rather than ladders, so they can bring their mates up to take in the view. But the rotor isn't budging today. Came up here to see why and, I don't want to get too technical here, but I think I'll have to get a man in.'

Elliot smiled at him. 'Aren't you the man?'

'I'm good at installing the things. Just like sticking the bits together on a giant Lego set. But see when things go wrong? Not my wheelhouse.'

'Your wheelhouse, eh?'

'Well, my wind turbine.' Talbot smiled back at her. He was a good-looking guy. The spiked hairdo was strictly 1988. The gouge taken out of his bonce wasn't nice looking, though. 'Didn't get your name, sorry?'

ED JAMES

'DI Andrea Elliot.' She glanced behind her to see Shunty still chewing his piece. 'This is DS Rakesh Siyal.'

'Morning.'

Shunty frowned. 'It's half past two.'

'Oh, right. Aye.' Talbot smirked. 'So.' His smirk disappeared quickly. 'You'll be wondering so I'll just confirm it. Yes, this is the turbine Napier Rattray fell off.'

Elliot frowned. 'Really? I was here investigating but I don't recognise it.'

'Very different time of year, eh?'

'And I don't remember you.'

'Spoke to a wee blonde lassie. Jolene something?'

'That'll be Acting DS Archer. Right.' Elliot couldn't stand looking at the ground behind him. 'Listen, do you want to come in from there?'

'Nah, I'm good out here. Get a bit claustrophobic inside.'

'Right.' Elliot didn't want to be anywhere near this height. Guy must've been raised in a tower block in the arse end of Glasgow and spent his days playing on the top of it.

'So, what can I do you for?'

'You know a Justin Lorimer?'

'He's the client, aye. He runs the farm. Deals with my boss. Try to have as little to do with him as possible, like.'

'Why's that?'

'Just a bit of a prick. He's not a man who can handle a lot of stress. And he was having to.'

'Must be hard, then.'

'Not really. Guy hasn't got a head for heights so as long as I'm up one of these bad boys, I don't see him.'

'Want to talk to you about Thursday.'

'Thursday?'

'Your visit to hospital.'

'Oh. That.' Talbot sniffed. Stared at the ground. Rubbed at

144

the mark on his temple. 'Guess you're more interested in what happened before that, eh?'

'Want to tell us?'

'Not really.' Talbot sighed. Then laughed. 'Suppose I better, eh? After all, you've climbed all that way just to speak to me.' He cleared his throat and ran a hand over his spikes. 'We got into a bit of a fight. Me and Justin. Daft, really. He was kicking off about people resting pints on the pool table. I mean, it is a bit annoying when people leave a glass there but boys are there to have fun and chat, you know? It's two shots, so if you're playing against someone who knows what they're doing, you really don't want to put your pint down. And he wouldn't listen to sense, kept ranting about it. So I challenged him on it and he went tonto. Dickhead hit us with a cue.' He pointed at his scar. 'Right there.'

'That's going to add character.'

'Got more than my fair share of that.' Talbot looked right at Elliot. 'Not my proudest moment but I hit him back. He wouldn't leave, though. Big Archie called the cops. Pair of them came over and chucked him out.'

'Then what happened?'

'I got taken to hospital. Sitting in A&E, blood splashing on the floor from my cut. Cops recommended I should press charges. No chance. Then who should walk in but Justin Lorimer.'

'You had another fight in the hospital, didn't you?'

'More a continuation of the first one.' Another sigh. 'He started on me. Cops broke it up. Nothing much to it, to be honest. Lorimer's a hard man in one place and one place only – the inside of his head.'

'And you?'

'Kyle Talbot's just here to do a job, Inspector. That's it.' Aye and when people talked about themselves in the third person, they hadn't lost it. 'We both got seen by the doctor, then that big Irish cop took me home to the Stagehall.' Talbot chuckled. 'Call it the Stagecoach because it's as rough as something from the Wild West.'

Shunty's mobile blasted out some Ed Sheeran nonsense. He checked the screen, then grimaced. 'I need to take this.'

Elliot focused on Talbot, grinding her teeth. 'Have you seen Mr Lorimer since then?'

'Not on Friday. Did my day's work, then got off home to Glasgow on the two o'clock train from Stow. Through to the West Coast by the back of four. In the boozer at half past.' He snorted. 'Lorimer's a persistent sod. Managed to avoid him all week. Then he's in the Stagecoach again last night. Same story as Thursday. Lorimer just wouldn't let it lie. Shouting at everyone. And I didn't rise to it this time. Archie chucked him out.'

'Any idea what happened to him after?'

'Why would I?'

'You might've followed him down the street.'

'Nope. Why do you think that?'

'There's a reason we want to speak to the guy who battered him.'

'Hardly battered him. Just smacked him with a pool cue after he got me. All's fair in love and war.'

'Which was this?'

'Closer to love than war, that's for sure. Bottom line, love, I don't really give a shit about the boy. He's a wanker. Learnt a long time ago to stay away from wankers.'

And yet trouble seemed to keep finding him. 'What did you do after that?'

'Finished my pint, like I do every night. Then went upstairs to my scratcher to watch some telly. Like to sober up by the time I get to sleep – don't want to be up one of these bad boys when you're still pished.' Talbot bellowed out a laugh.

Shunty reappeared, smiling. 'Can anyone back that up?'

'Called the good lady wife when I got into the room, aye.' Talbot swung over and into the turbine's interior, then pulled out his phone. 'See the call log. Video call? That.' He winked. 'She gets lonely when I'm away so things can get a bit saucy.'

Shunty scribbled something down, hopefully a note to check with Mrs Talbot and not to masturbate in front of a video camera. 'You didn't think to invite her to stay with you here?'

'In the Stagecoach?' Another laugh. 'No way.' The grin faded. 'Two detectives following me up a turbine to ask about a fight in the boozer is a bit of a weird one. What's this about?'

'He's one of the bodies found earlier on the Stow-Lauder road.' Elliot glanced over in the direction, not very far away, but the world seemed to spin around as she moved her head.

'Kidding me.' Talbot stared down at the ground. 'Christ. That was him?'

'Right.'

'Ah, shite almighty.'

'You know anything about what happened to him?'

'Me? News to me, like. After that video call, I went to bed. Be around midnight.'

'See anything around the time Mr Lorimer left?'

Talbot frowned. 'Now you mention it, aye. I did. I was having a smoke outside and I saw a van revving. Ford Transit, I think. Had GoMobile signs on the sides.'

'GoMobile?'

'Aye, same network I'm on. Headed off up the hills towards here.'

Where Lorimer's body was found...

Elliot smiled at him. 'Thanks, sir. We'll be in touch.'

'Don't mention it.' Talbot ran up the rotor blade.

Elliot had to turn away and walk over to the staircase.

'Shunty, if you're not going to turn your mobile off, at least have some better music on it.'

'What's wrong with Ed Sheeran?'

'What's *right* with him?' She chuckled, but that descent looked brutal. The mesh seemed to just … disappear. 'Actually a big fan of him. Seen him twice now.' She gestured for him to go first – last thing she needed was him seeing her falling. 'Who was that on the phone?'

'Kirsten. They've found a big vehicle buried in a snow drift.'

'You think it's this van?'

CHAPTER TWENTY-THREE

Marshall stood in the formal hall in Balfour's home, more a castle than a house, looking out of the giant window down to the landscaped grounds carved out of a forest of evergreen trees climbing the hill. Giant boulders marked out the split between garden and wilderness. An ornamental pond was frozen over, with some ducks shivering at the side. The only sign of a patio was the slight indentation in the snow at the edge, criss-crossed by pheasant prints, but no sign of the birds. The only human footprints led from the two cars on the drive: theirs and Balfour's. The long lane led down to the minor road they'd been stuck on.

The Tweed was a mile or so to the south but was hidden by the hills. Behind, the horizon was cut off by the gentle curve of Elibank's forest. Where some bodies had been found a few months back. Hard to imagine climbing the woodland on a day like this.

Aye, this was pretty much the middle of nowhere.

Marshall turned back to face into the room. The walls were lined with paintings hanging from a rail – old hunting images, going back hundreds of years. Whatever message Balfour Rattray wanted to convey, it had something to do with destiny.

Continuity.

That was the language landowners used. They saw themselves as servants of the lands, not owners. Custodians. Meant that the blood from any atrocities their ancestors carried out wasn't on their hands. Meant their estates weren't taxed when they died.

Over the other side of the room, Jolene sat on a mock-Regency sofa that looked as comfortable as the giant rocks lining the drive. Perched on the front, with an erect posture. Notebook out, ready. Waiting.

'Here we go.' Balfour barged in, lugging a tray laden with a teapot, mugs and milk. He carried it over to the table with the grace of a waiter or waitress in a café. 'I've only got oat milk, is that okay?'

Jolene smiled. 'That's great for me.'

Marshall joined them and took the armchair next to her. 'Suits me.'

'Excellent.' Balfour tipped milk into the cups then started pouring out the tea. 'Just opened this bag of tea yesterday. Hope you enjoy it.' He handed Jolene her cup and saucer first. 'Assam.'

'Thank you.' She set it down on the coffee table. 'I would've thought you'd have a butler for this stuff.'

'Butler!' Balfour laughed. 'No, it's just me here.'

'You're not married?'

'Not even seeing someone.' Balfour passed Marshall his cup. 'Here you go, Roberto.'

That overly familiar name again. Not a nickname he had at school. Odd.

'Still can't believe it about Justin.' Balfour sipped his tea. 'I was speaking to him just yesterday.'

Marshall set his cup down on the coffee table. 'You didn't notice him not turning up to work?'

'I've been distracted with all the snow, to be honest. Disrupts everything. They're still working on the wind farm, though. I swear, those boys will work through the zombie apocalypse. Hordes of the undead will be walking up the Gala Water valley and they'll still be trying to install a rotor.' Balfour laughed. 'I've got a good team at the farm. Place kind of takes care of itself. Or used to. It's going to be next to impossible to replace Justin. I'll have to roll up my sleeves and see what knowledge he's distributed amongst the others.'

Marshall nodded slowly. 'I know what it's like when you lose a good member of your team.'

'Aye.' Balfour sipped his tea, his gaze shifting between them. 'Can't believe Justin's dead. He was a great worker and a good friend. Knew the farm inside out. Planned it all. Scheduled everything.' He took a biscuit from the plate and bit into it. 'You going to find who killed him?'

Marshall took a drink of tea, but desperately wanted a biscuit to stave off the hunger. 'Depends.'

'On what?'

'Whether the killer or killers have left behind enough clues.'

'Come on, Roberto. That sounds a bit wishy-washy.'

'We're investigating a number of strands.' Marshall put the teacup back down again and grabbed a biscuit. A basic digestive. Beggars can't be choosers. 'I'm sorry to hear about what happened to your father.'

Balfour couldn't make eye contact. 'Aye...'

Marshall bit into the biscuit. 'I still chuckle about that talk he gave the school all those years ago.'

Balfour looked across the giant room to the window, swallowing hard. 'You know, this is going to sound daft, but... I still text him. Like he's not in a coma in hospital. Send him the usual crap we'd talk about. Rugby news, jokes, run things on the farm past him. Used to go and see the Falcons down in Newcastle a lot with him. Not the same without him so I stopped going.' He swallowed down some tea. 'Stupid old goat got obsessed by this app on his phone. Measured the output from the wind farm up Torsonce Hill, just south of Stow.' He burped into his fist, then took another sip of tea. 'Windiest night of the year, he called me up, saying we're not generating enough. One turbine wasn't turning.'

'Windiest night of the year and it wasn't turning?'

'It's a safety feature. Locks the rotor so it doesn't tear itself apart. Father didn't believe me. Told him we'd fix it in the morning and I went to bed. We lost forty acres of trees that night. All gone.' He shook his head, eyes staring into space. 'Next thing I know, I get a call from Mother, telling me he's gone up the wind turbine. He's seventy-five!'

'He climbed up?'

'On the inside. All of them have ladders for access, but that one had a staircase. Father went up there to see why it wasn't turning. I *told* him, but would he listen?' Balfour picked up his teacup but didn't drink anything and put it back down with a slight clatter. 'I know why you're here, Roberto. Police investigated it, cleared everyone on the farm. It was an accident. And I wasn't even in the country.'

Marshall nodded. 'I get it. It's a tragedy, like I say.'

'Whatever else you're thinking, my inheritance is all caught up in a trust. This house is the only thing I own outright. Marks out the western edge of our land. The Elliots own everything further west of here, but us Rattrays own most of it east towards Langshaw and north to Stow.'

'So all across the north of Gala and Melrose?'

'Right over to Earlston and Lauder, even.'

Jolene's mobile rang. 'Sorry. Thought it was on mute.' She put her cup back on the saucer and checked the display. 'Actually, better take this.' She left the room and her voice echoed around the hallway.

Balfour watched her go, but without hunger or lust in his eyes. He trained his gaze on Marshall. 'Roberto. Mate. I wanted to say how sorry I am for being a grade-A arsehole at school. I was an embarrassment to myself. You didn't deserve half of the shite I gave you. My position and birthright are a privilege and I didn't appreciate that at the time. It's taken me years to realise that. For our civilisation to flourish, it's incumbent on people like me to not abuse our entitlements.'

Spoken like his own mother's platitudes.

'Balfour, we all acted like dickheads at school. It's what being a teenager's all about. We get corrected, we adjust our positions. We learn, we grow. No lasting harm done.'

'Maybe not to you or your sister, but... I've done things I'm not proud of and I've tried to make amends for going above and beyond typical teenage dickheadery. I'd already been expelled from two other schools. I was out of control. I punched down to people like you, Roberto.' He raised a hand. 'Sorry, I don't mean that you're lesser than me, just... our social statuses might be deemed to be that way.'

'I get it. I had a happy time at primary, but high school was a different kettle of fish. Gattonside High was... Thank God it's closed.'

'I think Satan had more of a hand in that place than Him.' Balfour grinned. Then it faded. 'The bullying was awful. I'd never seen anything like it. It was... It was a prison, right? I came in and was... What do they call it in American films? Oh yeah. Fish. I was the fish. The new fish. It was them or you. You had to tear someone else apart before you were mauled. Always lash out. That culture seemed to be in bricks and mortar of the place. One of the reasons it was closed down. I mean, I don't know why it was so bad, considering where it was. Kids from Gattonside, Melrose, Darnick, Newstead and the surrounding farms all up this way.'

Marshall didn't know what to say. He took another biscuit and covered his discomfort by scoffing it very slowly.

'Roberto. I mean it when I say I'm sorry. I was a dickhead. A total dickhead. That time where I had a go at you... I didn't expect you to punch back. Remember when we got taken to the PE teacher's office? What was his name? McArthur? Aye, Peter McArthur... He threatened us with expulsion. "You're both smart laddies, so don't act like thugs." You... You acted the big man, Roberto, offered to shake my hand... But I didn't. I said it wasn't over. It'll never be over. Or something like that. Had seen too many hard-man films. But you just ignored me and got on with it. I soon got disinterested in you and focused on some other poor bastard. And I got expelled *again*. That was the final straw. The old man sent me to a boarding school down south. It sorted me out, once and for all.'

Marshall reached over for his tea. It was lukewarm, but he drank it anyway, draining the cup.

'Here.' Balfour refilled him and topped up his own. Jolene's was still intact. 'I mean it, Rob—'

The door opened and Jolene walked back in. 'Sorry about that.' She sat and sank her tea. Eyes shifting between them. Like she'd picked up on something unusual going on. 'Mr Rattray, I gather you held a function last night?'

'A function?' Balfour frowned then smiled. 'Ah, the Burns supper. Well, I wouldn't go so far as to call it a function. Merely a hundred people in for a wee dance. For a cancer charity I was asked to be patron of.'

'Who asked you?'

'Dr Louisa Baird. She was Mother's oncologist. Charming woman.'

Jolene held his gaze. 'I'm afraid her body was also found this morning.'

Balfour was just about to sip some tea. Narrow escape from spraying it everywhere. 'My God.' He set the cup down. 'Near Justin's?'

'Nearby, yes.' Marshall shot Jolene a look that said he was taking charge. 'How well did you know Dr Baird?'

'Not well at all. Just through Mother. Her care was first class, I have to say. I mean, I was honoured to be asked but I'm not sure what I can do as patron. I'm not famous.'

'But you are wealthy, right?'

'I might seem well off but my finances are held in a trust and in this place. It's not like I can drop a hundred grand into the charity.'

'A hundred or so people who'll attend your Burns supper over others. Sounds like you have connections.'

'There is that, I suppose, but most of them were Louisa's friends or donors.'

Jolene looked around the room. 'Seems a bit small to have a ceilidh.'

'The function wasn't here.' Balfour looked over at Jolene. 'It was at Father's place.'

'We need to dig into Dr Baird's movements last night. Do you have an idea of when she left?'

Balfour got to his feet. 'No, but I can show you.'

CHAPTER TWENTY-FOUR

Elliot got out of the pool car and stomped over the snow to the crime scene. She didn't hear any following footsteps, so she stopped and turned around.

Shunty was putting his second coat on. At least he was out of the car now. How much longer could they let that clown stay in the force?

'Come on, you.' She waited for him to daintily tiptoe over the snow. 'You'd think you'd never seen snow before.'

'Of course I've seen it, just not like this.'

'Oh, that's right. It was just icy when you shunted that car off a bridge, eh?'

'Aye, very good. Haven't heard that one before. Know the guy who books people at the Stand in Edinburgh. You should work on some new material, give the comedy routine the chance it deserves.' Shunty stopped beside her and rubbed his gloved hands together. 'Seriously, is it like this every year?'

'Every year, aye. Sometimes for a few months.'

'Bloody hell.' Shunty finished zipping up his overcoat, a

lime puffer. 'I mean, we had snow in Glasgow, but this is pure mental. I don't know if I can hack this.'

Elliot knew he couldn't. Try as she might, she couldn't get him done on a disciplinary. Trouble was, he was competently incompetent. She tucked her fringe behind her ear and gave him a motherly smile, the kind she'd give to any of her kids when they were at it, or to someone a few bricks shy of a full load. 'I get it. You were supposed to be based in Edinburgh, but they sent you down here. It's like buying a Brie in Tesco and getting home to find a big lump of mouldy blue Stilton in there.'

'I like Stilton.'

'Aye, bless your heart, but you know what I mean.'

'Suppose so. Thanks.'

'Don't mention it. Come on.' She continued on, avoiding the trail of footprints, now all melted and slushy, and instead walked on virgin snow, savouring the crisp cracking. 'Good news is there's a fresh fall due overnight.'

Shunty just groaned. Idiot was walking in the well-worn slush – while he wouldn't fall over, he'd have spray up the back of his breeks.

Getting dark now. Reminded Elliot of that time she visited Iceland in November, way before the kids. Never seemed to get light. Wasn't that bad here, but still, January in the Borders wasn't January in Tenerife, was it?

Any sunshine would be nice.

'Who called you as we drove, Shunty?'

'Big Jim. He's been onto GoMobile. Said there's no planned works down here. No vans south of Edinburgh out at that time anywhere.'

'Didn't think of telling me?'

'I was trying to live your advice – don't come to me with problems, come to me with solutions.'

Cheeky sod.

'So, what solutions have you thought of?'

'That's got to be the van that took him. Looks like someone snatched him from outside that pub and brought him up here.'

'Way I'm thinking is they slipped on magnetic signs to make it look like a GoMobile van. Pretend they're installing a new 5G mast or something. Could swap it for BG or whatever British Gas are called these days. Either way, I'd say we're looking at a pro.'

'A pro, boss?'

'A professional. A hitman. An assassin.'

'Sure?'

'I think so, Shuntster. But priority number one is tracking down that van.'

'I don't know how, boss. All we've got is it was a navy Transit.'

'Here's the lad who'll do the donkey work for you.' Elliot walked up to DC Jim McIntyre, standing outside the crime scene tent and dicking about on his mobile. 'You found the van yet?'

Big lump didn't look comfortable in a fighting suit. Too big for it, making it strain at the chest. Probably be better to be back in uniform. His hair was soaking for some reason. Was he sweating in the cold? *How?* He shifted his gaze from Elliot to Shunty and seemed to relax a bit – he realised the shoeing wasn't going to be that severe. 'What van?'

Elliot glared at Shunty. 'Tell me you called him and—'

'Aye, I did.' Shunty got himself between Elliot and McIntyre, like he was jumping on a bomb. 'The van that left Stow at eight thirty-two.'

McIntyre nodded. 'Right.'

'Right?' Elliot barged past Shunty. 'What's that supposed to mean?'

McIntyre took a halting breath. 'It means I'm on top of it, ma'am.'

'You're on top of it? Great.' She threw her arms up in the air. 'Case solved by the big man!'

McIntyre clenched his jaw. 'I put in a request for all the CCTV in Lauder. Nothing's come back.'

'And you've phoned to chase?'

'Not yet, because I've been too busy here.'

In the name of the wee man...

'I've been trying to speak to Rakesh, ma'am. The forensics team want approval to take down their tent.'

'Fine, I'll sort that.' Elliot let out a sigh and tried to centre herself, just like her meditation teacher told her to. 'As for the CCTV, we're not going to get anything from the council. Only thing you'll get is a speed camera on the A68 heading north. You of all people should know, as well as I do, how many rat runs come out of Lauder.'

'I do, ma'am. Which is why I haven't prioritised that work.'

Elliot stepped away from the numpty. 'Okay, Shunty, here's what I need you to do. Search for any cameras on that stretch into Lauder.'

Shunty frowned. 'But you just said there aren't—'

'There are about twenty houses facing the road. At least some of them will have those doorbell cameras.'

Shunty rolled his eyes at her. Daft sod.

One of the problems with that generation – they were all afraid to think for themselves and anything that involved "work" was to be avoided. Walking five miles in every direction, knocking on every door, leaving a card when nobody answered, then following up until you got an answer... that was police work, the traditional kind.

'But we can't just ask them to—'

'Shunty! Someone's died. Two people. You need to get

them scared for their own lives and, before you know it, they'll be grassing about their neighbours and everything.' She waited while the daft sod scribbled it down, like the list of infractions in that grotty pub. 'While you're at it, check in garages to see if nobody's got a navy Transit conveniently hidden away.'

'Okay.' Shunty put his notebook away and tilted his head towards McIntyre. 'Can you do the doings, Jimbo?'

McIntyre's nostrils were flaring. 'I'll do it, but I think it's a forlorn hope. Started snowing around that time so surely the plates will be covered in snow.'

Elliot tilted her head to the side, wanting to snare him in a trap. 'Why's that a problem?'

'No officer who isn't a total prick is going to do anything about snowy plates.'

'Why?'

McIntyre scratched his neck. 'Chances are their own registration is covered or grimed over with frozen road spray. Bottom line, we'll struggle to get plates.'

'Well, Jimbo, I've been that prick.' She clapped him on the arm like he was a pet dog. 'Make sure my plates are always clear. And stop people who don't. Old-school police work. It's not an exercise in shafting everyone you pull over, but learning the things you might need to know by asking the questions right in front of you. Can you ticket them? Of course. Would you? Best not to. No amount of goodwill surpasses the officer who had a citizen dead to rights on a charge but didn't give them a ticket. "Listen, you seem sound. Do me a favour, brush off your plate and drive safely home." Or even better still, "I've brushed off your plate for you, take care." Ask around your old uniform chums, Constable, and see if anyone's got anything. Sure there's bound to be a prick or two there.'

'I'll find that bloody van, don't you worry...' McIntyre trudged off across the snow.

Useless git...

'He's not. He's a good cop.'

She'd said that out loud, hadn't she?

Great.

She swung around to Shunty. 'Talking about myself here. I should've been here first thing to get my arms around this case and not allow Dr Donkey to let it get this bad.'

'McIntyre's a good cop.'

'A decent *plod*, maybe. Should never have been made a detective.' Elliot stomped over the snow towards the crime scene tent, ruing Pringle's decision to over-promote. Technically, PC to DC wasn't a promotion but he'd got a pay rise. And Elliot was sick of being saddled with Pringle's decisions, often as inscrutable as his language. Something needed to change on that score and soon. 'Word of advice, Shunty – make sure he doesn't screw this up. It reflects badly on you when people under your supervision don't manage their tasks well. Or at all.' She opened the tent flap and peered inside.

Sally the CSI was busy stuffing some gear into a box. She looked up and smiled at Elliot. 'Oh, hey! How are you doing?'

'I'm fine and dandy, Sally.' Elliot stepped inside, ready to berate her for the lack of a result on the forensics.

But she saw a much better target.

Kirsten Weir, sipping a coffee. Smelled glorious too, the coils of dark fragrance stretching across the tent. She was halfway out of her crime scene suit. 'Afternoon, Andrea.'

'McIntyre said you need approval to bring your tent down?'

'Oh, that's a bit out of date. I called Rob and he okayed it.'

'Initiative, I like it. Now, about this vehicle...'

Kirsten zipped the suit up to her chin. She finished her coffee and set it down, then grabbed a mask and goggles. 'You're welcome to tag along, but if you want inside, you'll need to suit up.'

Aye, and that would take up precious minutes...

Elliot had to step aside to let Sally out with a box of gear. 'Nice try. Wanting to get there ahead of me, eh?' She smiled. 'I'll follow you.'

'Fine, but you're not getting in.' Kirsten left the tent then headed over to the road, tracking a pair of prints in the snow.

The snow was coming up to halfway up Elliot's shins. 'Found anything here I should know about?'

'Not really.'

'What about stuff I shouldn't?'

'None of that either. But I never expected to get anything. The only forensics will be on the bodies, if at all.'

'Thought you'd be over there with Owusu, Kirst?'

'Should be. I'm over here because I thought you'd be attending the post-mortem.'

Elliot laughed. Almost stumbled over. Christ, the snow was up to her knees here. 'We've missed you down here, Kirst.'

'If I'm honest, DI Elliot, I'd say I missed you too, but we both know I'm full of shite.'

Cheeky cow. Who needed enemies with friends like Kirsten Weir?

Slow going through this stuff – she could feel the cold gnawing through her wellies. Maybe Shunty had the right idea with all his gear – thermal socks would be nice. 'Need to have a word with you about Sally.'

'It's okay, Andrea. Your official complaint is still in my inbox. It's being handled.'

'Handled, right. Okay, but between friends... Is she a drunk?'

'I can't speak about personnel matters. You know that.'

'And off the record?'

'It's never off the record with you.'

Speaking of personnel matters...

Up by the road, Shunty was in conference with McIntyre. Hopefully he'd be giving him guidance on how to best discern the difference between one's elbow and one's arse.

Probably moaning about her, though.

Sod them.

Sod the pair of them.

Elliot followed Kirsten down a hollow heading towards some old shepherd huts that looked like they hadn't been used since the times of Rabbie Burns.

Trevor guarded a ditch, resting on a snow shovel. 'There you are.' Skinny bugger with a mullet, as tightly wrapped up as Shunty. Not as useless as Sally, but he'd given her a good run for her money on occasions. 'Managed to dig it out.'

A black Audi SUV sat behind him, gleaming. Not quite like one of those alpine photos they'd use to sell the buggers, but it looked pretty against the snow.

'You've done a good job of clearing it.'

'Absolutely class motor, this.' Trevor waved a hand at it. He was practically drooling over it. 'Audi Q5. Four point five litre TDI. Goes like shit off a shovel.'

Kirsten crouched behind it. 'Four-wheel drive, right?'

'No. But yes. But no. And... Look. *Technically*, it's got the Quattro *all*-wheel drive system, which is pretty much the best of the best. But only for AWD systems. A proper four-wheel drive will wipe the floor with it.'

'I don't need the details. But it should be able to handle this kind of place in the snow?'

'Should do, aye. And it wouldn't slide into a bridge like what Shunty did.'

Kirsten smiled. 'Seriously, though – would you be able to go off-road with it?'

'This would handle all the heather and sheep crap you throw at it.'

'Need to figure out how it got here, then.' Kirsten crouched to peer in the window, but it was all misted up. 'You been inside?'

'Waiting for you.'

'Good lad.' Kirsten snapped her goggles and mask in place, then opened the door. 'Her coat's here.'

'That's a good find... Anything in the pockets?'

'Not that I can see.'

'Figures.' Elliot looked back the way. Maybe a hundred metres to the road. 'Think she was forced off down here?'

'I'd say so.' Trevor shone a torch back the way, all the way to the private road down to Blainslieshaw Mains farm, away from the direction she'd travelled from the Stow-Lauder road. 'If you look closely, you should be able to make out the faintest indentations in the snow. Her path from the road.' He adjusted it to a narrow beam, right at the spot where some sheep huddled together. 'Took a minor swerve there.'

'So she could've just avoided a sheep?'

'That's one theory. Doesn't explain why she ended up tied up and dumped on top of a frozen body.'

'True.' Elliot could see an alternative – the navy Transit sitting on the wrong side of the road in the dark, waiting for her to leave. Turn on the lights, scare her off the road. Grab her. Dump the car.

Trouble with that theory was it relied on knowing when she would be there.

Elliot frowned at Trevor. 'Just one set of tyre prints over here?'

'So far.'

'Any footprints?'

'Won't find them, I'm afraid. The snow's been blowing all day. Smooths it all out. Lucky to see that track. How we found it, basically.'

'Typical.' Elliot grunted. It fitted together like clockwork, but she still had no idea why anyone would want to kill the good lady doctor.

A light flashed from inside the car, then Kirsten got out. 'Found a purse in the glove box. It's Dr Baird's.'

CHAPTER TWENTY-FIVE

Marshall couldn't tell if it was snowing again or the wind was blowing the flakes in a horizontal blast across the fields towards them. Either way, visibility was low and his speed lower. At least now he had the four-wheel drive engaged and the pool car was chewing through the icy roads.

The temperature was as high as it was going to get, just above freezing, which meant it was going to tip back overnight and anything that'd melted would become black ice. Shunty'd earned his nickname in similar conditions last winter – Marshall really didn't need another one on top of 'Dr Donkey'.

Balfour Rattray was driving ahead of them with a plough on the front of his Land Rover, piling along the road like the conditions were normal.

'Seems like a nice guy.' Jolene was casually looking out of the side window across the pure white vista, like they were a couple on a normal drive. 'A lot older than you, though.'

'Boarding school must've straightened him out. He was an absolute bastard at school. Full of all that alpha-male bullshit.

Top of the pecking order. I tried to keep myself to myself but it didn't cut it with someone like him.'

'After thirty years, I think you need to bury the hatchet. And not in his neck.'

'Thirty? How old do you think I am?'

She shrugged. 'Forty-five?'

'I'm thirty-six!' Marshall steered around the bend onto the straight running past the crime scene. The tent was being taken down now – given the radio silence from Kirsten, Marshall assumed they hadn't found anything of note. Or maybe she'd found something that needed that level of focus.

'You ever have a high school reunion?'

'If there was one, I wasn't invited.'

'What about your twin sister? She would've invited you.'

'True. What about you?'

'Had one last summer. Straight out of the pandemic, so I thought it'd be okay. Nope. The people who organised it wished they were back in the glory days. Back where they peaked.'

'And you?'

'It made me remember why we hadn't stayed in touch.'

Around another bend and Marshall had lost sight of Balfour's Land Rover. 'Bollocks.'

'What's up?'

'Nothing.'

The sign for Blainslieshaw Mains hung from a private road sign and pointed to the right. Clear of snow, with its cute drawing of a few sheep in a chalk style on a deep blue background.

Marshall took the turning. The surface had been gritted and had that overly dry look to it, like it was now desperately seeking moisture. He ploughed on down to a crossroads in woodland, with giant farm sheds on both sides, then went straight on. The number of potholes increased so he took it even slower. Maybe fixing the road was lurking on a to-do list in Justin Lorimer's office. Maybe Balfour didn't care.

Marshall drove on into a wide circular drive, immaculate pebbles surrounding a frozen pond in the middle. He pulled up behind Balfour's Land Rover and got out.

The hulking farmhouse loomed over them. As big as the stately homes open to the public around here, all built from money made in the slave trade, but this was still functioning as a home and a business. The estate office was probably in there too.

Balfour Rattray was already out of his car and chatting to a rugged guy, a big bruiser with a suntan even in January. Probably spent all day every day outside. 'Guys, this is Jock. He's Justin's number two, so he'll be stepping up in his... absence doesn't cut it, does it? Departure?' He shut one eye then opened it again. 'Anyway. Reason we're here is Jock has access to my father's elaborate security apparatus, which I'm afraid absolutely baffles me.'

'Alright?' Jock didn't seem to be. Puffy red eyes, a gaze that wasn't quite there, a smile that seemed stitched on. 'Here's the CCTV from last night.' He held out his phone and the screen was filled with a shot from the top of the house. Floodlights cast a glow across the pebbles. The now-frozen fountain bubbled. 'Had a break-in at the farm three years ago, lost tons of equipment, so Napier got me to install this so he could access it on his phone.'

'Father's obsessed with technology.' Balfour smiled. 'Whereas I'm a bit of a luddite. Got a rugged farmer's phone in case it falls in a puddle somewhere. I prefer to focus on the here and now. The real world. Nature. I believe in the traditional methods espoused by our new king and prefer to invest my time and efforts into those aspects of farming rather than enriching some Silicon Valley firms. But such is the modern world.'

Spoken like a true pompous git, as much as Marshall might agree with some of the sentiments. Virtue signalling of the highest order.

'Anyway.' Jock wiped a shovel-like hand across his cheek. 'Balf said you're looking for an Audi Q5? Well, here you go.' He handed the phone to Marshall.

The video showed a jet-black SUV pulling up and parking in the long rows of cars on both sides of the pond. Louisa Baird got out, wearing the same little black dress they'd found her in, but with a coat draped over her shoulders. Must've been freezing. No sign of the snow, though. She walked over to the house and met a man who checked her off a list, then she went inside.

Marshall looked over. 'Do you have anything indoors?'

Jock shook his head. 'Napier didn't want that covered, sorry.'

Figured – he wanted to protect the family from what was going on outside, but his own privacy was paramount. Especially if someone like Jock had access. And while Jock might be trustworthy, what if his phone got into the wrong hands?

Jock jumped forward in time. 'She left alone at ten.'

Sure enough, Louisa stepped out of the house into the maelstrom of snow and hurried over to her car, shrugging off the coat as the exhaust plumed. She raced off up the private road, heading out of the camera's angle.

Jock shrugged. 'That's it.'

Marshall had to face his disappointment. 'Okay, this is great. Can you send the CCTV to Jolene's team?' He gestured over at her. 'We'll need to go through all of the attendees to try and find any witnesses. It's crucial we find out where she went after she left here.'

'Of course.' Balfour beamed at Jolene. 'Happy to help.' Almost too happy, maybe. 'Have your people reach out to mine. And I mean Jock here.'

Jock produced a business card from his pocket. 'This has all my details. Day or night. Anytime. Of course, I could send you an NFC link from my smartphone?'

Jolene snatched the card out of his hand but smiled like she knew what one of those would be. 'This'll be fine. Thanks.'

'I'm serious.' Balfour focused on Jock, like the words were more for him than them. 'Whatever I have is yours.'

Marshall returned the smile. It was absolutely freezing outside – they might be used to it, but the chill was making his bones rattle. Was there a reason Balfour wasn't letting them inside? 'It's great that we've now squared off part of her movements last night, but we really need to know who she spoke to inside. Do you have a guest list for last night?'

He knew they did – the big guy checking everyone off on the video – but sometimes a little trap was needed.

'Of course. Follow me.' Balfour nodded at Jock. 'Please share the footage with Ms Archer.' Then he entered the building.

Finally.

Marshall followed him, though it wasn't that much warmer inside. A fire flickered in a room to the side, a drawing room or a sitting room.

Balfour marched down the long hallway's parquet floor and opened a door at the back.

Any hotel would kill for a ballroom on this scale. Fifteen or so ten-seat tables were dotted around in a gradual arc. Windows on three sides looked across snow-dusted gardens towards ornamental woodland.

A man stood in the middle of the room, hands on hips, shaking his head at the floor. Haggis was scattered across it, with big splodges of neeps and tatties. He didn't seem to know where to start.

Balfour walked across the flooring. 'Gundog, there you are.'

The tall man looked up from assessing the damage. 'What's up?' Home Counties accent.

'This is DI Rob Marshall. Rob, this is Gundog.' Balfour's eyes were full of mischief. 'I met him at school.'

'Fergus Ross.' The name was incongruous with his accent. 'I ran the event last night. I organise many parties and events in the Borders. Firm's based in St Boswells.' Gundog shook Marshall's hand with the force of a soldier.

Marshall gripped it just as tight. 'Looks like a lot of fun was had?'

'Struggling to get the cleaners up here to clear the place because of the roads. Or that's their excuse.' Gundog winced. 'So we'll be a while tidying the place up today. Had a ceilidh band in, local lot who do a few events for me a month. Trouble was, two groups got into it over the correct direction to do Dashing White Sergeants. Clockwise or anti-clockwise. Wouldn't settle on an answer and things started to escalate. After that amount of whisky and cava, what started as a few sarcastic words led to a push, then to someone throwing handfuls of haggis. Followed by neeps and tatties.'

Balfour laughed. 'Hey, any Burns supper where the haggis is the only thing skewered with a big knife is a success.'

Marshall knew all about toffs and their food fights from school and university. They didn't seem to have the same behaviour modifiers as council house scumbags like him, never having been hungry unless Papa was exhibiting tough love. Didn't seem to care who cleaned up their mess. 'Need to ask you a few questions about Dr Louisa Baird.'

'Ah, yes. One of the patrons of the event. Lovely woman.'

Balfour scratched at his neck. 'Gundog, she passed away this morning.'

'Heavens.' Gundog frowned. 'But she was so young and vibrant.'

'We believe she was abducted after she left.'

'Abducted?' Gundog's eyes bulged. 'By Christ...' He looked around the room. 'I only spoke to her briefly as she was incredibly popular on the night. She gave an impassioned speech about her cancer charity. My job was to make sure it ran smoothly, and that everyone paid attention. Before you ask, she'd gone by the time this all happened.' He waved around the midden.

'Do you know when she left?' Marshall knew but he wanted to make sure her leaving this room tallied with her leaving the event.

'After ten. Just after, I think.'

'Alone?'

'Think so.'

'You think? Anyone else leave around the same time?'

'Not to my knowledge, no. But I was in charge of letting them in until the event started. We had cabs turning up all evening.'

'Any record of who was here?'

Gundog walked over to a table and picked up his clipboard. 'I signed everyone in, personally, and had a trusty lieutenant sign them out.' He handed it to Marshall. 'This is yours to keep, should it prove helpful.'

'Cheers.' Marshall checked through it. Bloody hell, it was even more precise than a crime scene log. He scanned through the list of names and one jumped out at him.

Dr Benjamin Rougier.

Lying bastard...

And the two below it made his gut clench.

CHAPTER TWENTY-SIX

Elliot marched up the embankment towards the pool car. Much harder going than coming down, that's for sure. Cheeky sods had taken down the tent already. Eager to get out of the cold and into the warm of the room they'd claimed in Gala nick.

Ah, who could blame them.

Even with all that snow spreading the faint sun's glow, it was getting too dark to see so she needed to switch on her phone's torch. Battery was suspiciously low, like it hadn't charged overnight. One thing she prided herself on was never getting into shit with the boss – she didn't want to give Pringle any ammunition – so she needed to be contactable at all times. She'd have to remember to charge the buggering thing when driving.

Shunty was by the roadside, watching McIntyre drive off like a jilted lover. Or one who feared he was being used. Good that he was finally getting the hapless arsehead to do something. It didn't have to be this difficult. It shouldn't be.

If she'd ended up with Jolene rather than him...

Aye, keep dreaming. Focus on the task at hand.

A Land Rover pulled in next to Shunty. Marshall got out. Big, ugly bugger was the one who'd taken that car.

Well, not that ugly but big and certainly a bugger. Acted like he had all the answers and clutched them so tightly to his chest.

Wanker.

Elliot managed to speed up through the snow, now she was at ankle height. 'A sleigh pulled by huskies would be ideal.'

Marshall looked over at her. 'Oh, hey. Didn't see you there.'

She ploughed on. 'I said, a sleigh pulled by—'

'Aye, I heard. Sure it would be.'

Jolene was still in the car, talking on her phone.

Let's see if Dr Donkey even realises...

Elliot waved behind her. 'Just been down in the gully there with Kirsten.'

Marshall stared past her, then focused on her. 'Heard you found Dr Baird's car? XJ72 ZLO, right?'

Bloody hell, was nothing sacred?

So Marshall could recite the plate from memory. Wonder of wonders – he actually was a cop. Fair dos.

She stopped by the car and resisted the temptation to lean against it. That climb was harder than she was used to. And her trousers were all manky. Great. 'Got a theory of what happened here?'

'Not yet.' Marshall narrowed his eyes at her. 'But I'm guessing you do.'

She smiled back at him. 'You show me yours first, Marshall.'

He scratched at his neck. 'We think we've narrowed down the window of abduction from the CCTV at Blainslieshaw Mains. Jolene's just checking it over now but it looks like she left the Burns supper at three minutes past ten. A taxi left not long after. Need to tally that with Owusu's findings, but I'd suggest it looks like someone stopped her up here and killed her.'

'That's interesting. Ties in with my thinky, as Pringle would say.'

He craned his neck to look at her. 'Go on?'

'Shunty and I did some digging down in the village, then... Then up in one of the wind turbines. We have a sighting of a navy Transit abducting Lorimer at the back of eight. Drove him up here and must've dumped him.'

'Makes sense.' Marshall was nodding along with it. 'But we need to drill down into what happened. What's your thinky?'

'I'd suggest the occupants of this Transit did both. Abducted them then dumped them both. Him first, then her, a few hours later.' Elliot pointed back to the sets of footprints she'd left in the snow, barely visible in the fading light. 'We've squared off some more of the story. Looks like her motor's been driven off the road.' She let it sink in. 'Picture it, Marshall. That van's sitting on the wrong side of the private road up from the farm to this road. It's dark, lights are off. Engine idling. They're waiting for her to leave the Burns supper. See her headlights approaching. Turn on their lights, check it's her, then shoot forward and scare her off the road. Her car seems to cope in the snow, but even that's going to struggle in a deep drift on top of heather. They grab her, get her out, then dump the car. Or maybe they just had to leave it down in that hollow.'

'Okay, I can see that.' Marshall scanned the frozen vista darkening before them. 'Some big gaps, though. First, there are two hours to fill between his abduction and hers.'

'Big Jim McIntyre's looking into that for us. Getting door-bell footage in Lauder.'

Marshall frowned. 'What if they went to the Stow end?'

Elliot glanced at Shunty long enough for him to get the message. 'We're on top of that too.'

'Excellent.' Marshall clapped his gloved hands together. 'If we can pin those movements down, then we can start to understand what happened here.'

Sanctimonious twat.

Elliot stuck her tongue in her cheek to stop herself from saying it out loud. 'What's the other thing?'

He frowned again. 'Other thing?'

'You said there were two issues with my theory.'

'Oh, right. Not necessarily an issue.' He smiled. 'They'd need to know when she left.'

Elliot couldn't help but roll her eyes. 'Already thought of that.'

'And?'

'They've got someone on the inside. So we need to speak to the catering and bar staff. Anyone working security at the event.'

'We could do that.' Jolene couldn't help smiling. Elliot hadn't seen her approach. 'Or we could ask Dr Rougier.'

'Eh? The lad who was stalking her?'

'Correct.' God, Jolene could be a smug prick when she wanted. 'He was at the Burns supper.'

Elliot couldn't process it at all. 'Why the hell would *he* get invited?'

'Turns out he's helping with the cancer charity. Probably so he can get close to her.'

Elliot exhaled slowly. 'I'm sick to death of people lying to us.'

Marshall frowned again. If he kept doing that, he was going to get big ruts on his forehead. End up looking like he had a ploughed tattie field on his bonce. 'Who else?'

'Kyle Talbot. Got into a fight with Lorimer on Thursday,

ended up in A&E. Wasn't that forthcoming with you lot, was he?'

'You think he's a suspect?'

Elliot shrugged. 'I mean, we don't really have any theories, do we?'

'Say Louisa and Justin aren't connected by anything other than dying on the same night by the same method. Say Talbot and Rougier paid the same people to off their enemies.'

'On the same night?'

'Why not?' His turn to shrug. 'Maybe it was designed to throw us off the scent.'

'Throw us off the scent...' Elliot laughed. 'Or maybe they weren't very good at it.' She couldn't help but glance at Shunty. 'Just because someone's got a job, doesn't mean they're any good at it.'

'Okay.' Marshall clapped his gloved hands together. 'Theories are like belly buttons, everyone has one and they all stink. I used to say arseholes, but I'm trying to be less coarse nowadays. But I suggest the following division of labour. You and Rakesh speak to Dr Rougier about him still stalking Louisa Baird. See if he slips up.'

'Fair dos. And you?'

Marshall looked at Jolene. 'We have another suspect to speak to.'

CHAPTER TWENTY-SEVEN

'Just look at him, Rob.' Jolene was behind the wheel, waving at the car ahead of them. 'Shunty might've passed advanced driver training, but look at him. He's slower than my mum. Hands at ten and two, signalling every turn. Unbelievable.'

Marshall hadn't really paid attention all the way down from Lauder. He was sick of the road, had travelled it so many times.

He couldn't get Elliot's theory out of his head.

What if the murders weren't connected?

What if someone had paid to bump them off?

Now he had his own pet criminal profiler, Pringle was desperate for this to be some sexy serial killer case. A chance to make himself look important.

The prospect of someone having prior knowledge of her leaving the function nibbled at Marshall.

Rougier was the obvious candidate, but could a doctor in A&E seriously pay someone to kill his lover?

Anything was possible, sure, but was it likely?

'Sick of this place...' Jolene followed the other pool car around the arc that approached Borders General and pulled in behind them.

For some reason, Siyal's reverse lights came on. He didn't move back, though. Just sat there.

'Come on, then.' Marshall got out into the bracing darkness and led along the gritty pavement towards the hospital. 'I'll catch you up.'

Jolene stopped to glare at him. 'Where are you going?'

'While you're speaking to people about why Rougier was at the Burns supper, I've got a message to run.'

'A personal one?'

'Kind of.'

'Jesus, Rob, you don't help yourself at times.'

'What's that supposed to mean?'

'Hiding stuff from me isn't cool.'

'Okay, that's not my intention.' He gave her a reassuring smile but was feeling a bit edgy that Elliot would get out and ask what the hell was going on. 'It's about Rougier. Believe me.'

'Hard to at times.'

'Look, I'll catch up with you.'

She scowled at him. 'You're the boss.'

Marshall slipped into the separate A&E door, feeling like everything in his life was under surveillance, and charged through to the treatment area. Like before, it was heaving like a nightclub at half two in the morning on a Saturday when everyone was making sure they'd definitely catch that last train to Oblivion Central. He pushed through to the office at the side and there she was.

Jen was tucking into a sandwich at her desk. She looked over, scowling, a splodge of mayonnaise dribbling down her chin. 'Rob? Christ, are you on payroll here or something?'

Marshall sat in the chair next to her. Took a few seconds to collect himself and centre his thoughts. 'We've known each other all our lives.'

'Jesus, is this one of those chats where you come out to me, or something?'

Marshall couldn't help but laugh. As hard as he tried. 'Jen, one thing you should know about me is how much I hate being lied to.'

She rubbed the sauce off her chin then licked her finger. 'Who's been lying to you now?'

'You, Jen.'

'Eh?'

'I'm giving you one chance to do this the easy way. You tell me the truth now and it's fine.'

'Truth about what? Rob, have you gone mental?'

'Jen. You were at the Burns supper at Blainslieshaw Mains last night.'

She put the lid back on her sandwich tub and sat there, staring at her blank computer screen. 'Rob, you've got a bloody cheek. I'm a single woman. I'm allowed to go to events I'm invited to.'

'Was it you who was invited?'

'What do you mean?'

'It could be that, say, Dr Rougier invited you. That I could buy. He's a colleague. Or it could be Dr Baird herself. Either works.'

She kept her silence. Thing with her was she knew when she was trapped. And when to shut up.

Marshall leaned close. 'It's a bit of an odd one to read through a guest list and see your name there. Your married name. And to discover that you were with Paul.'

She buried her head in her hands. 'Shite.'

'Jen... Why were you there with your ex?'

She leaned forward, then sat back, kneading her hands through her hair. 'I can explain.'

'You'd better. And you'd better be able to explain to Thea too.'

'Rob, I've made such a mess of everything.' She slumped back in her chair. 'I've accidentally rekindled my marriage.'

'How the hell did you manage that?'

'That night you were looking after Thea for me... Three weeks ago. Friday night. Me and Sally from Kirsten's team were in a pub in Melrose. Last orders came and went. We ended up in a taxi to that club in Gala. Haven't been there since I was, like, twenty-five. We were both too pissed to get in, so we went for chips next door.' She looked over at Marshall. 'Who should walk out with a kebab but Paul. He was out on the lash with his mate, Jamie. Started out pretty frosty, but we ended up getting a cab back to Jamie's place in Clovenfords. Other side of the village from us, near the school.' She started fiddling with the clasp on her sandwich tub. 'And one thing led to another...'

The room was silent. Somewhere, someone started screaming the British national anthem, but stuck to the words about saving the queen.

'It's a disaster, Rob. I'm so lonely. I've *been* so lonely. The sex is good. Always has been. Paul's a good laugh and a good shag, but I divorced him for a reason. He's a terrible father and, when I'm sober, I can see that he's just a dickhead. I can see that. But... I hate being lonely, Rob. I just can't do it. I've been with someone since I was fifteen. This is the longest time I've been single. I know you... held a candle for years, but we're not the same person, you and I, and...' Tears slid down her cheeks. 'I can't do it alone, Rob.'

Marshall gripped her hand. 'Let's talk about this later at Grumpy's thing.'

'Okay.' She wiped a tear out of her eye. 'Thank you. I hate

secrets too. I hate… lying to people. Especially you. Especially Thea.'

'I hate it too. We've been so distant from each other at times. I'm glad we can have this chat without you slapping me.'

She raised a hand. 'You're skating pretty close, buster.'

Marshall jerked his head back away from her, playfully. 'Thanks for being so honest with me, but I need to ask you some questions about last night.'

'You pervert.'

'Not about that!'

Jen frowned, maybe realising this was serious. 'I thought we were going to talk about this later?'

'Your feelings, sure. But if you were at the event, I need you to tell me what you saw.'

'Okay. I saw a load of toffs getting wankered on whisky and wine then doing the gay Gordons badly. What specifically do you want to know?'

'Did you see Dr Baird there?'

Jen nodded. 'She gave this speech. Made me tear up a bit. Talked about how she'd treated Rhona Rattray for cancer, but also about her ladyship could afford for some stuff over and above what the NHS provides. The charity wants to make sure everyone gets that same level of care. Hence the charity, which is to provide a support network for sufferers and their loved ones. The event was to help fund renting a space in Gala. Paul dipped his hand in his pocket. Probably just trying to impress me.'

'Did you speak to her?'

'Just to say hi.'

'Was she with anyone?'

'I mean, she spoke to a lot of people, but I can't remember seeing her talking to anyone specifically, no.'

'When did she leave?'

Jen looked away. 'Not sure.'

'Come on...'

'I'm serious. I saw her, Rob. That was it.'

'When did *you* leave?'

She unclipped her sandwich tub again. 'After midnight.'

Marshall left a space, filled with a fumbling attempt at the second verse of the national anthem.

She stared at him and swallowed hard. 'We got a cab at midnight and went back to Paul's. Big mistake. Got into this big argument first thing this morning.'

'About what?'

'He wants to get Thea a tutor.'

'That's not a bad thing.'

'I know, but... He's just an arrogant shit, Rob. It was pretty tough getting a cab from Cardrona to Clovenfords at that time in the morning, especially in the snow.'

'So you weren't getting bacon and rolls this morning.'

'Well spotted, genius.' She sighed and it turned into a deep yawn. 'I'm so bloody tired, Rob.'

'Not surprised. You were out on the lash until after midnight on a school night, then you were back home very early after a night of shagging.'

She slapped his arm.

'Were you drunk?'

'I was a bit pissed, admittedly.' She looked at him then glanced away again. 'Might've started a food fight.'

'A food fight?' Marshall didn't let on that he knew about it. Didn't let on that he was both disappointed and amazed that his twin sister had been the one instigating matters. 'What happened?'

'The numpties started going clockwise in Dashing White Sergeants. That's wrong!'

'True. Anti-clockwise then clockwise.'

'Exactly! Everyone was falling over each other. Absolute chaos! And this red-faced arsehole with a kilt a couple of sizes too small for him started saying I was wrong. So I flung a spoonful of haggis at him. He flung some back.'

'Did you get chucked out?'

'Hardly. Thing with toffs, Rob, is they just get stuck in without caring who clears it up because it sure as hell won't be them. I found haggis in my bra this morning.'

Marshall stifled a laugh. 'Was Dr Baird involved?'

'No, she'd already left. Most people there were pretty wankered by this point.'

'Dashing White Sergeants isn't exactly one of the more advanced dances. Third or fourth?'

'Things got delayed. That arsehole Balfour Rattray was a bit wankered and did a talk, kept going on about how much he loved his mother. Pretty weird, to be honest.'

'Did you speak to him?'

'A bit. Thing with Balfour is he was mentally abused as a kid by his father and he took it out on the world. On you and me and everyone else. Aye, he was a dickhead in high school, but he said that's what high school's all about... be a bully, get bullied, decide who you are, who you stand up to, who you ignore, why you do what you do. We come from the generation where a punch in the mouth might be earned or might be the answer.'

'That's a bit much.'

'You don't agree?'

'I don't know. Do you?'

'I think so. You're who you are because of people like him. Same with me. We're both resilient people. Be thankful for that. We're the sum total of both our DNA and our experiences, plus or minus. What didn't kill us, made us stronger.'

Marshall wished that applied to everyone. 'Did you see Dr Rougier speaking to Louisa?'

'Opposite ends of the room all night.'

'Seriously?'

'Seriously. Why are you asking this?'

'Dr Baird's car was found in the snow, half a mile away from the farm. She died just after midnight. Left about ten o'clock.'

'Shit. Really?'

'Really. In that time, someone abducted her, tied her up and dumped her on top of a corpse.'

'So when I was leaving... She...' Jen swallowed. 'She was dying?' She tugged at her hair. 'While I was throwing food around?'

'Looks that way. But it's not on you, Jen. Okay? We're looking for anything, though. You're the only person who was there who I can trust. Anything that can help us find her killer. Anything at all.'

'Listen, the taxi driver who picked us up said they'd already been there that night. Got into a shouting match with someone who was leaving. A big Audi. Kept moaning about Audi drivers.'

'That's interesting. Do you know who the driver was?'

'Dr Baird drives an Audi, right?'

'No, I mean the taxi driver.'

'Sorry, no. But why did you ask me about Ben Rougier?'

'Because he told us he wasn't there.'

'Did he?' Jen shook her head. 'He was there, alright. I wanted to speak to him but he'd gone.'

'Was he involved in the food fight?'

'God no. He'd slipped off early too.'

Shit. This wasn't looking good. 'Any idea what time?'

'Must be about ten.'

CHAPTER TWENTY-EIGHT

Elliot had to step aside to let an orderly push a poor sod on a gurney past. Looked like someone had been at his skull with a chisel.

The A&E department buzzed like a broken fridge. Too many people and so much noise. Someone was screaming somewhere like they were being drilled into. Maybe they were. Someone else was singing the British national anthem but was still stuck in the days of a queen.

Snowy days like this were hell – car crashes and slips on pavements brought in the punters in their droves. No wonder all the staff looked like they'd been on a pretty aggressive hen weekend.

Elliot grabbed Shunty's arm and stopped him entering the doctor's office. 'Okay, sunshine. Here's how we're doing this. I'm good cop. You're a bad cop.' She grinned. 'I mean, bad cop.'

He winced. 'Sure we should do it that way?'

'I want to see if you can, Shunty. Prove you've got what it takes, eh?'

Shunty stood up a bit taller. God, the kid was a giant. 'Will do.' He opened the door and swept inside.

Some boy.

Marshall stormed out of another office and disappeared into the throng.

What the hell was *he* doing down here? Him and Jolene were supposed to be up seeing Baird's oncologist boss. The plot thickened...

She knew that big guy was shagging someone, but she thought it was someone in the force. Maybe it was a nurse or doctor here.

Elliot followed Shunty into the office.

He stood over Rougier like he was going to smack him one. Barely two feet between them. 'We. Know.'

'Woah, woah!' Rougier pushed his chair back and squirmed to his feet. 'What the hell?' He clocked Elliot. 'Who the hell are you?'

'Police, sir. DI Andrea Elliot.' Elliot held out her warrant card with one hand and dragged Shunty back with the other. 'This is DS Rakesh Siyal.'

Rougier nervously eyed the door. 'I spoke to two other police officers earlier.'

Elliot nodded. 'Colleagues of ours. DI Marshall and DS Archer.'

'I think that was them.' Rougier frowned, then shifted his gaze between them. 'What's going on?'

'Sergeant, why don't you be helpful and tell him what you know?'

'Right.' Shunty stepped over to Rougier, towering over him again. 'We know about the HR case against you.'

'HR case?'

'Seems like whoever investigated it missed the point of what you're up to.'

'What I'm up to? What the hell are you talking about?'

Shunty prodded him in the chest. 'Don't deny it.'

'Don't you *dare* touch me!'

'I didn't.'

'Don't gaslight me!'

'Gaslighting?' Shunty laughed. 'You should know all about psychological manipulation, right? Stalking Dr Baird is just the start of what you're—'

'I wasn't stalking her.'

'Oh?'

'Seriously.'

'Oh, cool.' Shunty turned to look at Elliot. 'We can get ourselves out of here, ma'am. He's just told us the truth and clearly isn't involved in her murder.' He turned back to Rougier. 'We need the truth out of you, now. You were stalking her. Admit it.'

'I wasn't!'

'The HR case would beg to differ.'

Rougier shifted his gaze between them. 'You want the truth?' He let out a deep breath and seemed to deflate. 'I took the rap in that case.'

Shunty folded his arms. 'Sounds like bollocks to me.'

'I wanted to help her.'

'You put a permanent blot on your record to help her?'

'Right. I wasn't the instigator. I told your colleagues. She kissed me, twice. Came onto me. Sent me signals.'

'Messages?'

'No. She was careful. Paper notes. I haven't kept any of them.'

'Convenient.'

'You're trying to finger me as her killer, aren't you? Fuck it, I'm not being Mr Nice Guy anymore. I took the fall to save her career and her marriage. You know what it's like to do that? To pretend you're the fucking creep? Eh? To have everyone think you're this weirdo loser?'

'I do, actually.' Shunty smoothed a hand over his face. 'I had a situation a few months ago that... Well, it turned toxic. I'm sure you can understand what I went through.'

What the hell was the big oaf talking about?

And so much for being Bad Cop.

Elliot pushed her way between them, forcing Rougier back against the wall. 'Listen to me, you sick bastard. You lied to us. Told us you were at home last night. Went to the gym, eh? Why do we find you attending a Burns supper where the woman you were stalking was just before she was murdered?!'

'I didn't... I didn't...' Rougier couldn't focus on anything. He seemed to crumple like one of those imaginary love notes from Dr Baird. 'I didn't kill her.'

'Maybe, but you probably know who did, eh? Whoever you paid to bump her off!' Elliot grabbed him by the arm. 'You're now the lead suspect in the case, sunshine. Get your glad rags on.'

'What?'

'We're taking you into the station to formally interview you.' She looked him up and down. 'We'll let you get yourself changed out of your scrubs into your civvies.'

Rougier stood there. 'I want a lawyer.'

'Excellent. Do you have a lawyer?'

'I... I do, as it happens.'

'Give them a wee tinkle and we'll make sure whoever it is meets us there.' Elliot opened the door. 'We'll be waiting out here.' She held the door for Shunty to leave, then left the room herself. 'Some boy, him.'

Shunty looked at her, shaking his head. 'So much for you being good cop.'

'Aye, that's not my strong point. Let's settle for "worse cop".'

CHAPTER TWENTY-NINE

Marshall sat on the toilet and got out his phone. Elliot hadn't responded to his text or called him back. She was a sneaky devil, always capable of hiding stuff from him.

He gave the cubicle door a good stare.

He'd got her with that number plate trick back at the crime scene. She thought he was useless, someone without her experience of solving crimes from the youngest age. Experience came in different shapes and sizes.

And it hit him – this was pretty much the only place he would get peace. Down here in the hospital basement, where no mobile signal could reach. Well, not quite none – they could reach you in Owusu's lair.

He needed to stop calling it that. Especially to her face.

He hadn't even needed to go to the toilet, just to think and process things. And there was so much noise inside his head today.

He needed to get a handle on just how stupid his sister was being. Turned out he didn't have the monopoly when it came to idiotic behaviour in the Marshall clan. Hell, the family motto should be whatever the Latin was for 'Bloody Idiot'.

He googled it, but of course his phone was offline.

He hoped Jen told Thea. And soon.

Poor kid had been through enough.

Actually, poor kid nothing. She was more mature than either parent, which was the whole problem. Aye, those two were living embodiments of being a bloody idiot.

Marshall got up and flushed the toilet, then walked over to the sink—

His phone rang.

Jesus, was nothing sacred?

He checked the screen.

Jolene calling...

Bollocks, he'd left her upstairs on her own. He stepped over to the sink and answered it. 'How's it going?'

'Just wanted to give you an update. And see where you were.'

Next to impossible to wash your hands one-handed, but he tried as good as he could. 'I'm down in the basement.'

'Why?'

'I want to check on the PM to see if we can tighten the timeline any further.'

'Right. So, I'm stuck here.'

'I won't be long. How did it go with Rougier's boss?'

'Didn't get anywhere. He didn't attend. Doesn't really know about her and Rougier.'

'Even though it was an HR issue?'

'Well, that's the game he was playing.'

'Okay, can you focus on Rougier's alibis, please?'

'I've got people doing that already.'

'He's our main suspect now. I expect *you* to be keeping on top of all of that, okay?'

'Okay, Rob. I'll see what's what.' Click and she was gone.

The joys of managing people... Like shepherding kittens.

Marshall set his mobile down and gave his hands a good wash this time. Dried them on his trousers as he walked through to Pathology.

The door was wedged open and lowered voices drifted through.

'She's just impossible.'

Pringle.

Marshall stayed in the corridor, listening. He really should have just walked away but something kept him there.

'I just can't... Can't seem to get through to her.'

'Jim, she's your daughter.' Owusu, sounding distracted. 'Though nobody knows about her, right?'

'Absolutely right. I've wound them up about it, but... It's a constant challenge. I find it all so difficult. The whole thing.'

Weird hearing him talking without the constant whistles and coded language only he understood.

Weirder still hearing him talking about his daughter. Kirsty. Everyone thought he was just a piss-taker, but Marshall started to worry he was losing his mind and convincing himself she was real.

Or he could just be trying to wind up Owusu too.

No, she was the one person who called him out on his nonsense.

Shite – Marshall had left his mobile in the toilet. He rushed back and found it sitting on the edge of the sink.

Unlocked, his screen showing:

Cruenta stultus

Took him a second to remember. Latin for 'bloody idiot'. The Marshall family crest. Well, Google Translate's version. Whether that'd pass muster with someone who actually spoke it was anyone's guess.

Still, it was proof that he was one, though – leaving a phone full of sensitive information unlocked.

He pocketed it and went back through, trying to ignore the trickle of sweat running down his back.

Pringle was in the doorway, scratching his cheek, eyes almost crossed as he stared into space. Then he saw Marshall and seemed to change entirely, growing taller. 'Aha, Dr Robert! Come into Dr Owusu's lair.'

Marshall followed him into the freezing cold space.

'Jim, I keep telling you...' Owusu was standing beside the corpse of Justin Lorimer, resting on a slab. 'I hate this being called my lair. Makes me sound like some kind of ghoul.'

'I totally get it, Belu. You're welcome to kick me in the goolies the next time.'

She looked up, rolled her eyes, then went back to slicing away at the corpse.

Marshall joined her but kept a good distance.

Lorimer looked almost peaceful, as though his death hadn't been an ordeal like so many. Almost smiling, even. Incredibly unsettling, worse than a brutal stabbing or car crash. Dying with a smile on your face...

Marshall looked over at her. 'How's it going?'

'We've narrowed down their times of death.' She took a deep breath and let it out as a rasping sigh. 'I say narrow them down, but really... it's just the same information as I had at the crime scene.'

'So a few hours apart?'

'Correct. Two, at most.' She waved a hand at Justin Lorimer's corpse again. 'He died first, around about ten o'clock.' She couldn't seem to bring herself to gesture at a former colleague's body, even though it was hidden in one of the storage racks. 'Her death is a bit trickier, eh? I'd say... between midnight and one.'

Marshall nodded. 'That fits with what we've found.'

Pringle tilted his head to the side. 'Oh?'

'It's all in an email to you, sir.'

Pringle patted his pockets. 'I don't have my jiggery pokery doodah here with me.'

'You haven't got your mobile phone?'

'No, my computer. Can't remember how to log in on my phone. And besides, I don't get reception down here.' Pringle looked over at Owusu. 'Is there anything to indicate if they were done by the same people?'

Marshall had to stop himself frowning – what the hell was the point in him being here for hours if he asked such basic questions.

'Possibly.' Owusu walked over to the corridor. 'Kirsten!'

Footsteps slapped closer. 'What's up?'

'Your time in the spotlight, dear.'

Kirsten stormed in, face like a blizzard. 'You need to have a word with your staff, Belu. Someone's left the toilet in an absolute state.'

Owusu waved a hand at Pringle. 'It's probably a copper like him, eh?'

'Not funny. My waterworks might be a complete disgrace, but I give you my deepest and truest testimony that it wasn't me, because I'm touching cloth right now and in dire need of an imminent departure.'

'Jim!' Owusu waved over at the door. 'Get out of here!'

Pringle strode out.

Owusu shook her head. 'I'd apologise for him, but he's nobody's fault but his own.'

Kirsten stood there, her face as cold as the icy air. Seemed to thaw when she spotted Marshall between the corpses. 'Hey, Rob.'

'Hi.'

Owusu shut the door and stomped over to the body. 'Anyway. I didn't get an update from you before you rushed off earlier?'

'Right. We found her car, so I was supervising to make sure it was done to my exacting standards.' Kirsten stood by Marshall and seemed to shiver. The hairs on her arms were standing to attention. 'Two things.' She held up her thumb. 'First, Trev is an expert on knots.'

Marshall laughed. 'Knots?'

'Big sailor, so he knows his knots. As he put it, as the bonds on their wrists and ankles were basic granny knots. Closer to shoelaces than a reef knot.'

'Any conclusions on that?'

'Well, you're not dealing with a master craftsman, are you? Someone tying someone up wants to make sure they're not getting away. Zip ties or at least a proper knot. Not those.'

'Makes sense.' Marshall scribbled it down. Hopefully his brain would be able to decipher 'knot — amateur' at a later point.

'Next, the blood toxicology came back when I was up there. Both victims show signs of alcohol. Hers was below the drink-drive level. His was way above it. But I don't think he was thinking of getting behind the wheel. He was pretty pissed and maybe he wouldn't have felt much when he died.'

That tallied with what Marshall knew – he was a heavy drinker last seen in a pub, whereas she was someone hosting a fundraiser who maybe nursed a glass of bubbly all night to appear sociable.

'Okay, that's all good. What about other substances?'

'Nothing.'

'No coke, weed, ketamine, speed?'

'Nope. Not even prescription painkillers.'

'And her?'

'Both of them.'

Marshall looked over at the door. He wanted to talk about how Pringle had been insistent this was a drugs case, despite there being no sign either was a user. Sod it, that was one for Pringle to hear himself. 'You said earlier that his death would've been euphoric. And if he was half-cut, that probably adds to it. But what about her?'

'Hard to say, Rob. She was dumped on top of a corpse. That's going to have been a gruesome death, though her system would've been flooding her with euphoric substances towards the end.'

Those last few hours must've been brutal. Feeling the ice of another body next to you. Hoping someone would find you, but the snow falling would... It'd kill off any hope she had. Then her endorphins would kick in and her death would've been a form of euphoria.

Jesus Christ.

Marshall locked eyes with Kirsten. 'What's the second thing?'

'Second thing?' She seemed to notice she was still raising her thumb. 'Oh, right. I was going to say that we've got nothing from the crime scenes.'

'Nothing?'

'Nothing.' Kirsten shook her head. 'No prints or hairs. Certainly nothing we could potentially tie back to the murders.'

'So someone abducted two people and killed them but they didn't leave any traces?'

'Big load of nothing. No prints on the bonds, either. The car might be better, assuming they forced her out of it. Trev's taking it up to Edinburgh to run a full assessment.'

'But you're not hopeful?'

'If I'm never hopeful, then I can't be disappointed.' Kirsten smiled at him. 'But it's not the first time someone's been bound like that, is it?'

'Precisely my point!' Pringle was back in the room, rubbing his hands on the wall like he was drying them. 'I've asked Doctor Donkey here to focus on the other crimes where someone was tied up, to see if it's someone escalating to serial murder.'

Marshall leaned against the desk and let the cold steel rise up through his wrists. 'I don't think that's going to yield anything.'

'Why?'

'I tend to go on evidence. There's nothing to suggest this is related to—'

'I think we need to at least investigate.'

'Sir, I have been and neither of them has—'

'You haven't really tried yet, have you?'

There was no winning this one. Easier to just do it than to argue about why he shouldn't.

'I'll get on it, sir.' Marshall stood up tall and sucked in a deep breath. 'I'll head back to base and do some digging, sir.'

'That's illegal.'

Marshall frowned. 'Eh?'

'Oh, digging! I thought you said *dogging*!'

Nobody laughed.

Pringle cleared his throat. 'Okay. I think we need to work on the basis that Mr Lorimer's death is gang stuff spiralling out of control. Maybe they didn't expect the snow and it caught them unawares.'

Marshall stared at him. 'And what about Dr Baird's?'

'Well, of course she...' Pringle yawned into his fist. 'Gad-zooks, is that the time?'

'You don't have an answer for that, do you?'

Pringle's eyes swept across the room, landing everywhere but on Marshall. 'Could be she drove up and interrupted the gang members shortly after they dumped him. Or she saw them with the body, so she was collateral damage.'

'Okay.' Marshall folded his arms. 'But we don't have any evidence for that. There's a big time difference. Two hours. Are you seriously telling me you think someone saw her witness a murder, then let her go to a party before killing her?'

Pringle glared at Marshall. Real fire in his eyes. 'I've asked you to focus on this being done by serial killers. I want a list of potential suspects before you bugger off home for the night. More snow on the way tonight so I suggest you pull the finger out, okay?'

CHAPTER THIRTY

Bugger this.

Marshall got up from his laptop and walked over to the window. Snowing again, just like Pringle had promised. Cars crawled towards the centre of Melrose, but a numpty in a Nissan took it way too fast, not just for the conditions but for the twenty limit. The town had a weird feeling about it, where it was dark but the snow on the park made it seem like a perpetual twilight.

He went back over to the desk and stared at the PNC query. Rows and rows of data, with each line opening up to another world of information about a particular case. Aye, this was going to be a long night. A long, boring one.

He exported the data so at least he had it on his laptop for working at home.

The office door swung open and Elliot swung in, grinning wide. 'Evening, Marshall.' She walked over to her desk and plugged in her phone. Stared at the screen. 'There. Bastard thing died and I got into shit for it from Pringle.'

Marshall reached into his drawer. 'Catch.' He flung over a

little black box. 'Spare portable battery pack. Never know when it'll come in handy. Keep it charged up.'

'Eh, well. Thanks, Rob. That's, uh, kind of you.'

He sat back, arms crossed. 'You seem in a good mood.'

'Am I not always?'

'Not if you've had a bollocking from the boss. What's happened?'

She brushed a hand across her lips. 'Just had a fish supper.'

'What's the real reason?'

'Had half of Shunty's battered haggis. Daft sod thought it was vegan. I mean, it's offal...'

'Come on, spill.'

'We've brought Dr Rougier in for questioning.'

Marshall felt his eyebrows shoot up. 'Wow.'

'You think that's a mistake?'

'No. It's just... Wow.'

'Don't give me that. What do you mean?'

'Just not sure we've got anything on him, have we?'

'We'll *get* stuff.'

That old chestnut...

Tunnel vision. The end justifying the means. Case being led by the desired destination, not by the evidence.

Cruenta stultus.

'Do you need any help from me?'

'Do I look like I need help?' Elliot burped into her fist. Classy. 'Just waiting on his sodding lawyer to come in.' She checked her watch. 'Thought he'd be here by now, but bloody lawyers, eh?'

'It is snowing.'

'He's coming from Gala, not the Sahara.' Elliot sat behind her desk and picked up her battered stress ball then started tossing it in the air.

Marshall walked back over to the window and stared out.

Seemed even brighter. 'Andrea, why are you so sure Rougier's our killer?'

'Because he's not talking.'

Marshall couldn't hide his laughter. 'Seriously?'

'Seriously. Feel it in my blood, Robbie.'

'Sure that'll stand up in court. "Your honour, our first witness will be DI Andrea Elliot's water." Come on...'

'He's not talking. And when he does, he's lying about his whereabouts.'

'That's not enough.'

'Okay but say this HR issue was an affair.'

'Wait.' Marshall felt a throb of pain in his brain. 'What the hell are you talking about?'

'Rougier said he took a fall for her.'

'That doesn't make any sense.'

'Rougier told both of us she was the aggressor in the matter. That she hit on him. Twice. But suppose she ended it. And he doesn't take no for an answer. Like you said, he was trying to woo her, like he was in a Hollywood film. And Hugo found out. They had it out. Hugo realised what was going on. He got someone to kill her. Or Rougier did.'

God. She had Rougier sitting waiting to be questioned over this with absolutely bugger all to go on. This wasn't going to explode in her face, was it?

'Andrea, this whole theory seems pretty far-fetched to me.'

'Robbie, I'd put actual money on one of those two paying some numpties to do it for them. Stands to reason.'

'Twenty quid it's neither.'

'Deal.' Elliot got the note out of her purse and slammed it on the desk. 'Let's see the colour of your money, Marshall.'

Thank God she'd reverted to surnames.

Marshall walked back to his desk and found his wallet in his coat pocket. 'There you go.' He got out two tenners and put them down. 'I don't really need to put the cash down. Should just come over and take yours from you.'

'Why are you so confident?'

'Because your theory doesn't cover why either of them would kill Lorimer.'

'Who says they did?'

'True. Someone did. Same MO. Same van. Same people.'

'Co-inky-dink.'

'Andrea, this really doesn't seem like a coincidence.'

'Come on. It could be. Hitmen aren't evil masterminds. They're stupid people who are just luckier than average when it comes to killing. Like that Robert Carlyle film about that hitman in Dundee. Not the brightest, was he? So good he was lucky and so lucky he was good.'

Marshall laughed. 'Andrea, you should write a screenplay. You've clearly got the imagination for Hollywood.'

'I'm serious.' She looked it. 'What's your take on the husband?'

'My take? Hard to get a read on him.' Marshall sat back in his chair. 'You spoke with him too, right?'

'Aye. Me and Shunty. Some kind of wake thing going on there. Party food and bottles of wine. I was the one who finally persuaded him to see his darling wife's body. So.' She stared at him, tossed the ball and caught it without looking. 'What do you make of him?'

'Well, at risk of upsetting people, I think theirs was a marriage of convenience. Separate rooms, both workaholics. Co-parenting, basically.'

'Tell me about it. Had a nanny, for God's sake!'

'Still haven't spoken to her.'

'Oh, we did. When you and the golden girl were off chasing up any number of leads on Lorimer.'

'The golden girl? Jolene?'

'God, don't tell her that.' Elliot slumped forward, touching her forehead to her desk.

Even her best mate got a nickname...

Classy.

'What's your take on it, Andrea?'

'Like you say, marriage of convenience. Hugo's old enough to be Louisa's dad. Not that I'm judging, but still...'

'Do you think there was something going on with the nanny?'

'What makes you say that?'

'You mentioned her.'

'Nice-looking lassie. Tall and thin. Willowy, they say, right?'

'But?'

'But we've got nothing to suggest he was at it with her. Still, their marriage seems so contrived it...' Another burp. 'Hugo told us he got an heir out of it, while she got money. An oncologist must be on a fair whack, eh?'

'Decent salary, for sure.'

'Know how much?'

'Depending on experience, you're talking a hundred grand to a hundred and fifty.'

'Seem to know a lot about that?'

'Had the same thought as you, so I googled it half an hour ago.'

She smirked. 'Call it a hundred grand. Down here that's a lot. Like being on a million in London.'

'Not sure. You don't get much for your money down there. A million quid would buy you a one-bed flat in Islington.'

'Okay, but you catch my drift. Right?'

'Right. I think so. She had her own source of money.'

'That's it. And is he likely to be on that much more?'

'Named partner in one of the three biggest firms in the

Borders. Offices in Gala, Melrose, Peebles, Duns, Berwick, Kelso and Carlisle.' Marshall was counting on his fingers and was sure he'd missed one. 'Probably takes home three or four times what she does.'

'And he lives on an estate in Lauder like I do?'

'What's wrong with that?'

'Nothing, it's just... Doesn't feel right to me.' Elliot dug a pinky nail into her teeth. 'Tell you what else doesn't feel right to me. She went to a function for her charity last night, while he worked.'

'They were sticking together for the kid. Right?'

'Right. When Pringle called me up and told me, that was my initial take on it too. Thing is, his wife's died and all the family were round at his mother-in-law's house. Hugo's not just taking work calls but making them.' She slapped a hand to her forehead. 'And bloody Shunty asked him if it was an open marriage.'

Marshall laughed. Sometimes he just had to admire Siyal's bluntness. 'What did he say?'

'Didn't really answer, but it made me feel like it was at least half open, on her side.'

'What are you saying?'

'Say he wanted it to be an actual marriage, but she was fed up. Didn't want to divorce for the sake of the kid. And she was shagging Rougier behind his back. He found out and was hurt.'

'Enough to kill his wife?'

'Seen it happen, Robbie.' Well, at least it wasn't an educated equine reference. Were donkeys equine? Marshall didn't know, but guessed they were – and he didn't want to ask her. 'Hugo's not really got an alibi for her time of death. In his office last night. Had some lads around who can't find anyone there later than seven.'

Marshall could see that. The logic. But it all fell apart. 'Okay, but the problem I've got is why kill him too?'

'Lorimer? I'm thinking it's a co-inky-dink.'

Cute...

Not.

'This again...' Marshall sighed. 'It's a coincidence if, like yesterday, we'd picked up Rory Tait in that park, and there was another guy there trying to groom another kid. A coincidence isn't when someone dumps another body in the same place someone else has, on top of them. In that amount of snow, that's ridiculously preposterous.'

She sat there, breathing hard and slow. 'Right.'

Thinking wasn't her strong point. Analytical reasoning. She went on gut instinct and would blunder in without a care for what she trampled on.

But her fingers were drumming the table. 'Wouldn't mind a word with you. One of those on-the-record ones.'

'Sounds ominous.'

Elliot got up and walked over to his desk, perching on the edge. She looked around at the door, like they were being listened in on. 'Have you got the guest list from last night?'

'That's the word?'

She shook her head, dislodging her long fringe. 'Changed my mind. Have you got it there?'

He pulled out a sheet of paper and she had a look through it.

'So Rougier was definitely there.'

'Aye. Lying to us isn't a good look.'

'Never is, Robbie. What are you working on?'

Marshall wanted to pursue what this word was about but decided to just play along. Besides, she knew a thing or three about local gang crimes. 'Pringle asked me to work up a criminal profile. He was raging. Never seen him like that,

Andrea. No whistling or "benefarts" or weird phrases. Just... fire.'

'He's a DCI; what did you expect? He had to do stuff to get where he is. Have you got anything?'

'All I've got is a list of all cases where the victims were bound like Louisa and Justin. I've found it as an MO in quite a few assaults and abductions. But also in auto-erotic suicides, robberies, thefts... but most of those are... incidental. The victims were tied up to facilitate what happened. An assault or a robbery. Especially the accidental suicides.'

'But?'

'But I'm thinking that with Louisa Baird and Justin Lorimer, the binding was the beginning, middle and end.'

'The whole Burns supper.'

'Right, exactly. There was nothing fetishistic about the knots or the binding. Very utilitarian – wrapped around a whole bunch of times and tied in a granny knot. Ankles and wrists. No gags, no blindfolds or hoods. No fuzzy handcuffs even. Good enough, but nothing to base any behavioural analysis on.'

Elliot was nodding along with it. 'So you don't think there's an escalation path?'

'That's precisely it. With deliberate murders, you'd expect there to be a few cases where people had been tied up and dumped as warnings. Maybe even a near-miss where someone was found and pulled through.'

'Or a murder where that happened by accident.'

'Exactly. That would be easy. An MO of some guy in Glasgow or Aberdeen or Newcastle, say. We could pick him up, question him. Might get a result.'

'But you've got nothing.'

'I've got a lot of knots. The whole thing doesn't feel like a granny knot so much as some elaborate thing used by sailors.'

'Meanwhile, Jim's asking you to dig deep into it?'

'Precisely. The cases I've found are all... He's going on this assumption it's a drug gang. They take people out into the wilds, rough them up and let them walk back. But what they don't do is tie their wrists and ankles. Nobody I've found matches that.'

'And Jim's all excited by it.'

'Only joy he seems to get these days is when a case looks like it might be a serial killer. I feel like a trophy wife to him.'

Elliot laughed. 'You're nobody's idea of a bit of eye candy on the arm.'

He joined in laughing. Couldn't help himself. 'No, but I'm this exotic creature he's come across. A profiler-turned-cop. I can do both and he sees it as an opportunity to seem more important.'

'And the trouble with him having a hammer is suddenly every problem looks like a nail.' She frowned. 'At least, I think that's how the saying goes.'

'Exactly. He's seeing this as a serial killing. But this doesn't have any links to the world where daft kids get in over their heads to the local drug gangs.'

'Not everyone who learns a lesson tells the police how much smarter they got as a result. Sure it won't lead anywhere but still, there's maybe something in two unconnected victims with the same MO happening on the same night.'

'Oh, I agree. Which is why I'm doing this. And it's why I'm betting against you.'

Elliot checked her phone. 'Bingo.' She hopped up to her feet. 'Lawyer's here. Time for me and Shunty to haul Rougier over some very, very hot coals.'

'Be careful with him.'

'Come on, Robbie. Shunty needs to be—'

'Not him. Rougier.'

'Right. I think he knows something.'

'I don't think he does.'

'He left the Burns supper about the same time as Louisa. He lied to us. He's got a history of stalking her. That's a lot.' She walked over to the door and left Marshall in silence.

Just the swishing of cars on the street. And Elliot's strong perfume, mixed with chip vinegar.

He felt a lot like he was trapped between two officers. His boss and her. A dick and a hard cop. Or someone who thought she was.

She was right about something – this whole case didn't add up. There had to be a connection somewhere, but looking at old abductions... was that going to provide it?

The door opened again.

Not Elliot, but Kirsten. Smiling for once. 'Hey you.'

'Hey.' He leaned back in his chair. 'How are you doing?'

'End of another day.'

'You're finished?'

'Finished anything active.' She nibbled her lip. 'Wondered if you wanted me to stay over?'

'I'd love to.' He winced. 'Trouble is, I've got work to do at home.'

'Well, I have too. Let's go.'

CHAPTER THIRTY-ONE

On the screen, watching Rougier and his lawyer chatting. Couldn't hear a word from them, mind. Client-lawyer privilege and all that shite.

Shunty sat in the observation suite, shaking his head, his long fingers gripping his thighs. He looked up at Elliot, his forehead all twisted into knots. 'Don't you think we should've been speaking to him by now?'

'Have patience, Shunty.' Elliot shifted her focus to stare at the screen again. He was right – time should've been up. 'I want to let that creepy bugger simmer on a low heat a little longer. His lawyer's just reminding him of his rights and telling him to say "no comment" to everything, like that helps anyone.' She looked at Shunty. 'And I want a word with you about being good cop *or* bad cop, not both. And not shifting halfway through. Okay?'

'Consider the word had.' Shunty pointed at the screen. 'I've got a concern over this. We're missing a smoking gun.'

'We'll find spent shell casings, though. And do some

detailed ballistic analysis.' Elliot was fed up with the analogy already. 'Come on, let's in there.'

Shunty hauled himself to his feet and towered over her. Christ, he was really tall. 'Why do you think we'll get him to speak?'

She opened the door and held it there. 'Because somebody knows something and I'm determined to find out who.'

'I don't follow that.' Shunty crossed to the other side of the corridor and politely rapped on the door then stepped inside.

He would never follow her logic – not in a million years as a serving officer. The one thing Shunty didn't have was intuition. No amount of experience would hone that into something that made him a proper cop.

Elliot followed him into the interview room but didn't take her seat, instead standing in the doorway and glowering at Rougier. 'Evening, Ben.'

Out of his scrubs, Rougier was a sight. Aside from looking like he'd been in a POW camp for weeks, rather than an interview room for an hour, he wore green hiking trousers and a red polo shirt. A baby-blue coat hung from the back of his chair.

His lawyer wasn't someone Elliot recognised. She offered a hand. 'Maddie O'Neale.' Edinburgh accent. Edinburgh suit too, probably from Harvey Nicks. Too much makeup on and her blouse was a button too low. Not a trick that was going to work on Elliot. Or Shunty. Poor thing had grossly misread the room.

Actually, Elliot had no idea which way Shunty swung. That situation he'd alluded to earlier, could've been a boy or a girl or an ostrich. Who knew with kids these days?

Shunty was leaning forward into the microphone. 'And DI Andrea Elliot is also present.'

She took her time sitting down.

Shunty sat back to whisper, 'We're recording.'

Little light blinking away tells you that...

Elliot smiled at Rougier, holding his stare. Pretty intense for a young lad. Hard not to think of him as a kid, he looked so fresh-faced. 'Thank you for agreeing to attend this interview, Dr Rougier. You're free to leave at any point, but I've got to stress there's a reason you're here and we're doing this on the record. We believe you have information material to the murder of Dr Louisa Baird.' Keep it that side of the line, that he's here to help, not here to defend himself. 'Hopefully your lawyer will have briefed you of your obligations and our expectations in a situation like this.'

Rougier gave her a brief nod.

'Do you know a Dr Louisa Baird?'

'No comment.'

'O-kay... Do you know a Justin Lorimer?'

He frowned. 'No comment.'

'See, Ben, we're trying to join the dots here. It's tough because all I see is someone who's lied to us.'

'Me?'

Bingo. Didn't take long to break him.

'Aye, you.'

'How have I lied to you?'

'First, you told DI Marshall and DS Archer you went home last night, via the gym. Members of their team have been investigating that alibi but have so far drawn a blank. And with good reason – you weren't there. Then we found out you were instead at a Burns supper, so I'm sure you can understand that it's pretty frustrating to be repeatedly lied to.'

He didn't say anything, just scratched at his neck.

'Were you present at the Burns supper last night?'

'No comment.'

She smiled. 'Okay. We *know* you were there. Your name's on the guest list and we've got CCTV of your arrival and departure.'

'No comment.'

'Got there at seven twenty-two in a taxi. Left at ten oh three.'

He looked at his lawyer and got a wink in return. 'I was there, yes.'

'Man like yourself, Ben, I bet you're on a decent salary, despite not being in the job long. Pay a fair whack of tax, sure. But the thing is, you've deliberately misled us and made us waste taxpayers' money. Worse, you've wasted time and time is more important. Because the time we wasted checking your alibis was time that would've been better spent finding out who killed Dr Baird. Don't you want us to find her killer?'

'Of course I do.'

'So why lie to us?'

'I just forgot.'

'You forgot. Well. I remember everything I did last night. Went home, fed the kids, had a glass of wine while I watched an episode of the American version of *The Office*. DS Siyal, how about you?'

'Worked until the back of eight. Then I got a takeaway and watched that film *CODA*. The one about the deaf family. Won the Oscar for Best Picture last year.'

'That's a lot of detail.' Elliot let a slow breath go. 'And yet, Dr Rougier here can't remember where he was.'

'Okay. I was at a Burns supper at Blainslieshaw Mains farm.'

'Excellent. See, that's helpful. Confirmation of your movements on the record.' Elliot left a gap. 'Said Burns supper was held in aid of charity. Were you just there to support an excellent charity?'

Rougier shrugged. 'No comment.'

'Because the charity that benefited, which is a great cause I have to say, was founded by one Dr Louisa Baird.'

Rougier swallowed hard. 'No. Comment.'

'Isn't your attendance at an event she hosted in contravention of the HR issue you've got on your record?'

'No comment.'

'I mean, the HR issue is officially on your record, isn't it? Only, we've got to seek a warrant to gain access to it, so if it's not and it's all just hearsay, now's your time to correct that and save us a bit more time.'

'No comment.'

'Saves us a job if you were to just admit what happened.'

'No comment.'

'Okay, so you admitted to being at the Burns supper. That's a start. But you're not exactly forthcoming about what happened afterwards. Why the silence, Ben? Why the lying?'

He jerked back in his seat. 'Because it looks bad, doesn't it?'

'How?'

'You think I killed her.'

'Do you want to admit to it?'

'No.'

'If you prefer to deny it, Ben, this is your chance to clear your name.' Elliot leaned back in the chair until the metal creaked. 'You can tell the truth. Move on with your life. Maybe even help us find who killed her.'

'Why do you think I know anything?'

'You were there. Either you're connected to it or you're a potential witness.'

'That doesn't follow!'

'But you spoke to her, right?'

'I didn't!'

'Okay. But you saw here there, right?'

Rougier looked away. 'Hard not to. She gave a speech.' He exhaled slowly and deeply until it sounded like there was no air left in his lungs. 'You want the truth? Fine. I loved her.'

'Dr Baird?'

He nodded. 'But that's all in the past. The affair. Not even that. Just a couple of kisses. That's all it is. All it was. And she tried it on with me both times, not the other way around.'

'And you didn't resist?'

'No. I'd spoken to her at work a few times. She was nice. Kind. Good at her job. And pretty.'

'Talk to us, Ben. Tell us what happened last night.'

'I left around ten. Got a cab. Got driven through the snow to the station at Stow. The village was beautiful, all white. The CCTV on the train and in the station will show I was there. Either Stow or Edinburgh.'

'We're checking that, of course. Good thing is we can now do it at the time you were there rather than the time you told us you were there.'

'Look.' Rougier thumped the table. 'I didn't speak to Louisa. I learnt a harsh lesson the hardest way. I didn't want to go anywhere near her.'

'Attending a Burns supper she hosted is a strange definition of "nowhere near her".'

He stared at her for a few seconds then looked away.

'Ben, you left just after she did.'

'That's not true.'

'No, it is. We've got it on CCTV. Your taxi went just after her car. Mere minutes.'

'Okay, but you're... The way you phrased it, it's like I deliberately left after her. I'd booked that taxi in the afternoon, so I could get the train home.'

Shunty scribbled something down. 'We'll check that out.'

'Good! It was Big Man Taxis, or something like that.' Rougier stared hard at Elliot. 'I swear I didn't know she'd just left.'

Elliot rested on her elbows. 'I'd love to believe you, Ben. I really would. Problem is it appears someone forced her car off the road around that time. They tied her up. Ankles and wrists. Then left her to die in the cold. Snow falling on her. That's a brutal way to go.'

Rougier frowned. 'They say it's a peaceful death. Euphoric.'

'They say it's the same if you're dumped on top of a corpse?'

He shut his eyes. 'Shit.'

'Come on, Ben. Did you see anything?'

'No. I swear I didn't. The taxi took me to Stow railway station. That's it. All I saw was snow.'

'See, the thing I'm struggling with is why you'd get confused about that... Most people just tell us the one truth. You're on your second now. How am I to know there's not a third or a fourth?'

'I swear. That's what happened.'

'I'm not accusing you of killing her with your own bare hands. But you could've paid someone to do it for you. Someone you told when she was leaving. So they knew she was on her way. So they could trap her. Abduct her. Tie her up. Kill her.'

'No!'

'Who was it? Who did you pay?'

'Nobody!'

'It must be eating away at you. As a doctor, you have to pledge the Hippocratic Oath, right? "Do no harm". Arranging to have someone killed might be considered harm.'

'Believe me.' Rougier was blinking back tears. 'I didn't have her killed.'

'Right.' Elliot got to her feet. 'Come on, Sergeant. We're done here.'

Shunty looked a bit spooked by it, but at least he followed her lead instead of jumping in two-footed. Or giving Rougier a nice hug. He leaned over and spoke into the microphone. 'Interview terminated at eighteen forty-two.' He pressed the button and got to his feet.

Elliot chased him out of the door but gripped the doorknob of truth and turned around slowly. 'Here's the thing, Ben. I know you're lying about something. I don't know what and I don't know why. But when I turn this doorknob and walk out, I will investigate the what and the why. Mark my words, I will be back. At the bare minimum you'll be nicked for obstructing an official investigation, so whatever wee secret you're sitting on, it better be worth it.'

'I'm telling the truth. I swear. I didn't kill her.'

'So why lie about going home and going to the gym?'

'I never. It's an honest mistake.'

'It's what you told colleagues, wasn't it?'

Rougier shut up again.

Aye. He was hiding something else.

Elliot twisted the door handle. The lawyer charged through first – she wasn't impressed with her client.

It left just Elliot and Rougier in the room.

'I'll tell you.'

Elliot shut the door and turned around. 'Tell me what? What you're lying about?'

'No. Something that might help.'

'Why not do it on the record?'

'Because I don't want anything getting back to me.' Rougier sighed. 'I saw Gary Hislop at the Burns supper.'

Elliot felt her stomach wound throb at the mention of the name. 'And who's he when he's at home?'

'You telling me you don't know?'

'I'm asking you what you know, Ben.'

'He's a local gangster. Or so I gather.'

'Did he wear a T-shirt reading "Local Gangster"?'

'Don't be so facetious.'

'How do you know he's a gangster, Ben?'

'I work in A&E, okay? I've treated a few people who work for him. And I've treated a few other people who have got on the wrong side of him. They know not to blab, but when they're out of it on morphine, it's a stronger truth serum than ten pints of lager.'

'So you're telling me an alleged gangster's doing the gay Gordons with a bunch of toffs between courses of haggis. So what?'

'I saw Hislop speaking to Dr Baird.'

'Lot of people spoke to her last night.'

'For a while. Seemed pretty heated. Look, I'm telling you in good faith what I saw last night. People think I'm a stalker, but I really liked her. She seemed to like me. A good woman like her being dead is a tragedy. Her poor son... Toby...'

She nodded at him. 'Thanks for telling us that. I'll see how it goes.'

'May I leave?'

'Of course. You might be able to catch the train to Edinburgh soon if your lawyer's happy to give you a lift.'

Rougier opened the door and ran down the corridor.

Shunty was waiting outside. 'You just let him go?'

'For now. Dig into his story, would you?'

'Already got the team on it.'

'Someone other than McIntyre, I hope?'

'I have other people, yes.' Shunty glared at her. 'What did he tell you?'

'When?'

'Now.'

'Nothing. Just asking me the train times back to Edinburgh. Had to look it up on my phone.'

CHAPTER THIRTY-TWO

Snow was falling, landing and lying everywhere. Their street was like something from a Scandinavian furniture catalogue.

Marshall got out into the cold air. 'Thanks for the lift. I was going to get a cab home.'

Kirsten waved over at his car. 'Please don't even *think* of taking the roller skate tomorrow.'

'I'll see how the road is in the morning.' Marshall looked over at the house, saw the lights on and heard raised voices, so he crunched over to the spiral stairs leading up to his lair. Aye, it worked better when the lair-dweller used that word. 'I'll need to see what I've got in the freezer.'

'Told you we should've ordered a pizza.'

'Bit sick of pizza.'

She glared at him. 'How can anyone be sick of pizza?'

'The state of my guts just now...' Marshall crouched low in case Zlatan made a run for it, then unlocked the flat door. No escaping moggies so he stepped inside. 'I really need to improve my diet.'

She didn't follow him in. 'Wait, was that you?'

'What was?'

'In the Pathology toilets?'

Marshall kicked the snow off his shoes, then nudged them off. Laces still on, which was bad form. 'Don't ask, don't tell.'

'Jesus, Rob. You need some prebiotics. Or probiotics. Or a bowel transplant.'

'I definitely need something that isn't a pizza or a fish supper.' Marshall hefted up the monster of a cat and carried him over to the counter then tipped out some biscuits for him in his bowl. 'Here you go, matey.' He knelt down and started transferring the little presents from the litter tray to the bin. 'Someone has no issues with their toileting.'

'You're right, though. Slim pickings in here.' Kirsten was at the fridge. 'I'll order us a takeaway. Hopefully they'll get through all that snow.'

Marshall finished washing his hands and reached into his wine rack, the only thing in the place that was well-stocked. 'Speaking of prebiotics, do you want a Malbec or a Puglian?'

'Not sure, Rob.' Kirsten was staring at him like she wanted a *chat*. 'Word is you were at school with Balfour Rattray.'

Marshall left the wine decision for later. What paired with a curry and pizza weren't necessarily the same bottle. 'You've met him?'

'He helped pull Baird's car out of the snow.'

'And he just told you about me?'

'No. Trev mentioned your name and he seemed to know you.'

'Mentioned my name?' Marshall sighed. 'Look, Balfour's a posh idiot. Was at our school for a couple of years before he got expelled. He bullied me.'

'Some people are shits in school and in life.'

'Don't I know it. Thing is, don't have to dampen my

emotions or shut down anymore. Used to be I saw Balfour as a threat, mainly because if it wasn't mental torture it was physical abuse. But now, I can see him for what he is. Or was. A sad little boy, who wasn't loved at home. So he took it out on the world and I happened to be in the way. And others. He was only at school for, like, a year until he went elsewhere and got sorted out. No long-term harm done.'

'Sure there's no harm?'

'Of course not. I've had twenty years to get over Balfour bloody Rattray.'

She walked over and held his hand. 'But I know the family. His brother, Dalrymple, was in my year at school.'

'In Gala?'

She nodded. 'Dal had been expelled from a couple of places in Edinburgh.'

'Same as his brother.'

'Real wild child. Kind of behaviour that would catch up to him sooner or later.'

'Didn't even know Balfour had a brother. When I spoke to their mother, she was giving us this chat about believing in the NHS and state education, but that's only because both of her sons were expelled from fee-paying schools, right?'

She raised her eyebrows. 'Sounds like inverse snobbery to me.'

'Hardly. Look. Me and Jen came from what people would consider a broken home, but I was willing to be the better man. Unlike Little Lord Fondleboys.'

Her face twisted. 'Seriously?'

Marshall was blushing. 'I'm not proud of the name, but it was the late Nineties. Different times. Woke-ism wasn't a thing. Political correctness had come and gone mad then gone away again. But I'm serious – I overcame all the shit our dad had put us through by him not being in our lives. I tried to be a grown-up and treat Balfour with derision. My granddad told me to ignore him. I did and he went away. Pricks like him thrive on attention, so starving them of it is the best defence.'

'For a guy who's fucked in the head, you seem to have it all figured out ...'

He walked over to her and cradled his arms around her. 'Hey.'

'Hey.'

'GO FUCK YOURSELF, YOU OLD SLAG!'

Peace hadn't exactly broken out down in the house...

Marshall heard footsteps thundering up the internal stairs.

'Rain check on that, then.' Kirsten hurried through to the bedroom. 'I'm going to the toilet. Assuming it doesn't look like a nuclear test site.'

Marshall walked over to the door and opened it to a crack.

Thea stood there, bottom lip quivering. 'Can I come in?'

'Thea, I'm kind of busy just now. I texted your mum that I have company.'

'She didn't tell me. Please, can I come in?' She had that look, like she needed to talk.

Marshall opened the door wide. 'Come on in, then.' But he really needed to get that door at the bottom of the landing to lock from the inside, so neither of them could angrily stomp up the stairs and interrupt anything.

Thea stormed in and perched on the sofa, arms folded, legs crossed, pouting. Silent.

How great it was to have absolutely no privacy...

Marshall walked over to her but didn't sit. 'You okay there, Toots?'

She scowled at him. 'You haven't called me that in years.'

'Sorry about that. Are you okay?'

'Haven't you heard?'

Marshall felt that tingle at the back of his neck. 'Heard what?' Like he didn't know...

'Been arguing with Mum.' Thea huffed out a sigh, then slumped back in the sofa. He doubted she'd ever heard of the Ramones let alone could hum a bar of 'Blitzkrieg Bop', but she wore a T-shirt with the band's logo splashed over the front. 'Turns out Mum's shagging Dad again.'

'Seriously?'

'So you didn't know?'

Marshall sat in the armchair. 'I found out today. By accident.'

'Jesus. *Every*one knows except for me!'

'It came up in a case, Thea. And believe me, I was pretty pissed off when I found out.'

'Just pretty pissed off?'

'Aye. Really. Your mother's...' He ran a hand through his hair. 'Let's leave it there, shall we?' He smiled at her. 'How are you feeling about it?'

'Fucked off, to be honest. They split up because *I* found Dad in our hot tub with that floozy. How Mum described her, not me. Not exactly sex-positive, is it? And now I found she's shagging him again? Going to *Burns suppers* with him?'

'I get it.'

'Do you?'

'Your granny... She's not that dissimilar to your mother. Bad luck with men, is how she puts it.'

'Bad luck?' Thea spat it out. 'Bullshit.'

'I agree. You make your own luck. People who believe in luck cede their own responsibilities for their actions.'

'Totally. The shit I've been through because they can't sort out their nonsense. Going to a new school. Hating it. Going back to the old one and everyone acting weird to me. Jesus.'

The toilet flushed and Kirsten came through. 'Oh, hey,

Thea. Didn't hear you coming in.' She sat next to her on the sofa and mirrored her defensive body language. Leg crossed, arms folded. 'How are you doing?'

'Hey, Auntie Kirsten. Didn't know you were here.'

Kirsten seemed to flinch at the use of the A-word. 'Just having some food with your favourite uncle.'

Thea grinned. 'Is Uncle Steve coming around?'

'He will do, once he starts to exist.' Marshall laughed. 'I'm just explaining to Thea that adult life is a bit messy.'

Kirsten's eyebrows flashed up. 'Isn't it just...'

Thea re-crossed her legs. 'My bloody parents...'

Kirsten nodded. 'My folks were a nightmare. Always moving in and out. Mum took me to London for two weeks once in a school term to stay with someone she went to uni with. Absolute nightmare. But they're still together and things are a bit more stable. It's not easy, is it? People do things because they think it's what's best for you but you don't get any say in it.'

'Right, exactly. I mean...' But Thea didn't say what she meant. She just sighed again.

'What would you say to them?'

Thea thought it through for a few seconds. 'It's simple. I love you both, you love each other, let's just live together under one roof and stop all this bullshit. Or stop it.'

Marshall missed the black-and-white truth of being a teenager. Shagging someone equalled love, love equalled marriage and marriage equalled happy family. Nobody mentioned arguments about whose turn it was to run the dishwasher or driving to let the other drink at family gatherings.

Not that Marshall had ever been in that situation himself, but he'd seen domestics escalate from the scope of dish-washing into something much worse. At least twice.

'It's sadly not that simple, Thea.'

'Isn't it? They can shag all they—'

The door thumped open and Jen stomped in. Dolled up in her purple dress with those purple Doc Martens. She looked like she'd fallen in a giant glass of Ribena in Willy Wonka's factory. 'What are you lot doing?'

Marshall frowned at her. 'Are you looking for the great glass elevator?'

'Eh?' She scowled at him. 'You're all just sitting around.'

'And why's that a problem?'

'Because it's Grumpy's birthday dinner!'

Marshall slumped back into his chair. 'Ah, crap.' He slapped a hand across his forehead. 'I forgot.'

'Useless sod.' Jen pointed a finger at Thea. 'You're coming, missy.'

'Fine, but I'm going like this.'

'Whatever.' Jen play-punched Marshall's arm but there was menace in her eyes. 'I'm not driving.' She stormed over to the door. 'Come on, then. Outside in five!'

Thea got up and followed her, shaking her head. Exact same body language, but Marshall couldn't decide if it was nature or nurture...

He looked at Kirsten. 'You're welcome to come.'

'To what?'

'It's my granddad's birthday. Dad's dad.'

'Wow.' She grinned. 'Aren't you a bit old to have a grandfather?'

'Well, I don't have a father, so having a granddad wasn't too bad. He's a daft old coot and is still clinging on. He'll be ninety next year. Look, I promise it'll be short and we can pick up where we left off when we get back.'

'Rob. Of course I want to meet him.'

CHAPTER THIRTY-THREE

Not that she was hungry after that fish supper, but all Elliot could think of as she drove home was food. Not for herself, but what she was going to feed her kids and husband. Because, let's face it – the useless sod wasn't going to bother cooking, was he? She loved Dave but he could be bloody lazy.

She came up to the Old Melrose roundabout and the snow was buggering up the traffic. Queues in most directions and nobody taking lead. Her indicator flashed yellow on the virgin snow to the left. She flipped it to the right, then cut into that lane and piled around the roundabout. Not the conditions for a bit of cheeky driving, but she did it anyway and powered south on the A68. Heading away from home, but she needed to—

Her phone blasted out of the dashboard.

Shunty calling...

She hit the answer button. 'Evening, Shunty. What's up?'

'Boss. Just ringing to say I've caught up with Jolene. Rougier's alibi checks out for last night. He left just after Baird did. She reckons the taxi driver shouted at Baird on the way in, got into a honking war. He got to Stow twelve minutes later, almost missed the train to Edinburgh.'

'Spoke to the cabbie yet?'

'No, why?'

'Well, if they got into a shouting match...'

'You don't think—'

'No, but I'm the kind who dots my Is *and* Js, Shunty. You should be too if you want to get on in the job.'

'Okay. Fine. I'll see where she is with—'

'No. *You* take charge. Okay? You. Get your guys to sort it out. You've got a team. Use them.'

'Will do.'

Elliot took a right turn into Newtown St Boswells, winding through the old village until another right turn by the old school.

'Boss. Are you sure we should've let Rougier go?'

She thought he'd gone. 'You thinking we should've kept him in?'

'No, but—'

'Aye, I'm sure.'

'Before we spoke to him, you were insisting he did it, so I don't understand why—'

'Just wanted to make him think we thought that. See what spilled out. We've got nothing much to go on, so sometimes you have to shake the tree and see if any pineapples fall out.'

'Pineapples?'

'Shunty, I'm not sure the laddie's capable of murder, either by his own hands or by paying someone.'

'Well... If you're sure...'

'I am. Have a good night, Shunty. Don't stay too late.'

'I won't.' Click and he was gone.

At least the lad was keen and put the hours in. Maybe he'd brute force being a decent copper just by the effort he put in.

Aye, who was she kidding?

Elliot killed the engine and took a deep breath. She looked along the row of houses, mostly council and ex-council, and saw one that still had its Christmas decorations up, a month after the event.

Bingo.

Okay. Time to do this. She got out into the fresh snowfall and walked along the gritted pavement. Heart thudding in her chest.

This was a bloody stupid thing to do.

Still, what choice did she have?

She should turn around and leave. Go back to her car, drive home and make sure the kids had veg with their chicken nuggets and chips.

Aye, should became could, then became wouldn't.

She walked up the icy path and pressed the doorbell. Chimes erupted from inside. Hard to place the tune, an old pop song. She stood there, waiting, her breath misting in the air, snow falling on her shoulders.

Stupid...

She made to walk away.

The door opened and he stood there, head tilted. The years had been kind to him. The same boyish face, the little kiss curl, but a few streaks of grey at his temples. Didn't exactly look like a local gangster, with or without the T-shirt proclaiming that fact. 'Andi?'

Her heart was in her throat. 'Evening, Gary.'

'Been a while.' Gary Hislop shoved his hands into his pockets. 'You standing there in the snow like that is like something out of a film.'

She gave a flash of her eyebrows. 'I'm imagining a horror film and I'm the final girl.'

He laughed. 'I'm not that bad, surely?'

'You're not that good.' She held his stare. 'Are you going to invite me in?'

'No, I'm not. My boy's watching some shite on YouTube. Don't want him asking any questions about you.'

'Not like you'd have to lie. We're just old school friends, aren't we?'

'That all, eh?' He stepped outside and shut the door behind him. Wearing slippers. Socks that read "BEST" and "DAD". His sigh seemed to solidify in the freezing air. 'Why are you here?'

Elliot waved at the building. 'You bought your mum's old house?'

'She died a few years back and I took over the tenancy. Bought it and next door came up, so I merged them. Council didn't like it, but I got my way in the end. I'm a man who always gets his way.'

'That right, aye?'

'Aye.' He was someone who could maintain eye contact, that's for sure. 'Why have you come to my home, Andi?'

'Wondering why you think I have.'

'Well, we might've gone to school together, but it's been a while. I know all about you. Your job, your career, your husband, your kids... Your youngest is ages with Tyler. Surprised we never met at all those maternity courses.'

'You a hands-on dad, Gary?'

'Have to be. Cheryl died not long after the boy was born.'

'Sorry to hear that.'

'We all have our crosses to bear, eh?' He laughed, but there was nothing in it. No bitter sadness, no wise warmth. Might as well be chatting to a robot. 'I knew you'd come to me eventually. Been waiting.'

'Oh? Something you want to tell me?'

'I go to the church for confession, Andi. Let me guess. Someone's trying to pin a load of shite onto me?'

'What shite might that be?'

'Don't play games with me, Andi.'

'Maybe you could speculate about why I might be here on a night like this.'

'Not just here to speak to a legitimate businessman, are you?'

'Legitimate businessman? You?'

'That's right, and don't you forget. I run a few local businesses. Own a few properties too. My hardware shop is prizewinning. Innovative, they call it. Talking with some people about expanding it into a franchise. And not Scott Street Hardware everywhere but say Roxburgh Street Hardware or Forth Street Hardware. You know?'

'Sounds promising.' Elliot left a long pause. 'And yet you live in an ex-council house.'

'Some of us are proud of where we came from, Andi.'

She waved at the snow-covered Mercedes parked on the drive. 'Expensive car for an honest businessman.'

'I'm nothing if not honest.'

'Private license plate too.'

'Just because I've got one doesn't mean I haven't paid my dues.'

She stared hard at him for a few seconds. 'This is Louisa Baird.'

'Right.' He nodded along to some silent beat. 'Awful business, saw it on the news.'

'You know her?'

'I was at her Burns supper last night.'

'Funny, because we've got the guest list for it and your name isn't there.'

'Last-minute addition. Had another booking but that fell through, so I decided to go along. I donate to her charity. Spoke to her. Can't believe she's gone.'

'Know anything about her death?'

'Me? Why would I?'

'Or Justin Lorimer's?'

'No idea who that is.'

'His body was found next to hers. Underneath it, in fact. Froze to death. Both of them did.'

'That's horrific.'

'What was she trying to pin on you?'

'Nothing.'

'Really?' She'd made a mistake here. She had no leverage and he was giving her well-practised silence and diversions. 'Reason I'm here, Gary, is that what happened to these two shares an MO with people who owe money to nasty people around here. Assaults. People dumped in the countryside after having the crap kicked out of them. Looks like it's escalated to murders now.'

'Andi, I don't know what you're talking about.'

'All I'm wondering is if you remember anything from last night which might help us find who killed these poor people.'

'I don't, really. Night was a bit of a blur, in fact. Lot of whisky and some daft lassie started a food fight.' Hislop narrowed his eyes. 'But I could ask around and see what I can dig up. I mean, it's the least I can do seeing as how we go way back.'

'You're an awfully well-connected man.'

'Am I not? We're two Gattonside High former pupils who

are both civic-minded folk. We should be able to help each other from time to time. Right?'

'Right.' Elliot held his gaze for a few seconds. 'Cheers.' She nodded and walked back to her car.

As she brushed the snow off her license plate, she couldn't shake the feeling she'd just made a deal with the devil.

CHAPTER THIRTY-FOUR

Marshall hated being over this side of the Tweed, away from Melrose. It felt wrong and on so many levels.

Gattonside was a long strip of houses, with some others climbing into the hills. The village where he went to high school, traipsing across the chain bridge from Melrose every morning while loving parents dropped others off in cars. More than once he'd ended up in the river, twice at Balfour Rattray's hand.

He'd forgotten that.

So much of his youth had been wiped from his memory, like rubbing out pencil from an old jotter. There wasn't much left from that period in particular.

The tall Victorian buildings sprawled in the space between the river and the road through the village. The playground was swallowed up by grass like it was in a later series of a zombie TV show, with weeds growing in the cracks in the tarmac. Theirs was one of the last years before it all got merged with Gala Academy but, just like him, the old school was a desolate husk, sold off to property developers who hadn't done anything with it in twenty years.

Hard to think how much had happened in that time.

Marshall walked away from it towards the low-slung sheltered housing. He was first at the door, so he pressed the button and waited for the gongs to finish chiming. 'I want to hold your hand. Is that okay?'

Kirsten stood next to him, her citrusy perfume giving him some reassurance. 'Of course it's okay.'

He gripped it, warm and soft, and gave it a slight squeeze. 'Thank you.'

'You don't need to thank me for anything, Rob.'

Thea and Jen were still in the car, arguing about something. Marshall could take a guess, but their silence all the way over meant there was a whole lot to be said about last night.

Kirsten was smiling at him. 'Can't believe your granddad's still managing to be in sheltered housing at his age.'

'Oh, you'll see—'

The door opened and Marshall gripped Kirsten's hand that little bit tighter.

Mum stood there, smiling wide. 'Robert!' She frowned. 'And Kirsteen? So nice to see you again!' She smothered Kirsten in a hug.

Marshall didn't want to correct her on the name again, so waited for the love assault to hit him. The soft smudgy smell of her cherry lipstick reminded him of this youth and made him cuddle her tighter. Sod it. 'It's Kirsten.'

'I know. She's lovely.'

'No, her name's Kirsten. Not Kirsteen.'

'Are you sure?' Mum broke off. 'Where's your sist— Ah, there she is.' She tottered off across the pavement towards the car, her kitten heels completely impractical for these conditions or her age.

Marshall made a face at Kirsten. 'Sorry about that.'

'Hey, she's fine. She's way better than my mum.'

'Believe that when I see it.'

Mum stormed back over, gripping Thea's hand. 'Come on inside, little one.' Incongruous given Thea was about six inches taller than her. 'Grumpy's desperate to see you.' She barged between them and led her granddaughter into the small home.

Jen trudged over. 'Bloody teenagers...' She blinked a few times then her scowl vanished. 'Okay. Sorry if I'm being a cow, just... Lot going on right now.'

Marshall patted her on the arm. 'It's okay, just make sure Thea's alright.'

'I—' She sighed. 'I try, Rob. Believe me. I try.' Another fake smile, then she passed them and went inside.

Kirsten shook her head. 'See why I don't want kids?'

'Totally with you on that score.' Marshall gestured for her to go first, then shut the door behind them.

Grumpy's flat was a reasonably sized space with a massive telly stuck to the wall, currently playing a rugby match. If Grumpy had his way, the telly would constantly play rugby, but Mum wrestled with the remote until the screen switched to *Eastenders* then BBC News then finally went black.

The small kitchen area was just about accessible for wheelchair use and had more appliances than Marshall's own humble dwelling.

The room had almost enough chairs for them, with Mum and Thea taking the red sofa. Jen claimed a seat by the window, wistfully looking outside.

And there was no sign of their host, but his mobility scooter took up pride of place by the door.

Mum got up and fussed around at the side table, laying a tray of beige party food out for them. 'Now. There we go.' She looked over at Marshall. 'Robert, can you fetch us an extra chair from Grumpy's room?'

'Sure.' Marshall went through to the bedroom.

A single bed was pressed against one wall. A tall wardrobe stood sentry over the bathroom door. The suitcase on top was covered in a thick layer of stoor, not that Grumpy was going anywhere.

The old bugger sat by the window on his electric wheelchair, peering out like Jen through next door. He slowly shifted his focus to Marshall. 'Bob? Is that you?' His mouth drooped, his eyes empty. 'Bob? My son, have you come back to see your father?'

Christ, he'd declined a lot in the years since Marshall last saw him. Ravaged by time and by loneliness during the pandemic and its lockdowns.

Marshall stayed by the door. He spotted the chair he needed to transport through, though. A high-backed thing next to his grandfather. 'No, Grumpy. It's Rob. Your grandson.'

The face hardened and tightened, all sign of his senility vanishing. 'I know bloody well who it is, Rob, you bloody idiot!' The old sod cackled, then put his glasses on. 'But I had you going, eh?'

'You old bugger!' Marshall walked over and gave him an awkward hug – hard to get access to him with the wheelchair, and when he did it was all bones. He stood up and got a better look at him. The towering presence of Marshall's youth had wasted away to a saggy sprawl. Nothing much worked anymore, except his pin-sharp mind. And those eyes still twinkled with mischief. 'You're looking well, Grumpy.'

'Am I hell.' Another wicked cackle. 'Thinking I was losing my marbles!' He tapped the side of his head. 'All still here! Count them every morning! Can hear them rattling!' Then the grin settled into a hard stare. 'Haven't seen you in years, Rob. You're looking alright for someone pushing forty.'

'Not quite that old, Grumpy. And I would've been back sooner but—'

'Don't bother lying to me about the pandemic, sonny. I know you've been arguing with your mother. She tells me it all, whether I want to hear it or not! And believe me, I don't!' He laughed. 'Reason I'm still on this mortal coil is your mother. Not even her flesh and blood, but she's looked after me for years. I'm only her father-in-law, son, and she's in here most days, unlike my actual son.'

Marshall knew the feeling. He pointed at an armchair by the window. 'Mum's asked me to take that through.'

'Can't quite fit it on the scooter, son! And I've tried!' He navigated the wheelchair out of the way and whizzed through to the living room.

Marshall hefted up the armchair and carried it through, placing it behind Grumpy's parked scooter. 'You get many miles to the gallon on that thing?'

'It's electric, you daft sod!' Grumpy reversed into a space between Thea and Jen. 'Here we go. Me and my two favourite girls.' He grabbed their hands and grinned at Mum. 'Don't tell Janice here!'

Mum took a quiche out of the oven. 'I know I'm Grumpy's number one.'

'Robert, Jennifer. Your mother's a saint.' Grumpy squinted at Kirsten. 'Oh, hello. Who's this?'

'Kirsten Weir.' She held out a hand to him. 'I'm Rob's... friend.'

Grumpy raised an eyebrow. 'Oh, aye.' He grinned. 'That sort of "friend" is something I like having. Not that anything works downstairs these days!'

Marshall deposited the chair next to her and couldn't get any eye contact to reassure her.

Kirsten was blushing. 'Happy birthday, Grumpy.'

'Thank you, doll.' Grumpy cackled again. 'Keep thinking I'll not see another one. I was in the hospital with pneumonia for a month, but not even that finished me off!' He looked at Thea, then pressed his glasses further up his nose. 'The Ramones! See this, Janice?'

'Aye, Robert. I see.'

Kirsten leaned over and whispered, 'He's a Robert too?'

Marshall dipped his head low. 'I'm Robert Marshall the third.'

Kirsten smirked then covered her mouth with her hand. 'That's good, though.'

'There won't be a fourth.'

Mum was frowning at them. 'What was that?'

'Nothing, Mum.'

'I'll be the judge of—'

'Janice.' Grumpy was grabbing at Thea's sleeve. 'I saw the Ramones in Edinburgh. 1977.'

'Grumpy, are you sure?' Jen counted on her fingers. 'You'd have been forty-three. And the Ramones were punks so—'

'Aye, definitely. Got the ticket stubs somewhere. Had their first two LPs.'

Jen laughed. 'Good wind up.'

'I'm serious, hen. Took your father to see them.'

That shut Jen up. Her mouth hung open. 'Okay.'

'Place in Tollcross.' Grumpy clicked his fingers like that would help him remember. A soft, dull sound. 'Clouds! That was it. Bob was seventeen and he loved the gig. Wouldn't shut up about it.'

'And you?'

'Thought they were okay, aye! My toes were tapping. Like I

say, I bought their LPs. More of an Elvis guy myself, but you can't knock the young lads. You could see what they were doing, how it all came from Elvis. Music was shite when I was a laddie, but the King tore it all up. For people like the Ramones.'

Thea was wide-eyed. 'So my granddad saw the Ramones?'

'Aye. And your great-granddad too! Who loves you!'

'Wow.'

Grumpy looked Marshall up and down. 'How are you, son?'

'I'm well. I think.'

'Don't sound so sure about that?'

'Worked in London for a bit but I'm back home now.'

'And this is the first time you've popped in to see your favourite grandfather.'

'Sorry. That's not—'

'It's fine, son. Laddie like you must be up to your nuts in guts, eh?' He shot Marshall a wink. 'You must be shagging your way up to Edinburgh and beyond.'

'I'm not like that.'

'Oh come on, you look just like your daddy. He was a one!'

'Do I.' Marshall hadn't heard that from him every time he'd met him. 'Have you—'

'Nope. Haven't heard from him in years. He's living in Plymouth or Portsmouth, can't remember which one. Get a Christmas card, mind.'

Jen rolled her eyes. 'That's more than I ever got...'

Grumpy pointed at Mum. 'Your mother gets one, too.'

Thea nodded. 'I got a box of stuff last year.'

Jen was scowling. 'I didn't know about that.'

Thea dipped her head.

'Jennifer, she's Bob's only grandchild.' Mum raised her hands. 'I told her not to tell you in case it upset you.'

'Well it did! It has! He never did anything for me or Rob!'

Grumpy looked away from her, shaking his head. 'So, Kirsteen. Are you going to marry Rob? Give Janice another grandchild?'

She laughed. 'I don't think that's on the cards.'

Grumpy cackled. 'He shooting blanks, eh?'

'That's not what—'

'Ah, it's like playing snooker with a rope.' Grumpy cackled. 'You can take a pill for that, Rob!' He shut his eyes, unable to see Marshall blushing. 'I'd love it if you'd give me some more great-grandkids, not that the little punk rocker here isn't the apple of my eye. Not getting any younger, Rob, but I'm relieved to see you with a lady. Starting to think you played for the other team.' He lifted his feet up into the air. 'Studs up!'

'GRUMPY!' Thea shot to her feet. 'That's, like, *so* offensive!'

'Not that there's anything wrong with it, my darling. Whatever makes your flag wave.'

Mum clapped her hands together. 'Who wants a bit of quiche?'

CHAPTER THIRTY-FIVE

Marshall felt a rumble in his pocket. The quiche and scotch eggs were doing a number on his guts, but he didn't want to burp. And Thea was still in the toilet, doing God knows what in there. Probably avoiding more pressing questions from Grumpy. He got his phone out and glanced at the notification.

KIRSTEN:

Want to get train at twenty past nine

Marshall put it away and got to his feet. 'Well, I need to get this young lady to her carriage.' He smiled at Jen. 'Just borrowing your car for a few minutes.'

'They're going to have sex in it!' Grumpy bellowed with laughter. 'And I ken the best site in the Borders!'

Jen laughed. 'Do you take your scooter dogging?'

Grumpy frowned. 'What's dogging?'

'You don't want to know.' Marshall tried to stifle his laughter. 'And no, we're not doing anything like that.'

'Here.' Jen tossed her keys over. 'Come back soon.'

'Sure thing.' Marshall walked over to Grumpy and gave him a big hug. 'Good seeing you, you old rascal.'

'And you. Don't be a stranger!'

'I'll try.' Marshall patted Kirsten on the arm. 'Let's get you to Tweedbank.' He grabbed her bag and carried it out into the cold, then shut the door. 'Thank you. And sorry.'

'Hey, I had fun. Your granddad's a laugh.'

'He's a bit coarse.'

'Our parents are one thing. His generation are a whole other one. And when they get to that age, they stop giving any fucks at all, don't they?'

'True.' Marshall unlocked the car and opened the door for her.

She stayed standing. 'You okay?'

'I'm fine, why?'

'Well, you seemed a bit quiet in there.'

'Sorry.'

'Stop apologising. I get it. You're just a bit weirded out by all the stuff about your dad.'

'What? No. It's work. This case.'

'Really?' She raised her eyebrows. 'Because it feels like—'

'BRRRRRRRRRRRRRRRRRMMMMMM!'

Marshall swung around. 'What the hell was that?'

'BRRRRRRRRRRRRRRRRRMMMMMM!'

'Sounds like someone moaning.'

'Come on.' Marshall slammed the door and tried to find the source of the sound. 'It does, but—'

'BRRRRRRRMMMMMM!   BRRRRRRRMMMMMM! BRRRRRRRRRRRRRRRRRMMMMMM!'

Marshall set off towards the old school.

A man sat on the edge of the wall, staring into space. Thirties, but dressed like a teenager. Superdry hoodie and T-shirt, those twisted seam jeans and bright white basketball shoes. Something wrong with his movements, though. Everything was slowed down, worse than if he was drunk. Or high. He looked up at them. 'I'm going for a ride! BRMM! BRMM! BRRRRRRRRRRRMMMM!'

'Jesus.' Kirsten grabbed Marshall's arm, stopping him. 'Do you recognise him?'

'No. Who is it?'

'It's—'

'BRRRRRRRRRRRRRRRRMMMMMMM!'

'It's Dalrymple Rattray.'

Marshall frowned. 'Balfour's brother?'

'Right. I haven't seen him since he left school... Heard he'd been in a motorbike accident and had permanent brain damage.'

That all made sense. Marshall's only recollection of him was as a little version of Balfour, but possibly even worse. Not so much mischief in his eyes, but armed assault.

'Poor guy.'

'Must be staying in the same sheltered housing complex as Grumpy.'

Dalrymple rubbed his stomach. 'My tummy hurts.'

'Either way, it's far too cold for him to be out dressed like that.' Marshall set off towards him. 'Dalrymple?'

He looked up at Marshall, then hopped off the wall and crossed the road. 'My tummy hurts. I need a jobbie.'

A quiet rumbling came from behind.

Marshall swung around and saw a silver Skoda trundling over the icy road. Big Man Taxis glowed in yellow. It pulled in and a woman got out, looking all harassed and stressed. She looked at Marshall and he recognised her but couldn't place her. 'Mr Rattray?'

Marshall pointed over at Dalrymple. 'That's him over—'

'I need to do a jobbie!'

'We'll get you to hospital soon.' She scowled. 'DI Marshall, isn't it?'

Then he got it.

Rachel Lorimer. Justin's wife.

'Hi, Mrs Lorimer. How are you doing?'

'I'd love to say I'm doing okay but my husband's just died. I've been sitting in the house, staring at the wall, playing through the last time I saw him. Everyone's shouting at me, asking me all these questions I can't answer and I can't...' She clamped a hand over her mouth. 'And I can't stand it. So I'm out working. Driving is the only time I don't think about him. I can lose myself in the roads or a conversation. And I'm supposed to take Dalrymple here to hospital.'

'Is he okay?'

'Not A&E. It's some family thing. His dad's in there.'

'Right, sure.' Marshall smiled at her. 'Let me know if you need a hand.'

'Handled way worse than this guy.' She smiled at Dalrymple. 'You want to sit in the front?'

'YES!' He ran over to the car like an eager five-year-old and jumped in the passenger side. 'I don't need anymore!'

Rachel walked over and got in. She leaned over and helped him buckle in. 'Oh, Jesus.' She slammed the door and covered her mouth.

Kirsten stopped next to Marshall. 'Who was that?'

'Rachel Lorimer.' Marshall watched her drive off. 'The day her husband died, she's working. Same with Louisa Baird's husband.'

'Tough for some people, I guess.'

'He owns a law firm, so feels like he has no choice. She's a cabbie and the noise when she's not working is too great. What a world...'

'People cope in different ways. Just so happens theirs is the same.'

'True.' Marshall smiled at Kirsten. 'About you getting the train... Wondering if you'd like to come back to mine...?'

CHAPTER THIRTY-SIX

'Here you go.' Marshall pulled up in the station in Tweedbank. The car park was massive but only had ten vehicles in it. 'I've never seen this more than ten percent full. At some point, maybe it'll become a transport hub, with trains heading west to Peebles, east to Berwick and south to Carlisle.' But for now it was like an IKEA car park without the smell of hot dogs and MDF or the sound of screaming kids and parents. Two trains sat there, but only one had the lights on.

And Kirsten wasn't listening to him.

Marshall killed the engine. 'Here you go.'

'Thanks.' She leaned over and kissed his cheek. 'Guess I'll see you tomorrow.'

'I guess.' His stomach was burning. 'Are you okay?'

She smiled wide. 'I'm fine.'

'You're being... Look. It's okay. I get it.'

'No. What am I being?'

'Nothing. It's fine.'

'Come on, Rob. What am I being?'

'I'm worried you're being weird about stuff.'

'Weird? Stuff?'

'Well, you won't talk. At work, you were keen to stay at mine, but now you're going back to Edinburgh.'

She sat there, nostrils flaring. 'The train's going to—'

'You've got ten minutes. Please. Talk.'

'Right...' She sighed. 'Truth is, I am a bit weirded out.'

'Go on?'

'When Thea called me Auntie Kirsten, it...'

'Okay, but that could be because you're friends with her mum as much as you being my lover.'

'Your lover, eh?'

'You know what I mean. Girlfriend and boyfriend at our age seems a bit strange. Partner always feels like a euphemism.' He held up a hand. 'And we're nowhere near that, yet. But it's spooked you. I can see that.'

'Right. I love the good times, Rob. The shagging, to coin a phrase. The food. The drinks. The company. But I'm not here to be a wife, a mum, or even an aunt. I know women who are all three but that's not me. Like I've said before, if you want to heat up the sheets anytime, I'm down for that.'

'But tonight isn't any time?'

'Shit's just got way too real. Especially with your mum and your granddad. And him asking all those questions...' She ran a hand through her hair, fanning it out. 'And the stuff at your flat... Thea's logic...'

'What logic?'

'That shagging implies love implies marriage... It stuck in my craw.'

Marshall sat there and watched her breathing, trying to avoid doing psychological analysis of her. Just listening to her words. Trying not to feel hurt that she didn't feel love for him. That it was just shagging. Maybe it was for her, but voicing it made this difficult. 'Look, I get all of that. It's okay.'

'Rob, you need to put a few boundaries around your life. Like your flat being off-limits. And the domesticated life of dropping children off and attending family gatherings, it's anything but a bit of fun.'

'You seemed to have fun tonight.'

'Up to a point. But family functions aren't mandatory for our rel— level of interaction.'

'You almost said "relationship".'

'Right. But that's part of the problem too.' She smiled. 'I'm not going anywhere. You take time to process it.'

'Okay. But I'll ask you one last time, though.'

'What?'

'The offer of a bed for tonight is still there.'

'Thanks, Rob.' She leaned over again and kissed him on the lips this time. Then grabbed her bag and left the car. 'Sleep tight.'

'Text me when you get back, okay?'

She spun around and laughed. 'Two rings, aye.' She shut the door, then walked over to the platform and the waiting train.

Marshall sat there in his sister's car, wanting to run after her. Grab her, kiss her, hold her. Some Hollywood romcom moment.

But that was the sort of fantasy Ben Rougier had confused with reality.

Marshall wanted to respect her boundaries, her desire for distance. Let her process her thoughts.

God knew he needed to process his own.

As soon as she stepped onboard, the train slipped off into the frozen night.

CHAPTER THIRTY-SEVEN

Balfour Rattray struggled to keep his eyes open. He was tired, sure. Absolutely exhausted, even. All from a solid day of manual labour, pulling cars out of the snow like this weather didn't happen every year, and it was somehow beholden on him to winch the unprepared out of a drift.

Like Robert Marshall...

His eyes stung with tears. And opening them meant looking down at the wraith lying in the hospital bed. Father. His body still breathed, the light flashing in time with his pulse, but whatever passed for a soul had long since departed this mortal realm – the King had left the building. The room's lights weren't even on. Those rasping machines were the only things keeping him alive. The solid pulse of his heart rate was a constant reminder that he'd died long ago.

He was a vicious old bastard.

But one who'd taught Balfour everything he knew and had turned him into the man he was now. Whether that was a good thing wasn't for anyone but St Peter to decide. Balfour fully expected to be reunited with Father somewhere a bit hotter than Heaven. Or at the very least over a few hundred years in Purgatory.

Footsteps rattled like buckshot out in the corridor. The nurse going about her daily business. Nightly business. Not many patients up here. Father was getting as good care as you could on the NHS and Mother wouldn't countenance going private... But she wouldn't agree that Balfour was right. That Father was already dead, his body just an empty husk where that vicious old bastard had been.

Other footsteps approached. Two pairs. One the steady rhythm of his mother, the other the stomp-slide of his brother.

Balfour leaned in and kissed Father on the forehead. 'Good night, you old bastard.' He stood up tall and tried to act like the family patriarch he had to become.

The room lights flickered on.

His brother just stood there, tongue flapping loose, wild eyes scanning the room. Truth was, he wasn't in a much better condition than his father, just had the luxury of being able to move around. Two vibrant men who'd lost themselves due to their own stupidity. 'BRRRRRRRRRRRRRRRRMMMMMM!'

Bloody hell.

Mother leaned in for a hug and he tasted her minty shower gel. 'Your brother doesn't understand what's going on, Balf.'

'No.' It was all Balfour had. 'No.'

Mother tapped his arm. 'It's time.'

Balfour nodded. He knew it and he'd already said goodbye, but... It felt like...

God, this was even harder than putting any of his dogs to sleep over the years. With them, you knew when it was past the point of no return, when you'd kept them alive for your own selfish reasons because you couldn't face the grief, and now you had to act kindly, supporting them through their final moments.

But with his father...

The reality was he'd died months ago. All that was left were his bones and what little flesh still clung to them.

Balfour looked at Mother, swallowed hard, then shut his eyes. 'It's time.'

'Okay.' She wouldn't look at him.

'You agree?'

'It's time.' Mother stroked his arm. 'I'll fetch the doctor.' She left him alone with his brother.

'BRRRRRRRRRRRRRRRRMMMMMM!'

Balfour walked over to him. For some reason, Dalrymple wouldn't go near Father's bed. 'How are you doing, Dal?'

'Went broom broom!'

Poor bastard was lost in that accident, like he was perpetually stuck inside that moment in time in some perverted and shortened *Groundhog Day*, reliving his bike hitting a car and him flying like an angel but crashing like a human being, head-first in a field next to the Tweed. His helmet saved his life, but what was left? What remained of that cheeky sod? That rascal, as Dad would put it? Dal had been so vivacious and eager. Served his country for six years in arid desert hellscapes. And what did he have to live for now? That ghastly little box in Gattonside, where a team of carers looked after him around the clock. Not that Balfour had visited in a long time. That awful school was next to it, the hellish place where those pricks had called Balfour 'Little Lord Fondleboys'.

Dr Heap swished into the room. 'Now.' If medicine failed him, he'd make an excellent supporting actor who specialised in playing aliens. Odd-looking ones at that. He pushed his glasses up his nose. 'Thank you for all being here.' He had that artificial distance to him, the one that certain types of doctors and vets had, like he was just about present enough to do his job, but having to think about what he was doing was asking way too much. Having to feel anything.

Balfour envied him that distance.

Heap licked his lips. Even his long tongue was like an alien's. Or a demon's. 'I understand how difficult this is for you all, but I think we all agree that now is the time. Yes?'

Mother nodded and Balfour followed his lead.

Heap looked at Dalrymple. 'And you?'

'My son is—'

'BRRRRRRRRRRRRRRRRRMMMMMM!'

Mother paused and waited for him to stop. Or to at least not start up again. 'As you can see, my younger son is unable to comprehend what's happening.'

'I do see.' Heap smiled at Dal like he was a small child. 'Well. Yes. Okay.' He walked over to the machines and inspected the readings, then started adjusting things. 'Okay. Your husband's life support has now been shut down.'

Father exhaled his final breath and lay there, deathly still.

Balfour looked at Mother and saw the same tears in her eyes.

'BRRRRRRRRRRRRRRRRRMMMMMM!'

Balfour grabbed his brother's cold hand and Mother's warm one. They stood there, waiting for Father to die.

The machine flashed.

And he breathed again.

Balfour looked over at Heap. 'Did I just imagine that?'

'No, you didn't. I'm afraid it may be some time before your father expires. That notion where the patient is like a consumer appliance who can be switched off at the wall is, I'm afraid, the Hollywood version of things. For many, they go on breathing just fine for hours, sometimes even days. Eventually, they all get too tired to breathe or until the...' He smiled. 'You don't need the details.'

'Please.'

'Well, they'll keep breathing until a pulmonary oedema fills their lungs. Then they make one last exhale and just never breathe in again. People always expect that it's "click" and then "eeeeeeeeeeeee". All done. Off to the funeral home we go. But no...'

Dalrymple laughed. 'EEEEEEEEEEEEEEEE!'

Made a slight improvement...

Heap sighed. 'Believe me, it isn't like that. And this isn't the first time this week, let alone this year. I have a lot of people just standing there, waiting for it to happen. Hoping it's over and done soon, but not knowing what to say or do. So I feel your pain, just like I feel theirs every single time.' He stared into space.

Mother frowned. 'Can he still hear us?'

'The science on that isn't as mature as—'

'Can he or can't he?'

'I believe there is evidence to suggest that it's possible, yes. Whether he can *listen* is another matter entirely.'

'Okay. Thank you. You don't have to stay with us.' Mother smiled at him. 'We can wait this out on our own.' She watched him leave them, then looked at Balfour. 'How about we each say goodbye out loud?'

Balfour had already done that but repeating it would fill the time. Not that there were any words left. He leaned over the bed and watched Father's breath lifting his chest. 'Goodnight, old man. Thank you for making me the man I am today. For being there for me when I needed it. For being strong when I strayed from the path. For loving me and my brother in the only way you knew how.' He leaned over and kissed Father's warm forehead, then stepped away.

Must've had something in his eyes so he shut them. His brother's fingers reached over and held his.

'Napier. I'll miss you. You old sod. You just had to go up that turbine, didn't you? Trying to eke every last penny out of the electricity. Tight to the end. And it caught up with you. I'll never forgive you for that. Never. But I loved you, you old rogue. Since we first met at that dance until now, I've loved you with every fibre of my being. How am I going to go on without you?'

Balfour opened his eyes and checked his watch. This could go on for hours. His heart was already broken into thousands of tiny pieces, but now it was being trampled. How much longer was this going to take?

'Say goodbye to your father, Dalrymple.'

The fingers let go. 'Papa, I went in a car again. It was great. Snow was everywhere! The lady skidded at one bit and it was so cool. I love you, Papa. Night night.' Dalrymple leaned over and planted a big kiss on Father's lips.

Balfour stood there, watching the chest moving. Might be his imagination, but was it slowing down?

Mother beamed at them, but tears were streaming from her eyes. 'How about we sing a song to comfort him?'

Balfour just knew this was going to go on and on, but he had no choice – he wouldn't leave until Father took his last breath. 'How about we sing "Flower of Scotland"? Father loved singing it at the rugby.'

'Okay.' Mother gripped his hand tight and Balfour did the same to his brother. 'It's in waltz time, so after three. One, two, three.'

Balfour shut his eyes. 'Oh, flower of—'

'Happy birthday to you!' Dalrymple had his head back, screaming away. 'Happy birthday to you! Happy birthday, dear Papa! Happy birthday to you!'

Mother leaned over and whispered, 'It's the only song he knows. Please just play along.'

Fuck it.

Balfour took over. 'Happy birthday to you! Happy birthday to you! Happy birthday, dear Papa! Happy birthday to you!'

Dalrymple was swinging his arms up high. 'How old are you now?'

Balfour joined in. 'How old are you now? How old are you on your birthday? How old are you now?'

'Happy birthday to you!' Dalrymple was laughing. 'Happy birthday to you! Happy birthday, dear Papa! Happy birthday to you!'

Balfour couldn't sing any more. He was laughing at the surreality of it all. He couldn't remember laughing. Couldn't remember feeling happiness. Or joy. And here he was, standing at Father's deathbed, with tears streaming down his cheeks. Happy tears, or not ones borne by tragedy.

He sang on, staring at Father's body. He'd lost him months ago, and Mother had clung on to the hope that he'd wake up and it'll be like it was before. Balfour had insisted they turn the life support off as soon as Heap broke the news and now here he was, winning, but it felt like a defeat.

All he wanted was his father back.

'—old are you on your birthday? How old are you now?'

Father's chest stopped moving.

Balfour took a look at the display, then nodded at Mother. 'That's it.' He wrapped his arms around her and Dalrymple, then let the grief consume him.

CHAPTER THIRTY-EIGHT

'Good night, Freddie.' Elliot leaned over to kiss her youngest on the head, just as her stomach wound decided to scream in pain. Everything clenched as she tried to stand up without shrieking. 'Sleep tight.'

'Please, Mummy. I don't want to go to school tomorrow.'

This again. She stifled the sigh. 'It's okay, little one. The teacher won't bite.'

'I know, but she'll shout at me.'

Elliot smiled as she leaned over again, trying to take it easier this time. 'You do as your mummy tells you. Okay?' She planted a final kiss, then tucked him in up to his chin. 'Now, I'll see you in the morning. Light on or off?'

'Off please, Mummy.'

'Night night, my sweet prince.' She flicked off the side light, then left the bedroom and kept the door open. She stood there, listening to three sets of slow breathing coming from all three rooms. Only one of them would be waiting to secretly WhatsApp their friends or watch TikTok. One of out of three wasn't bad. Pretty good, in fact.

Chances were the bloody schools would be shut again tomorrow anyway, but Elliot really needed to have another word with that teacher about her attitude.

She crept down the stairs and went into the kitchen.

The sounds of the dying embers of a football match came through from the living room. Loud enough to wake the dead, but the kids were acclimatised to it.

She glanced at the clock. Ah, the minute hand struck wine o'clock. Excellent. She poured a glass of the South African Shiraz and gave it a short sniff, then spent a few long seconds soaking up its glory.

Hallowed be thy name, eh?

She sipped it, then slurped and gurgled like a wine snob.

Beautiful. That spicy, fruity assault was hard to beat.

Elliot picked up her glass and walked through to the living room and ten minutes' peace sitting on the sofa.

Her phone rang before she left the room.

She could ignore it. Let it ring out, sitting on the counter. Leave whatever crap Pringle or Marshall or Jolene or Shunty wanted until the morning.

This was her ten minutes of solace with a glass of wine, after all.

But she couldn't. Two people were dead and their killers still at large.

She stomped over and set her glass down without spilling any, then checked the display:

Unknown caller...

One of those...

Could be anyone. And that was the problem.

She picked it up and unplugged the cable. Then answered it. 'Hello.'

'Andi, hi. How are you doing?'

She'd recognise the voice anywhere – sounded like a local radio DJ in 1993.

'Evening, Gary.'

'Evening, yourself.' Sounded like Hislop was outside. 'Having a nice night?'

'Got a recovering school avoider trying to bunk off again, so not really, no. How are you?'

'Got a similar dilemma. Hard when the little ones just don't want to go in, eh?'

'Isn't it just?' Elliot eyed her glass of red, gleaming under the kitchen's spotlights. 'If you've called to share parenting tips, can we do this later?'

'Oh, it's not just that. Like we agreed earlier, I've done some asking around. Seeing as it's you, I've decided I'll help you out by passing it all on.'

She took a big gulp of the wine. 'I'm all ears.'

'Word on the street, which I'm hearing from pals in the rugby club, is both murders were done by the same pair.'

'We know that. Any proof?'

'That's *your* job, I'm afraid. I'm merely a concerned local businessman helping out another pillar of the community.' Sounded like he actually meant it. 'But what's more, Andi, whoever did those two... They were the same ones who did Napier Rattray.'

Elliot slammed the glass down on the counter. Some wine splashed back onto her hand. 'That was an accident.'

'An accident?' Hislop laughed. 'Good one. Nope. Well.' He laughed again. 'It actually *was* an accident, truth be known. My pals at the rugby club say they were just meant to scare him, but they were too good at that. Whoever did it, they over-achieved. Old Napier wriggled and fought, then scrambled away. Trouble was, he fell. Lucky to survive, to be perfectly frank, though he isn't exactly surviving, is he? Visited him not long after in BGH and saw him, rotting away in a hospital bed. Hate to see it. Happened to my old boy too, so it's maybe been a bit triggering for me.' He paused long enough for her to lick her hand clear of spilled wine. 'But what I'm raising with you, Andi, is that they got away with it.'

'Who was it?'

'Come on, Andi. You're not much of a detective if I have to give you all the answers, eh? Is there a better cop I should go to?'

'None better than me, Gary.'

'Rightio. I only hear murmurs and rumours. Reason I'm telling you this is because you came to me, Andi, cap in hand, asking what I know. Now, I'm humble enough to admit I knew nothing then, but I'm telling you what I've heard this evening from the lads at the rugby club. I trust you to do the right thing.'

'Come on, Gary. What's in this for you?'

'Nothing. These are just rumours I'm hearing at the rugby club. But what if they're all true? Ask yourself that, Andi.'

'Not like you to give up two of your guys.'

'My guys?' His laugh was a bellow. 'Andi, I don't have guys other than the lads working in the shops. In business, it's always good to have an ear to the ground.'

'Okay. So, I'm thinking these guys have gone a bit off-piste of late and are over their skis just now.'

'Nice metaphor, Andi. Well, it's two married together, right? But I hope this information helps bring clarity to the awful events up near Rattray's farm. What's it called?'

'Blainslieshaw Mains.'

'Right, aye. I hope you get to the bottom of it.'

'Seriously, though. Why are you doing this? Aren't you worried about blowback?'

'Blowback? You talk like I'm some kind of gangster. I'm just an innocent businessman who's helping out an old girlfriend.'

'Girlfriend? We snogged once or twice in the park.'

'Still counts for me. Besides, we both know you aren't going to source this tip to me.' He let out a deep sigh. 'Now, I hope you get a good night's sleep and your wee one goes to school in the morning. Ciao, baby.' Click.

Elliot tossed the phone down on the counter.

Why the hell did she go to him? Him of all people.

What a bloody idiotic move.

She tore off a strip of kitchen roll and dabbed up the wine spillage.

Thing was, she now had a lead on the case.

Problem – she really needed to keep the source to herself because Pringle would be up her legs like a ferret.

What she couldn't fathom was why Hislop gave her that info about Rattray.

Nobody treated it like a murder, not even the family. To reopen it, while his body was still plugged into the mains and breathing, all she'd achieve would be to rub salt in their wounds.

Balfour Rattray and his mother might be toffs, but they were good people. Community-spirited and kind.

What worried her was how easy the information came from Hislop's lips. Whoever killed Lorimer and Baird must've outlived their usefulness.

But the biggest worry was what the personal cost was going to be.

Anything could happen with a man like Gary Hislop. She'd have to be more careful – starting now.

She grabbed her wine glass and walked through to the living room. 'What's the score? Nothing's up?'

'Aye, been a bit boring, to be honest.' Davie put his beer mug down and looked over at her. 'You look like you need to talk.'

CHAPTER THIRTY-NINE

Galashiels might be a small town that punched above its weight, but it sure as shit wasn't like any city that Chunk knew. Nowhere in the UK would you be able to go to somebody's house at three in the morning and not hear the deep thump of dubstep or suck in the sweet smell of ganja. Wood Street was the main road running west out of the town, but it was quiet as a judge's home in a Cotswold village.

Chunk was in the passenger seat. 'Time to do this.' He let his seatbelt go and got out.

Baseball just got out. Daft sod never wore a seatbelt. Some machismo bullshit, proving how hard he was. Or just that it cut into his giant belly. 'You leading?'

'Of course.' Chunk walked up the path to the home, right at the end of a long row of council houses all split into quarters. Some would've been sold off over the years, but not all. And not this one. Steven Beattie's door was on the ground floor, but his flat was on the top. Chunk looked across the road, past their van masquerading as a painter-decorator's, and saw no internal lights, no twitching curtains. 'Three a.m. eternal.'

'Eh?'

'Never mind.'

Baseball waved across the road at the low-slung church. 'Think there are any Scientologists in?'

'What are you talking about?'

'It's a church of Scientology in there!'

'No, it's not, you daft bastard. It's Jehovah's Witnesses.'

'Fuck you.' Baseball got out his mobile and tapped at the screen. 'Both wrong. It's the Church of Jesus Christ of Latter-day Saints, whatever the fuck that is.'

'Mormons.'

Baseball scowled at him. 'You can't say that word these days.'

'Eh?'

'You can't call them... Mormons?'

'I can. That's what they're called. Mormons. Based in Utah or something. Some lad found some stone tablets in his back garden and set up the religion.'

'You're talking shite.'

'Google that, if you don't believe me.' Chunk thumped the door with his fist. He was glad the daft sod had taken his phone and used it. Did another full circle to see if that had woken anyone up. Nobody was watching them. Nobody he could see.

'Washing lines are all full of clothes, man.' Baseball was shaking his head. The tip of his bat clonked off the ground. 'Basic mistake, that. *Basic.*'

'Not here for any of that thieving, though, so don't get any ideas.'

'Wasn't.'

'Good. Keep it that way.'

Another thump, much louder. Still no sounds from inside, so he gave it one last go.

Baseball took a drag from his jazz cigarette. 'Absolutely perishing here, man. Never felt so cold. Even last night, when we were... you know...'

'Aye, I know.' Chunk took a toot on his vape stick. 'Feel the cold deep in your bones, eh?' The vapour didn't heat him up any. He craved a real cigarette. 'Down in the marrow.'

'Damn right.' Baseball picked up his bat and thudded the end against the door. 'Come on, Mr Beattie! We know you're in there.'

Chunk put his vape stick away and walked around the gable end, sniffing. 'Can you smell smoke?'

'Yeah, man. I'm smoking this bad boy.'

'No, not your joint.' Chunk stopped in the back garden and sucked in another lungful. Definitely something being burnt.

The upstairs windows glowed a tell-tale orange.

Chuck groaned. 'His bloody flat's on fire.'

Baseball joined Chunk. 'Alright, Stevie?'

Chunk had to squint, but he saw him.

Steven Beattie was dangling from a first-floor window. 'Fuck off! Pair of you, fuck off!'

Chunk walked over to stand just below him. At least Beattie was dressed. Black trackies and a Rangers shirt from three seasons ago. Big desert boots too. 'This is no way to treat old friends, is it?'

'What do you want?'

'Why don't you come down from there?'

'Stuck.'

'Was it a chip pan?'

'No, man.'

'Come on. We've all been there. Smoking a J while making

some chips and a bomber gets in. Next thing you know, thing's totally out of control.'

'Mate, I'm fine.'

'So why are you telling us to fuck off?'

Beattie's legs wriggled. 'I'm falling.'

'I'll catch you. We both will.'

'Look, I don't know if—'

An explosion erupted from inside the house.

Beattie dropped, slipping between them and landing on the concrete with a dull thud.

He yelped. 'Ah, you bastard!' He looked up at them, sucking air across his teeth. 'Landed foot first! Thought you pricks were going to catch me?'

'Didn't say when you were going to jump, did you?' Baseball pressed his joint into the wall then pocketed the butt. Good lad – don't leave a trace. 'Anyway. You need to come with us.' Still spoke like a cop, didn't he?

Beattie stared up at them. 'Why do I?'

'Pal of yours got himself arrested for noncing a girl. Only a matter of time before he starts talking.' Baseball held out a hand and hauled him up to standing. 'Can you walk on it?'

Beattie tried to put some weight down. He yelped again, like Chuck's mum's wee Jack Russell. 'Think I've broken it.'

'Come on.' Baseball wrapped Beattie's arm around his neck and started walking him away. 'Let's get you to hospital.'

'No hospitals, man.'

Chunk raced ahead, scanning the buildings opposite. Coast still looked clear. Despite a neighbour's flat being on fire. 'We know a guy in Walkerburn. Name's Columbo.'

'Columbo?'

'Well, Colin. Used to be a vet. Now he helps people like you. Columbo'll fix you up.'

Baseball stopped at the end of the path. 'Just one more thing?'

Beattie frowned at him. 'Eh?'

'You're supposed to laugh.'

'Why?'

'It's Columbo's catchphrase. From the TV programme!'

'Never seen it.'

'You're hopeless.' Baseball passed him to Chunk and opened the van door.

Beattie stopped. 'Eh, mind if I ride up front with you lads?'

'Only two seats up top, champ. To make it fair, I'll be with you in the back.' Chunk grabbed his left arm and leg, then helped Baseball get him inside. 'Just sit there and be a good boy.'

Beattie laughed. 'Which of you boys has been shagging on this mattress?'

'We both have, Stevie.'

'Each other?'

Baseball laughed. 'It's not gay if it's in a threesome, eh?'

'It is if it's with another laddie.' Beattie shifted his focus between them. 'That what's going to happen here, eh? You going to tie me up and fuck me, eh? That your kink?'

'Of course not.' Chunk got in and looked up at the burning flat. He still couldn't fathom the logic, so he pulled the door shut and hit the switch to leave the light on.

The engine roared into life and Chunk braced himself against Baseball's ludicrous driving. Taking it way too fast.

Chunk pointed at the house. 'What was the plan there?'

'Plan?'

'You set fire to your house.'

'Ah, that.'

'Why, though?'

'Thought you were the cops. Needed to create a nice

distraction. Time to get away. But I got stuck, eh? Couldn't jump down.'

'You've got neighbours. Nobody else in?'

'Jock downstairs is in hospital. Somehow got a chisel stuck in his bonce. Next door neighbours are grassing arseholes, so I don't care if they die.' Beattie shifted his position on the mattress and seemed to get a bit more comfortable. 'Made my way to the back window but the petrol caught before I could get to the front door.'

Chunk gripped the handle to stop him toppling over. 'You're a daft bugger.'

'Aye, should've done it the other way, heh? But you live and learn.'

'Guess some do.'

'Eh?'

Chunk stared at Beattie. 'We're not stupid.'

Beattie grinned. 'Baseball is.'

'He is.' Chunk smiled back at him, then let it fade. 'But I'm not. What are you thinking of, setting your own house on fire?'

'You don't want to know, man.'

'Of course I do. You're a good guy, Stevie. Got a lot of time for you.'

The van slowed down and Chunk had to push against the giant's hand pulling him.

'I know I'm a wanted man, Chunk. I was trying to fake my death.'

'Stevie. You need a body for people to think you're dead.'

'Eh?'

'If you burn your flat, the cops need to find a body that matches yours otherwise they'll know you're not dead.'

Beattie scratched at his neck. 'Right.'

'Is there someone in there?'

'No, man.'

'Seriously?'

'Seriously. Last time I had a bird in there was wee Emma. And they'd never mistake me for her!'

Chunk's guts were churning. That was a monumental disaster. He didn't agree with the chosen outcome either – they should've done this back then. 'True enough. Few months back that, aye?'

'Nah. Just before Christmas, aye.' Beattie stretched out his foot and yelped again. 'So why do you want to speak to us?'

'What makes you say that?'

'Pair of you turning up at three in the morning... It's not for a cup of sugar, is it?'

Chunk figured he deserved the truth. 'Well, you've been a bit naughty again, haven't you?'

'Wondered if it was something like that.'

'Maybe a bit more than naughty. Not paying our boss for a lot of drugs... How much did you use yourself?'

'You're not taking me to see Columbo, are you?'

'We'll see about that.'

'Does he even exist?'

'He does, aye. Walkerburn's not far, either. Five miles, I'd guess.'

'You're going to tie me up and dump me miles away, aren't you? And me with this buggered ankle. And it's freezing, man. It's a death sentence.'

'We've got no choice here.'

'I get it.' Beattie stared hard at him. 'Thing is. I know both your names.'

Nicknames, maybe.

'Steven. Mate. After what you did to that lassie – who was fifteen, remember – you're not in any position to be making threats.' Chunk stared him out, feeling the burst of acceleration again. 'Rule number one. When you kill someone, you tell nobody. Rule two, when someone finds out, you add to your tally.' He reached over and opened the side door.

The dark night air whooshed past. The banks of heather were a blur across the other side of the road.

'What the hell—'

Chunk grabbed Beattie's arm and pushed him out, head-first. He looked back up the carriageway and watched him bounce on the tarmac. Job done. Well. Half of it anyway. He shut the door and sat back, feeling the force of the van slowing. Braking would leave tyre tracks, so Baseball just took his foot off the pedal and let the clutch do the rest.

Another one bit the dust.

Chances were the next driver would be tired, drunk, bursting for a pee or just indifferent and Beattie would get run over a few times as well. But from the angle his bonce took relative to the rest of him, he was dead at the first drop.

The van slowed to a halt then Chunk opened the door and hopped out. He looked back up the A72, but there was nobody about at this time. Something lay on the carriageway. Not moving. Easy to mistake it for a deer. He got out his binoculars and looked back. Definitely a man. A smear of red ran along the carriageway under the lights.

Chunk opened the driver's door. 'How fast was that?'

'Eighty.'

'Good.' So Stevie definitely couldn't have survived that. 'Budge over.'

'Thought I was driving?'

'Aye, you were. Boss called me just before, gave us another job. Told me to drive, so shuffle over.'

'Fine.' Baseball jumped over. 'What's the gig?'

Chunk buckled in. 'Some wee twat in Innerleithen's lost two hundred grand of coke.'

'Why does he want you to drive?'

'Don't want you to know the addy, mate. Believe me, it's in your interests.'

'Right.'

Chunk put it in gear and drove off, taking a right at the Nest roundabout, then blasting along the A72. Didn't even spare another thought about Steven Beattie.

'Thought you'd take the back road?'

'Why?'

'No cameras along that route.'

'Schoolboy error, mate.' Chunk smirked at Baseball. 'Remember how they found some bodies up one of the forests last year? Well, there's more CCTV on that road than in your average Tesco's. This way's clear until Peebles.' He kept his eyes on the road but was scanning for the exact spot. Still a mile or so away.

Baseball kicked off his trainers and put his smelly feet up on the dashboard. Cheese and Marmite. 'Weird, this.'

'What is?'

'Killing. That's three people in two nights. Thought the boss would rather we spaced it out.'

'Way I see it, what we're doing is a gish gallop.'

'A what?'

'Know how in political discussions, sometimes someone will just talk utter, utter pish?'

'All the time. Politicians are wankers, man.'

'No, but like... I heard this thing on the radio the other day. About how someone will make so many comments and go off on a ton of weird tangents. Hundreds of them, right? That's a gish gallop. They flood the place with stinking bullshit. By the time the other punter's dealt with the first one, they've dropped another ten or twenty. Win by just drowning them in crap. "I'm glad you asked that, because nobody listens to us about ABC. People from DEF are flooding this country. Our mission is to stop the murder of GHI. We have a strong record for JKL. And, of course, who else do you think of when it concerns MNO." You see?'

'Sort of. So we kill so many at the same time that the cops are kind of flustered?'

'Bamboozled. Flummoxed. Exactly. They're stretched way too wide and far. You're an ex-cop, sure you must understand?'

'Didn't spend that much time on the force, mate.'

'Didn't know that.'

'How do you know all this shite?'

'Listen to a lot of podcasts when I'm working.' Chunk rolled his shoulder. 'Still, the fourth will be a charm.'

'Fourth?'

Chunk grabbed the baseball bat and slammed it one-handed into his face. A tooth flew out.

'What the fu—'

Chunk grabbed the wheel hard and pulled out into the lane for oncoming traffic, not that anyone was. Another sharp tug, then the van shot off the road and slammed into a stone wall.

Something thudded.

Baseball screamed.

The airbags hissed and smothered him in a giant marshmallow.

Chunk's heart was pounding. Felt like someone had branded him – searing pain, all the way up the line where the seatbelt made contact with his skin.

All those extra layers he wore as a precaution and it still hurt more than he had planned.

The bonnet was caved in and hissing. But none of the glass had even cracked. Hell, the windscreen wasn't even scratched.

Baseball was still in the van, lying upside down in the footwell. Blood poured down his face. He moaned, deep and loud. Boy was seriously fucked.

Worked like a treat – the airbags had driven Baseball's shins back, breaking both femurs as his head lurched forward, almost snapping him in half. He'd bleed out internally in a short period of time.

Chunk shot into action. He let his seatbelt go, left the keys in the ignition and slipped out onto the verge. He opened the back door to grab his backpack and the tin of white spirit. He unscrewed the top, tipped some white spirit out, dousing the back where that filthy mattress lay. Then a really good showering on top of Baseball. He slammed the driver door and lit a match, then tossed it on the doused mattress. Didn't even watch to see it catch, just slid the door shut again and checked the handle. Locked.

Baseball was hammering the window. 'Let us out, you prick!'

Chunk stepped back away from the van, then stood there, watching as the flames crawled over the van like fingers.

The begging turned to screaming as the flames hit the front.

The driver door opened and Chunk kicked it shut.

Felt the heat coming off the van, though.

The can in the back exploded and Baseball didn't scream any longer. The van was now an inferno.

Not long before the fuel tank went up, so Chunk hoisted his backpack on, then started on the long walk back towards home. Not dissimilar to any of the stupid wee neds they'd done that to over the years. Soon enough, he'd be passing the fire engines at Beattie's flat.

The Tweed bubbled in the cold night, his companion as he walked. He broke off the road and hiked up into the woods, climbing the hill towards the fields, his feet crunching in the snow. Cutting cross country didn't make that much difference to when he'd be home. Absolutely freezing out, so he put on his gloves.

Just as his phone rang.

Bloody typical.

He slid the right glove off and answered it, still walking up the hill.

'Is it done?' Her voice, cold like the Tweed on a night like this.

'It's done, ma'am. Aye. Just like you wanted.'

'Great.' She breathed out a deep sigh of relief. 'Got another job for you tonight.'

CHAPTER FORTY

One day Marshall would track down that mirror he'd broken, but the seven years of bad luck weren't hard to find. Like having to run the morning briefing because Pringle couldn't be arsed to attend.

Pick up, fuck off.

Aye.

Some talked a good game, but still did their jobs. Him? Completely different story.

'So, yeah. That's pretty much it.' Jolene looked down at her notebook again. 'Oh yeah. We got hold of the CCTV from inside the perimeter of the wind farm construction site and it's a dud.'

'A dud?'

'Shows nothing for the times we're interested in.'

'Long shot, I guess.' Marshall smiled at her – he knew all of this, but the rest of them didn't. 'That you?'

'One last thing. The CCTV from the Stagehall Arms doesn't show Talbot as being there when he said he was.'

Now that Marshall didn't know... 'That seems weird.'

'Not really. There's a beer garden that doubles as a smoking area. Place has two exits. He must've been in the garden but there's no CCTV there.'

'Can you follow up on that?' Marshall waited for a nod, then looked around the room, settling on Siyal. 'Rakesh, you're up last. Can you give us your update now?'

'Sure.' Siyal looked at his notebook and read, like the thing just contained longhand detail. 'Bottom line is we have lost our prime suspect.'

The groan rattled through the room like a missed Scotland penalty at Murrayfield.

'Dr Rougier's story checked out, unfortunately, so he was unable to have killed Dr Baird.' Siyal raised a finger. 'Himself, of course. And I mean directly. We'll still investigate to see if there's anything linking him to the killings.' He turned a page. 'The CCTV at Stow and Edinburgh railway stations—'

'What?' Jolene was scowling at him. 'Shunty... My team have been doing that.'

Siyal blushed. 'DI Elliot ordered me to.' He looked around the room for confirmation and support but of course she wasn't there. 'Okay.'

'I mean, you *knew* Rob and I... Sorry, DI Marshall and I were leading on that, right?'

'I did, but...' Siyal let his head dip. 'I did.'

Christ, don't let yourself get bullied like that.

And not in front of so many people.

Marshall clapped his hands together. 'Okay, we clearly need to get better at working across the streams here. But bear in mind this is a complex case with two victims and an overlapping MO. The worst case would be if neither of you did it. Let's focus on that.' He stared at Jolene, then at Siyal. 'You were saying before you were interrupted?'

Siyal opened his notebook again and shuffled through the

pages. 'The CCTV matches Dr Rougier's account of that evening. Additionally, my team have spoken with a few other attendees of the Burns supper. It's our understanding he didn't speak to Dr Baird, so there's even less reason to suspect him.'

'Okay.' Marshall had expected something along those lines. But Jolene still looked like she wanted to throttle him. 'We have just as much interest in ruling people out as in finding the guilty culprit. Important to focus on the fact that Dr Rougier's able to go back to work now because of the hard graft your teams have put in.'

Didn't seem to pacify Jolene or uplift Siyal.

'Anything else, Rakesh?'

Siyal was scratching at his neck. Nervous as hell. Just great... 'Better news, I guess, is that Kyle Talbot's wife confirmed his story. They *were* having video sex.'

Laughter rattled through the room like a missed England penalty at Murrayfield.

Siyal seemed to smile at that reaction. Learning to work a room was one of the toughest tricks you'd master as a cop. Getting laughter from so many egos and alphas was one of the best tricks in any cop's kit bag. Police officers – well the good ones – were natural born storytellers. So much of the job was based on forming that quick bond, finding common ground and telling someone to go to hell in such a way that they looked forward to the trip.

Siyal, of course, wasn't a natural, but he could learn, imitate, adapt and overcome. At least, that was the plan.

'Talbot's call logs back it up too. And both of them were sufficiently embarrassed, of course.'

'Cool.' Marshall walked over to the incident room's whiteboard and scored out Talbot. Both of them admitting to having video sex was good enough for him. 'Is that it, Rakesh?'

'No. DC McIntyre has been searching Ring cameras at the

Lauder end of the Stow-Lauder Road. He's found a Transit van arriving in Lauder not long after Justin Lorimer's time of death.'

Marshall couldn't see McIntyre anywhere in the room. He scribbled it onto the timeline, though it was really squeezing the data in – someone needed to update it with the latest picture and with good enough handwriting that hopefully anyone could read. 'Did they just dump Lorimer and leave?'

'We can't know for sure, but the timeline makes it look that way.' Siyal walked over to the board. 'This van had the GoMobile livery. However, at Dr Baird's time of death, a similar van went back that way from Lauder towards the farm, where she was picked up and dumped, but it had Craven's Heating signage.'

'Have you checked with them?'

'Indeed. They didn't have any vans out at that time. But it's harder to pin down as they've got four vans that stay with the drivers overnight.'

'I take it you're picking up with them, Rakesh?'

'Correct.'

Marshall focused on McIntyre. 'Do you have anything on it in the interim?'

'Nope.' McIntyre appeared through the fug of people, hands in pockets. 'The plates were obscured by snow...'

'Still, this is good work.' Marshall smiled at McIntyre, trying to show he meant it. 'A lot of time went into this. I appreciate the work and the effort.'

McIntyre nodded. 'Not just me, sir. DS Siyal sat in with me until midnight.'

And Marshall had warned him about pulling all-nighters after that brutal cold he got after Christmas...

'Okay, well, our highest priority is finding that van. If we get that, we get the killers. Or a solid trail to them.' Marshall

ED JAMES

took his time looking around the room. His gaze settled on Kirsten. He hadn't noticed her arriving. Sally had given her non-update. 'Kirsten Weir, welcome to the party. Have you got anything to add?'

'Not sure what Sally's told you, but I've just had word from the vehicle inspection compound in Edinburgh. No other prints in there.'

'None?'

'None.'

'No fingerprints or DNA traces in a car?'

'Right.'

That sounds like shit to Marshall.

'Who was—'

'Sir, I asked her husband.' Siyal was scratching at his chin. 'He said Louisa was meticulous.'

Marshall arched an eyebrow for effect. 'There's meticulous and there's this...'

'That was *her* car, was how he described it. Never gave anyone a lift. Only ever drove their kid in his.'

Some people were freaky about being clean.

'Okay, guys, let's get to it. We've got a clear focus here. We don't understand the why, but the who is feeling that bit closer. If we get this van, we'll catch them. They won't kill again. Let's do it. Dismissed.'

Marshall settled back against the wall and watched them disperse, heading back to their desks to get coffee or finish half-eaten bacon rolls. That post-performance buzz fizzed around his head, the sheer immediacy of living in the moment and being on your feet all that time, even if the audience were half-asleep.

Kirsten walked over and leaned against the wall next to him. 'Well done there.'

'I've led briefings before.'

278

'Aye, true. But this is a bastard of a case, Rob. Feels like you've made some progress.'

'It does, actually. We have.' He laughed. 'I'm just so used to disappointment.'

'Is that a dig?'

'No. If I was giving you a dig, you'd know.' He locked eyes with her. 'Are you okay?'

'I'm fine.'

'No, it's just... Last night...'

'Sorry I'm being odd. That's just me.'

'It's okay, Kirsten. We're both getting used to things. There's going to be stuff that throws us both. I try to hide some of the annoyances from you.'

She snorted. 'Like what?'

'Like your dickhead neighbour.'

She smiled. 'Todd's okay.'

'That's the problem. He's a seedy creep.'

She arched an eyebrow. 'Is that all you're hiding from me?'

'I try to talk through the rest of it. Like you leaving on the train last night.'

'Sorry about that, Rob. That whole thing weirded me out.' She patted his arm and gave it a little squeeze. 'Look, I'm heading out to an accident on the A72.'

'Car crash?'

'I wish. No, someone got chucked out of a moving vehicle last night.' She held up a hand. 'Or fell out. I'll have to determine. Either way, they're dead.'

'You know I worked the Serious Collisions beat in the Met, right?'

'I've heard word of it.' She grinned. 'Several words. I'll call you if I need you, Rob.'

'Offer's there.'

But she didn't leave. She let out a deep breath. 'But I do want to clear the air with you about last night.'

'The air's clear, isn't it?'

'Doesn't feel like it. I've been thinking about your granddad asking if we're getting married.'

'Kirsten. I'm happy with where things are. I don't let other people's expectations change mine.'

'What are you trying to say?'

'Just that I'm here. I'm listening. We're taking it at our pace. Sod everyone else. If it's just sex, then the sex is getting better.'

She looked around at him, then up and down. 'I agree. Your sex *is* getting better.'

'So, it was that bad at the start?'

'No. You're that good now.'

Marshall glanced around the empty office, then leaned in for a sneaky workplace kiss.

'Woah.' She pulled back and gave his balls a squeeze. 'Save it for later, tiger. Traffic's backing up on the A72.'

'I'm pleased there is a later.' He watched her go.

What a woman...

CHAPTER FORTY-ONE

Marshall stood up, desperate for a second coffee of the day, and walked through to the tiny incident room to have another check of the whiteboard. Progress had been made. Sometimes you had to settle for that.

But it was definitely for want of trying – the room was empty. What was the point of having an incident room if no bugger used it? Maybe things would be better when they moved to Gala.

'Ah, Dr Donkey as I live and breathe!' Pringle.

Marshall turned towards the door.

Pringle was standing, hands on hips. And he wasn't alone. Elliot was staring at the floor. Arms wrapped around her body. Completely unlike her.

Pringle shut the door and leaned back against it, arms folded. 'Need a word with you both.'

Marshall stared at Elliot, but she didn't look up. That square of floor tile was incredibly interesting. 'Is this about what you wanted to discuss last night?'

'Not to my knowledge.' Pringle shifted his gaze between

them, but he seemed to think better of chasing down that rabbit hole. 'I just want a meeting with my two favourite DIs in the world to better co-schmordinate the reassignments. Word on the mean streets of Melrose is that Shunty and Jolene both ended up trying to interview the same witness at the same time.'

Ah, so that's what Elliot was in a huff about. One of them had told her, she'd told Pringle and he'd bollocked her.

'That's correct, sir.' Marshall nodded. 'I've nipped that in the bud. Hopefully it won't happen again, but like I said to them, better it happened twice than not—'

'How's the profile?'

'The profile? It's virtually non-existent, sir.'

'Virtually? Or actually?'

'Actually. We're not dealing with a serial killer.'

Pringle deflated. 'A spree killer, then?'

'Nope.'

'Tell me it's a hitman, hitwoman or hitthem?'

'Well, maybe. They're a different breed of both spree and serial killers. They don't do it for a compulsion, but they're paid to do it. They're professionals.'

Elliot was looking at him, her eyes narrowing. Didn't say anything.

'And a professional is what we're looking at here, correcta-mundo?' Pringle stood between them, blocking Marshall's view. 'We have similar MOs with no connection between the victims. Isn't that more in that column?'

'Even so. Justin and Louisa were dumped, like the ten or so other cases Andrea helped me validate. All were assaults, none were murders. If you'd solved your abductions and assaults, then I'd love to solve our murders with them. But we don't have any kind of clue relating to them.'

Pringle nodded like Marshall wasn't disagreeing with him.

'This could be their escalation. Or it could just be a miscalculation.'

'A miscalculation?'

'Leave them overnight in the cold then grab them at, say, three in the morning having learnt their lesson. They didn't expect them to die. They didn't expect the temperature to plunge to minus twelve and for it to snow.'

'But if they're professionals, we—'

'What have you seen that suggests professionals?'

'Well, you just suggested that?'

'I suggested it, but you're the lord of the evidence settee.'

Marshall clenched his jaw. 'Okay. Abducted without a trace, both on the same night, then bound and effectively killed.'

'But you don't think this is the work of a professional?'

'I'm seeing two bodies dumped by the side of the road. If you want to kill people and get away with it, you bury them somewhere wild animals will get at them.'

'Like a fox?' Pringle waited for a nod. 'Trouble is, this has outfoxed us. We've no idea who did this.'

'Those other cases are drug-related crimes.'

Pringle seemed to brighten. 'So you think these two are drug dealers? Or users?'

He was clinging to this being a sexy crime.

Marshall hoped he hadn't promised anything to any senior officers. 'If there are other cases that are drug-related, why aren't we shaking those trees to see who falls out? Who *did* they have drug dealings with? They might be coming after them next.'

'Good point. Okay. So we need to ask those questions, then.' Pringle walked over to the board and wrote it up.

Marshall tried to engage Elliot, but she was back to staring at the floor. 'Sir, I don't—'

'Now, about the other thing.' Pringle stared at Marshall. 'Robert, have you got something you want to tell us?'

Marshall felt heat searing his neck. Lying, even by omission, never worked. 'Well, my sister and someone else I know were at the Burns supper. I didn't tell you last night and I'm sorry.'

Pringle leaned back and laughed. 'I was just winding you up.' He wagged a finger at him. 'I don't like you keeping secrets from me. Bad boy! Get in your bed!'

'Sir, it's all logged. DS Archer's team were following up with detailed statements from them.'

'It's okay, man! I get it.' Pringle reached into his pocket. 'Why won't this infernal machine ever stop?' He checked his phone. 'One second.' He charged over to the doorway. 'Hey, it's me.' Then he was gone.

Marshall looked over at Elliot. She was watching him now. 'Are you okay?'

'Of course I'm okay! You think I'm some little snowflake who'll melt in the sun?'

'Come on. You're clearly not that, but something's happened. What's up?'

She shook her head. 'Dickhead.'

'It's okay. Whatever it is. What's got you so rattled?'

She shut her eyes. 'Like you'd understand.'

'Come on. I'm capable of listening, you know?'

'Robert, Robert, Robert.' Pringle came back in. 'Just had a request for some of your time, Dr Donkey.'

'Profiling?'

'No, a serious collision on the A72.'

CHAPTER FORTY-TWO

'Second time in two days I've been back near home during work hours.' Marshall passed his poky wee flat on the right, then continued on the long road to Peebles, heading out of Clovenfords through farmland on both sides, still dusted in solid white. The towering hills of the Southern Uplands crowded them in on all sides. Couldn't even see the Tweed from up here. He floored it to get past a slow-moving tractor. Nice to have worked out the four-wheel drive – it cut through any amount of cold conditions like a hot knife.

Red light.

He braked hard and pulled back in behind the tractor. Just as the row of cars moved off. Gave him a few seconds to clock out what was going on – the traffic lights directed the oncoming traffic around a crime scene tent which filled that lane and the crawler, for those wishing to overtake during the climb from the Tweed down at the bottom. And on this road, everyone wanted to overtake.

He spotted Elliot and Siyal as they passed.

Marshall approached the roundabout, then took the right lane and carried on towards Peebles. Behind the tractor.

'Are you paying attention there, sir?'

'Sorry. Just didn't get much sleep last night.'

'Join the club. Bet you didn't have an unwelcome visitor in your bed.'

'I wish.' Marshall finally managed to get past the tractor, then settled into a steady sixty on the single carriageway. He slowed as they crept towards another set of traffic lights.

Jolene wound down her window and let in a blast of freezing air, then flashed her warrant card at a waiting uniform. Poor sod. 'Should be expecting DI Marshall and Acting DS Archer.'

'In you go.' The uniform pointed towards a space at the side of the road.

Marshall pulled up and got out into the biting cold. He walked over, desperate to get it out of the way. Fifty metres until the locus, with a good two hundred cordoned off behind.

A burnt husk of a van was pressed against a wall. Hard to tell the make and model, and the plates had long since melted off. Next to impossible to tell the colour. But the fire service were here – this was their bread and butter.

The nearest uniform was that Irish guy from Gala nick. Warner. He smiled at Marshall. 'Morning, sir.'

'Night shift?'

He nodded. 'Still on. Three days off, though.' He clapped his hands together. 'Be able to put in the mother of all overtime claims too.'

'Just make sure you're not burning the candle at both ends, aye?'

'Wouldn't dream of it, sir.' Warner put his cap on, like that made him any more serious. 'A van's hit a wall.'

Jolene laughed. 'I can see that.'

'O-kay... But then it was either torched or it blew up.'

'*Blew up?*'

Warner nodded. 'Exactly.' Uniform always thought a car blew up. Spent way too much time watching TV.

'That what the fire service are telling you?'

'Aren't telling me anything.' Warner pulled his hat off and flattened down his hair. 'Weird thing, though. We got called out to an incident a few miles away.' He waved back the way Marshall had driven. 'Down between the Nest roundabout and Clovenfords. My colleagues found someone chucked out of a moving vehicle. Then we have this.'

Marshall walked around as much of the van's perimeter as he could. The front bumper was shattered and the bonnet had taken the brunt of the collision, with half the engine hanging out. Easier to see the paint was navy here.

Which matched the van they were looking for.

Jolene pointed at it. 'That's the same make and model that dumped Lorimer and Baird, isn't it?'

'Eagle eyes.' Marshall pointed at it. 'Okay, can you find a VIN number and track down who owns it, check if it's been stolen. All that jazz. Speak to DS Siyal and sort it between you. No doubling up on effort. I'll square it all off with DI Elliot.'

'Sir.' She got out her notebook and jotted something down. 'The two events happening so close together...'

'Aye, it's not sitting well with me, either.'

'Someone covering their tracks, maybe? Killing the killers. Or just... more killing.'

'Could be anything.'

The van rocked a bit. A suited figure was in the front. She looked up at them through misted-up goggles – Dr Owusu. She was inspecting a body, still in situ. A man, big too. Whoever it was, he was badly burned from the fire. Bent forward, though. Arms up in the pugilistic post Marshall had seen a few times with burns victims in cars during his lost years in Serious Accidents down in the Met. Up and looking like he was trying to fight the fire with ungloved fists.

Marshall smiled at her then focused on Warner. 'Talk to me about that?'

'That?'

'Up the hill.'

'Well, I don't know much. Been here since half three, sir. Dr Owusu's just finished up there, so she can see this.' He exhaled slowly. 'The victim landed on his head, broke his neck and so he isn't talking to anyone about anything. Dr Owusu's taking him for a post-mortem.'

'Thanks.' Marshall looked at Jolene. 'Do me a favour, would you?' He tossed the keys to Jolene. 'Head back up there and dig into what happened. You're right – I don't like this.'

'On it.' She marched over to the car and got in.

Marshall walked back around to the van's driver's side.

Owusu stepped out and tore off her mask. 'Hi, doctor.'

'Hi, doctor yourself.'

Owusu laughed. 'Have a look at that, Dr Robert?'

An improvement on Dr Donkey, at least.

She pointed into the van.

Marshall just saw charring. Everywhere. The body was even stranger up close. 'What am I looking at?'

'He's been sitting on the seatbelt. The rest of it's burned away.'

'What the hell?'

'Firefighter said there was an explosion from the rear, which put the fire out.'

'And him sitting on the seatbelt?'

'Weird, right?'

'Right. Exactly.'

'Don't want to get in your way, Belu, but I've got a few questions.'

'I don't have a time of death, if that's what you're asking.'

'It's not that.' Marshall pointed at the body. 'Leaning forward like that, but arms raised... Sitting on the belt, though. Wasn't he wearing one?'

'Good question.'

'Have you got a good answer?'

'I might have. He wasn't wearing a seatbelt, judging by the injuries. So he's been tossed around. It's not all about being flung forward through the windscreen. Internal collisions, and I mean those inside the passenger compartment, are common for people who don't buckle up. Both femurs are broken... pretty tell-tale.' She pushed the corpse back, then lifted up a big belly that was surprisingly well-preserved considering the fire and the explosion. 'Aha. I think he's been preserving a tattoo.'

Of all the things...

Marshall reached his phone in and took a snapshot then held it out. Sure enough, the victim's giant belly was all twisted and distorted, but the words were still easy enough to read:

GI' IT
SOME
WELLY!

'What the hell does that mean?'

Owusu shrugged. 'I'll have to dig into it. As will you.'

'Right.' Scores of missing persons reports. Criminal intel. Press releases. All of the joys. 'Still, it's pretty distinguishing for a distinguishing mark.'

She laughed. 'That's true.'

'Holy shit.' Warner was right next to Marshall. 'Is that who I think it is?'

'I don't know. Who do you think it is?'

'A numpty I dealt with in the past... Iain Caddon, AKA Baseball. Lives in Burnfoot in Hawick. To Gala lads like yourself, that's the equivalent of Langlee. Bit of a dark fucker. Alleged to break knees with baseball bats. Never owned a baseball.'

'Interesting.' Marshall smiled at him. 'Any next of kin?'

'None who'd speak to the police.'

'Got it.' Marshall looked at Owusu. 'Can you fast track DNA on him? Would be good to confirm an ID.'

'On it.'

Warner folded his arms. 'You know, you just need to ask any number of cops in Hawick. That's Caddon. I mean, he was a cop.'

'Was?'

'Long before me, aye. Didn't last long.'

'Thanks for that.' Marshall shifted away from him and called Jolene. 'How's it going up there?'

'You want the truth?'

'Always.'

'Well, it's shite.'

'Why?'

'Because one of Andi or Shunty have sent McIntyre up here and he's acting like he's the SIO.'

Marshall knew that would come back to bite someone. 'Does the name Iain Caddon AKA Baseball mean anything to you?'

'Big fat guy with a baseball bat, right?'

'Right.'

'Got chucked out as a probationer for all kinds of shite. Witness intimidation. Nothing proven, but the powers that be took a dim view of it. Why?'

'He's the victim down here.'

'Holy shit. That's the only time in his life he can be described as a victim.'

'Need you to get people around at his friends and families. If he works, get them there too. Be good to confirm the ID.'

'On it.' Jolene sighed down the line. 'Give me a sec.' She muffled the receiver.

Warner was standing way too close, grinning.

'Haven't you been relieved yet, Constable?'

'D'you know, I went in the field. Always have some packs of hankies in the car, just in case.'

'I meant your shift.'

'Right. No.'

'Get your sergeant to call me, immediately.'

'On it, sir.'

Jolene came back on the line. 'Listen, McIntyre was just saying they've identified this victim as Steven Beattie.'

'Who's he?'

'Wee bam from Langlee. Been caught with a bit of dealing. Occasional pub assault. Suspected underage sex, but nothing proven. Current address is Wood Street in Gala.'

Marshall knew it – the long road heading out this way. Made sense if you were going to drop someone out of a moving car you'd—

'Wait a sec.' He frowned. 'I don't like that two headbangers are dead on the same night, about a mile apart. Can you get McIntyre to work his magic on the CCTV? I want to know if this van is the vehicle Beattie was dumped out of.'

'On it.' Her scribbling was loud and furious. 'One other thing, though. The fire service got called out to Beattie's home in the wee sma' hours.'

'Curious.' Marshall could picture it. Torching a flat, torching a van. 'I don't get why they abducted the occupant of the flat, only to turf him out of a van, though. Why not leave him in the flat to die?'

'Aye.' Jolene sounded distracted. 'Sir, got an issue. McIntyre said Shunty's not answering his calls.'

'So how am I supposed to help with that?'

'You might want to know – Shunty called McIntyre to say he's found the taxi driver who was seen arguing with Baird when she left the Burns supper.'

'The one blocking her off.'

'Right.'

'And?'

'It's the same one that dropped Lorimer off at BGH on Thursday night. Sent you a picture.'

Marshall pulled the phone away from his face and checked the display. A message from Jolene. He tapped it and opened up a photo.

A silver Skoda with Big Man Taxis in gold.

Paul Armstrong's firm.

His bloody sister's sometime ex-husband. Thea's father.

CHAPTER FORTY-THREE

'Come on, Shunty.' Elliot charged along the hospital corridor. No response from him. No footsteps behind her. She turned and saw the big lump had stopped to talk on the phone.

He raised a hand in apology and turned away.

Sodding hell.

She hadn't even heard it ring. He hadn't asked if it was okay. Aye, she needed to assert more authority over him.

She spotted Balfour Rattray there too, phone pressed to his ear. He clocked her, waved and walked off towards the stairs. Presumably he wasn't on the phone to Shunty.

'Andrea.'

Elliot swung around in the direction of the fierce voice.

Jen Marshall, looking that little bit more like her brother every day. Pretty tall, but nothing like the size of her big brother. Well, they were twins, so bigger brother. 'Thanks for screwing up my day.'

'What have I done?'

'You arrested one of my doctors.'

'Rougier?' Elliot smiled at her. 'He isn't *your* doctor, Jennifer.'

'That's my ward, though. If we're a doctor down, that means we're in deep doo-doo on the nursing side.'

'Good news is we released him from custody last night, so—'

'Jen!' As if by magic, Dr Rougier appeared. Dressed for a hike up Ben Nevis. Orange jacket, lime trousers, salmon scarf, black hat. Aye, Mountain Rescue would be able to see him from space. Bit out of breath. 'Sorry I'm late. Just ran over from Tweedbank station.'

'Get into your scrubs, Ben.' Jen patted his arm and walked off, shooting daggers at Elliot.

Rougier stood there, eyeing her. 'Have you got anywhere with that case?'

'Not yet, but I appreciate the lead. Thank you.'

'Don't mention it.' Rougier raced off towards A&E.

Jen was frowning. Christ – Elliot thought she'd walked away. 'What lead?'

'Just wanted him to think he's given us something useful in our interview. Making someone feel important's all part of the job. Sure you get it when you speak to the doctors, eh?'

'Oh, I do.' She smirked. 'I'll see you around, DI Elliot.'

'See you too.' Elliot watched her go, hoping that little nugget of information didn't get back to her brother. Certainly not before she told him.

Aye, she should do.

She got out her mobile, ready to call him.

'Boss.' Shunty appeared, phone finally away from his skull. 'Is that who I think it was?'

'We're not doing this dance again, Shunty. It was Dr Rougier and I don't know if that's who you thought it was. Still not sure about the boy, but hey ho.' She set off towards the stairs down to Pathology in the basement. 'Who were you on the phone to?'

'McIntyre.'

That chump. 'What did he want?'

'Well, he's still out at the crash sites. Jolene and Marshall were there.'

'Aye.' She stopped at the landing halfway down. 'Wait a sec. You said they *were* there?'

'They've got an ID for both victims. Stevie Beattie and Iain Caddon, AKA—'

'Baseball?' Elliot felt like she'd been stabbed in the guts again. 'Christ. Had to sack that wanker from his probation. Long time ago, mind. He's dead?'

'Body's heading here once forensics are finished with the van.'

'Someone torched it, eh?'

'Marshall said he'd seen a few like that in his time. The fire originated inside the vehicle, not from the engine or the fuel tank.'

'What a way to go.' Elliot allowed herself a grin. 'Truth is, Shunty, I'm glad to see the back of that big bastard.'

'Hopefully Beattie's already here.' Siyal knitted his brow. 'Didn't we have him fingered for underage S-E-X?'

'First, please just say sex. And second, don't use fingered and underage sex in the same sentence, Shunty. You pervert.'

'Didn't we, though?'

She cleared her throat. 'PF didn't bite on the evidence.'

'Unlike with Tait.'

Elliot sighed. 'Just be glad someone's doing the Good Lord's work for us, eh? Clearly CrimeStoppers is upping their game.' She skipped down the steps to the basement and held the door.

But Shunty was looking like a fortnight's holiday in Langlee.

'What's up with you now?'

'The phone call. Jolene asked Big Jim to take a lead in a few things.'

'Such as?'

'Tracing the van ownership.'

'Okay.'

'Thought you'd fight it?'

'Trick to succeeding in this game, Shunty, is knowing when to pick your battles. This benefits us.'

'You talk like you're playing a game against Rob.'

'Life is a game, Shunty. Some win, some lose. Some don't even know they're playing. Has McIntyre actually got anything, though?'

'The back plate was like the inside of a cheese toastie, but forensics and the fire service managed to get a read off the front one. Jim's traced it to a lease company, but they're playing silly buggers. He's escalated it to management but they're not playing ball without a warrant.'

'Seriously?' Elliot let the door shut again. 'Haven't we got data access agreements in place?'

'With all the national firms and mid-sized local ones. But Happy Baz's Vans in Hawick are neither of those.'

'Has anyone spoken to Happy Baz?'

'That's who I was on the phone to afterwards. Finbar Mulligan. I got told the same story, then I pushed back to explain what's happening. What the van's been used for. He relented and said it's going to be an hour.'

'An hour? It doesn't take an hour to—'

'Fire drill.'

'Fire drill, my arse.' Elliot opened the door and stormed through into the maze of corridors around

Pathology. 'Shunty, this sounds like absolute bollocks to me.'

But she could see that Marshall's van fire was clearly related to the body dumped out of the van. And she wanted to be the one to figure out precisely how.

Elliot pushed through the door to Owusu's lab.

Place was empty. No sign anyone had been here. At least it was clean and tidy.

Shunty joined her in the room. 'Must be still out at the crash site, eh?'

'No, I'm here.' Owusu hopped up from between two beds. 'Just got back.'

'What were you doing there, Belu?'

'One of these beds has a squeaky wheel. Interferes like hell with my dictation machine. I'm so bloody busy just now, I can't have any more hassle from my PA.'

'I'd love to have a PA.'

Owusu winced. 'Isn't Shunty the next best thing?'

'There are some miles between the next best thing and Shunty.' Elliot laughed. 'You okay there, Belu?'

'I'm fine. Just a stitch.' She pressed at her side. 'It'll pass. Just stood up too quickly.'

Elliot wasn't too sure about that, but she wasn't the medical professional here. 'You done any more thinking on the A72 incidents?'

'Just that I've got a lot to deal with, Andrea. That's four bodies in two days. Unless we're coming down with some kind of zombie plague, that feels really unusual for here.'

'Not the first time, though, and it won't be the last. Last lot did for your predecessor.'

'So I gather.' She waved a hand at the body. 'Anyway. I've been asked to prioritise Caddon.'

'Who by?'

'DI Marshall.'

'And he's in charge?'

'Jim Pringle said he's the deputy SIO, so we must all dance to his beat.'

Pair of wankers.

'How can I help you, Andrea?'

'Got a few questions about the blood toxicology of both victims.'

'Kirsten did that last night.'

'Aye. But did she do it well or did she get Drunk Sally to do it for her?'

'Kirsten did it herself. She's great, Andrea. One of the best I've worked with.'

Elliot didn't believe that, unless she hadn't worked with anyone. 'As Pringle would say, refresh my non-existent.'

Owusu rolled her eyes. 'Dr Baird was pretty much clean, just drinking too much caffeine.' She winced again. 'Then again, she's a doctor so it's par for the course.'

'Pretty much clean, though?'

'Some alcohol there. I gather she was at a function where prosecco was served.'

'We believe she even had some, aye.' Elliot leaned on the counter. 'No coke? No hash?'

'Sorry.'

'Bloody doctors. What about him?'

'He was drunk at time of death. We think six pints of lager. Probably five percent.'

So, whatever pish they had on tap in the Stagehall... Not that Shunty would've noted that down.

'No drugs?'

'No.' Owusu was scowling at her. 'Andrea, why are you so interested?'

'Want to know if they were both users.'

Owusu laughed. 'These two? Drug users?'

Elliot couldn't look at her. 'Jim wants to pin these to being drug cases.'

'That's an incredible reach. These two were not drug users. Blood toxicology would show if they'd been using in the last two weeks.'

'Bugger.' Elliot stared at Shunty. 'Told you this was a long shot.'

'It's not my fault they weren't getting high on their own supply.' Shunty laughed like he'd just invented the phrase. 'By that I mean... It's possible they were just dealing. And not partaking. I mean, if they were—'

'Rakesh.' Owusu's sharp tone was like a whip crack. 'Are you seriously investigating Louisa Baird as a drug dealer?'

Shunty couldn't look at her. 'Boss's orders.'

Owusu drilled her gaze into Elliot. 'Yours or Jim's?'

'Him.'

'Hmm. Listen. I knew Dr Baird pretty well. She was a good woman. A great doctor. Kind. Gentle. Compassionate. There's no *way* she's a drug dealer.'

Shunty still couldn't look at her. 'Weird how she was dumped in the same way as plenty of them are, though.'

'She's just not, Andrea. Look, I'll have a word with DCI Pringle.'

Elliot laughed. 'Why's he going to listen to you?'

'He's not. It's just... if he's not listening to you or Rob, then maybe he'll see sense if I talk to him.'

'All I can say is good luck. And I truly mean that.'

Owusu was frowning. She didn't say anything, though.

Elliot stared at Shunty. 'Okay. Assuming Belu isn't successful in persuading our numpty-in-chief that this is numptyism of the highest order, can you get your lot prioritising the bank details? Look for big cash payments in or out, that kind of thing. Money going to odd accounts.'

'I'll see what we can do, but surely they'd be good at covering their tracks?'

'Never assume the kind of arseholes we investigate are any good at anything, Shunty. Do the basics right.' She clapped his shoulder. 'There's a good lad.' She watched him trudge off like a wee laddie, then smiled at Owusu. 'Can't get the staff, eh?'

'He's a good guy, Andrea. Heart's in the right place.'

'Aye, but he's not got a brain.' She let a slow breath out. 'Thing is, I'm here because I don't really know where else to go. Sure, the blood tox came back last night but I'm here asking you in case there's something in Jim's wee theory.'

'You do seem a bit at a loss.' Owusu stared into space, then shifted her gaze to Elliot. 'Did you get anywhere with that hotel card?'

'With that *what*?'

CHAPTER FORTY-FOUR

'Let me get this straight.' Jolene was in the passenger seat, watching the traffic pass as Marshall eased along Channel Street towards the cinema. Shoppers milled about in the darkness, even at this early hour, with a few well-dressed folk off to work. 'This firm is owned by your sister's ex-husband?'

'That's right.'

'And your sister and him are at it again?'

'Unfortunately.'

'Why unfortunately?'

'He's a bit of a dickhead.' Marshall pulled in and let an old man cross, newspaper tucked under his arm. Even got a doff of the imaginary cap for his trouble. 'No. I'll correct that – he's a total dickhead.'

She laughed and ran a hand through her hair. 'In what way?'

'You'll see.'

'Come on, Rob...'

'I mean it. Always hated him since the day I met him. He's arrogant, barbaric, psychopathic...'

'Sounds like your sister's got terrible taste in men.'

'Terrible would be a massive improvement.'

She side eyed him. 'What about you, Rob?'

'I like my men with ginger handlebar moustaches and leather dungarees.'

'That's not what I meant.' A frown pulsed on her forehead. 'Unless this is you finally coming out?'

'I'll never tell.' He laughed. 'But my taste in women... It's a long story.'

'We've got time.'

'Not now, we don't.' Marshall pulled up on Bank Street. 'That's his office there. I can't go in and ask about my former-and-possibly-future brother-in-law in any official investigation, so I'm asking you to do it for me.'

'But yesterday you went off and spoke to your sister about the Burns supper?'

'Aye, but I asked you to follow up and obtain a statement, then to check that statement.'

'Still, you spoke to—'

'I just needed to have a word with her about it first.'

'Fair enough.' She huffed out a sigh. 'Be back in a minute.'

Marshall sat back to watch her cross the road and pop inside the office. Not like any other taxi firm, with neon signs and smoke stains. No, it had pebbles and potted plants like some Japanese business.

Hang on, there was that Japanese pharmaceutical company over by Aldi. He drove past it every day. Place was unassuming, but a multinational sitting in humble Gala was something else.

Bank Street's gardens were pretty much the only part of the

town not buried in snow. They faced a row of upmarket shops, cafés and a couple of bank branches, though the name came from the sluice from the Gala water running the other side of the gardens.

At least, Marshall thought that.

He googled it.

Weird. Turned out the name wasn't because the street was on the bank of a river, but because the National Bank of Scotland had had a branch there. Became part of the Royal Bank of Scotland, which was now NatWest.

Huh. You live and learn.

Someone rapped on the passenger window and got in.

Paul Armstrong. Jeans, black shirt, brown leather jacket. Clean shaven and stinking of smoky aftershave. 'Morning there, Bobby.'

Marshall looked away from him. No sign of Jolene inside his office. 'Why does nobody call me by the name I want? It's Rob. It's been Rob since I was born. It'll stay that way until I die.'

'I see. Sorry about that, Rob. Your dad's a Robert too, eh? And Grumpy too. That old bugger's a Robert, isn't he?'

'I'm Rob. He's Grumpy. Dad was Bob.'

'You say was. That mean he's dead?'

'I hope so.'

'That's not very nice.'

'I'm not.'

Paul laughed. 'So you're third generation Robert Marshall? Landed gentry, mate.'

'Far from it. And I'm not your mate.'

Paul looked over at him, then did the old up and down. 'Why are you sitting outside my office?'

'A colleague's gone inside to speak to you.'

'That's interesting. When I saw you, I thought you were here as the big brother to warn me off your sister.'

'Paul. You need to listen to me. We're twins, you daft bugger. Neither of us is older.'

'Well, that's a relief.'

'What is?'

'About you not coming here to warn me off.' Paul let the words settle on the upholstery. 'Otherwise, we'd have had to have words. Maybe more.' He licked his lips. 'Thing is, Rob, I had enough of you years ago.'

'Oh aye?'

'Aye. Remember how you tracked me down in my taxi and started giving me shite about how I'm not good enough to go out with your sister?'

'We both know that, Paul.'

'Turned that cab into a twenty-car business. Expanding into Midlothian next month. Hopefully get a few licenses in Edinburgh after that.'

'You say that like it's a rags to riches tale. We both know your dad died and you inherited twenty-five cars, but ten drivers hated your guts and set up their own firm.'

Paul laughed. 'You've got a bloody cheek.'

'Paul, we hate each other. That's fine. But this isn't about you and Jen.'

'What is it, then?'

'You're both old enough to at least pretend you know what you're doing. Just take into account Thea's feelings, okay?'

That seemed to hit Paul in the stomach. The hard-man wide-boy facade slipped away. Then it flashed back. 'Don't you *dare*—'

'She's my niece. I want to look after her.'

'That right, aye?'

'That's right. Given you two don't seem to be able to. Don't forget about her needs. That's all I ask.'

Paul laughed. 'So you are here to warn me off?'

'No. Just don't screw her up with your selfishness.' Marshall caught a flash of movement from outside. 'My colleague needs to ask a question.'

The passenger door opened and Jolene stood there. 'Sir, he's not in.'

'DS Jolene Archer, meet Paul Armstrong.'

'Ah.' She grinned. 'The very man.'

'I'll let you two get acquainted.' Marshall got out of the car and walked off towards the RBS branch. The building wasn't that grand, certainly nowhere near fancy enough to name a street after. Still, in this day and age, having any branches open was a good thing. Not that he'd had cause to use one for years. Not since his mum last sent him a cheque.

'Let's start with if you saw anything at the Burns supper.'

Marshall was still in earshot. He didn't move away from that spot, even though it was freezing and dark. Caught a glimpse of them in the reflection.

Paul was out of the car now, hands in pockets. 'Didn't see anything, darling. Too many whiskies. Got splattered with neeps and haggis.' A passing car swished over his speech. 'Then someone chucked up their stovies.'

'You drive home after that?'

'In my game, you don't drink and drive. You don't even have a drink the night before you're supposed to drive. Got a cab home with that prick's sister.'

Marshall had to fight hard not to look over at the allusion to him. Still, being called 'that prick' was the kindest thing he'd ever said. And someone like Paul Armstrong was always looking for a reaction.

'Take it you didn't drive yesterday?'

Paul laughed. 'Aye.'

'We're interested in a silver Skoda, registered to Big Man Taxis.'

'Well, I'm the big man.' Paul grunted. 'Must be one of mine, eh?'

Marshall chanced a glance around and saw him inspecting her mobile.

'Not the first time that car was there that night. Big Balfour Rattray asked me to put on a few. Ferry his toffs in from far and wide. Few coming from Edinburgh, so they got the train to Stow. Most were from around these parts. Always a good piss-up, though, so taxis are essential. Still, it was a nightmare with all that snow. My fleet's just not cut out for it up there in those conditions. We managed, but three are in the garage now.'

'So this cab picked you up?'

'Aye, definitely. Why are you asking?'

'The driver allegedly got into a dust up with someone who was subsequently murdered.'

'Ah, shite. Heard all about that. Awful business. Louisa Baird, eh?'

'That's right. You know who was driving the taxi?'

'Right. It was Rachel. Rachel Lorimer.'

CHAPTER FORTY-FIVE

Chunk yawned into his fist. Felt like it'd keep on going. So bloody tired. Two hours' kip after that long walk home this morning, then back out now. A coffee and a tin of liquorice and lime WakeyWakey didn't cut the mustard on that front.

The house was in the throes of morning activity – daddy dearest getting the kid ready for school. Shouting and thumping.

Chunk laughed at that. Nobody'd got him ready for school in the morning. Just did what he wanted. Which wasn't school. Chunk didn't have a nanny growing up. Had both parents, but the sick bastards would rather drink themselves to death than look after a kid. Not that anyone else stepped in when his old man did die and his mum even managed to increase her intake afterwards.

It was a wonder he'd even made it to this age.

The front door opened and Hugo Baird stepped out, looking like death warmed up. Held his wee lad's hand and walked him over to the car. On a phone call. As ever. The company man. He ended the call and pocketed the phone.

Something weird about taking him to school the day after the pigs found his mother's body.

A wee lassie stood on the top doorstep.

The little brat's live-in nanny. Quite tidy too, but young. Super young. Barely eighteen. Chunk wondered if Hugo was boffing her on the side. Who'd blame him?

Crass to talk about a grieving widower like that, but grief didn't really change people. Just made them more distilled.

She'd be helping out with all the domestic crap now the good lady wife was dead.

Bit of a shame, really, but Chunk didn't regret doing it. A job was a job. Some were justifiable, others were a shame. They both paid about the same though. Most of the people he'd killed were complete bastards, but she seemed to be a bit of a saint. Running a cancer charity. Curing the disease in people.

Still, a job was a job.

The front door closed.

Hugo was belting his kid into the back seat. He shut the door and his breath hung in the cold, catching in the street-lights. He clapped his gloved hands together and got in the front.

Brilliant – maximum leverage.

Chunk let Hugo drive off through the estate, then slipped his car into gear and followed at a distance. Caught sight of Hugo indicating right to enter the A68, so Chunk pulled in and waited a bit. Give him some space. Not feel like he's being followed.

Not like he was in the middle of Glasgow or anything, where you could lose yourself in traffic. None of that two-car distance shite here – barely two cars on the roads in the whole of the Borders. No, down here he had to keep it brazen, mixed with absolute caution.

Chunk eased off and followed Hugo's path onto the main road, a few yards shy of the national speed limit sign. The morning was cold and dark, with snow piled up at the side of the road. Surface seemed decent enough, so he wasn't worried about sliding off. Chunk was more concerned about Hugo, to be honest – he didn't want him escaping his clutches.

He floored it to catch up with him. Not quite bumper to bumper, but not far off.

The Old Melrose roundabout was clear of traffic and he followed Hugo all the way round, heading for Melrose and Gala.

Chunk had no idea why the old Melrose was so far from the new one, but hey ho. He wasn't from around here so he only needed to know the geography of the place, not the history.

The traffic was thicker on this stretch, the main road to the largest Borders towns, with a few cars piling on at the junctions. Cutting it fine to shave those extra seconds off the commute, despite the conditions.

The first big roundabout loomed, and Hugo was indicating right.

Chunk knew precisely where he was headed – the mother-in-law in Darnick. Then he'd be going into the office.

Well, he wasn't getting to either of them.

Chunk got right up his tail as he slowed, then followed him around, skipping the exit for Galashiels, but he floored it and blasted round him, then hauled the wheel in to block him off at the next exit.

Hugo honked his horn. No room to brake and stop, so he took the turning for Tweedbank.

Fly, meet spider web.

Chunk followed him down the long straight, then repeated

the trick, overtaking him and forcing Hugo off the main road and into the industrial estate.

Chunk bumped the kerb and followed him around, then stopped the van, parking across both lanes. He tugged on a balaclava and got out into the freezing air, pulling out his knife.

Hugo stepped out of his car with almighty fury. 'What the fuuuuuuuuuuck!' His eyes went wide.

Chunk was on him in a flash but didn't stab him. Instead, he pushed him over onto the rough patch of ground. Then tore the back door open and pressed the knife to the kid's throat. 'You want the boy to live?'

Hugo nodded. 'Please! Don't!'

'I won't. I'm not a monster. But I can do monstrous things, if pushed. Are you going to play ball here?'

'Of course! Just don't—'

'Do what I say.' Chunk reached into his coat pocket and flung over a roll of duct tape. 'First, you're covering your mouth well by going around your noggin four times.'

'Please. Don't do anything to him.' Hugo tacked his thumbs against the end of the tape, then he hauled out a length and covered his mouth.

'Not going to.' Chunk handed him two zip ties. 'Wrists and ankles. Suggest you do it ankles first.'

Hugo bent over and wrapped it around his ankles, then tightened it. He was out of breath just from that. He slapped it around his wrists and took a few goes to tug it tight.

Chunk should've got Baseball to use them on the other two, but he wouldn't listen. 'Good lad.' He pointed at the van. 'Now, bunny hop over there.'

Hugo's eyes went even wider.

'Dude, this is in exchange for your kid's life.' Chunk held up the knife. 'Okay?'

Hugo glanced back at the car, then hopped over to the van. Almost comical. Totally unnecessary too but fuck it – Chunk needed a laugh as much as anyone else.

Chunk pushed him back against the van's door, then took the phone from Hugo's pocket. He dialled 0800 1111 and held out the phone to Hugo. 'Childline.' He walked over to the car handed the phone to the kid. 'Explain to the nice man what's going on.' He slammed the door and walked back over to the van. 'By the time Childline get done hugging trees and think to call the police, we'll be long gone. But your wean's safe.' He slid the van's side door open and pushed Hugo in.

He landed on top of Rachel Lorimer, struggling against her zip ties.

CHAPTER FORTY-SIX

Shunty bumped up onto the pavement outside Baird & Cruikshank. Whether he'd intended to was anyone's guess. 'What's the plan here?'

Elliot put her mobile away and stretched out. Might be a wee back street, but a fair few people were using it to get down from the posh houses to the train station. At least the trains were still running in all this snow. 'We're going to pay Dr Baird's husband a visit and see if he knows anything about her dealing drugs.'

Shunty killed the engine and yanked the key out. 'I don't see why a hotel key card implies that?'

'Because... It fits, Shunty.'

'Boss...' Shunty was shaking his head. 'Do you really?'

She couldn't even look at him.

'Boss, I think this is a bad move.'

'We've got a hotel keycard, but we don't know which hotel it belongs to. Now, while your lot are pulling a finger out of their collective bums to call around and find anyone matching her description, we're going straight to the man.'

'Seems like a long shot.'

'Of course it is. But we need to tick all the boxes, don't we?'

'I didn't join the police to tick boxes. I don't see a shred of evidence to suggest either her or Justin Lorimer were involved with drugs. We've nothing to suggest these two have even so much as inhaled second-hand marijuana smoke, let alone—'

'Call it "hash", Shunty. Christ.'

'My point stands. Why are we jumping in here to ask a grieving widower about his wife's drug deal?'

She didn't have a solid answer, but she had an unanswered question. 'You don't think Mr Grieving Widower here going to work after his wife's body's found is suspicious?'

'Didn't say that. But... Look. Boss. All I'm saying is we need to go easy on him. Dr Owusu said he was crying in there yesterday.'

Elliot scowled at the office. 'Him? Crying?'

'After we left, apparently. She said he was in floods of tears. Had to get her PA to go to the shops to pick up more Kleenex.'

Elliot couldn't see it. But it wouldn't be the first time she'd come across crocodile tears in the wild. 'I hear you, Shunty. And actually, I'm commending you on raising those concerns. Your role isn't just about doing the doings, it's about making sure I'm challenged.'

'Thank you.'

'And Hugo Baird's either going to know about that card or he's not.' She opened the door and got out into the freezing darkness. 'Come on.' She walked towards the office.

He jogged to overtake her. 'Seriously? After that, you're still ploughing in?'

'Shunty, Shunty, Shunty. This comes down to whether he denies it or not. I think he's going to. Lad seems to be full of it.'

'Lad? He's about ten years older than you.'

Cheeky bastard. 'Twenty. At least. You Millennials don't know you're born.'

'What are you?'

'I don't care. All that Gen X, Boomer, Zoomer, Millennial shite is the new horoscopes. It's all bollocks, Shunty.'

'You raised it!'

She tried to move past him, but he was still blocking the way. 'Shunty. Out of the way.'

'Can I just go on record as saying I think it's a bit much to be going into—'

'Aye, Shunty, I hear you. I heard you in the car. Thing is, you need to learn the virtues of the cop's instinct. After twenty years on the job, you develop this second sight. Call it a Spidey-Sense. A deep gut instinct. You and Marshall don't have it, mind, as it has to be earned.'

He grinned wide. She didn't expect that. 'You were stabbed in the guts. You didn't see that one coming, did you?'

Cheeky sod.

'Maybe you're improving a wee bit since I rescued you from Dr Donkey, but if you have any hope of staying employed, sunshine, you need to do as I say and stop trying to out-think situations. Less thinking, more doing, as I say.'

'I hear you.'

'Are you listening, though?'

'Of course. I'm always listening.'

'Good.' She stepped back to let someone through the office door. They shouldn't be having this chat in the street, but the big bugger wouldn't stop and listen, would he? 'Have you got someone going through his bank records?'

'Told you I would.'

'Aye, but have you?'

'Yes!'

'Who?' She raised a finger. 'If you say McIntyre, Shunty, I swear I'll...'

He was bright red. 'Paton's looking into it.'

'Good.' Elliot had no idea who Paton was. 'Come on, then.' She opened the door and held it for him.

Shunty was too busy texting, probably inventing a DC Paton or finding one with that name.

So Elliot went inside.

The place was heaving, tons of young professionals running around like someone had called in a bomb threat. The queue at the printer was longer than the one at the coffee machine.

She smiled at the receptionist and showed her warrant card. 'Wonder if we could speak to Hugo Baird?'

That got a polite smile, all eyelashes and fake tan in a Gala winter. Elliot would bet anything the lassie was all over Instagram and TikTok. 'I'm afraid Mr Baird isn't in yet.'

'Thought he was an early starter.'

'Sure, but I don't know if you heard... There was a death in the family.' Spoken in an undertone. 'His wife.'

Great.

Should've gone to the house...

Shunty appeared next to her. 'Is Mr Cruikshank here?'

'Just over there.' She got to her feet and her perfume was a citrus wash over them. 'Donald!'

A guy in his late thirties swung around and raised his head. Electric blue shirt open to the neck, black suit. Shiny brogues. 'What's up?'

'Police.' Shunty walked over and shook his hand. 'DS Rakesh Siyal. Just need a word with Hugo.'

'He's on his way in.'

'Even with—'

'Even so. Hugo's... Hugo. He's driven, as I'm sure you know.

I told him to take all the time he needed and he said he already had.' Cruikshank swept a hand through his immaculate quiff. 'We're up against it on one of his clients, to be honest, and we're all looking to him for direction. So he's coming in after he drops the boy at his mother-in-law's.'

'Haven't they got a nanny for that?'

'No idea what to say to that. Sorry.'

'Did he say how long he'd be?'

'That's just it.' Cruikshank tapped his watch, plain silver but studded with jewels. 'Should be here by now. Spoke to him just as he was leaving the house but that was half an hour ago. Just tried calling him, but he's not picking up.'

CHAPTER FORTY-SEVEN

Jolene was driving like a demon, hammering it up the A7 despite the conditions being even worse than the previous morning. The sun was creeping up over the hills to at least light up the morning. A little bit.

They passed a sign:

DON'T BE A "TOSSER" – TAKE YOUR RUBBISH HOME!

Hard to disagree with that.

'Let me get this straight, Rob.' Jolene slid out to overtake a silver Citroen. 'Rachel took her husband to hospital after a pub fight, then she cleared off. Later, she's getting into an argument with a woman whose body just so happens to get dumped on top of her husband's. Seems a bit massively strange to me.'

Marshall gripped the handle above the door that little bit tighter. 'Elliot would be talking about that being a co-inkydink.'

'I hate it when she does that.'

Marshall let go of the handle and looked over. 'Go on?'

'It's just annoying, isn't it? She's getting as bad as Pringle with all his whistles and weird phrases. Like the power's gone to her head and she thinks she can get away with whatever she wants. Perhaps she's dressing for the part she wants – she's made it no secret she wants to be the DCI in Gala.'

Marshall smiled. He was warming to Jolene. Didn't hurt that she was probably the only person in the world who actually called him Rob. 'You don't think it's a coincidence?'

'Do you?'

'Hard to say, isn't it? With Louisa leaving... Rachel's a cabbie, so she could've been working. Paul told you his firm put on a load of taxis for the function.'

'I didn't tell you that, though.'

'I've got very good hearing.' Marshall smiled, but she was too focused on the road to notice. 'You don't think it's a co-inkydink?'

'Please...' She sighed as she slowed to the village's twenty speed limit. 'Okay, I do think it's possible. Probable, even. Taxi drivers turn up where you least expect them.'

'So why didn't she say anything about dropping her husband off?'

'That's a very good question.'

'Let's see what she's got to say.' Jolene took the left and wound her way up past the Stagehall Arms to the Lorimer home, parking just past it. 'Her car's there. The taxi in question.'

And her husband's van was next to it.

Marshall got out into the bracing cold and walked over to the door. He waited for Jolene to join him, his breath misting in the air and seeming to linger.

Always felt that little bit colder in Stow and he didn't know why. Wasn't that much higher than Gala and the wind didn't seem to cut through. Maybe it was that lack of air that did it.

Jolene hadn't joined him.

He turned around.

Jolene was peering in the big living room window. 'Nobody's in, Rob.'

Marshall joined her on the front lawn and peered in. A big living room, looking through to a dark kitchen at the back. Lights off. L-shaped sofa in this corner, facing a big telly in the opposite one.

He heard someone shouting for 'Mylo' somewhere nearby. Whether that was a man, boy or dog, he couldn't tell. Either way, Jolene was right – no tell-tale signs of anyone being inside the house.

A door opened.

Next door. Attached to Rachel's.

A wee man tugged his thick coat around him. Scarf, gloves, hat – dressed for the elements. He tugged on a lead. 'Come *on*, Mylo.' Then he set off down the street, yanking an overweight Westie behind him. He stopped to scowl at Marshall, standing in the middle of the front garden. 'Can I help you there, son?'

They probably looked like Jehovah's Witnesses to him, keen to press the locals on the impending apocalypse of which the snow was a harsh reminder. Assuming that was what they did.

'Police, sir.' Marshall got out his warrant card. 'Looking for Rachel Lorimer.'

'Awful business, son.' He walked past them. 'Sorry, but I need to walk the dog before work. Hope you find her.'

'Wait a sec.' Marshall jogged across the garden then blocked him off on the street. 'When did you last see her?'

'Saw her come back late last night around midnight.'

'Sure of that?'

'Aye, aye. Taking Mylo out for his widdle last thing. Getting to that age where he'll pish on the carpet if I don't. Mind you, he's always been a bit of a bugger like that. Haven't you, son?' He crouched as low as he could get to tickle his dog on the chin. Clearly the only thing he had in his life, and it was receiving all of the love he had.

'Did you speak to her?'

'Spoke to her, aye. She told me what happened. Like I say, awful business. Justin will be missed. He was a good lad. Always good for a laugh in the Stagecoach. Always stood his hand.' He looked at the Lorimer house and shook his head, then frowned. 'Should've left for school now. Eh?'

'That's what—'

'Mind, the kids will be off school the day.'

'Because of the snow?'

'No, because their dad's died!'

'Of course.' Marshall gave him a tight smile. 'You haven't seen her today, then?'

'Nope.'

'Would you normally?'

'Well, aye. She's usually hanging out clothes in the morning, eh?' He pointed at a side gate. 'Usually have a wee chat about stuff. I'll get her some messages. Work security at the Ashworth's at Tweedbank, you know? She'll look after Mylo if I'm late.' He looked around the gloomy skies. 'Not a great day for it the day, mind. Sheets'll freeze on the line.' He looked Marshall up and down. 'You mind if I...?'

'On you go.'

'Sure thing, son. You know where I live, eh?' He laughed then tugged at the dog's lead. 'Come on, Mylo.' And off he toddled.

Marshall waited for him to go, then walked past the cars and went down the side of the house. The back garden was filled with kids' toys. Cars and castles, all in primary colours. A giant trampoline was on its side at the back, probably blown over by the strong winds last year. A small shed lurked in the corner – looked like it was older than the house and probably had a gateway to a mystical realm inside.

Marshall peered into the window and got a better view of the kitchen. Nice new units and appliances. Wee table with four seats at it.

And three half-eaten breakfasts.

Two half-drunk glasses of orange juice.

A cup of tea up to the brim, a little bit of scum on the top.

Aye, this looked suspicious.

'Jolene.' Marshall beckoned her over from the shed. 'Have a look at— SHIT!'

Through the door at the back, he saw into the living room and could make out what was on the purple L-shaped sofa in the corner by the window.

Two children.

Taped up. Back-to-back, their ankles bound.

Marshall kicked the back door below the handle and it exploded into the house. He stormed in and charged through the kitchen into the living room.

The kids were wrapped up with duct tape. It wouldn't budge. 'Shite.'

Their eyes were wide, both staring up at him. A boy and a girl. Six and seven, if Marshall had to guess.

Jolene ran back into the kitchen. Whacked the drawer around a bit, rattling the cutlery.

'Hey, it's going to be okay.' Marshall smiled at them. 'I'm a policeman. I'm here to help you. Just let me try to get you free, okay?' He reached out and tried easing the boy's tape from his mouth.

The lad's eyes bulged.

'Sorry, I know it's sore, but I need to get that off.' Marshall reached out again and the little guy screwed his eyes up tight. Marshall gave it a sharp tug and managed to get it free. 'There you go.' He looked at his sister, who must've been older. 'Now your turn.'

Jolene ran back through with two pairs of kitchen scissors.

Marshall braced his hand against her shoulder and ripped her mouth tape off. He grabbed a pair of scissors from Jolene and started cutting away at the wall of tape between them. 'Hey, who did this to you?'

'The bad man!'

'He took Mummy!'

Shite.

Another abduction. He hoped Rachel Lorimer was still alive. 'What happened?'

'The bad man made Mummy walk around us twenty-five times with the tape, then did our hands and feet and then around our mouths!'

'Twenty-five times, eh? That's a lot.'

'It's not as high as I can count! I can count to *two hundred*.'

'That's very impressive.' Marshall smiled at the lad. 'Did you see the bad man?'

'He was wearing a hat over his head. One that just showed his eyes.'

'A balaclava?'

The kid shrugged. 'I had one when I was little. Daddy used to say I had to put on an accent and I don't know why.'

Marshall could spot an off-colour joke a mile off. 'Did you see—'

'The bad man had evil eyes.'

'What colour were they?'

'Don't know. Wait. Green?'

'Brown?'

'Maybe blue.'

Perfect. They didn't see anything. Or just didn't remember it.

'Was he tall like me?'

'He was big, but...'

'Was he as tall as Jolene here?'

'I don't know. He was a bad man, that's all. Daddy told us to not speak to bad men. So we didn't.'

Marshall tore off the last strip of tape. He balled it all up and dumped it into the middle of the floor. He took Jolene aside. 'Okay, you stay here with them. I'll call this in and get uniform around here. Get them to go door-to-door; I want to know what happened.'

She was nodding. 'Where are you going?'

Before he could answer, the kids wrapped their arms around his legs.

'Please, Mr Policeman. Can you take us to Granny's?'

CHAPTER FORTY-EIGHT

Elliot got out and crunched up the gravel path towards the house. 'You lead here, Shunty.' Despite her words, she wanted to show him how it was done. Be dynamic. Always be doing. But he needed to show that himself. 'Okay with that?'

'If you'll let me.' Shunty hammered on the door and waited.

Elliot took in the neighbouring area. Just a few streets away from her home, but this was the posher part of Lauder. The new houses. A few estates that sprung up in the last twenty years. Calling them estates would get you lynched by some of the occupants.

She could remember them being built more easily than she could playing in the fields as a kid, even drinking there as a teenager.

'His car's gone.'

Elliot saw what Shunty meant. Just a little Fiat 500 sat on the gravel. Hugo's big Lexus was gone. And, of course, Louisa's Audi was at the yard up in Edinburgh.

The door opened and Nancy the nanny stood there. Skinny wee waif of a thing. Red eyes like she'd been crying all day. What was her name?

Shunty smiled at her. 'Hi, Becky.'

Right, aye. Not Nancy. Of course.

She frowned at him. 'What's happened?'

'Just need a word with Mr Baird, that's all.'

'Oh. He took Toby off to his mother-in-law's. Said I wasn't capable of looking after him today.' She wrapped those skinny arms around her torso. 'Which is fair enough, I suppose. Been a mess since I heard about Louisa.'

This was just amazing. Need to speak to him and he's gone walkabout.

A squad car pulled into the street, then drove right up to the drive.

'Stay with her, Sergeant.' Elliot raced down the steps to meet them.

The driver's door opened and PC Liam Warner got out. That big Irish lump of gristle. What he was doing still on shift was anyone's guess.

'Constable, I thought you were sent home?'

'Sarge told us to do this last one wee trip.' He opened the back door.

A child sat in the back.

'Toby!' A shout rang out from behind Elliot. A blur of teenage limbs and hair shot past, burying the boy in a big cuddle. 'What happened?' Becky looked up at Warner.

Now the nanny was in the car, Elliot beckoned Warner away. 'What the hell is going on?'

'Don't know, really. We've got what we think is a bogus story of his dad getting abducted.'

'Who told you that?'

'The kid...'

'Wait, what? Where is Hugo?'

'We don't know. Got a call from Childline.'

'*Childline?*'

'Aye. The dad's phone was on a call with them. They eventually called us. Me and Stish turned up and we found the wee lad in the back seat, holding his dad's phone, thinking this is a brilliant game.'

Nothing like cynical cops to ignore everything a kid said.

'And there's no sign of him?'

'Not that I could see. I'm thinking the wee bugger stole the car and made the whole thing up.'

Shunty was speaking to the nanny. 'Awful business.' He clocked Elliot's glare, then crouched. 'Becky, what happened this morning?'

'This morning?'

'Last time you saw Mr Baird.'

'Hugo drove off first thing. He dropped Toby off at his wife's mother's in Darnick. Let me clean the house. Thing is, I'm in a bit of a state just now, so it's... It's tough. Should I take Toby there?'

'Why do you think that?'

'Well, it's obvious Hugo's been abducted. Just like what happened with Louisa.'

That made Elliot's wound throb a bit. She stared at Warner. 'Where's the car?'

'Relax. Stish is still with it.'

CHAPTER FORTY-NINE

Marshall should've had a car seat for each of the kids, but he was only driving three streets away. Trouble was, Stow was a long road with only a few coming off, so he had to go past two garages, a tractor salesroom and the old pub, now a former tearoom and on sale as a house. For once, he was glad of the hard twenty limit for all settlements in the Borders.

He couldn't spot the turning. Not many streets left, just a couple of ultra-modern developments that had somehow got past planning.

There.

He took the right. 'Be there soon, kids.'

'Thank you, Mr Policeman!' Her face beamed in the rear-view, smeared in chocolate. She picked out a giant crisp and put it in her mouth. Quite why someone had left all that in the pool car's boot was baffling, but it was a lifesaver. 'Don't you have a hat?'

'Or a costume?'

'I'm a detective. Uniformed officers are the ones who wear caps.'

'Josh wiped a bogie on your car!'

'Well, Josh better wipe it off.' Scratch that – he'd just smear it into the upholstery. Marshall knew he wouldn't be the one cleaning the car, but he had to wipe that off before he turned it in at the end of the shift. Knowing what some of his colleagues were like, Josh's may not have been the first. People always asked what it was like being in a police car – the truth was it was like any other car, only less hygienic.

He pulled in opposite a post-war bungalow. The lane seemed to lead way off into the hills. Maybe a favourite with dog walkers like Rachel's neighbour, but this morning it seemed like a scene from a frozen version of Hell, the ruts covered in black ice. 'Okay, kids. You'll be good for your granny, okay?'

'Sure thing, Mr Policeman.'

Marshall opened the door like he was letting Zlatan out of his box after a visit to the V-E-T.

Josh shot out of the car and raced up the path to the house. He thumped on the door and did a nose trumpet at his sister. 'I won!'

Kids had that capacity to amaze him. They were totally oblivious to what'd happened to their parents. Sure, they'd bear the scars for the rest of their lives, but right now...

Marshall had to find their mum.

The door opened and a slender woman stepped out. Jeans and tight T-shirt that exposed a lot of arm. Could easily pass for Rachel Lorimer's sister. Marshall wondered if it actually was, except for the fact the kids wrapped themselves around her and shouted, 'Granny!' She narrowed her steely-grey eyes at Marshall and patted their backs. 'In you go, kids. Telly's on.'

'Yay!' They raced inside the house and the TV volume

swelled with the inane chaos of a morning show. Very different from the tedious old-person gameshows Marshall would have to endure on days off school.

She folded her arms. 'You don't look like a friend of my daughter's.'

'DI Rob Marshall.' He held out his warrant card. 'Need to talk to you—'

'Aye, I know about Justin. Some female came yesterday with Rachel, saying how he's dead. Saw the body myself yesterday.'

'Right.' She hadn't been there when Marshall had taken Rachel in. Must've been Elliot or someone in Siyal's team. 'I'm not here about that. Sorry, I didn't get your name?'

'Joan Glisson.' Her eyes narrowed that little bit further. 'Kids are here, but my daughter's not. Where is she?'

'We believe Rachel's been abducted.'

'What?' She screwed up her face. 'What are you talking about?'

'When did you last hear from her?'

'Last night. She was working the late shift. Covered the last train from Edinburgh. Sometimes she can pick up a drunk from Eskbank or Gorebridge who's fallen asleep and she'll drive them back up there. Can be quite lucrative.'

'Were you with her kids?'

'Free babysitting, aye.'

'Have you heard from your daughter this morning?'

'Aye, first thing. Back of six.' She pulled out a high-end smartphone from her jeans pocket. 'Said she'd call when she was leaving.'

'And did she?'

'No.'

'That didn't concern you?'

'Thought she wasn't up yet. Falls back to sleep a lot. Late

shift takes it out of her.' She dug her fists into her hips. 'Besides, her husband's dead.'

'And I'm truly sorry about that, Joan.'

'Still, even I found it a bit odd how she was out working last night of all nights. I tried talking to her, but my girl's very headstrong. She said she needed to work. Things are super tight with them. And it'll only get worse.'

'Sorry to hear that.'

She flared her nostrils. 'What do you think's happened?'

'We believe she's been abducted.'

'You can't honestly think that?'

'We do.' Marshall stared hard at her. 'Those two grandchildren of yours were taped up and left on the sofa while someone took her away.'

Joan looked back into the house, her forehead pulsing.

'Do you have any idea why someone might abduct her?'

'I've no clue, son. None at all. And I'm completely mystified over what happened to her husband too.'

'Do you look after them a lot?'

'Evenings when they're both at work, aye. Usually three nights a week. Sometimes four.'

'But he works on a farm. That's seasonal labour.'

'Justin was in the pub a lot. If you ask me, I think he was an alcoholic. Rachel was a bit worried. He said the pub is where a lot of business gets done.'

'What kind of business?'

'I don't know.'

Marshall could see the little gap in the case being filled if he wasn't careful. Pringle would plunge both hands in and make the hole wide enough to drive a conviction through. 'Joan, if that business relates to drugs, then—'

'*Drugs*? Justin? No way.'

'Are you—'

'How dare you?' She lurched forward like she was going to slap him but seemed to think better of it. 'How *dare* you?' Her voice was thin and shrill.

'It's a possibility. The people who killed your son-in-law and another victim used a similar methodology to criminal gangs who—'

'There's just *no* way he was involved in drugs. He was a churchgoing man.'

'Persuade me.'

'I will.' She was shaking her head hard enough to jostle her hair. 'Justin? Drugs? No way.'

There wasn't anything to back up her assertion.

'You said things were tight.'

'They were. Raising two kids on their wages... But really? If he was bringing in drug money, they'd have plenty to go around, wouldn't they?'

Fair point, but also far from conclusive.

Marshall saw a woman who didn't know who her daughter had married.

Maybe.

Or he was clutching at the same bundle of straws as Pringle.

'Did Justin ever talk—'

His phone blasted out.

Shite.

He should've muted that. Highly professional... Still, the welfare of those kids had to take precedence.

He slid it out of his pocket and checked the display:

DS Jolene Archer calling...

'Sorry, I better—' He looked up, but all he saw was the door slamming.

That was going to bite him on the arse, no doubt.

He answered the call. 'Hey, what's up.'

'Rob, I'm still at Rachel's. Forensics aren't here yet, but uniform have arrived.'

'Okay. Do you need me to call Kirsten?'

'Sally's on her way now, so no. But I'm going door-to-door with DC Paton and we might have something. Neighbour on the other side from the wee man we spoke to earlier, Mylo's owner. She saw Rachel getting out to defrost her car. Back of seven. Then a van turned up. Thought it was a delivery. Next time she looked out, the van was gone.'

'Did she get a plate?'

'Hardly. Black Mercedes one, though.'

'Definitely?'

'Definitely.'

'So, it's different to the one we found burnt out.'

'Obviously. Doesn't mean it wasn't the same person or people.'

'No, that's very true. It's looking like she's been abducted. Get McIntyre to update the street CCTV for this morning and find that van.'

'On it. Oh, hang on.' She disappeared and all he heard was a muffled voice. 'Shunty's just called Paton. Hugo Baird's been abducted too.'

CHAPTER FIFTY

Marshall pulled off the roundabout but didn't have to look too far to spot where he needed to be.

The blue-and-yellow Battenberg livery of two squad cars glowed in the low light levels. Daylight, sure, but only just.

He pulled in behind them and got out. Mercifully it was raining – hopefully that'd wash away the snow throughout the day and not leave the whole county slicked in black ice. The air was heavy with the fug of fuel from the cars whizzing past on the Melrose bypass.

Elliot stood between the squad cars, hands on hips, as she berated some poor sods just trying to do their jobs.

Behind her, the industrial estate clanked and clattered. Kind of places that started and finished early. Maybe people saw something, maybe not. Marshall only knew the brewery there from a lost afternoon in the tap room with Jen and Kirsten.

'You daft bastard!' Elliot prodded one of the uniforms. 'You need to find that fucking van!'

'Hey, hey.' Marshall got between them. He recognised the uniform – Stish. Geordie lad, mate of Liam Warner. Colleague, anyway. Whether they were friends was a stretch. But he looked like he was going to lamp Elliot. 'Can you two canvass the businesses and get hold of the CCTV?'

'Sure thing, sir.' Stish's mate clamped a shovel-sized fist around his arm and hauled him away.

Elliot was struggling to control her nostrils. 'Fucking hell, Marshall. They'll let anyone join the force these days.'

'You need to calm down.'

'Me?'

'Aye, you. Shouting at those guys won't help anyone. They're just doing their job, same as you. Give them a bit of respect and they'll repay it with hard work.'

'Sounds like bull—'

'*Andrea*. Why aren't you answering your phone?'

'Because I'm trying to shepherd cats here! Swear, those two couldn't find their arses with both hands and a torch.'

'I need you to focus.'

'You *need* me to, do you?' Elliot laughed. 'You're not my boss.'

'No. But if I'm having to do your job for you as well as my own, then we're not going to find them.'

She scowled at him. '*Them?*'

'Them. Both Hugo Baird and Rachel Lorimer are missing.'

'What?'

'Seems like they were abducted around the same time.'

'Shite.' Her mouth hung open. Weird seeing Elliot shocked. Seeing her humbled for a second. Looking older, beaten down, haggard, not sleeping, consumed by this case. Bloody hell, was she human after all? 'Shite.' She looked up at Marshall. 'What happened?'

'Jolene and I found the kids tied up and left on her sofa. She's running a door-to-door search around Stow and we're trying to access this morning's CCTV. Early reports are it looks like Rachel was bundled into a van. How about you tell me what's happened here?'

'We have a witness here.' Elliot waved at the nearest squad car. Marshall hadn't noticed the two people sitting in the back, out of the rain. 'Mike Hay there was cycling to Tweedbank station for the eight fifty train to Edinburgh. He saw a van nudge a car off the road. Happened really quickly.'

'Eight fifty's a while ago. Why's he here to tell you about it?'

'Because he stopped to call it in and missed the train.'

'Better to have a conscience later than not at all, eh?'

'Right. Exactly.' She swept a hand across the industrial estate behind a thick wood. 'A lot of development going on. Engineering firm are fitting out a massive new building. That huge pile of earth... Rumour was it will become a Lidl. Or a Premier Inn. Or a drive-through Greggs. Doubt we'll get any CCTV here. Pretty quiet too. Everyone's either going into Melrose or through to Gala. The big Ashworth's is at the next roundabout, a few miles away. Pretty much the perfect spot to abduct someone.'

'I can think of a lot better ones.'

'Aye, but he was on his way to his mother-in-law's in Darnick. Think they nudged him off the road here. Grabbed him, left his kid with his phone. From what the little guy says, the bad man shoved him in the back of the van.'

'Where is he?'

'Back with the nanny.'

'Right.' Marshall tried to picture it. The car was up a little side lane leading to some factories. At an odd angle, like it had just stopped rather than the driver parking. 'You think Rachel Lorimer was in there too?'

'Hard not to, eh? And if she wasn't, I think it's the same people who did it. Same MO. So they probably know where she is.' Elliot stared hard at him. 'Listen. That thing last night, the matter I wanted to discuss with you... it's about Shunty. More importantly, his appraisal.'

She was picking a weird time. Then again, she seemed a bit thrown by this, looking around the scene, clearly out of her depth. Tugging at her hair. The almighty Andrea Elliot, looking more wounded than when she had a knife in her and half her guts hanging out on the floor.

But sometimes people lashed out when they were backed into a corner.

'Can we do this later?'

'Paperwork's due in today, Marshall. As you know.'

'Jolene's was filed two weeks ago.'

She smirked at him. 'Swot.'

'I don't see why his appraisal affects me.'

'You were his line manager while I was off sick for a few months. Bottom line, Marshall... I don't think he's cutting the mustard. But I'm worried about putting him on an actioned contract.'

Marshall felt the news like a jab in the guts. 'That's a big step.'

'It's needed. He's not a cop and needs some hard lessons to become one.' She tucked her damp fringe behind her ear. 'Thing is, that whole generation make a lot of noise about the tiniest thing. Micro-aggressions. They're constantly harping on about their mental health. Seriously, don't do a job where you might have to scrape a junkie off train tracks then inter-view a child molester if you're that—' Her gaze was caught by something.

Marshall swung around and saw a classic BMW pull up. 'Let's park this, shall we?'

Pringle got out of the car. 'Ho-chee mama.' He sucked in a deep breath. 'This is a hot damn mess and a half, Charlie.' His gaze wildly flitted between the pair of them. He'd finally cracked. 'Riddle me this – why has someone targeted both couples?'

Marshall smiled to try and bring him down to planet Earth. 'That's the key question for me, sir. The day after we find two bodies, their spouses get taken.'

Pringle laughed. 'What some people won't do for a little marital peace and quiet!' He fixed Marshall with a hard stare. 'If they're both dead, we're goosed...'

Marshall saw a guy who was out of his depth. All the crazy banter and joking was just bluster. There was a reason he'd been shoved down here – he could do the least harm in a backwater like this. Having someone exotic like Marshall on the payroll made him seem useful to the brass. Police Scotland's own criminal profiler. But he wasn't capable of dealing with a complex inquiry like this. 'Look, sir, I've been thinking about the drug angle. There are pieces missing here, but these two being abducted at the same time and in the same way shows there's a connection. Andrea talks about it maybe being a coincidence, but I think we can rule that out. This is being done for a reason. Trouble is, we don't see why yet.'

'So you think it could be drug-related?'

Marshall stood back and thought it all through. The cold rain poured down on him, soaking through his coat and his suit jacket. 'Let's build a hypothesis about that. Justin worked at Blainslieshaw Mains farm. A farm's a good way to get drugs in, right? Lots of big deliveries of stuff in bulk. Plenty of places to store stuff, even to grow it. Nobody around most of the time, so it's discreet. And Rachel worked as a taxi driver, which is a good way to distribute drugs.'

'A-ha!' Pringle grinned wide. 'See, even Dr Donkey agrees with my gut instinct.'

Marshall raised both hands. 'Hang on. I'm just spit-balling here.'

'But I like the spit and I *love* your balls.'

Marshall glanced at Elliot, but she was staring into space and barely paying attention. 'I don't see how it connects to an oncologist and a local lawyer. There's got to be a connection. But we just don't see it.'

'Were they swingers?'

Elliot laughed. 'Seriously? No. We've asked around and not one single person on either side knows the other.'

Marshall frowned. 'That's not quite true. Louisa Baird was Rhona Rattray's oncologist. Justin worked for the family.'

'Right, but that's Kevin Bacon degrees of separation, there.'

'Mmm, bacon.' Pringle slapped his hands together. 'I want all of those statements printed out and put on a table, then the three of us, the brains trust, can smack our noggins together and see what we're missing.'

'Maybe.' A thought jabbed Marshall like an ice-pick to the brain. 'Look, Rachel's mother babysat for the kids most nights. She said Lorimer was doing business most evenings, the kind you do in pubs.'

Elliot rolled her eyes. 'Drinking?'

'That's what she thought. But what if he was dealing to people who drank. The Stagehall Arms is a busy pub, fair amount of trouble. Barman in there turns a blind eye to most infractions.'

'That's not true.' Elliot grinned. 'Shunty's got a long list of them, most of which are actually enforced.'

'But shifting grams of coke from the toilet? Bags of skunk? Heroin? Ecstasy? Spice?'

'We've nothing to suggest they're doing that.'

Pringle nodded. 'No, but we need to find out the art of the possible on this, the absence of "no" vis-à-vis "maybe, yes". If you know what I mean, say no more, say no more!'

Marshall stared hard at him. 'Okay, I'll pick up with Drugs on that and—'

'You can piss right off on that, Robbie.' Elliot was shaking her head. 'Drugs is my world. Sat through all those stupid meetings, so I should at least get some of the action.'

Pringle folded his arms. 'Number one priority is finding them.' He looked at Marshall. 'For Andrea. I've got something else for you, dear doctor.'

'Wait, what?'

'It's something *shiny*.' Pringle smiled at Elliot. 'Fly free, my lovely! Go and see what carrion your birdies have called forth.'

Elliot narrowed her eyes a bit, then seemed to process it. 'I'll let you know.' She turned around and walked off towards the industrial estate.

Pringle wrapped an arm around Marshall's shoulder. 'Rob Marshall. Robbie Marshall. Bob Marshall. Robert Marshall. Marsha Roberts. Bobo Mar Shall. Marshall Law!'

'It's Rob, sir. Thanks.'

'Sure.' Pringle sniffed. 'That was some very quick thinking there. I love the cut of your jib. We'll be able to put some colouring in between your pencil lines.' He laughed. 'Actually, Andrea's not quite graduated to crayons yet, but she does her best.'

Marshall put his hands deep into his pockets. 'What's up, sir?'

'Hate to take you off that strand, but we're a bit stretched and I need your expertise.' Pringle licked his lips. 'Napier Rattray died overnight.'

'Oh. What happened? Was he murdered?'

'God no! Nothing untoward. At least, not on that score. They just agreed to turn off his ventilator. Beep beep beeeeeeeep. End of story.'

'Okay, so why's this sitting with us?'

'Because Andrea and I worked it back when he fell. And we're treating it as a murder now.'

'Why?'

Pringle leaned in. 'Because Andrea heard from a little birdie that it was murder...'

'A little birdie?'

'She received some credible intel.' Pringle's mobile rang. He checked the screen and put it away again. 'Do I have to spell everything out to you?'

'It'd certainly help, sir. What was the nature of this?'

'According to said avian informant, it was no accident, but an attempt to scare him. Sadly, it resulted in him falling from a wind turbine. So that part's true – was an accident on that score. But we gather someone forced him to take a fall. Pride goeth before the fall... *Pride and Prejudice.* Pride in the name of love. Not that it's the fall that kills you, mind, more the last several inches... That's what she said!'

'Who gave her that info?'

'It's a CHIS, Marshall.'

'This all sounds like bollocks. I need to—'

'Nope. You know I can't just give you the name of another officer's covert human intelligence sources.'

'Come on. If I'm to treat it as a murder, then—'

'It's all in the log. Captain's log, stardate January 2023.' Pringle whistled and made shadow puppets with his fingers. 'Now, the sooner you can tie this back to the drugs stuff going on at the farm, the better. Right now, Napier Rattray's body is lying in BGH. Do we send him to a funeral home or to pathology?' His phone rang again. 'Buggeration.' He scurried off back to his car, putting the phone to his ear, then getting in and driving off.

What the hell was that all about?

CHAPTER FIFTY-ONE

'I don't get it, Rob.' Jolene was in the passenger seat, arms folded. 'I worked that case with them. Why do they now think it's a murder?'

'Intel.' Marshall powered up the brae through the driving rain. The hills up here even had some green breaking through. Good to get away from all that bloody snow. 'According to Pringle, it's come from a confidential source.'

'So we've no idea who it is and we have to investigate?'

'Doing our duty.'

'I don't get how Pringle thinks this is connected to the case, though.'

'He's clinging to a drug angle. I mean, I kind of fed him it, but...' Marshall passed the spot where the bodies were found. Aside from an indentation in the snow, now partly replaced with yesterday's fresh fall, you wouldn't know anything had happened here. Deep time, as his former therapist would say – up on these hills, nothing much happened for thousands of years. Millions, probably. Not so much history or geography as geology.

'You fed him it?'

'Rachel's mum mentioned something to me. About how she didn't know what he was up to in the Stagehall Arms.'

'We've had people in there speaking to the locals and nothing's come up.'

'Sure.' Marshall smiled at her. 'People who spend significant amounts of time in the same pub are very reliable and always tell the truth. About the only thing that lot are reliable about is polishing their seats with their bums.'

'I see your point.'

Marshall took the right turn, then powered down the road towards the farm, probably the best-gritted in the Borders, and passed into the thick woods, then out into the approach to the grand old house.

A cleaning van was parked there now. Mop Top Cleaning Services Ltd with a Beatles-esque cartoon chimney sweep.

Marshall pulled up between it and Balfour's Land Rover. 'Wonder if they're here to clear up the haggis?'

'Why do businesses do that?'

'Do what?'

'Put the "Ltd" bit as their branding. Nobody cares about how you manage your tax affairs. Just call it Mop Top Cleaning and be done with it.' She sighed and got out, then crunched over the gravel towards the Blainslieshaw Mains farmhouse, head low like she could duck out of the rain.

Marshall followed her over and pulled the chain for the door, which set off a cascading series of bells inside.

The door opened and a familiar face popped his head out. Kyle Talbot, wearing his work gear. 'Alright. DI Marshall, isn't it?'

'That's right. Wondering if—'

'Just getting my lunch, eh? You looking for me?'

'Not this time. You heading off?'

'Aye. It's a bit shambolic today. The snow's all melty, which makes things a bit precarious. Going to head off, as my Xbox is getting lonely. Boss approved it, before you ask.'

'Is Rhona Rattray about?'

Talbot nodded. 'Left us all a massive roast lunch, then headed to the chapel.'

'You know where that is?'

'Nope. Just a sec.' He disappeared back inside.

Marshall stepped up to the top step.

A familiar face appeared – Gundog, Balfour's mate. But his forehead was all creased. 'Can I help?'

'Looking for Balfour or Rhona.'

'Ah, yes. Well, Rhona's in the chapel. Asked not to be disturbed.'

'Okay. And Balfour?'

'That's the thing.' The forehead creased even further. 'I've been looking for him for a while. Need him to pay my cleaners, otherwise they won't start.'

'When did you last see him?'

'About an hour ago. He was going to do a bit of mechanical work. Fix up the old motor. Needed to clear his head after, you know...'

Marshall nodded. Seemed to be the way of it here – solve your grief by losing yourself in work. 'You know where?'

'There's a big garage out the back. Come on.' Gundog set off across the pebbles, heading away from the cars.

Marshall struggled to keep up with his very, very quick march. 'How did he seem?'

'Balf? Broken.' Gundog shook his head. 'I've known him a few years and he's usually able to put a brave face on stuff. But today... Nope.' He stopped and pointed at a ramshackle brick garage. 'Might be in there.'

'Thanks.' Marshall walked over. No sounds of clanking or

clattering, but the deep rumble of an engine. He tried the door and it squeaked as it opened.

A classic BMW sat there, headlights on full, engine running. The room tasted of bitter petrol. A pipe ran into the driver's window.

Marshall raced across the frozen ground and tore open the door. Coughing hard.

Balfour was slumped forward.

Something clattered and fell out. A silver hip flask. Empty, but putrid whisky dribbled out.

Marshall shook him. 'Balf!'

'Roberto? Is that you?' Balfour focused on Marshall. 'I see three of you, Roberto. Which one is you?'

'All of them.' Marshall grabbed him and dragged him out of the car, across the pebbles. 'Jolene! Get an ambulance! Now!' He focused on Balfour. 'What are you playing at?'

'Father!' Balfour grabbed Marshall's sleeve. And passed out.

He was clutching some papers.

Marshall picked it up. Legal letterhead.

CHAPTER FIFTY-TWO

Elliot pulled up on Scott Street in Galashiels. A long row of tenement flats, with various businesses operating on the ground floor. Mostly hairdressers. Way too many, in fact. And she'd lived down here most of her life but didn't know anyone who had their hair cut here.

Shunty looked up from his phone. 'This is where I arrested that guy.'

'What guy?'

'Drug dealer.'

'Oh, right, aye.' Elliot knew who he was talking about. One of the links in the chain that led to her guts being opened up like she was on a butcher's block.

The paper shop on the corner was doing brisk business, with two older couples lurking outside to discuss the weather. Probably.

Mercifully, Scott Street Hardware was open. Sacks of wood and coal were stacked up on both sides of the door. Big pipes of snow salt. And Gary Hislop stood in the middle of the doorway, the maroon apron covering his shirt and trousers matched the shop's logo. Looked even more like a car salesman.

Elliot looked over at Shunty and made eye contact. 'You're staying here.'

He glowered at her. 'Why?'

'Because I said so. Adults are talking.' She reached into the door pocket and grabbed a bag of crisps, then tossed them onto his lap. 'Here.'

'I'm not a child.' Still, he looked at them. 'And these are bacon flavoured!'

'Aye, flavoured! There's no bacon in them.' She grabbed them back and tapped on the little green symbol on the back. 'Not even vegetarian – they're fully vegan!' She flung them back at him, then got out.

Useless sod. Even worse than her oldest.

Aye, that contract was going to be an action one. He needed to shape up or ship out.

Elliot walked up to Hislop, tucked her hair back, then smiled her best smile. 'Morning, Gary.'

'Morning, Andi. Been a while.'

She gave him a flash of her eyebrows. 'Hasn't it just?'

'What are you after?'

'Got this smell I can't seem to shift.'

'In your car?'

'No, it's everywhere.'

'Got a few things that could help with that.' Hislop walked inside the shop.

The place was a rabbit warren of tight shelves, at least two rows more than there should be. Each shelf was filled with a view to maximising the variety of products. Twenty-odd flavours of air freshener, all in a row, one by one. All the shapes and sizes of screw you could want.

'Have to say, Gary, I'm astonished this business can survive with that B&Q in Gala.'

'Screwfix opened in December too.' Hislop stopped at the end of the row and squatted low. 'Some folk like things done the old-fashioned way. It's not just about selling stuff *to* them. It's about telling them what to do with their purchases. Helping them solve their problems. Or just listening to them.'

Elliot joined him in the crouch. Made her stomach wound throb a bit. She tried to battle through it. 'So, if I bought a load of duct tape and some cable ties, you'd tell me how to abduct two people?'

Hislop stared at her, then laughed. 'That's a good one. Give me a saw and some wood, and I'll tell you how to build a coffin.'

'Will you help me bury it?'

'Depends who you've killed.'

'Not talking about murder, Gary.'

'Oh? It was that yesterday.'

'That was then. This is now. Two abductions this morning.'

A frown flashed across his forehead. Seemed genuine. Whoever did it, Hislop didn't know. He rose to his feet. 'That's worrying.'

Elliot stood up again. 'You know—'

'Nope. I don't know anything about it. Any of it. Am I making myself clear?'

'Crystal. Smeared and wiped clear with some of your best products. Thing is, we did have another two murders overnight. Someone was dumped out of a moving vehicle. And someone else burnt to death.'

He looked away, rubbing at his neck. 'What's happening to this town?'

'Poor sod who was barbecued goes by the name of Iain Caddon.'

Hislop swung back to focus on her. 'What?'

'Goes by "Baseball". You know him?'

'Aye, big daft sod from Hawick. Known him for years. He came in here at the start of the pandemic. Just before the very first lockdown. He'd been smoking this really strong stuff and was paranoid as hell. Convinced himself the world was going the full *Walking Dead*. Wanted to hammer some nails into a bat like the boy from that. The evil one. The boss.'

'Negan.'

Hislop clicked his fingers and pointed at her. 'That's the boy. See, you and me really do have similar tastes.'

'Hardly. I gave up watching at that point.'

Hislop chuckled. 'Anyway. Had to explain to Caddon that you can't hammer nails into a metal bat.' He laughed. 'Not the sharpest tool in this shop.' He picked up a battery-powered jigsaw, navy and lime green. 'No idea if he ever did it, but he did buy a pack of nails.'

'Sad to say, your pal's dead.'

'Not my pal, Andi.'

'Know anything about his death?'

'Nope.' He put the jigsaw back down. 'When did he die?'

'Early hours of this morning.'

'Like midnight?'

'Three, we think.'

'Right. Who was the other murder?'

'Steven Beattie.'

His eyes went wide. Another genuine shock. 'Wow.'

'You know him?'

'Had to ban him.' Hislop picked up a hammer from a rack. 'Tried stealing one of these.'

'You stopped him?'

'Aye. Not difficult. Off his face, to be honest. Drink with

that one. Fell over on his way out the door. Last time I saw him.'

She waited for him to look up from his wistful memories. Took almost a minute. 'You can understand that the powers that be are a bit concerned over how we've had four murders in two nights, then two abductions this morning. Especially when these two abductions are related to Wednesday's.'

'How so?'

'Husband of one, wife of the other.'

He shook his head. 'You're kidding me.'

'Nope. Hugo Baird and Rachel Lorimer.'

Hislop gave a shrug. 'Don't know either.'

'Abducted first thing. School run o'clock, really. Both cases, looks like their kids were seemingly used as leverage.'

'Maybe Baseball was right – this world's getting worse and worse.'

'I'd appreciate if you could ask your mates in the rugby club about them.'

'Sure.' He looked at her and nodded. 'Of course.'

'Let me know what it costs.'

'On the house, Andi.' He held her gaze, his tongue tracing the bottom of his top lip. 'You do anything with what I gave you yesterday?'

'I passed on the information.'

'Oh.' Hislop's eyebrows shot up. 'That's interesting.'

'How?'

'Didn't take credit for it yourself?'

'I'm a team player, Gary.'

'Sure. I believe that.' He chuckled. 'You're a self-centred woman, Andi. One of the things I love about you. Means you're driven and focused. But also means you're selfish.'

She leaned in close. 'Level with me here. Are you playing me?'

'Someone who was playing isn't going to level—'

'I'm serious.'

'Why would you think that?'

'We're building up a picture. Seems like everything centres around Blainslieshaw Mains farm. Thing is, we wouldn't have that clue if it wasn't for you talking to me about Napier Rattray last night.'

'That was just me passing on rumours, Andi. Old lover to old lover.'

'That wasn't love.'

'Sure felt like it, though.'

'Gary.' She stepped close enough to taste his aftershave. 'Was Rattray running an operation rivalling yours?'

He laughed. 'Running a hardware store from a farm?'

'Drugs, Gary. Was he running drugs?'

'I don't run drugs.'

'Bullshit.'

'I'm a legitimate businessman and you can't prove otherwise. Now, maybe the Rattrays *are* up to no good, but I don't know anything about it. All I've done is speak to some people and get you a lead. What you choose to do with that is up to you. Did it get you anything?'

'Not sure yet. Napier Rattray died last night.'

'Oh, that's sad.' He huffed out a deep coffee-breath sigh. 'I'll have to pay my respects to Rhona and Balf.'

'You told me it was a threat gone wrong. That whoever tried to intimidate him went over the score. Was it Caddon?'

'I don't know, Andi. My information is anonymous.'

She brushed her hair out of her eyes again. 'It's a big coincidence that you grass up someone doing something, then the likeliest culprit is found burnt to death in a van.'

'Listen to me. I don't know anything about that.'

'That how you're playing it, eh?'

'These are just rumours. And I'm just trying to help you.'

'Well, I appreciate it. I do. But if you could ask around about these abductions.'

'Consider it done.'

The door tinkled.

A tall old man shuffled in. 'Morning, Gary. My shovel's broken. Handle snapped clean off.'

Hislop narrowed his eyes. 'See you around, Andi.'

'You've got my number, big boy.' She left the shop but had to wait for a car to pass.

'You shovelling snow yourself, Davie? Told you to get some salt instead. Come on.' Hislop popped back outside, not far from her. 'Pipe of this snow salt will last you till next winter. No sliding around on your path. Your postie will thank you for it.'

'Sure about that?'

'Aye, wouldn't sell it if I didn't use it myself. See when someone comes to your door in the dead of night, they'll not complain about the snow and ice.' Hislop looked over at Elliot and winked. 'You get your will updated, Davie?'

What was he playing at?

'Not yet, Gary. No. Been a wee bit under the weather. That cold that's going around.'

'Aye, had it myself. Makes it all the more important, Davie. I've been doing a bit of estate planning.'

Davie laughed. 'Never know when you might pop your clogs, eh?'

'Exactly. Want my affairs to be in order. Went to Baird & Cruikshank down on Overhaugh Street. Strong recommendation from Napier Rattray.'

Bingo.

Wait.

Napier Rattray was a client of Hugo Baird?

How the hell had that not come up?

Elliot darted across to the pool car. Had to wait for another car to pass, then she got behind the wheel.

Shunty was folding his crisp bag into a weird series of triangles. 'What was that all about?'

She put the key in and twisted it like a neck. 'You enjoy them?'

'Not bad.' He put the tiny triangle into his pocket. 'Seriously. What were you doing in there?'

'Needed some screws.'

'Come on. You might think it, but I'm not an idiot.'

She set off into the traffic, heading for the centre of Gala. 'Shunty, you have no idea what I think. Bless your heart, you never will.'

CHAPTER FIFTY-THREE

Jesus Christ, what a mess.

The blue lights of the ambulance pulsed across the snow.

Marshall swallowed another freezing breath and looked across to the garage. The paramedics with Balfour. Heard their voices. Talking to him. Still alive. Still lucid.

Why the hell had he done it?

Losing his father was one thing. Anyone would be traumatised by that long, slow death. Well, most people would.

Thinking about it made Marshall's brain melt. He walked over to the garage.

The lead paramedic clocked him and raised his hands. 'Sorry, mate. Need to get him to BGH now.'

'How is he?'

'He's very lucky to be alive. Another few minutes and the carbon monoxide would've got him. As it is, well... It'll be touch and go about long-term brain damage.' The paramedics raised the gurney up to full height.

'Thank you.' Marshall stood there, watching the paramedics wheel Balfour away over to the ambulance.

Such a tragic waste. Both of Rhona's sons would be taken down at their own hand: Dalrymple by his lust for speed, Balfour by some hidden guilt.

And Marshall still clutched the document Balfour had been holding. He spotted a sign for the family chapel, so set off across the gravel, away from the garage and the flash of the lights.

Straight ahead, down a wee lane between two bum-height beech hedges. The chapel nestled in a small garden, hidden by towering trees on the other three sides. The polished sandstone walls glimmered in the sunlight, the arched stained-glass windows glowing.

'Sir.' Jolene crunched along behind Marshall. 'A lot of death around just now. Bet you thought it'd be quiet working down here.'

He didn't know what to say, so just nodded.

She led across the flagstones and inside the grand folly.

Candlelight cast shadows on the carvings of angels and saints decorating the walls. Rhona sat on her own in front of the oak altar. Dressed in black, except for a gleaming pearl necklace. She looked around at them, nodded, then returned to her grief.

Marshall walked over and sat along from her. 'Sorry to hear about your loss. I don't mind saying I really liked Napier. And that comes from the heart.' His voice echoed around the space like a hundred monks whispering scripture.

'Thank you.' Rhona smiled as Jolene sat on the other side, boxing her in. 'This place hasn't been used for years, not since Napier's mother passed away back in 2008.'

'It's beautiful. You must take great solace here.'

'No way.' Rhona looked around and seemed to shiver.

'Awful place, this. Ostentatious doesn't even begin to cut it. This family, I swear...' She shook her head. 'I go to the church in Stow. The minister is excellent and the community are very welcoming. I sat near Justin Lorimer and his family. They were very kind and accepting.'

'That must be a great comfort.' Marshall sat forward, still clutching the notepaper. 'I've got some bad news about Balfour.'

She looked around at him. 'What's happened?'

'There was an incident... in a garage.'

She put her hands to her mouth. 'Oh my.'

'Your son's on his way to hospital.'

She frowned. 'He's alive?'

'He survived what we believe is a suicide attempt.'

She got to her feet. 'Spend most of my life down at that infernal place.'

Marshall looked up at her. 'Rhona, the paramedics said he'll be a while getting treated.'

'Oh my.' She slumped back down on the bench with a crack. 'This luck I've had...'

'There's something else I need to discuss with you, unfortunately.'

Her fingers were twitching. Like most mothers, she wanted to be with her son. 'Go on?'

'We received some information suggesting your husband's fall wasn't an accident.'

'That... That can't be right.'

'Thing is, we really need to clear up the inheritance of this farm.'

'You think I pushed Napier?'

'No. I'm not saying that. But we received word that someone allegedly came to the farm to send your husband a message. We don't know what it was about, but word is it went too far. So your husband's fall was an accident, but not the way we've been led to believe.' Marshall waited until the monks stopped whispering. 'Do you know anything about that?'

'Of course not!' Her shout echoed around the room.

'Rhona, as I understand it, you and your son stand to inherit all of the money from the farm.'

She fixed him with a hard stare. 'You honestly come in here the day my husband dies and tell me my son's gone to hospital... Then you accuse me of murdering Napier?'

'Stands to reason, doesn't it?'

'I was the one keeping him alive!'

'And if not you, Rhona, then who? Who was behind it? Follow the money, they say. And it leads to who finally agreed to switch off his life support.'

'I can't believe I'm hearing this! I loved my husband. You've no idea just how much!'

Marshall unfolded the sheet of paper. 'Do you know what this is?'

She took a look at it. 'No.'

'A letter from your husband's solicitor, addressed to yourself. Is this him opening divorce proceedings?'

She was acting calm, but her bottom lip was trembling. 'If it was, that'd be news to me.'

'After your husband made this threat, the next thing we know he's fallen off a wind turbine. And the day after he actually dies, your son's trying to kill himself.'

'*Kill* himself?'

Marshall stared into space. 'He was drunk. Clutching this document.'

'I never received it.'

'You're sure of that?'

'Of course I am! As far as I'm concerned, what happened to Napier was a stupid accident.'

'Okay. I'll just have to take your word for it.' Marshall didn't move. 'Would help us greatly if you could give us some proof, though.'

'I know this game, Inspector.'

'It's basic detective work, yes. Follow the money.' Marshall looked around the chapel. 'Lot of it here.'

'And it's all tied up in complex trusts that I don't begin to understand.' Her head dipped. 'The truth is, nobody *inherits* Napier's money. They inherit the trust, which gives an income, sure, but a lot of pressure.'

'Would it be you or Balfour who takes over?'

'Not I.' She tugged at her white pearls. 'Napier removed me from his will and the family trust.'

'I'm sorry to hear that.'

'I doubt that very much.'

'So it's just your son who will inherit the farm?'

She shook her head. 'I don't know. My husband dealt with that side of things. Napier made it very clear that my role was to raise his children. Feed him and his men. Organise functions for his friends and family. But... When he removed me from the inheritance, it was...'

'That sounds like a painful experience.'

'It broke my heart.' She tugged at the pearls, so tight it looked like the necklace might snap. 'Listen to me. Whatever you think is happening here, it's not. You've painted me as some black widow figure who's paid someone to kill their husband after he initiated divorce proceedings.'

'I still need proof of what was actually happening.'

'That letter... I never received it, but I've seen it before. It's a draft version of what was to be issued. Balfour must've found it in his father's papers. I don't know. Napier was updating his will and the family trust. His legal documentation is all lodged with our law firm, so please take this up with them. I give you approval to access it.'

'That's very kind of you.'

'I have nothing to hide and the sooner you cross me off your list, the sooner you hold those responsible accountable for my husband's murder.' She stood up again. 'Now, if you'll excuse me, my son needs me more than you do. Good day.'

CHAPTER FIFTY-FOUR

Donald Cruikshank might be young, but he had that red-faced arrogance you got from all lawyers after a few years in the job. He even shut his eyes while he spoke, so sure he was that he was in the right here. 'Let me get this straight. You were here earlier and didn't ask anything about Napier Rattray, but seem to expect me to disclose an exhaustive list of not only all of *my* clients but *all* of my firm's clients? Is this supposed to happen every time a police officer visits a law firm, or just this office?'

'Not what I'm saying.' Elliot smiled back at him. She had that queasy feeling she got every time she dealt with a lawyer. Criminal defence were obviously the worst sort, but all solicitors were cut from the same cloth. Smooth, over-educated bastards who were just looking after the bottom line. Their own. Pretending to be protecting their clients, but Elliot knew it was all just to cover their own arses. 'Thing is, Donald, what you can't escape from is the truth of this matter. You're trying to make me look unreasonable, but you knew about this case. All about it. So when we turned up asking questions, you should've put two and two together. The lead labourer dies not far from the farm. An oncologist is killed leaving a Burns supper held there. Come on, it *must*'ve crossed your mind. Must've done.'

'Look.' He stared at her with the full force of his glare. 'I'm sorry, but what with Hugo going missing, everything's been a bit of blur.'

She smiled. 'I only just told you that now.'

'Aye, but... His wife died yesterday. And your oncologist. And him not turning up this morning...' Behind all the bluster, Donald Cruikshank was a man completely out of his depth. A good thirty years younger than Hugo Baird, he clearly looked to the older partner as a father figure and did everything he wanted. 'It's thrown everything up in the air. I'm holding the fort here, when the truth is I'm very much a junior partner.'

Elliot got up and walked around the office. The view looked across a little garden, some benches and tables soaking in the morning rain. Not a trace of any snow out there now. She turned around to face him but Shunty was in the way, so she shuffled over to the side a bit. 'When you join the dots on this case, Donald, it all seems to come back to a couple of things. First, that farm. Second, this law firm. Now, if I was in your shoes, I'd be—'

'Shouldn't you be out searching for Hugo?'

'We are. I've got thirty cops from this area and Edinburgh out doing precisely that. Takes a lot of mindless shoe leather to get a result on something like that. Mostly the explanations are prosaic and we can solve a case with just a little bit of knowledge. Someone saw someone doing something somewhere. But that's not all cases. Sometimes it takes an officer like me asking the right person the right question. Now, I'm confident we'll find your business partner, and hopefully safe and sound, but if I was in your shoes, Donald, I'd be trying to make sure none of this lands on your head.'

'None of what?'

'Any blame for what's happened to four people.'

'Four?' He drummed his fingers on the tabletop. 'Fine, I'll play ball with you, but just so you can get on with finding Hugo.'

'Great. So. My first question is, was Napier Rattray a client?'

'He was.'

'Did you know—'

'Rhona informed me this morning of her husband's passing.'

'Did you do anything in relation to their legal work?'

'Hugo was the lead on that client. He's been the family's lawyer since the Nineties. I know he took them and a few other clients when he set up his own firm with my father.'

That explained a lot – as her kids would say, Donald Cruikshank was a nepo baby.

He joined her in the window, looking out across the garden. 'We're hard up against it at the moment precisely because of Napier's ailing health. He'd asked for us to restructure certain aspects of the farming business in his will. Sadly, the matter of inheritance has now come to pass.'

'And that's what we're interested in.'

'I'm sorry, but that's going to need a warrant. It's highly sensitive material.'

'Is the sensitivity to do with the inheritance or your business?'

'Like I told you, anything more needs a warrant.' Cruikshank gestured towards the door. 'Now, I need to get on with some work. I've got clients waiting and I should be billing my time, not chatting.'

Elliot stared at him for a few seconds. He was bouncing off

the ropes. She'd get something else, then come back with a knockout blow. 'Fine.' She got up and left the office. 'Which way's reception?'

'Left, left, then right. Can't miss it.'

'Thank you.' She left the room and shut the door. But ignored the directions. 'The whole thing's perfect, Shunty. The way I see it, Hugo Baird worked indirectly for the farm as their lawyer. So Louisa's murder was a warning to him, taken too far. Justin Lorimer worked directly for the farm. His death was a warning to his wife and to Balfour. They were all in on it and whoever sent the warning wanted a piece of it.'

And she had a good idea of who wanted that piece. Gary Hislop. And she needed to flip this on its head and stop him using her.

Shunty was scratching his head. 'In on what?'

'Drug dealing.'

'Drug dealing?'

'There was a racket to bring drugs in through the farm, then distribute them through a taxi firm. How much of that is on the books?'

Shunty frowned. 'I've no idea.'

'I'm asking a hypothetical here. The money has to be some-where.' She tucked her hair behind her ear. Really needed to grow it out. 'Shunty, remember that call from Marshall I got you to bounce?'

'Right?'

'Call him back and see what it's about.'

He looked down his nose at her. 'What are you playing at?'

'Whatever he says, come back into that office and play along with me. Okay?'

'Okay...' Shunty got out his phone and put it to his ear.

Elliot opened the door without knocking. 'Mr Cruikshank,

I've got a few more things to run by you while my colleague chases up that warrant.'

Cruikshank looked up from his laptop then out at Shunty in the corridor, talking on the phone. 'Chases up?'

'I expected you'd be difficult, so we put in the request first thing. It'll be with us in less than an hour. Upshot is, it'd look pretty bad if you don't play ball. So. Are you going to answer my questions?'

Cruikshank sat back and slammed the laptop lid. 'Go on, then.'

'You're doing a lot of legal work for the farm. How can a dead man instruct you?'

'He didn't. Napier Rattray's wishes are documented, they just hadn't been formally actioned at the time of his injury. The requests for alteration came via the trust.'

'So they've been informally actioned?'

Cruikshank laughed. 'Sorry, I'm not following you here.'

'What work are you doing for them?'

'We're actioning them now. Blainslieshaw Mains has been governed under a trust for the last sixty years. It's standard practice for landowners on that scale. You save a fortune in inheritance tax. Sure, you pay a salary to the custodian, AKA this firm, but the legal side of things is boilerplate standard stuff. The taxman has a look at it and doesn't ask for a significant portion.'

'That's what you're working on?'

'Not entirely, no. Most of our work just now is in streamlining the trust for the twenty-first century. Removing layers and layers of caveats and subclauses. It'll be a much easier read for the layman or laywoman, trust me.'

'I'm not getting a warm, fuzzy feeling here.'

She heard Shunty stepping back into the room.

'You get that warrant, Sergeant?'

'Mr Cruikshank.' Shunty leaned across the desk. 'I've got a few questions to ask you about the inheritance of Napier Rattray's estate.'

'What do you mean?'

'Who's named on the will?'

Cruikshank looked away. 'I don't have the records to hand.'

'Sir, I'm a trained lawyer, so I'm happy to review them myself.'

'I can... That can be arranged.'

'But you've been working on it, right?'

'That's correct.'

'So you can at least summarise, right?'

Cruikshank sighed. 'What I know off the top of my head is we were to remove Dalrymple Rattray from the inheritance chain after his accident. We've created a separate trust to look after him in perpetuity, but that was funded by his insurance settlement from his accident. The car that hit him was deemed to be liable and the insurers had to pay millions.'

'Who is actually named, then? Balfour? Rhona?'

'Half of it goes to Balfour, but the other half...'

CHAPTER FIFTY-FIVE

Marshall trotted along Overhaugh Street as quickly as he could, tugging his coat collar up to avoid the horrible rain. The bright days of the snow had been replaced by the grim overcast of rain. Up ahead, the Baird & Cruikshank sign swung in the wind, creaking with each sway. He clutched his mobile as he walked. 'Sir, if you could give me a call back, I'd appreciate it.' He decided to follow it up with a text and started tapping it out as he walked.

> Jim, can you call me back? Cheers, Rob

He looked up and noticed Elliot and Siyal leaving the office, then heading away from him, lost in their own conversation.

Marshall ran after them. 'Andrea! Rakesh!'

Neither paid any attention and got into their pool car.

Two can play at that game.

Well, three can.

Marshall opened the back door and got in.

'Jesus Christ!' Elliot had her pepper spray out, ready to fire. 'Marshall? What the hell are you doing?'

'Just seeing how the aftermath to my little chat with Rakesh went.'

'Just a sec, Rob.' Siyal was scribbling something down in his notebook.

Marshall focused on Elliot. 'Are you okay there?'

'No. Some big lump's got in the back of my car.'

Jolene got in the other side, lugging a heavy bag that stank of fat and vinegar. 'Here we go.'

Elliot scowled at her. 'What's this?'

'Lunch. Rob was getting as grumpy as my son, so I thought I'd treat you all. I've got three fish suppers and a white pudding for Shunty.'

Siyal looked up from his notebook with a snarl. 'I can't eat that.'

'Why?'

'It's made from beef fat. And the chips are cooked in beef fat.'

Jolene smiled at him. 'Just as well there's a vegan fryer and that's a vegan white pudding. Gluten-free batter too.'

'Oh. Wow.' Siyal hungrily snatched the package from her and tore it open.

'Starving.' Marshall opened his container and his mouth was actually watering. He snapped off a hunk of golden batter and crunched into it – way too hot, so he breathed all the fire out. Probably burnt his lips. But it tasted incredible.

The heat was steaming up the window.

Elliot leaned back against her headrest. 'That's my favourite chippy in Gala.'

Jolene nodded. 'Which is why I went there.'

'So.' Marshall finished swallowing down a handful of tangy chips. 'How did it go with Cruikshank?'

'Usual difficulty when dealing with our learned friends.' Elliot took a bite of fish, eyes closed. The heat didn't seem to bother her. 'Usual pushback, but it's a murder case.' She nudged Siyal with her elbow. 'Should've seen Shunty in there, though. Like a wee terrier. Well, a six-foot four terrier.'

'Six five.'

'Fuck off, you are?!' She tilted her head back, frowning. 'Anyway. He stormed into the room and got Cruikshank to play ball. Couldn't have done better myself.'

Marshall finished chewing. 'What did he say?'

'Told us about the work they did for the Rattray Estate. Shunty?'

Siyal held out a sheet of paper. 'Have a look.'

'My hands are too greasy.' Marshall bit another chip in half. 'What's the gist?'

'This is a photocopy of the notarised copy of the will. There could be a later one lodged with another law firm, of course.'

Elliot stabbed the air with a chip. 'And that's a matter which Shunty will be getting his guys to look into.'

Marshall blew out hot air. 'Bottom line?'

'Before his tumble...' Elliot chewed the chip. 'Napier Rattray updated his will to remove Rhona.'

Marshall nodded along with it. 'That all checked out?'

'Correct. But the juicy part is, the will was updated to go fifty percent to Balfour and fifty percent to Louisa Baird.'

CHAPTER FIFTY-SIX

'Louisa Baird?' Marshall almost dropped his chips. 'What?'

Siyal waved the pages in the air. 'Seriously.'

Marshall sat back in the seat and stared down at his half-eaten fish. Golden batter snapped in half, steam still wafting off it. 'How? Why?'

'Took another bit of Shunty magic to get that.' Elliot rummaged around in her box for more little chips. 'Honestly, Marshall, it was like seeing two prize fighters going at it.'

'Why the hell is Louisa inheriting the farm?'

'Cruikshank says she's Napier Rattray's illegitimate daughter.'

'Seriously?'

'Seriously. Napier felt guilty about excluding her from his life. After all, she'd looked after his wife during her bout of cancer. Huge pang of guilt, so he updated it to replace his wife's share with hers.'

'How did Rhona take it?'

'She disapproved, of course. Said it should all go to their

son. Her son, of course. Not half to his "bastard daughter", as Cruikshank described it. But a prenuptial agreement prevented Rhona from inheriting anything unless expressly stated.'

Marshall ate the last soggy bit of fish and thought it all through. 'We've been looking at this from a spurious drug-dealing angle, when it could be that Balfour Rattray is the one who paid someone to kill Louisa so he inherited the whole farm.'

Jolene was about to eat a chip, but she slapped it back down. 'He just tried to kill himself!'

Elliot scowled at her. 'What are you talking about?'

'Hosepipe to the exhaust job.'

'Christ.'

Siyal held his white pudding like a cigar. 'That could be a ruse.'

'A ruse?' Jolene laughed. 'You don't try to kill yourself for a *ruse*.'

Elliot's gaze shifted between them. 'I think it's much more likely to be guilt. Tried to warn her off but it went to shit and she's ended up dead.' The gaze settled on Marshall. 'Stacking up for me here.'

He held her gaze. 'Andrea, this all stems from your intel about the murder.'

'I won't give up my source.'

Whoever she was protecting better be worth it.

Marshall picked up a chunky chip but didn't eat it. 'We're about to cause Balfour Rattray a world of pain. So I need to be on the same page as you.'

'You've got to trust me on this, Rob.'

'That's a big ask.' Marshall crunched a chip. 'Here's another question. Why were you at the law firm?'

Elliot glanced at Siyal. 'Just asking questions.'

'That old chestnut.' Marshall laughed. 'And in the real world, since we trust each other?'

Elliot couldn't maintain eye contact. 'The lad's business partner's been abducted, so of course we were here. I mean, it's basic police work.' She nudged Siyal again. 'Need to speak to the accountants and see how bent those books are. Going to take ages, Marshall. Shunty's going to follow up with them.'

She was still evading the truth but Marshall bet Siyal knew something about it. He'd prise the facts from him later.

'Okay.' Marshall took a tin of Irn Bru from the holder and popped it. 'We need to agree our theory regarding this case before Pringle can warp it into something else.'

Elliot grabbed her own can. 'You think there are still holes in it?'

'Sure. On the Justin Lorimer side. The same people have killed the guy who ran the farm and the woman who'd inherit half of it.'

'I think it's simple, Marshall. Someone paid these plonkers to abduct Lorimer and send him a message. Accidentally let him freeze to death. Same night, same story with Louisa Baird. Who was Balfour's half-sister and stood to inherit half of the estate. Despite what Pringle wants, they're not necessarily linked.'

Marshall sipped the cold drink. 'I'm happy to concede that whoever did this could've been sending a message to them both and things went too far. *Could've* being the operative word. But I'm still struggling to see what the message to Lorimer was.'

Elliot shrugged.

'So it's a coincidence?'

'You know I love a co-inkydink, Marshall.'

Jolene rolled her eyes.

'But, aye.' Elliot's mouth opened to reveal a half-chewed

mush of white fish and chips. 'Balfour was telling her to back away from the inheritance.'

'And, what, Kyle Talbot paid someone to teach Justin a lesson over some bar-room bullshit?'

'Hard to say. Thing is, we had a theory about drug dealing, but... This feels better. So much better. Louisa's side feels like something I can get my hands around.'

'Agreed, but Justin... It's just feels a bit nebulous.'

Jolene still had most of her fish left. 'The trouble is, he's dead now so won't answer any questions. Need to dig into his past. Could be he was responsible for the drugs.'

Marshall dropped a chip back into his tray. 'We don't actually have a single thread of evidence for drugs.'

'True, but this area has a massive drugs problem. The whole country does.' Elliot crumpled up her wrapper. 'They don't exactly put big signs up saying "pick your own heroin and crack" outside the farm, do they?'

Marshall laughed. 'Do I detect a note of sarcasm there?'

'Should do, cos it's dripping in it.'

Marshall sat back and chewed his chips, trying to think it all through. The confusion from hunger was now replaced with fatigue from over-eating. 'I do agree that we've got the spokes of a perfect drugs operation. Someone at the farm to bring the drugs in, someone in a taxi to sell them. And if Louisa's inheriting, then maybe...' No, it slipped out of Marshall's brain. He stared at Elliot. 'Who gave you the intel?'

'Not telling you that.'

'Come on. This is life or death. People are being murdered here. Louisa Baird, Justin Lorimer, Steven Beattie, Iain Caddon. Hugo and Rachel have been abducted, presumably dead. Balfour Rattray tried to kill himself. If the missing piece of this jigsaw is your source, then we should know that now.'

Elliot looked around and locked eyes with him. She stared at Siyal then Jolene. 'You two, can you give us a minute?'

Jolene swallowed a chip, eyes wide. 'Bugger off. It's pissing down out there.'

'Come on then, Andrea.' Marshall got out and waited for her. He had half his chips left and they could've done with more vinegar.

Elliot joined him in the rain and jabbed a finger at him. 'Don't question me like that in front of the children.'

'I'm just asking questions here, Andrea. We're building a house of cards and I need to know how sturdy those cards are.'

'The intel is legit.'

'So name your source.'

'I can't.'

'Come on, Andrea. This is critical to all of this. If this goes tits up, it's going to look bad on you. Nobody else. You.'

'Fine.' She walked over to the bin on the side lane up to Channel Street and stuffed her wrapper in. 'The intel came from Gary Hislop.'

Marshall let out a slow breath. 'He's not the kind of man who gives away intel lightly. Or cheaply.'

'He's bad news.'

'I know. Why's he told you about Napier Rattray?'

'Went to school with him. Year above me.'

'Andrea, the rumour is he's responsible for most of the drugs in the Borders.'

'Aye. Never shits where he eats, but he defecates everywhere else.'

Marshall looked at the dregs of his chips and couldn't face any more. He wrapped it up and stuffed it in the bin on top of hers. 'Lovely image.'

She was pointing at him. 'Don't you even *think* of going and speaking to Hislop.'

'Okay. We'll see what else we can shake out, but you better log it all.'

'Already done. That's what me and Jim were doing this morning instead of attending your dreary briefing.' She laughed. 'Way I see it, someone paid some of Hislop's guys to push Napier Rattray off that turbine.'

'You don't think it was Hislop?'

'Nope. I'm guessing the reason he's telling me is he found out way after the fact and isn't happy, so he's shoving them under the bus.'

'One of them being Caddon?'

She nodded. 'Almost literally. Assuming there's another.'

'You don't know who else?'

'Nope.'

'Fantastic...' Marshall laughed. 'That's all you got out of him? That someone pushed Rattray?'

'Aye, but it's opened this case wide, hasn't it?'

'Makes me think he wants that farm shut down.'

'Sure does.' Elliot tugged her damp hair behind her ear and stared at the ground. 'I've fucked up, Marshall. Bitten off more than I can chew for once. In waaaaay over my head.'

'Okay, but you've not done anything wrong. Right?'

She wouldn't look at him.

'All you've done is speak to an old schoolfriend, who's told you something and you've put some information into a log. You've opened up to me and Pringle about it.'

She made eye contact and nodded. 'Can't shake this feeling that I've sold my soul to the Devil and lost the receipt.'

Marshall smiled at her. 'Andrea, we're much better working together than as adversaries. We're all on the same side, okay?'

'Aye, fair dos. Robbie, you are a total bastard but you don't half talk sense at times.' Elliot walked off and got into the car.

Marshall looked up and down the street. He just didn't know what to think, other than for all her experience, she could be bloody naive at times. He got back into the car.

'Shunty!' Jolene threw a chip at Siyal. 'You weren't there!'

'You two!' Elliot was pointing at them both. 'Shut up!'

Marshall shifted his focus between their angry faces. 'What's going on?'

Jolene pointed at Siyal like a petulant child. 'He's calling you out for chasing after Balfour this morning.'

Marshall frowned at him. 'She's right, Rakesh. You weren't there. We might've saved his life.'

Siyal stared back at him. Looked like he was going to say something, but his phone rang. He checked the display. 'Better take this.' He answered it and looked away. 'What's up, Ash?' He turned back around. 'Got a possible sighting of Hugo Baird.'

CHAPTER FIFTY-SEVEN

Elliot hurtled along the snowy back road towards Langshaw, a tiny wee outpost between places. Might be all thawed out down by the rivers, but the snow was still lying up here. The dark sky even threatened a fresh dusting.

The Rattray clan owned the hilly fields to the left, but she'd no idea who the giant plantation opposite belonged to. And she should. It was her job to know this area and the people.

'How was your mealie pudding, Shunty?'

'My what?'

'Your white pudding.'

'Mealie?'

'Oatmeal. Mealie. White because of its colour and lack of blood.'

'Oh, right.' He grunted. 'First time I've had one.' The big lump burped into his fist. 'It was lovely.' He checked his phone. 'Next right.'

'Okay.' Elliot had to brake to take the turning down a narrow lane to a car park at the bottom of the plantation. A squad car sat in one bay, a red Volvo in another. A cop stood out in the rain, speaking to a man with two black dogs at the gate. She took the space furthest away and got out, then walked over and peered into the squad car.

Hugo Baird was on the back seat, shivering and naked save for a blanket. A female uniformed officer sat next to him, stroking his arm.

Elliot got in and knelt on the passenger seat. The engine was grunting away and the heating was up full. Felt hotter than her fish supper. She smiled at the female uniform, then rested a hand on Hugo's arm. Christ, he was freezing. 'Hey, there. How are you doing?'

'So cold.' When she'd seen him the previous day, Hugo Baird had been full of vigour, but right now, he looked his age. His skin was grey, his face washed out. 'So cold.' His teeth chattered, rattling like music coming from a drug dealer's car stereo.

'Did you see who took you?'

'Man in a balaclava. Tall. Big.'

'Did you get anything else?'

'Told your colleague here. He might've had grey or blue or green eyes.'

As useful as the description Rachel Lorimer's kids gave Marshall...

He looked up at her. 'Is Toby okay?'

The uniform stopped pouring tea into a Thermos lid and looked over. 'I told you, Hugo. He's fine. He's with your mother-in-law. She's looking after him.' She handed him his drink. 'Here you go. Should be cool enough to have straight away.'

'Thank you.' He sucked it and spilled some down his chin. 'So bloody cold.'

Elliot got a better look at him. Whoever attacked him had

really gone to town on him – big gouges taken out of his arms and legs. That wasn't just kicking and punching. It wasn't a baseball bat either. She couldn't see his ankles, but sure enough, he had the tell-tale marks around his wrists. The MO matched his wife's murder, and Justin Lorimer's. 'Hugo, I know this is maybe not the time, but I need to ask you a question.'

'Will it help you find who did this to me? Will it? Because if it does, I'll tell you my deepest secrets.'

'It might do, aye.' Elliot paused. Hard to word this without getting a slap for her trouble. Ah, she had an easier way in. 'You were updating Napier Rattray's will, weren't you?'

He frowned. 'I wasn't.'

'Sure about that?'

'Of course I'm bloody sure! Listen... It's complex. The whole thing is complex.'

'If you weren't, then who was?'

'Donald.'

'Cruikshank?'

A halting nod. 'He advised me to recuse myself from the work over a potential conflict of interest. We built a Chinese wall around that client, so my guys and Donald's guys weren't able to communicate on the matter.'

'What was it?'

'It'd be unprofessional of Donald or myself to share the nature of the conflict.'

'Napier Rattray was *your* client, though.'

'Correct. Had been for years. One of the first. Napier appreciated brutal honesty and good old-fashioned hard work.'

'So you've no idea what happened that required his will to be updated?'

'No. And I had to advise Donald on certain matters, going back to his father's time, but I never learnt the detail.'

'Is this true?'

'Completely. I... Listen.' Hugo huffed out a sigh. 'What's all this about?'

'Did you know that your wife was Napier Rattray's daughter?'

Hugo looked around at her with the confusion of a child. '*What?*'

'Was she—'

'I heard what you said.' Hugo frowned. 'Lou... What? As far as she told me, she never knew her father.'

'I get that. But was it Napier Rattray?'

'Lou was his daughter? That can't be true, can it?'

'We're trying to determine that, sir, but we believe so. Yes. She was certainly in his will and would've inherited half of the farm.'

Hugo stared into space and took another sip of tea. 'My God.'

'I'm not a lawyer, but I imagine you won't benefit?'

'A beneficiary dying before the deceased means the legacy they were due to inherit is kept within the estate and will be distributed to the surviving beneficiaries. I don't know who that is, but I presume it's Rhona and their sons?'

'It's just Balfour Rattray.'

'Well. Sounds like you've got a motivated killer, then, doesn't it?'

'Ma'am.' The uniform waved out of the window.

The paramedics had arrived, two green-clad muscle boys jumping down from the cab like firemen.

'Okay, Hugo. These two will get you warm but my colleague here will stay with you during that time.'

'Thank you. And please, I need you to promise you'll find my wife's killer.'

'We're doing our best.'

'But will you promise?'

'I can promise to only have one glass of wine tonight and I can promise to eat a salad. Those are things under my control. I can't promise to find the killer, no, but we are doing our best and we're peeling the onion, slice by slice.' Elliot paused. It seemed to be good enough for him. 'One last thing, though. You were abducted by someone in a van, right?'

'That's right.'

'Was there anyone else in the van with you?'

Hugo's brow folded up like a chip wrapper. 'A woman, I think.'

'Do you know what happened to her?'

'No. They just dropped me here. Kicked the shit out of me and left me.'

'They? How many were there?'

'I don't know. Felt like multiple people.'

'Okay.' Elliot gave him a smile, then got out of the car and let the paramedics at him. She stepped away and took in the scene.

The plantation climbed up the hill. Must be that big one to the north of Gala, the one that parts of Langlee crawled up. Must be. A big gate blocking access swung in the breeze – whoever had done this must've either snipped the lock or had access. Or it was just left open. Lot of forestry work going on up there, so could be as simple as that.

Rachel Lorimer was still missing. Was she in the woods somewhere?

Shunty was chatting to the uniform and the big dog walker. 'So, you were hiking up there and you found him?'

He laughed. 'Hiking's stretching it a bit. But I got a good sweat on, charging up the hill, then spotted him lying there. Middle of the path, moaning. About two hundred metres up.' He pointed at a pair of dogs in the back of a four-by-four. Elliot had missed him putting them away. 'Ran up to him and my bloody dog started licking his face. Called the cops, but I couldn't get any mobile reception so ran down here.'

Shunty nodded. Still so many black spots around here, even in 2023. 'Did you cut those bonds on his ankles?'

'Aye. Always have a wee saw with me. I do woodturning on my lathe at home. The wind usually blows some branches down and I can get a hold of them.'

Shunty looked like he was going to take detailed notes on the lad's lathe work. He smiled then noticed Elliot.

She stepped in and smiled at the dog walker. 'Did you see anyone else up there?'

'No. Just came back here to phone, like I say, then walked back up and helped him down here. He was in a bad way, so he collapsed. Your colleague was here soon after and she took over.'

'You saved his life.'

'Wow. Really?'

'Really.' She held the grin, but it was feeling forced. 'Sergeant, can I have a word?'

'Just a sec.' Shunty followed her away from him. 'What's up?'

'Get a detailed statement from him.'

'Seriously? You can't think—'

'Come on, Shunty. He's a suspect until he's not. Everyone is.'

'Fine.'

'And you need to scour that whole wood.'

'Why?'

'Because she might be there! Come on, Shunty. This is basic stuff. We've got two people missing. These people aren't impressionistic creative types. They dumped two bodies on top of each other by the side of the road. Stands to reason they might do the same here. Okay?'

'On it.' Shunty smiled at her, but that clown would never cut the mustard.

Whatever that meant. He'd put whole seeds of mustard on his ham sandwich. And he didn't even eat ham, did he? On his Quorn sandwich.

Bloody hell.

His phone rang. He got it out and checked it. He put it away, but let it ring out.

'Aren't you going to take that?'

'Don't recognise the number.'

'Answer it!'

'Eh?'

'Could be related to the case!'

'Probably about an accident that wasn't my—'

'Shunty! Answer your bloody phone!'

'Fine.' He sighed and got his phone out again. 'They've stopped calling. Oh, wait.' He put it to his ear and turned away. 'Hello?'

Honestly, that generation...

Shunty looked back at her. 'Got a name for who rented that burnt-out van.'

CHAPTER FIFTY-EIGHT

Marshall pressed the bell and waited. Inane babble came from inside the house, the kind of kids' TV noise Thea would've listened to when she was a lot younger. Hopefully it meant she was in.

Jolene was picking at her teeth. 'Bit disappointed by that fish supper, to be honest.'

Marshall hadn't been, but that amount of potato at lunchtime was starting to repeat on him. And he hadn't even been able to finish them.

The door opened and Ailsa Johnstone peeked out, shrouded by the smell of baking. 'Can I help?'

'DI Rob Marshall.' He showed his warrant card. 'We met at the hospital yesterday?'

'Ah, yes.' She looked at him, hope burning in her eyes.

'It's Ailsa, right?'

'That's correct.'

'I wanted you to know first. We've found your son-in-law.'

'Alive?'

'Alive, yes.'

She seemed to deflate. 'Thank you.'

'Don't you have a family liaison officer here?'

'I sent the laddie away. He was just getting in the way. And eating all of my scones.' Her laugh was short and sharp. She let out a deep breath and the news seemed to hit her.

'Would we be able to have a word inside?' Jolene smiled at her. 'Only it's raining.'

'Sure, sure.' She opened the door wide and ushered them in. 'I've been baking. Can I get you a scone? Butter? Cream? Jam?'

Jolene smiled at her. 'We've just had our lunch but thank you.'

'Okay.' Ailsa stopped in the living room doorway to look in. 'Toby, we're going to be in the kitchen, okay?'

Her grandson was lying on the floor, a Nintendo console stuck to his face, while the TV blared away. 'Okay, Granny.'

They followed Ailsa through into a bright kitchen that looked across a mature and well-kept garden, damp in the rain. 'How's Toby doing?'

'It won't hit him for a while. Just the way he is. Like his father. News like that... It seems to hit a rock face, but you can see the cracks later on.' She sat at the kitchen table. A cake stand was filled with massive scones that looked more like cakes. 'Baking's my escape. I've poured my grief on those. Not all of it, obviously, but it helps. I'll have to freeze them.' She looked up. 'Unless you want to take them to the station?'

Jolene smiled. 'They'll disappear in seconds.'

'Please, I insist.' Ailsa got up and went over to a drawer, where she pulled out a roll of freezer bags. 'Please, take them in. For finding Hugo.'

'Will you be baking some more?'

'Might do.' She sat down and started carefully filling the bag with the scones. The clear blue plastic puffed with warmth. 'I don't want this to sound selfish, but it's a blessed relief that you've found Hugo. I'm too old to raise my grandson. I was forty-two when I had Louisa. Raised her on my own. Can't do that again at this age. I just can't.'

Sometimes you had to ask the questions. And others you got the answers unbidden.

'Thank you.' Marshall took the bag of scones from her. 'What happened with her father?'

She looked away. 'He's dead.'

Marshall sat back and nodded slowly. 'They switched the machine off last night.'

Her mouth hung open. 'What?'

'We know Napier Rattray was Louisa's father.'

Ailsa got up and walked over to the fridge, then pulled out a pack of butter, a carton of milk and an egg. Then she got out a basket of Kilner jars filled with various flours. A bowl clanked as she took it from the cupboard. 'My cousin knew Napier Rattray from the rugby club in Melrose. Big drinking buddies. And he got me a job working at the estate. Secretarial work, but I'd worked in Edinburgh and London, briefly. I knew what I was doing. They didn't, so I went in and turned things around there. Did a lot of work with Napier... One thing led to another and... I thought I'd never have kids, but there I was – single, pregnant and in my forties. Of course, Napier would never leave Rhona. They had two boys and they took precedence over me. Napier was a gentleman about it. Said it was a mistake, but it was his and he took full responsibility. Offered to support me however. I couldn't have had a... a you-know-what. So he bought us this house and he contributed some money every year. A generous amount. I didn't have to work again, just focused on Lou... But the cost was high. He shunned us. Didn't want his wife to know. Or his boys. Or anyone. I'm a discreet woman, of course. One of the things you learn working in business, I suppose. And I saw them out and about at things. Not exactly the happy family. Those boys were out of control, weren't they? But they were a family. And I had Louisa all on my own. She grew up just fine without knowing who her father is, so I think I did a fine job.'

'But?'

Ailsa cracked the egg and poured it into a ramekin, then tipped flour into a bowl. She stopped and sighed. 'One day, Louisa came through that door in floods of tears. She was Napier's wife's oncologist.'

'So she knew?'

'I'd told her. One night when we'd had too much wine and gin.'

'Did she ever confront him?'

'One day, she went up to the farm and spoke to him. He was mortified, of course. And typical Napier – he gave her a chunk of money to go away. She didn't want it. She wanted a father. But she used the money to set up a charity. Seemed to pacify her about it. But she saw how cold he could be. Of course, none of that stopped my Louisa doing a grand job with Rhona's treatment and soon enough, she was in remission. Hasn't returned, either. So, I guess that Napier felt guilty about his actions, because the next thing I knew, Louisa stood to inherit half of his estate.'

'She told you?'

'Another time my daughter came through that door in floods of tears. The one time that wasn't because of Hugo's coldness. Last year. Napier was going to change it all around. Kick his wife out of his will and put Louisa in. Fifty-fifty with her half-brother, Balfour. I gather there was an accident with the other one, but he was well looked after. Still, I can't believe Napier would cut his wife out entirely.'

Marshall shook his head. 'He didn't. Our understanding is

Rhona will inherit the house, which was kept out of the estate. The land and the farm are what are at stake with the trust.'

'I didn't know that. Sorry.'

Jolene leaned forward. 'Did Napier ever meet Toby?'

'A few times, yes. He loved him. Suspect that's why he made the change. Balfour... He never married, did he? Not suggesting he's that way inclined, but some people... It just never works out, does it? I should know, after all. But Balfour Rattray never had children and Louisa did. And with his lawyer too. Toby would inherit the trust, eventually.'

'Did he know she was his half-sister?'

'Of course he did.'

'Are you sure of that?'

'Well, he'd met her. I think. And if you want my opinion, Balfour Rattray is a spoilt little shit. People like him have a tendency to take what they want from people.'

CHAPTER FIFTY-NINE

I f Marshall ever returned to this hospital again, it'd be way too soon.

His phone rang.

Elliot calling...

He wanted to bounce it, not least because he saw Jen in the middle of the ward and she had a habit of spotting him and buggering off to a hiding place. He answered it. 'Hi, Andrea. How is he?'

'Hugo's on his way to hospital. You get anything out of her?'

'All checked out. Louisa knew the will was going to change and Napier saw his grandson as a way of continuing his legacy.'

'So Balfour wanted her out of the picture?'

'Right.'

'You buy that?'

'I can. That amount of money could motivate anyone to do

anything, especially murder a secret half-sister.' Marshall stifled a yawn. 'Okay, I'm at the hospital now. I'll see if I can talk to him. What are you going to do?'

'I'm, eh, seeing what's what at the plantation. Got people scouring it. Maybe Rachel Lorimer's there. Maybe not.'

She was up to something. Hopefully if it exploded, it wouldn't do so in his face.

'Keep me posted.' Marshall killed the call.

Jen hadn't spotted him. She nodded at a nurse, who returned it and walked away.

He took a deep breath then tapped his sister on the shoulder. 'Hey.'

She grabbed his hand and bent his fingers back. 'Rob? What the hell?'

He took his hand back, all sore and twisted. 'Sorry. I shouldn't have done that.'

'No, you shouldn't.' She looked him up and down. 'Heard what happened with Balfour?'

He looked away along the busy ward. 'Right. I found him.'

'Bloody hell. He was trying to kill himself. Right?'

'Aye.'

She let her hair fall, then retied it. 'I saw him here. First thing. Must've been closing off stuff with his father. Arranging for the body to go to the funeral director.'

Marshall stared at her. 'How bad is he?'

'He's lucid, but... he almost succeeded.'

Marshall shook his head. 'I don't know what to think, Jen.'

'About Balf?'

'About any of it.'

She narrowed her eyes at him. 'Hasn't stopped you speaking to Paul.'

Some news travelled at light speed. 'Come on, Jen. *He* spoke to *me*.'

'Rob... You're not my dad. Okay?'

'No. And I'm not trying to be. But someone's got to look out for you.'

'I can do that myself, thank you very much.'

'Can you? Because it—'

'Shut up.'

'I'm looking out for Thea.'

She shut her eyes and snorted.

'Don't forget that her needs have to come first, Jen. Okay?'

'Right. Sure.'

'We'll discuss this later.' Marshall stared at her until she folded her arms. He wasn't going to get a nod or an okay, but that'd do. 'Listen. Is it possible for me to speak to Balfour?'

'If it's not, you've wasted your time coming here, haven't you?'

'Hardly. I've been able to spend some quality time with my amazing sister.'

She laughed.

'Seriously. I was just in Darnick and you weren't answering your phone, so it's not exactly out of the way.'

'I'm at work, Rob, so my phone's in my locker.'

He shrugged. 'Look, can I speak to him?'

She looked up and down the corridor. 'Why?'

'Because I think he arranged for Louisa Baird's murder.'

'Oh, shit.' She smacked a hand against her forehead. 'Seriously?'

'It's looking increasingly likely, aye.'

She stared up at the ductwork on the ceiling. 'Okay. But don't take the piss. Okay?'

'Okay. I never do.' Marshall followed her along the corridor to a corner room.

Dr Rougier stepped out, lugging a tablet computer under

his arm. He frowned at Marshall, then focused on Jen. 'Can I have a word, please?'

'Sure.' She led him away.

Giving Marshall a chance to look into the room.

Balfour didn't look as bad as he expected. Like he was drunk and sleeping it off.

Maybe Jen was right. Maybe Balfour was as much a victim as them of the whole system, of his oppressive father.

Focusing on Balfour as a suspect felt like the obvious thing but maybe it was trying to force a square peg into a hole. Trouble was, Marshall didn't know if the hole was square, round, triangular or that star-shaped one.

Easy to see Balfour as the man who stood to lose half of his inheritance to a sister he'd barely met and possibly didn't know about. Easy to see him pay for her death.

Then when she died, and the police knocked on his door and his father died...

He felt guilty – killing himself was the only answer his drunken, grieving mind could picture.

'Can see you standing there.' Balfour sounded drunk. 'My old pal Robert Marshall.'

Marshall stepped into the room. 'How are you doing, Balf?'

'A bit sore.'

'Sure that's not the morphine talking?'

'Had worse injuries on the rugby pitch.' Balfour smiled. 'Got to thank you for saving my life, haven't I?'

Marshall took the seat next to the bed. 'You were trying to kill yourself. I know that. You know that. But what *I* don't know is why. Why were you trying to kill yourself?'

'I was drunk and thinking about Father and... How he'd fallen from that turbine. It was too much.'

'It's okay, Balf. Whatever it is, you—'

'How can you say it's okay if you don't even know what it fucking is?!'

'Heard about your father.'

'Aye.'

'That it? That all you're going to say?'

'Roberto... Come on, man.'

'I'm serious. Must be rough losing him. You were close, weren't you? Remember you gave a talk at school to the class about Newcastle Falcons. How your dad would take you down there for every match. Most kids in school who were into rugby had a local team, but you wanted to see Johnny Wilkinson in the flesh. Right?'

'Some player. I should've saved Father. Should've stopped him going up there. I wasn't even in the country, but...' Balfour looked up and over at Marshall. 'I still talk to Father.'

'But he died last night, didn't he?'

'Doesn't mean I can't speak to him.'

'His ghost?'

'I'm not a simpleton, Robert. I told you I text him, didn't I? Well, I've left him voicemails too.'

'Are you angry with him?'

'Angry with myself. I can't keep going without him. Father wasn't an easy man to live with. Sent me to those private schools in Edinburgh. I was six. Mother would drive me up until I was ten. Then I had to go alone. On the bus. Things were... I didn't settle. And I was expelled, of course. Mother and Father had an almighty battle about it. She wanted to try me at the local school with you. And you'll know yourself, Robert, that I was an absolute prick.'

'That's true. You were a total arsehole.'

Balfour looked around at Marshall. Mouth hanging open. He didn't say anything, then he laughed.

Progress.

'Thing you need to focus on is you're not that arsehole anymore, Balf. And nor am I. Back then, I was an arrogant wanker, but we're grown men now.'

'You *were* arrogant. Needed taking down a few pegs.'

'And that happened. But we should be able to admit our failings as kids. Laugh at them, even. Over a whisky or a glass of wine.'

Balfour laughed. 'What sorted *me* out was boarding school. Tough place, but fair. Thing I always keep going back to is how cold it is to just cast out your child like that. I saw Mother and Father four times a year. Away on your own all the time for months, including weekends. It's... It's so *cold*.'

'Did you talk to them about it?'

'Father said it did him no harm.'

'And your mum?'

'She... A good parent fights for their kids, puts their needs first, like I'm doing with my brother. I look after him and make sure he's getting the best of help.' He let out a deep sigh. 'And the farm is too much for me to bear on my own. I've lost Father and the main worker at the farm. How am I supposed to cope with that?'

'Come on, Balf. You're a good man. You'll be able to sort it all out.'

'A good man. Hardly. At school, I was arrogant but it was all bluster. It's what you learn at those schools, how to bluff your way through the day. I don't have a clue what I'm doing.'

'Balf, I want to help.'

'Fuck off. You don't care.'

'I don't. Not really. But I'm here to help you. Right now. Thing is, you and I aren't that unalike. Me and Jen never even knew our dad. For all we know, he could be into *football*.'

Balf laughed at that.

'Our mum's lovely, Balf, but she's... She's Mum. She's

special in her own way. My granddad, Dad's father, he took on a lot of that role. Old sod's body's failing him. Hard to watch. But he did so much for us.'

Balfour smiled. 'Why are you here?'

'You want the truth? Fine. We're treating what happened to your father as murder.'

'Murder?' Balfour did a slow blink. 'But that was an accident!'

'We have credible intel that someone was paid to push your father off that wind turbine. Or to threaten him.'

'That's bullshit.'

'But what if it wasn't, Balfour? Who'd stand to inherit? You and your brother.'

'Not true – Dalrymple was removed after his accident. He got a huge settlement. A trust looks after it for him. But he won't inherit the farm.'

'Which leaves you and your mother.'

Balfour stared at him, ice cold. 'Is framing me for murder your revenge for what happened as kids?'

'Of course it's not. I'm not petty like that. That was high school. This is now. At the time it was bad, sure, but through the lens of twenty-odd years I should be thanking you for making my skin that much thicker... But I want to find out what happened to your father. If it's bogus intel, then fine – I'll walk away and clear you. I don't want a dark cloud hanging over you. Don't you want to put your father's ghost to rest?'

Balfour looked away. 'You know I was out of the country skiing when Father had his accident. Right?'

'Right. Balfour, you being in Val-d'Isère or Aspen or wherever doesn't stop you paying someone to warn him, does it?'

Balfour looked around at him and winced. 'What?'

'You paid them to send a message not to jeopardise your

inheritance. But they accidentally forced your father to fall from that turbine. And now he's dead.'

'I thought better of you, Robert.'

'Did you pay them to kill your sister too?'

'My *sister*?'

'Sorry. Half-sister.'

'What? I don't have a sister, half or not.'

'Louisa Baird.'

Balfour scowled at him like he'd gone insane. 'Mother's oncologist?'

'She was your half-sister.'

'I have no idea what you're talking about.'

'Balfour, stop lying to me. Your mother was removed from your father's will and was replaced by Louisa Baird.'

'I assume you've got evidence of this?'

'We do, aye. It's all stacking up.'

'Well, I don't believe it. You're trying to pin this case on me.'

'If you truly didn't do anything, you wouldn't be acting so guilty. I want to find the truth, Balfour, but I guess we'll just have to wait until you're back on your feet and able to sit in an interview room. With a criminal defence lawyer. On the record. As I present evidence to you.'

Balfour shook his head.

'Look, Balf, I get it. I found the document you were looking at when you tried to kill yourself. Must've been shocking.'

'I found it in father's things. I needed to know who to speak to about putting things in motion. I...' Balfour fixed him with a harsh glare. 'You want the truth?'

'That's all I want.'

Balfour leaned back in his bed and stared up at the ceiling. 'The truth is, I wanted out of the business.'

'You wanted out?'

Balfour nodded. 'I was working with Father to get some money in exchange for my share. They were to write me out of the family trust. The plan was then to sell the farm and land. Had a few buyers too.'

'So you did know about Louisa Baird?'

'No. Father told me he'd been unfaithful and he had another child. One who'd furnished him with the grandchild I haven't. But I didn't know it was her.'

'Just supposed to believe that?'

'It's the truth. I swear.'

'You better not be lying to me.'

'Why would I lie to you, Robert? Why? My life's a mess.'

'Inheriting a farm worth tens of millions isn't exactly a mess, is it?'

'Money can't buy love or happiness.'

'No, but you're not on the streets. Far from it.'

Balfour settled back and stared up at the ceiling.

But there was something nagging at Marshall...

'Do you know Gary Hislop?'

'Who?'

'Owns Scott Street Hardware. You don't know him from rugby or anything?'

'Nope.' Balfour frowned. 'I bought a shovel from there once when I was passing. My favourite went missing and I was stopped in traffic and, lo and behold, the exact same model was in there.'

Seemed a weird story to remember, but Marshall needed to do more digging on that score. 'Okay. I will return.' He stormed off, clutching his phone then tapped a contact and put it to his ear.

'Donald Cruikshank. How can I help?'

'I appreciate you answering.'

'When you give someone your personal mobile number, it's the least you can do.'

'Just got a question. Who knew about the changes to the will?'

'To my knowledge, the only living person was Rhona Rattray.'

'Plus Napier.'

'Of course.'

'And Louisa?'

'Either might've told her or their son. But I can say, categorically, that the leak didn't come from this office.'

Marshall waved at Jen as he passed, on his way out. 'Is Balfour Rattray a client?'

'Not of mine.'

'Of Hugo's?'

'I believe so.'

'Was there any work done on him receiving a payment in lieu of his inheritance?'

Cruikshank's sigh rattled down the line.

'Donald, I need a straight answer.'

'It's part of what we're working on, yes. The work wasn't completed during Napier's life and obviously won't be now. As it stands, Balfour will fully inherit the farm.'

'Okay. Thank you.' Marshall stepped out into the freezing cold and saw Jolene behind the wheel. He got in the passenger seat. 'Has Rachel been found yet?'

'Nope. How did it go in there?'

'He denies knowing her.'

'You believe him?'

'Maybe. And that's the hard part.' The doubt still nagged at him. 'Has Elliot ever talked to you about this info she got about the Rattrays?'

'No.'

'She got some info from Gary Hislop.'

'She *what*?'

'You know him?'

'I do, aye. He's bad news, Rob. Really bad news.'

'He's who put us onto this nonsense at the Rattrays, so how about we pay him a visit?'

'No. You really shouldn't. There's a strategic drug investigation into him.'

'We look like idiots for believing her bullshit story about the Rattrays.'

'How about you take this up with Elliot, then?'

'Okay, let's go back to the plantation.'

'Why? She's in Gala nick.'

CHAPTER SIXTY

One of those interviews where Elliot didn't want to sit down. Her whole body was fizzing with energy, like she'd been plugged into the mains. 'What were you going to do with her, Rory?'

Rory Tait was sweating like a sex offender. Because he was one, even though he'd only been charged with it and not convicted. His long greasy hair was dangling free. No Brylcreem in the cells to slick it back. Not due in Selkirk to plead until the morning so he was still wearing the same clothes from when he tried to pick up a teenager. He looked at his lawyer, then at Shunty, then back to the tabletop. 'No comment.'

'Been a few years since I've seen you, Rory.' Elliot hoped the way she was drumming her fingers was annoying enough. 'The silver hair poking through isn't adding any dignity or gravitas, is it? Just makes it all the more tragic to find you sitting in freezing parks trying to get young lassies to look at your wee pecker in exchange for sweeties.'

'Vape sticks.' He shut his eyes as soon as he said it. '*Idiot.*'

'Thanks for the reminder. Aye, you were going to give Kelly-Jane a pack of vape sticks and a Tango Ice Blast in exchange for a cheeky hand shandy.'

'No comment.'

The lawyer looked up from his notepad, blinking hard. 'Inspector, I appreciate that you were otherwise engaged when my client was accidentally arrested, but—'

'Accidentally?'

'His presence there was a mere accident. I don't blame your colleagues for assuming the worst and believing he was there to chat to a young girl. It's very noble of them and I think the world should know about the sterling work they're doing to keep the streets safe. But it was merely coincidental and I laud your officers' efforts.'

Elliot laughed. 'Merely coincidental that he'd been chatting her up online, eh?'

'You have read his statement, yes?'

'Sorry, not yet. Had a few murders to investigate. Not to mention the associated abductions.'

'My client was there with some vape cartridges and your colleague, a DS Jolene Archer, pretended to be a minor to ensnare him in a covert mission. That's entrapment.'

'That's not entrapment. The courts have ruled on it. If we picked his name out of the phonebook and solicited him, then yes, that's entrapment. But remember, *he* sought *her* out online. We took over the girl's account, sure, but the offer and the exchanges were brokered from his end. The bringing of vape sticks and frozen treats is for identification. If your client fell into a trap, it's of his inability to not send inappropriate messages to a minor, who he then lured to a park via a series of messages. It's all documented and above board. But he's playing silly buggers here.'

'Been in here for ages.' Tait smacked his fist off the table. 'Time to let me out.'

The lawyer rested a hand on Tait's arm. 'My client has only been charged with two crimes, both incredibly minor, and yet he's still here. Why?'

'Because your client's IT stuff is taking a while to process. Lots of it. And so many safeguards in place to prevent us getting in. Luckily, we've had an extension to your stay here while that goes on and, in some late breaking news, we've made a breakthrough in hacking your passwords.' She leaned on the end of the table and leered at him. 'Bet you like some colourful stuff, eh?'

'No comment.'

'Come on, Rory. There's no crime if it's on a computer, eh? Not like it's real kids being abused, is it?' She stood up tall and frowned. 'Oh wait. It is. They're real kids being abused for *your* enjoyment. Yours and thousands of other sick bastards.'

'No comment.'

She sighed. 'Well, this is exactly what I expected.'

'So you're letting me go?'

She laughed. 'Hear that, Rakesh? Thinks he's getting out of here.' Now she took her seat. Stared into his bloodshot eyes. 'Let's talk about this van.'

'What van?'

'The van that was used to abduct two people, who both died. A third was abducted and dropped out of said van at roughly seventy miles an hour. On his head. So another death. Then we found it, burnt out with someone else inside.' She left a pause, watching him wetting his lips repeatedly. 'And who should we find actually hired it from that back-street van rental place in Hawick? You probably won't get the deposit back.'

'I don't know anything about it.'

'Well, it was hired in your name, Rory.'

He looked up at her, then away. 'Still no idea what you're talking about.'

'We can maybe add a pair of accessory to murder charges to your pending charge sheet.'

'I didn't do anything!'

'*You* hired the van, Rory. That's not in question.' She sat back. 'Rakesh?'

Shunty slapped some photos on the table. 'We've got CCTV of you going in. We've got a photocopy of your driver's license. We've got your credit card being used. Not very smart, is it?'

'No comment.'

Elliot picked up the photos like she was examining them for the first time. 'Now, I know the people you muck about with. Rough as you like, keep themselves to themselves, only harm their own. Yadda yadda yadda. I suspect the deal your boss gives you is he'll make sure you get looked after inside, eh? Wait it out then get a nice wee nest egg when you get out. Live out your life in style. That about the size of it?'

'No comment.'

'Trouble is, Rory, you tried picking up a young lassie in the park. A lassie you'd been messaging and sending photos of your wee willy too. That's not going to sit well with that crew, is it?'

'No comment.' But Tait was sweating. He knew how fucked he was. Inside and out.

'Rory, you scratch our backs and we'll see what we can do.'

'No fucking way.'

The door opened and Marshall popped his big face in. 'Andrea, can I have a word?'

How the hell did he find out about this?

'Sure thing, Rob.' She got up, grinning wide, but she wanted to throttle the bastard. She was so close.

'DI Elliot has left the room.'

She shut the door behind her and walked along the corridor, then jabbed a finger at him. 'What are you playing at? I had him on the ropes there!'

Marshall folded his arms. 'I'm not the one who needs to explain what I'm playing at. What are *you* up to in there?'

'Thought I'd give Rory a little chance to confess to what he did to Kelly-Jane.'

'While we've got a missing person? Come on, I wasn't born yesterday. Don't lie to me, Andrea. I watched the last five minutes in the obs suite.'

She couldn't look at him. 'Right.'

'Andrea. Us playing off against each other isn't working. We need to pull together here. We broke bread in Gala, or at least fish suppers, and I thought we were on the same page. But now I find you going off on a solo mission here? It doesn't sit well with me.'

'Did Shunty tell you about this?'

'No. He didn't. And you should focus on telling me the truth, not on who grassed.'

'So someone did.'

'Of course someone did! Someone always does, and they'll always tell me. Andrea, we need to have both our teams working as one for the common good... all egos on the side line... And I really don't care about glory. You can take it all.'

'What?'

'I don't want to make DCI, but you clearly do, so you can have whatever glory you want.' Marshall stepped that little bit closer to her. She could smell his sour aftershave. 'But I do want to solve this case and if your game-playing jeopardises that, then I'll make sure you pay for what you've done.'

'What have I done?'

'Hopefully nothing yet. But are you in agreement to work together?'

She folded her arms too. 'I couldn't care less about the glory, Marshall.'

'So what's this all about, then?'

She didn't have an explanation for it. She'd focused on him taking Pringle's job before her. If he truly didn't want it... Maybe she'd got Marshall all wrong and he wasn't a threat, but a potential ally. She pointed at the door. 'That wee prick in there knows who did it, Rob, but he's not talking. He hired the van that abducted everyone.' Her voice was a croak. 'Forget about why and who for a minute. Rory Tait knows the fucker who killed Louisa and Justin. And Steven Beattie and Iain Caddon. So he probably knows who abducted Hugo and that means we can find Rachel Lorimer.'

Marshall stood there, silently staring at the wall. 'Okay.' He looked around at her. 'Does your ego mind if I have a go with him?'

'Let me ask it...' She walked over and opened the door, then beckoned Marshall to go first.

'DI Marshall and DI Elliot have entered the room.'

She followed him in but stood at the back and let him sit.

Marshall was mirroring Tait's defensive posture. Legs crossed, arms wrapped around his torso, staring at the table. 'Remember me?'

Tait looked up, then looked away again. 'Course I do.'

'You know you did wrong with Kelly-Jane. Don't you?'

Tait sighed. Then nodded.

'I know you're sorry for it, Rory. Much as I hope you're an honest man who'll take his fair punishment for what you did, well... Maybe there's a nest egg waiting for you when you come out, but maybe not. But that's all going to happen to you, okay? Right now, though, I'm here about your mum. See, I know

Edith. I know she goes to church every day. I know she loves you, and despite all you've done, and despite all you likely will do in the future, she believes you have good in you and you will one day go to Heaven. Here's the deal, Rory. You've got a chance to reunite Rachel Lorimer with her two kids, okay? Do that and I will personally tell your mum myself that I know St. Peter's going to let you in. Whatever you've done. And you and I both know how bad the stuff you've done is. It'll help reassure your mum. And you've got a chance to help us solve multiple murders. To help us find someone who's been abducted. Maybe she's dead, but maybe not. She could also still be alive, Rory. This is your chance to make good on the wrong you've done. Do you want to help us find Rachel Lorimer? To reunite her with her two kids?'

Tait looked up at him. 'Okay.'

'Good, Rory, good. Now, we know it was you who hired that van. Your paperwork, your money. But you couldn't have known what they were going to do, could you? Probably told you they were just transporting some stuff for a mate. Credit card stopped working. Easily done. You didn't think they'd abduct and murder anyone. You're as much of a victim as anyone, Rory, so please tell me – who made you do it?'

Tait rocked back in the chair and stared up at the ceiling. He glanced at his lawyer, then sat forward again. 'Chunk.'

Elliot didn't know the name. She stepped out of the shadows. 'Rory, who's Chunk?'

'He works with a kid called Baseball.'

'Iain Caddon?'

Tait nodded. 'Him.'

'Do you know his real name?'

'Aye, I do.' Tait scratched his chin. 'Thing I'm asking myself here is, what's that worth to you?'

CHAPTER SIXTY-ONE

Marshall kicked down the gears and blasted past a column of slow traffic, then headed on towards Stow. A police speed van sat at the side of the road, flashing twice as he passed. 'Well, that's going to be fun sorting that out.'

'Rather you than me.' Elliot was in the passenger seat, staring out across the Gala Water to the hills on the far side. 'How did you manage getting that nonce to speak?'

'You did most of the work, Andrea, I just tapped it in at the back post.'

She glanced over at him. 'Didn't think you were a football man.'

'Spent a while working with a West Ham season ticket holder. Not that he knows much about people tapping in at the back post. Unless it's against West Ham. Or it's a West Ham player scoring an own goal.'

She didn't laugh. 'But his mum? How long have you known her?'

'About five minutes. She hired the lawyer and I met her on

the way into the station. She was all aflutter. Her words, not mine. So it all just came pouring out. The poor dear poured her heart out, practically begging God to save her boy's mortal soul. You work with what you have, right?'

'You do. You were right about some things, though. I have been a dick since you turned up.'

'That's not true.'

'Come on, Marshall. I'm trying to apologise here. Don't deny it.'

'Okay. Right, you have been a dick, but it's only since you came back to work in November.'

'Ha. Ha. I mean it. I'm apologising and I'm not someone who apologises. Ever. So this is a strictly limited edition of one. I, DI Andrea Elliot, am very sorry. I'm a hardened cop and I don't have some of the skills you do.'

'Apology accepted.' He gripped the wheel tighter. 'And like-wise, there are things I can't do either but you excel at. I meant it when I said we should work together, not as adversaries. Deal?'

She looked over and locked eyes. 'Deal.'

Stow staggered into view and Marshall caught sight of the flashes of neon yellow on the far side, over by the train station. 'Looks like uniform are ready and waiting for us.'

'Good.'

'That intel you got about Rattray's death is paying off.' Marshall slowed for the twenty limit. 'We were fumbling around in the dark until then. Without it, we wouldn't have the why and now the who. Chunk AKA Kyle Talbot. I feel like a bit of a twat for scoring his name off the whiteboard.'

'You weren't to know. His alibi checked out. What else were you supposed to do? We had nothing pointing to him being involved. But you don't think Tait's leading us down the garden path here?'

'It's always possible, but even Rory Tait knows that he'll get a lot more out of being honest than by lying. The way I see it, Talbot worked for Napier Rattray, which gave him a perfect opportunity to kill him. Knew when he was up that turbine and it helped him cover his tracks. Must've known everything going on at the farm. Who to speak to.'

'What I still don't get, Marshall, is who paid him to kill them? Balfour? Rhona?'

'Could be anyone. But let's find him first, then give him a chance to confess.' Marshall pulled into the train station car park and waved at the ten cops lurking around. Laughing and joking in the freezing rain. He could see the Stagehall Arms from here. 'Let's hope he's here.'

'Shunty and Jolene are up at the farm. Said he's not there.'

'You could've told me.'

'Didn't I?' Elliot scowled at him. 'But it works, right? Talbot didn't go to work the same day these people are being abducted in... not quite broad daylight, but on the school run?'

'He was there earlier, though. I saw him at lunchtime.'

'Anyway. They're both on their way here, but I think we need to strike now.' She stared out of the window again, then nudged Marshall's arm. 'See... them... Is that a laddie or a lassie?'

DC Ash Paton was getting out of the next car, wedged too tight against the other one. Mid-twenties and androgynous. Short hair, but medium height and slight build.

Marshall smiled at Elliot. 'They're on your team, Andrea.'

'Aye, aye, but... It's so bloody hard to tell these days.'

Marshall knew what she meant. 'You're the one who keeps banging on about your non-binary child. Is that you just virtue signalling to stop Rakesh opening an HR case against you?'

'They bloody are non-binary. Don't know what to do about

it, Marshall, other than let them be. And having a kid going through that is why I want to find out before I blunder in and misgender... them.' She scowled. 'Is non-binary actually a gender, though? Fuck me, I just don't get the rules these days. And they're called Ash too. I mean, that's like Alex or Sam, could be either or neither. Or both. It's not like Mike or Daphne.'

'Thing is, if you'd actually taken the time to speak to the members of your own team, you'd know things like that.'

'That's what I've got Shunty for.'

'Why don't you ask?'

'Fuck it, I might.' She got out and walked over, offering a hand and a smile. 'It's Ash Paton, right?'

Marshall had meant asking Shunty... He took his time getting out into the pissing rain.

'Hi, ma'am.' Paton's voice didn't provide any clues either. 'Keep popping my head into your office but you're never there. Wanted to thank you for having me on your team. Only been a week, but it's been an experience already.'

'You've got Shunty to thank for that.'

'You know Rakesh hates that name, right?'

'Just like I hate being called Ballmuncher by him. It's all swings and roundabouts, young...' She coughed. 'Padawan.'

'Don't want to be an arse, but Rakesh told me to speak to you about the bank details?'

Elliot twisted her frown into a smile. 'And what about them?'

'Well, I've still got a few transactions to finalise for Dr Baird, but it's—'

'It's not finished?'

'No.'

'And why are you here?'

'Rakesh told me to come.'

'Right. Ash, that work's still a top priority, so can you please head back and finish it, please?'

'Sure.' Paton got back in the pool car and drove off.

'Quit laughing at me.' Elliot turned to scowl at Marshall. 'I've still no idea.'

'You know it doesn't matter, right? And at least you didn't generate another HR issue.'

'Still time. And I'm leading this, okay?' She clapped her hands together. 'Gather around.'

Marshall focused on the squad of six uniforms and three detectives. Should be more than enough to catch someone who'd allegedly killed five times and abducted twice.

'Okay, gang. We've got reasonable intel suggesting Kyle Talbot is the man we want for five murders and two abductions. I'll remind you that the whereabouts of Rachel Lorimer are still unknown, so we need to tread extra carefully here. We don't believe Talbot is armed or has any access to weapons, so the risk assessment leaves it as just us lot being necessary and sufficient.' She swept her gaze across them. 'Uniforms, you're serial alpha and you're with me. We are maintaining a perimeter around the pub. Nobody in, nobody out. Make sure we get a location for Kyle Talbot. Everyone got that?'

They all nodded.

'Good. Detectives, you're with Marshall. You're going inside. Marshall, I'll give you a notification that we're ready, then you're going in.'

Marshall watched them set off to establish a perimeter. He got out his police radio and sparked the line, letting her know he was there.

The only detective he knew well was McIntyre. Fresh out of uniform, so still physically fit enough to do battle with the best. And worst. The other two were big lumps of gristle in their early thirties. Great for both scouring through bank records and kicking down doors.

'Okay, lads, we're just a group of boys out after a funeral. Okay?'

Three nods.

'From memory, there are two doors in the pub. We're going in the front, so I want that guarded. As soon as we enter, I want one of you on the other door. Okay? I'm going up to his room. McIntyre, you're with me. Are we clear?'

Another three nods.

'Good.'

His radio chirruped. 'Serial bravo, this is serial alpha. Over.'

Marshall put it to his lips. 'Receiving. Over.'

'We're in position. We've found a black Mercedes van parked outside. We have reason to believe the target is here or has been. Over.'

'Received. Over and out.' Marshall looked around at them. 'You heard that. He's likely here. So let's do this.' He led out of the train station car park and crossed the road, checking his baton was safely stowed away. Slowly, casually, like a group of lads heading to the pub.

No sign of Elliot's lot, but that wasn't a bad thing.

Marshall walked up to the door, his heart pounding as he strode into the bar.

Lunchtime busy. Pool balls clicked and rattled. The karaoke machine pumped out 'New York, New York' but the singer didn't know many of the words. Or the tune.

Marshall scanned the crowd for any sign of their target.

Nothing.

McIntyre was doing the same. He clocked Marshall and gave a tight shake of the head.

The other two were in position, guarding both doors.

Marshall approached the bar and flashed his warrant card. 'DI Marshall. Looking for Kyle Talbot. He in?'

The barman shook his head. 'Not seen him since breakfast.'

'When was that?'

'Early one today, like. Sitting here at six, waiting for me to stick the fryer on.'

That tallied with the timeline. He must've walked back from the Nest roundabout, cross country past Clovenfords, then on to Stow. Ten miles or so. In the dark and cold.

Marshall could feel his frustration mounting. 'What room is he in?'

'Three. Up the stairs there.' He nodded over to a door at the side and past the second of the two big lumps guarding it.

Marshall nodded at McIntyre. 'Jim, you're leading.' He crossed the bar and pushed through the door into a tiny place with three doors. One was the gents, another led outside, presumably to a smoking area, so he took the other. No sign for the ladies' toilets, but a staircase. One of those places. He bounded up the steps, his legs pumping with adrenaline. He reached the landing and stopped, listening carefully for anything.

Nothing up here, just a roar of laughter from downstairs.

Marshall approached room three and paused, listening intently. Movement inside. His heart began to race again. This was it. He balled his fists and readied himself to take down his prey.

He nodded at McIntyre, then at the door.

McIntyre took a deep breath, like he was kicking a penalty for Melrose against Gala RFC at Netherdale. Then he burst into the room.

CHAPTER SIXTY-TWO

No word from Marshall.

Hard to hear if he was in some kind of fist fight with Talbot over the din of the karaoke machine, but at least they'd gone from murdering 'New York, New York' to stabbing 'Maggie May' in the back.

The Stagehall Arms beer garden would be a miserable place in the height of summer when Archie overcooked the burgers and undercooked the chicken. In January, though, it was like a post-apocalyptic hellscape, years after the nukes had fallen. That black mould growing on the walls could get into your lungs and turn you into a zombie mushroom monster like in that TV show.

'What's your name, son?'

The young uniform she'd picked didn't look around at her. 'PC Paul Buchan.' Skinny but not a beanpole. Hard to see him winning a fight with anyone. Might be a useful runner.

'That's an Aberdeen accent, aye?'

'Aye.' The long Doric version wasn't that dissimilar to the

local one. 'I know I'm a sheep-shagging bastard, before you start.'

'Wasn't going to.'

'Parents moved here when I was twelve, if that's what you're wondering. Never lost the accent.'

'Wasn't wonder—'

Her radio chirped.

'Marshall to Elliot. His room's clear. But the bong is warm and the Xbox is still on. Window's cracked open. Over.'

Elliot spotted Marshall in a window up on the first floor. 'Got you.' She put her radio away and scanned the area again. The shed and its lavender and plum paint job looked totally out of place here. Six picnic tables with built-in benches. Parasol stands, but no beer umbrellas. The only exit was the gate they were guarding.

Last time she'd been here, to pick up a flasher in the summer, everyone had been hiding under umbrellas advertising beers and ciders they didn't make anymore.

Those brollies had to go somewhere for winter.

That storage shed.

'Buchan, can you open that door?'

'Sure about that, ma'am?'

'Come on, son. We've all kicked in a door. That's an order.'

He took off his hat, ran a hand through his hair, then grabbed the door handle and twisted. 'Not opening, ma'am.'

'Give it some—'

He jerked it and hauled it open.

A bowling ball swung out on a pendulum, aiming for his head.

Buchan jumped out of the way.

It swung out and cracked him on the shoulder, knocking him down to his knees.

Elliot dashed over and pushed him out of the way of its second swing.

Talbot rushed out and punched her in the guts.

Searing pain burnt through her, like she'd been stabbed again. She stumbled back and sprawled over a picnic bench.

Talbot was racing over to the gate. He stopped, eyes wide, then turned and hopped up onto a bench, then jumped over the low wall.

Getting away.

She got up and tried to climb up after him. Everything hurt and her vision swam. She managed to clamber up onto the bench and spotted him running down the back lane.

She smelled fire.

She looked around at the shed and saw a flame burst out of the gas barbecue. The explosion pushed her over the wall and she landed on the grass verge.

Pain screamed out. Felt she'd reopened her wound.

She had to get him! Had to!

She pushed up to a kneel then a crouch, then she was upright, staggering forward, towards him. She had to lean against the wall at the end and suck in deep smoky breaths.

Next to a black van, a uniform lay on the pavement, clutching his balls. He got up and tugged at the driver's door. It shot open and knocked him over.

Talbot was behind the wheel. He clocked her and the van shot off.

She fumbled her radio. 'This is DI Elliot, requesting urgent police pursuit for a black Mercedes van leaving Stow.' She sprinted off after it, each step feeling like it tore something. 'License plate NJ69—'

A car smashed into the side of the van, knocking it into the front wall of the Stagehall Arms.

Elliot hobbled over, her guts burning.

Shunty staggered out of the pool car's driver door, then hauled open the van's door. 'Kyle Talbot, I'm arresting you for—'

CHAPTER SIXTY-THREE

Marshall reckoned it would take just an hour and a half to drive through from Glasgow, much longer if taking the train. Kyle Talbot's lawyer somehow managed the feat in fifty minutes. Marshall wouldn't even have cleared the Edinburgh bypass in that time. Maybe Colin Bannatyne-Fyffe was one of those arseholes in German cars who rampaged along the A72 regardless of what was coming towards them.

Might work for a top law firm through there, but Bannatyne-Fyffe looked like a PE teacher, just one dressed in a shabby suit. No shave could be clean enough to scrape the hair out of his cleft chin. 'This is a total farce and I expect my client to be let go.'

Marshall smiled at Jolene sitting next to him. 'Hear that, Sergeant? He's not answered a single question and he's expecting to be let go.'

'No. Doesn't have to. DS Siyal read him his rights. One of those is to silence.'

'It's not been the case for over ten years. He doesn't have to

ED JAMES

say anything, sure, but if he doesn't... That bit about it harming his defence if he later relies on it in court. That's what I'd be focusing on. And I'd be getting him to answer all those questions.'

Bannatyne-Fyffe smirked. 'And you should be focusing on the fact that someone smashed a police car into a van he'd rented, so you'll be facing a lawsuit.' He checked his watch. 'A junior colleague will be filing that just now. Not sure the Police Scotland coffers will stretch that far.'

'That's frivolous and you know it.' Marshall was getting nowhere and didn't expect to progress any further. Being stonewalled by the pair of them... It was... Change of tack needed. He focused on Talbot. 'Why did you run from my colleague?'

'Because you've been trying to pick me up for ages. Police intimidation, man.'

Finally, the dam had burst. 'That doesn't track. We've spoken to you a couple of times. You'll note how we didn't arrest you at any time.'

'Still stands.'

'What are you running from?'

Talbot laughed. 'I've sat here and listened to what you're saying. Got to admit yourself, man, this whole thing's a very interesting fiction. The last time I saw you was at the farm. I spoke to you and buggered off for the day.'

'Not very diligent of you, was it?'

'Don't know if you've heard, but the owner died. Old Napier Rattray. Nobody was really in the mood for work, so I went back home to my digs.'

'To smoke dope and play *Call of Duty* on your Xbox.'

'*Assassin's Creed*, actually.'

'Is there a point to this, Inspector?' Bannatyne-Fyffe dabbed at something on the table and inspected it, then flicked it away over his shoulder. 'Because you're wasting his time. And mine. Which is pretty expensive.'

'You'll be glad to know I'm getting to the point.' Marshall shifted his focus back to Talbot. 'When I turned up at the farm, you knew I was asking about a crime you'd committed, right?'

'Haven't committed any crimes.'

'You assaulted two officers.'

'Okay, but they were attacking me when I had a smoke.'

'We will charge you for their assault.'

'See you in court, then.' Talbot got to his feet.

'Sit down.'

'No.'

'We're done when I say we're done.'

Talbot grudgingly sat. 'You got a point here, champ?'

'Aye. I do. The reason you ran, Kyle, is because you're an assassin.'

Talbot leaned back and laughed. 'That's brilliant.' He prodded his lawyer. 'Hear that? I'm an assassin.'

'I don't mean the ancient Order of Assassins, like in that video game you're playing. No, you're just a common or garden hitman. Someone pays you. You kill someone or you abduct them.'

'Call your first witness, would you? Or how about you show me the forensics?' Talbot shifted his gaze between them. 'No? Thought not.'

'Like most assassins, you assume that one day people will come after you. The police or someone associated with a target. So you'd have a series of booby traps set to facilitate that escape. When you moved in there, you set up the shed as a hiding place.'

Talbot smirked. 'This is way more ludicrous than a video game.'

'Except this is real life. You almost killed someone. A

serving officer. PC Buchan's nineteen. His second year in the job. And you almost killed him.'

'An accident. Entirely his fault for barging in there without checking.'

'Answer me this, though. The nearest bowling rink is in Edinburgh, by my reckoning. And you had an elaborate pendulum system there.'

'Mate, you're cracked in the head. Got some items in storage in there, so Archie gave us a key. One of the items was my old bowling gear. Pretty decent player back in Glasgow. Noticed someone had been fannying about with all that stuff. Must've been Archie. Or one of his regulars. I wouldn't know where to start.'

'Care to explain the explosion?'

'Freezing outside, so I was smoking in the shed. Didn't know the gas was on in there. Whoever buggered about with my bowling gear must've knocked it.'

'You weren't running because you got Rory Tait to hire a van in his name?'

'Rory who?'

'Tait.'

'No idea who that is.'

'He knows you.'

'Lot of people do. Doesn't mean the reciprocal's true.'

'You pushed someone out of a van last night. Headfirst.'

'Not me.'

'Then you burnt it, with a pal inside. Iain Caddon.'

'No idea who he is. Sorry.'

'AKA Baseball.'

'Baseball?'

'His nickname. Like you're called Chunk.'

'Chunk?' Talbot scowled. 'Do I look like I should be called Chunk?'

In truth, he didn't. 'You might've been fat as a kid.'

'Hardly. Been skin and bone all my life.'

'But the thing is, you do know Baseball. Archie at the Stagehall Arms said you were in a pool league with him.'

'As good as I am at bowling, I'm even better at pool. Can beat anyone. All about the break, you know? Make sure I pot both colours every time, so I can choose depending on the lay of the land. But being in a league with someone doesn't mean I know their names. Or push them out of a moving vehicle.'

'You're getting confused here. Baseball is the one who you burnt to death after you crashed a van into a wall.'

'This is such bullshit. Fanciful bullshit, I'll give you that. Do you get ChatGPT to write these questions for you?'

'I'm much better than any artificial intelligence.' Marshall held his gaze until the smile faded. 'What about Louisa Baird?'

'No idea who she is.'

'Steven Beattie?'

'Who?'

'Someone set fire to his home. Then pushed him out of the van.'

'Heard it was him who set that fire.'

'Oh? How did you hear that?'

Talbot looked away. 'Some boy at the farm was saying.'

'What about Justin Lorimer?'

'That prick deserved what he got but I didn't give it to him.'

'So you know him?'

'Played pool with the boy, aye. You know he attacked me.'

'Then this morning, you abducted Hugo Baird and Rachel Lorimer.'

'Mate!' He slapped the table. 'This is priceless.'

'We found Hugo up Ladhope Moor. Rachel's still missing, though. Where is she?'

'Dude, listen to yourself. According to you, I've killed four people in two days. And abducted another two. At the same time, I've been working on installing a wind farm *and* helping you lot with this investigation. I can't have done all that in that time, can I?'

'Aye, you can. Where were you?'

'Not telling you anything more. I'll just wait here while you lot make up another chapter in your narrative.'

'Come on. You weren't at work this morning. Where were you?'

'No comment.'

Stonewalled again.

'How about the crime formerly known as the attempted murder of Napier Rattray.'

'What about it?'

'Well, it's now known as the murder of Napier Rattray. Just because it takes months for a victim's loved ones to decide to switch off the life support machine doesn't make it any less murder-y. But it was just supposed to be a warning, wasn't it? You didn't *mean* to kill him, did you?'

He laughed. 'That wasn't a murder. That poor old bugger was up a hundred-foot wind turbine in the middle of a storm. He fell. Stupidity doesn't make it a crime.'

'Sure. That's what you told the police. After all, you were there.' Marshall smiled at Bannatyne-Fyffe. 'While you were driving through, I refreshed my memory on that investigation. Reviewed the statements given at the time, which now seem to be complete nonsense.'

'Mate. He fell. Nothing to do with me.'

'Don't you feel any guilt at all these people dying? *Five* people, Kyle. You might justify to yourself about some of them deserving it. After all, Justin Lorimer hit you with a pool cue. Who knows what Baseball or Beattie did. But one of those victims of yours was definitely innocent. Dr Louisa Baird. She was an oncologist. Lovely woman. A mother. A wife. Ran a cancer charity. And you abducted her husband.'

'I really want to help you, mate, but I've no idea about any of this. Sounds bloody awful though.'

'And Justin Lorimer? Father of two. Rachel's husband. Worked at the farm. All-round good guy. You seem to have fallen out with him. So why abduct his wife after you killed him? Where is Rachel Lorimer?'

'I've no idea who you're talking about.' Talbot sat back, arms folded. 'Okay, I've had enough of this. I'll tell you exactly what I know right here and now, then you let me out. I can see you're quite dug in on this caper but I can't waste any more time playing around.'

'You give me your truth, Kyle, I'll see if it matches anyone else's.'

'Right.' Talbot looked at his lawyer and got a nod. 'Justin *was* a mate. Worked with him, of course – he was the client, so I had to deal with him a bit when my boss was off. We'd eat with the farm lads at lunchtime. Always had a lovely roast dinner on. Ate like a fucking king in there. And when that caravan got a bit too cold in winter, I moved into the pub and used to see him in there. Have a drink with him. Shoot some pool. Even did a duet of Robson and Jerome at that boy's karaoke night. The lad with the mullet and the piano-keyboard tie. But we fell out last week. Too much to drink. Too much aggro. But that's it. That's all it was.'

'That's a good start, Kyle. It matches up with what I've heard so I can buy that. Why did you kill him?'

'I never. But I could see why someone would want to.'

'Go on?'

'Justin was in there every night, right. Guy would speak to anyone. I mean, *anyone*. One night, he was speaking to a guy. Kid called Baseball.'

'So you do know him?'

'I know who he is, aye. Wannabe gangster type. Seen a lot of them in Glasgow. Boys who are all mouth and no trousers. Anyway, this Baseball lad was mouthing off about how he did a deal with someone. A woman. She paid him to send Napier Rattray a warning. He ended up pushing him off a wind turbine. "Fucking scary up there, man." Those were his words. I can handle it up there, but not a lot of others can.'

'You were there that night, though.'

'I was. Trying to secure all the equipment. Absolute bedlam, man. But I didn't know what was going on up there. Didn't even see this Baseball guy.'

'Sounds like complete bullshit to me.'

'Swear, that's all I know.'

Bannatyne-Fyffe smiled at Marshall, like a snake away to eat a mouse. 'He's given you it all. How about you let him go?'

Marshall smiled at him like a mongoose away to eat a snake. 'I'll have a think about it.'

'No. Here's what's going to happen. My client will be released on the charges related to attacking the police officers who tried to detain him.' He opened his briefcase and put a sheet of paper on the table. 'I am formally presenting you with a draft copy of a civil action for the damage to my client's van.' His grin widened. 'I understand the driver of the police vehicle has had a few vehicular mishaps in recent memory?'

CHAPTER SIXTY-FOUR

Marshall regretted not having those last few chips earlier. He was starving now. And his laptop wasn't exactly helping his mood any. Buggering thing should be smart enough to solve the case for him, but he was having to deal with it constantly restarting to update. There it was again.

Useless.

He got up and wandered over to the window. Rain hammered the glass. Dark outside, but the park was filled with dog walkers, letting their pooches mill around after a day of work. Where the gossip would flow.

'Did you hear about Napier Rattray?'

'Heard it was his son who did it.'

'Or his long-lost half-sister.'

Marshall had less idea than those people out there. So many open questions and no real avenues left to explore.

And he saw the pool car sitting there. With all the biscuit crumbs and Josh's smeared bogies on the back seat. He needed to clean that up.

Later.

Poor kid. Hard to imagine what Josh's life was going to be like now. Him and his sister had lost one parent and their mother was still missing.

Poor kids.

'Evening.' Elliot swung into the room and he caught her smile in the reflection. 'You hungry?'

'Starving.'

'Well, auntie Andrea's got you a nice wee treat.' She flung a sandwich through the air. 'Don't say I'm not good to you. Or the whole team.'

Marshall unwrapped the cling film and opened it to peek inside. He'd expected cheese and tomato or egg mayonnaise on dry white, but he got a pastrami, Emmental and gherkin on rye. 'Thank you.' He tore at the wrapper and took a mouthful. 'This is very kind of you.'

'Got Davie to rustle up some rounds for the team. Kids are all playing on their games, so he was just sitting on his arse watching Sky Sports News. Moaned about having to go to Ashworth's at this time, but their bread's the best.'

'All the same. Thank you.' He took another bite then walked over to his desk and washed it down with still-warm coffee. 'Where have you been?'

'Home. Getting these sandwiches.'

Even after all those chats, she was still evasive to the end. 'Before that?'

'Ah, went to the hospital to speak to Hugo Baird. He doesn't have any leads on where they've taken Rachel Lorimer. It's like they didn't even know each other.'

'Certainly seemed that way.' Marshall finished chewing. 'This sandwich is fantastic. Davie should set up a café.'

'I'll pass that on.' Elliot was staring into space. 'The longer it takes us to find her, the lower the chances of finding her alive.'

'I know that. I hate this, Andrea. The lack of... She's out there, somewhere. And I'm sitting looking through all the files we've got on Kyle Talbot, Iain Caddon, anyone. All of their known associates. I've been through the file from when you investigated Napier Rattray's fall. Hell, I've even picked up the half-arsed profile I did for Pringle.'

'Anything?'

'What do you think? It was half-arsed for a reason – this isn't a serial killing.'

'I expected nothing, but are you sure it's not a serial killing?' She was smirking. 'He had a hard on for that, didn't he?'

'He really did.' He took another big bite of his sandwich. 'It's nonsense, though. Feel like I'm just an exotic pet for him. Something to make him look good.'

'Still, I heard you got Talbot talking.'

'A bit. Mostly denying it all. Thing is, it all fits, but Talbot didn't give us a smoking gun. Except... He did speak about Baseball. Alleging he was the go-between between them and their client.'

'Them? So he was involved?'

'I'm assuming so, but he didn't admit it.'

Her eyes narrowed. 'You think this client is Hislop?'

'No. A woman. Paid to kill Napier Rattray as well as the rest.'

'Rhona Rattray?'

Marshall shrugged. 'It's crossed my mind. Getting Louisa Baird out of the picture would be good for her. All of the money would go to *her* son, rather than being split with Napier's daughter. But something doesn't feel right about it.'

'We should take a drive up there and speak to her.'

'Already been up there today. Poor woman's grieving. Don't want to piss her off into making a complaint.'

'Never stopped me in the past.' Elliot grinned, like it was a point of pride. 'And it doesn't mean she isn't behind all this. Six down: something, something, who gains, something, something, hide behind grief.' She slumped behind her desk. 'Or I could speak to Hislop again.'

'Sure that's wise?'

'Not really. I'm already in too deep with him. I could pick up with Gashkori in Drugs, but he's a big sweaty mess and he'll just go tonto.'

'Be careful using that word around Rakesh. It's a micro-aggression, apparently.'

'How?'

'It equates Native Americans with psychopathy, allegedly.'

'Jesus wept.' She hauled her hair back out of her eyes. 'Hislop knew something we didn't. He probably knows a lot more.'

'I'm worried for you, Andrea. Someone like Hislop has no limits.'

'He won't harm me.'

'Glad you're sure of that.' Marshall took a final bite of his sandwich. 'Okay, so we need to charge Talbot, then let him go.'

'Let him go? He punched me in the stomach!'

'As it stands, we've got nothing on him save for the word of a child sex offender. And Rakesh smashing a car into his van while we arrested him.'

'So you're thinking we charge him with something minor to get him on the books. The assault on—' She clicked her fingers a few times. '—Buchan. Bowling ball to the chest and a kick in the goolies.'

'That's right.' Marshall hoisted himself up to standing. So

bloody tired. He didn't want to start yawning. 'Besides, we don't have anything else on him, do we?'

Someone knocked on the door.

Siyal stood there, hands in pockets. 'You guys got a minute?'

'Speak of the devil and he shall—' Elliot shut up.

Ash Paton followed him into the room. 'Hi, I'm Ash.' They walked up to Marshall and shook his hand. 'Pleased to meet you, sir.'

'And you.' Marshall returned the smile.

Paton nodded at Elliot.

'Ash has been going through the bank details for the victims.' Siyal waved a hand at them. 'Asked her to pick up McIntyre's work.'

Marshall clocked a glance from Elliot, but she didn't say anything.

Siyal scratched his neck. 'Thing is, she found a funny thing in there.'

'I'm not very good at it, sir. Ma'am.' She was blushing. 'But I went back through Louisa Baird's records and found a strange debit card transaction. Jim had— That's DC McIntyre. He'd queried it with the bank but hadn't heard back, so I followed up on it. The business name is Tutzing Enterprises. Sounded a bit funny. Turns out to belong to Wedale House in Stow.'

Marshall knew it. 'That's the fancy B&B, right?'

'Boutique hotel, yes. Anyway, I called them and they found a booking matching that transaction.' She held out a giant smartphone showing the website of an upmarket hotel, lots of moody night shots with a lit-up garden. 'Two hundred quid a night.'

Elliot laughed. 'For a place in *Stow*?'

'Aye. Dr Baird prepaid for three nights.' Siyal pulled out another evidence bag. 'We found a hotel keycard on her body, remember?' He glanced at Paton. 'We think she was planning on leaving her husband.'

'Hold your horses, Shunty.' Elliot raised her hands. 'Who was she there with? That's the million-dollar question. Let's pay them a wee visit, shall we?'

CHAPTER SIXTY-FIVE

Marshall wished there was a police station in Stow, because he kept having to hurtle up and down the A7 towards that infernal town. Not a bad place by any stretch, but everything seemed to centre around there.

'I suppose if anyone's going to get her pronouns precisely right, Rob, it'll be Shunty.' Elliot was in the passenger seat, nibbling at her nails. 'Seems like a decent cop, though. Never heard of her, mind.'

'You didn't interview her?'

'Hired while I was off, Rob. Pringle and Shunty did it. She only came in last week. Been swept up with all the crap with Drugs up in Edinburgh so haven't had a chance to speak to her.'

'Why did it take her that long to start, then?'

'Search me. Still, I'm glad we know her gender now so that's another mystery closed.'

The way she talked, that HR referral gained complaints by the hour.

Marshall spotted the grand three-storey house a few doors

along from the modern church, and pulled into the lane between the old, ruined church and the manse. He parked opposite the arched entrance and got out, immediately shivering in the cold dark.

The house sign was stuck to the gable wall, lit up from all corners and glowing in the dark:

Wedale House
Putting the "you" in boutique

'That doesn't work.' Elliot walked through the entrance into a courtyard. A wee bothy sat to the side, opposite the house, with some plinky-plonky piano music playing. 'Funny it just being you and me, eh?'

'That's only because you won't let me out of your sight in case I find something you don't want me to.' Marshall yanked the heavy oak door open, a creak piercing the air, and he held it for her. 'Ladies first.' He followed her into the soft glow of the reception area.

Flames leapt and danced in an ancient fireplace, casting flickering shadows over the antique furniture and Persian rug. The intimacy was stifling, every detail whispering secrets and history, but smelled of fried cod and vinegar.

Marshall approached the front desk and rang the bell. No sign of anyone, but he felt the walls were silently sizing him up.

A tall man flounced out from behind a curtain. 'Grüß Gott!'

Elliot scowled at him. 'Excuse me?'

'Ah, forgive me.' He bowed. 'I am from Bavaria and that is a common greeting. It means... I think the English would be "God greets you".'

'Very nice to finally meet God, then. DI Andrea Elliot.' She held out her warrant card. 'This is DI Marshall. We're looking into a transaction relating to a booking here.'

'Do you have the name?'

'Dr Louisa Baird.'

'One second.' He sat down and unlocked his computer. 'I don't have a booking under that name.'

'Interesting.' Elliot reached into her pocket and produced a sheet of paper. 'This is when the transaction was made.'

'Ah, ja. Superb.' He hammered the keyboard. 'The booking was for Mr and Mrs Smith. Three nights.'

Elliot frowned at Marshall then at the hotelier. 'Did anyone check in?'

'Ja. At six o'clock on Wednesday. I gave her two keycards. She left at seven, I think, but she didn't come back.'

Marshall jotted it down in his notebook – that pinned down Dr Baird's timeline that little bit more. 'She hasn't checked out?'

'No. I will remove her possessions tomorrow at noon.'

'We wonder if we could have a look at them?'

'Ja, that shouldn't be a problem. The room's presently empty.' He set off past them, limping badly. 'Forgive me. I cracked my knee running.'

'Sounds painful.'

'Ja. I ran seven marathons in a week.'

'In a *week*?'

'It's not so bad once you get going.' He opened a door and took the steps one by one. 'The hills here are not as unforgiving as where I'm used to.'

'You ran *twenty-six miles* every day for a week?'

'Twenty-six miles and three hundred and eighty-five yards.'

'Of course. How remiss of me.' Elliot was shaking her head

like the idea of those yards being too much for her, let alone the miles.

The owner stopped at the top of the steps and shoogled his knee until it clicked. 'We had a bit of, eh, mischief when the previous owner died. The estate let us buy the place for a greatly reduced fee.' He opened another door leading into a hallway. A lot less salubrious up here than the reception area. 'She was a politician. We renovated it and opened it as a boutique hotel. Still needs a lot of work up here, but my wife is a wonderful designer.'

Marshall thought he heard Elliot say, 'Wife?'

He limped along the corridor again. 'If you look at our website, we mention the ghost. I haven't seen him myself, but I believe old Hamish haunts this particular room.' He stopped outside a door with a Do Not Disturb sign hanging. 'We have a podcaster coming to record it next month. I hope you listen for it!' He swiped a card and the reader clicked green. 'Be my guest.' He belched out a laugh.

Marshall opened the door.

A woman sat on the bed facing the door, dressed in a white gown.

Rachel Lorimer.

CHAPTER SIXTY-SIX

'Just a second, sir.' Elliot shut the door behind them and leaned back against it. No way was the hotelier getting into the room. Or Rachel Lorimer out. 'Been looking for you, Rachel.'

'Shit.' She swallowed hard and collapsed back onto the bed, which filled most of the room. The place had a kind of chintzy charm to it, but not what Elliot would describe as boutique. The ceiling was a giant map of the world from hundreds of years ago. Heavy wooden cabinets surrounded the bed.

Elliot picked up a chair and rooted it down, facing Rachel, then sat, folding her arms across her chest.

Marshall walked over to the bathroom and peeked inside. A swish of the shower curtain then he gave a short shake of the head.

Elliot tilted her head back. 'Just you here, Rachel?'

She nodded. Didn't sit up, though.

'First thing we need from you, Rachel, is for you to explain what you're doing here.'

'They abducted me. Tied me up. Brought me here.'

Elliot scanned her arms and wrists – sure enough, there were marks from bonds. 'Who did?'

'I don't know their names. There was more than one of them, I think.'

'Sure about that?'

'No. I only saw one, but... I think I heard him talking.'

'Him. Sure about that?'

She sat up now. 'Sure. They abducted me! The day after my husband was killed! In front of my kids!'

Elliot played it all through and it just seemed like absolute gibberish. 'Guess we need to look through our list of known offenders, looking for someone who abducts people and dumps their bodies inside boutique hotels. In dressing gowns.' She had a different answer to who the mystery woman was, the one paying Baseball. 'You paid them to abduct you and Hugo Baird, didn't you?'

'No!'

'Rachel.' Elliot rocked back on the chair legs. 'How the hell did you have a keycard for this room?'

'What?'

'You have a keycard for this room, which means you got it from Louisa Baird somehow. Now, if that was when she was alive, it's a different matter to when she was dead. Or is it? I don't know, Rachel.'

'I'm saying nothing.' Rachel's eyes danced across to Marshall, then back to Elliot. Her shoulders sank.

'Why did you do it, Rachel? Why?'

'They were having an affair.'

'Affair?'

'Justin and Louisa.' She coiled her damp hair around her finger. 'Louisa was at this Burns supper where Justin worked. She left and was on her way to meet Justin here when she was abducted. They each had a keycard when they took them.'

'How did you know they were coming here?'

'Because the cards were in these little cardboard sleeves. Putting the "you" into boutique. And a room number.' She folded her arms around her shoulders. 'This was Hugo's idea.'

'Hugo?'

'Baird. Louisa's husband.'

'You paid for him to be abducted?'

'No. Well, yes. Look, my dad used to play rugby with him so I've known him for years. Ever since I was a girl. Friend of the family. He never married, then he met Louisa and... And she was taking him for a ride.'

'Can you explain how?'

'I can try...'

'Go on.'

'Hugo's the lawyer for the farm. He knew all about the change to Napier's will. Napier's wife was being written out and Louisa was replacing her. Thing is... Louisa hadn't told Hugo and that freaked him out. They had a loveless marriage, just staying together for their kid. Toby. Nice boy. Anyway. It was only a matter of time before Napier Rattray died and Louisa would get the inheritance. Half of that farm. Hugo was going to divorce her and get half of the money. He'd split some of it with me.'

'Seems very generous of him, Rachel.'

'I had the connections. I knew people who could... do stuff. So I arranged for the accident on the wind turbine. When Napier survived, we panicked.'

'It wasn't a warning?'

'What?' Rachel scowled at him. 'No. Of course not. We wanted him dead, so Louisa got her inheritance. But things were getting more and more strained between Louisa and

Hugo. She was shagging some young doctor at the hospital. I picked them up once from a pub in Melrose. Very hands-on. You see all sorts in the taxi game... And I did. Hugo didn't want them to divorce until he got his hands on the money in the settlement. But he got wind of Louisa arranging to meet a divorce lawyer in Gala next week. So we had to act.'

'What did you do?'

'Like you said, I hired someone to abduct them both and delay the divorce until Napier died and Louisa got the money. Didn't mean for them to *die*.'

'So that was an accident?'

'I swear, I didn't want them to die. Just to receive a message. To freak them out, make them delay.'

'Who did you hire?'

'A guy called Baseball. Turns out he knew my husband from the pub. Said he'd sort it out. I swear, it wasn't my intention for them to....' Rachel brushed tears away from her eyes. 'Then you lot started circling so we... I arranged for us to get abducted to make it look like we were both innocent. In front of our kids too.' She tugged at her nose. 'I hate to think what it's done to them.' She looked up at Marshall, then over at Elliot. 'Hugo was beaten up worse than I'd expected. The man who took us was a real sadist.'

'It wasn't Baseball?'

'No.'

'Good, because his body was found this morning, so we know you're not lying. Who was it?'

'I've no idea. He dropped me in Stow. I didn't know what to do. I had a keycard for this room, so I sneaked in and... I'm so fucking sorry.'

CHAPTER SIXTY-SEVEN

Marshall stood in the window, looking out across the dark town centre. The snotty pool car was still there. Still needed cleaning. That'd wait until tomorrow. Or maybe he should do it tonight.

'You know, Marshall, I'll miss this place.'

He frowned at Elliot, standing next to him. 'Eh?'

'We're moving to Gala soon.'

'Are we?'

She laughed. 'Do you actually read your emails?'

'Not if I can help it.'

'Well, you better brief Jolene and the rest of your team, because come April, we'll be based there.'

'Will do. Shit, I didn't know.' He rubbed the back of his neck. 'Easier commute for me.'

'Aye, extra ten minutes for me. Traffic can be a bastard in Gala too, especially at that end. Ever since they put that one-way system in, I swear...'

'That was over twenty years ago.'

'Aye, exactly. The council are so bloody stubborn.'

The door opened and cracked back off the wall.

Pringle stormed in, face like thunder.

'Evening, sir.' Elliot turned to face him. 'Good result, eh?'

He stopped in the middle of the room, hands on hips. 'Is it?'

She glowered at him. 'We caught the killer.'

'No you didn't.'

'Eh? Stop messing about, sir.'

Pringle looked her up and down with a sneer. 'You caught the woman who paid the killer to do it. I don't see anyone in the cells in Gala who fits the bill of our abductor-murderer.'

Marshall walked over to him. 'What's up, sir?'

'The pair of you are acting like we've caught DB Cooper and Jack the Ripper with Madeline McCann.' Pringle walked over to Elliot's desk and picked up a sandwich. He dropped it, then got out his phone and tapped out a text. 'You don't have the killer.'

'We will find them. Rachel's been co-operating with us. We've got phones to trace and—'

'That's beside the point!'

'No, sir.' Marshall got between them. 'It's simple. Two people got greedy. Paid the wrong person to do something and they fucked it up. Then they paid the price.'

'Marshall, you're not hearing me.' Pringle shook his head. 'Until we have our killer behind bars, this case isn't over. Okay? And I want you to go through the profile and—'

'Jim! It's not a serial killer.' Elliot jabbed a finger in his face, almost touching his nose. 'Rob's told you that! I've told you that! It's a load of idiots making a mess of—'

'Andrea! Shut up! Shut the fuck up!' Pringle stepped forward. 'It's always about you, isn't it? Nipping my head. Moaning and moaning and moaning. Well, just shut the fuck up for once and listen.'

Her mouth hung open. 'You can't talk to me like that!'

'Not usually, no. You're usually too busy giving people fucking nicknames and belittling them.'

Marshall had only seen flashes of him like this. Right now, the whistling weirdo was away somewhere, cowering in a corner, while this Lovecraftian monster exploded with rage. 'Sir, I agree with Andrea. We've got a confession from Rachel Lorimer. Rakesh and Jolene are documenting it all. We've got people in the hospital speaking to Hugo Baird. I've contacted social services about the Lorimer kids, to make them aware. There's a good chance—'

'Fucking hell.' Pringle collapsed onto a desk. 'Those poor children.'

Elliot exchanged a look with Marshall which captured his confusion. 'What?'

'Rachel and Justin had two kids.' Pringle gripped his thighs tight. 'Hugo and Louisa had one. They've each lost a parent, while the other is going to prison for a long, long time. As a proud father, it breaks my heart.'

Elliot shook her head. 'You can't keep winding us up about that.'

Pringle looked up at her with red eyes. 'I'm not winding anyone up.'

'Shut the fuck up about that.' Elliot squared up to him. 'You don't have a kid. Never have, never will. It's not a joking matter. I've got three bairns myself and do you know how fucking hard it is? Do you?'

'Of course I do.'

She swung out with her fist.

Marshall clocked the movement and grabbed her wrist. 'Come on, Andrea, give us a minute, would you?' He dragged her over to the door and pushed her out into the corridor. 'Don't. Okay?'

'Don't what?'

'Don't punch your boss. Go and chase up Shunty or get home. I'll see you later.' Marshall slammed the door without a reply, then turned back to Pringle. 'I'd apologise for her behaviour, sir, but I agree with her sentiment. What the hell is going on with you?'

'Nothing's going on.'

'Come on, sir. We haven't seen you all day and you come in here biting our heads off. What's going on?'

'Do you want the truth?'

'No, sir. I want you to keep lying to us.' Marshall smiled. 'Of course I want the truth.'

'You can't handle the truth!' The old Pringle reappeared, laughing at his joke. 'Can I ask you to brief Andrea about Shunty?'

'His appraisal?'

'His appraisal?' Pringle frowned. 'What about it?'

'She was going to put him onto an actioned contract.'

'Was she? Bloody hell. Well, he's no longer her problem.'

'You're sacking him?'

'God no. Young Shunty has proved himself as a capable officer. One of my favourites, just not necessarily murder squad calibre. He's secured himself a move to Professional Standards and Ethics, based up in Edinburgh.'

'Wow.'

'You don't think he's up to that?'

'No, I think he'll be ideal for it. He's very good at checks and balances. I'm both surprised and pleased for him. I'll pass on the news, sir.'

CHAPTER SIXTY-EIGHT

Another day over and Elliot strode down the street towards her car. Be so much better to be in Gala with its proper car park, rather than having to rely on street parking like in Melrose. They were police officers – people targeted cops' cars.

Christ, had she really thought that anything could be worse than being in Gala?

Her phone rang:

Dr Donkey calling...

Nah, she was over that noise for today, so she bounced it.

A text popped up:

> Need a chat about Rakesh when you've got a minute

She didn't need any of *that* noise either.

Obviously bollocks. He wanted to speak to her on the false

premise of persuading her to get out of putting Shunty on an action contract, so he could talk to her about how she almost lamped Pringle.

Aye, he'd saved her there. She owed him one.

Still, she wasn't going to be talked to like that by anyone. Least of all Pringle. Coming in like that and hitting hard. After all she'd done for him over the years.

Aye, she'd take him down a peg or two. She tapped out a reply:

> Tomorrow. Have a good evening

She put her phone away, zapped her car and got in. Be home soon, then a glass of wine. She smelled something wooden. That sharp sawdust smell.

A case of wine sat on the passenger seat. A posh one, stamped with a vineyard she could sort of read but didn't know how to pronounce.

Some fucker had broken into her car.

She tore the envelope off and opened it.

A card, showing a chintzy painting of the snowy Borders countryside.

> Gather you're into your French reds just now

Had to be Gary Hislop. Had to be.

She rested the box in the footwell and got out her phone.

Something dropped out of the envelope.

Photos of her, Davie and the kids at the donkey sanctuary in the summer.

A shot of them arguing in Ashworth's on Saturday.

Her hands were shaking. Everything was. That sleazy

bastard wasn't the first to threaten her. Hell, this wasn't the first time *he'd* threatened her.

Probably watching her right now.

She kept her cool and hit dial on her phone.

'Hislop.'

Elliot laughed. She wasn't going to let him get any satisfaction. 'Not a very imaginative way to punish me or attempt to control me.'

'What are you talking about?'

'Breaking into my car to leave behind a box of wine. Photos of me and my family.'

'Don't know what you're talking about.'

'This your way of showing me you still love me?'

'Oh, I'm like a sixteen-year-old laddie on a promise with a filthy older woman.'

She laughed. 'You're not sixteen and I'm not that filthy.'

'You used to be.'

'You try having three kids and a drink problem, then see how filthy you are.' She smiled. 'What's the message you're trying to send?'

'Someone gives me a case of French red, I'd say thank you.'

'Didn't say it was French red. Just wine.'

'An educated guess, Andi. That's all it is. But it wasn't me. Though I do want to thank you.'

'What for?'

'You've done me two favours, Andi. You reminded me I needed to sign my revised will. No use updating it if you don't sign it, eh?'

'That right, aye?'

'Aye.'

'And the other thing?'

'You got me to speak to lads at the rugby club. One of them's selling his shop in Earlston, so I'm taking over the lease.

Earlston Hardware, here we come. Same business model, same happy customers. Local success story of the year.'

'Hardly local if you're spreading out that far. I mean, Earlston's, what, ten miles from Gala?'

'More or less.' He held the silence for ages. Pretty creepy. 'My pal, let's call him Innes. He—'

'Surname or first?'

'According to Innes, word on the street is Baseball was coming to the end of his usefulness, which is why his paymaster binned him. Heard he did a few homers too, as I'd say in my trade. You know, when a wee laddie tiles a bathroom for cash in hand but doesn't tell his boss?'

'I'm well aware of what a homer is.'

'Right. Right. I mean, Innes's take on it is it's fair enough if it's a homer against people in the trade, but against the general public, it really isn't cool.'

'I love how you can make assassination sound so prosaic.'

'Assassination?'

'Come on, Gary. Cut the crap. There is no Innes. It's you. And Baseball worked for you, didn't he?'

'He didn't.'

'And Chunk?'

'Chunk? Oh, you mean Kyle Talbot?'

It hit Elliot right where her stitches had been. 'What?'

'Everyone calls him Chunk. Aye, he's a solid worker. Heard he installs wind turbines, would you believe? Renewables aren't the future, Andi, they're the present.'

'He's the one who's been doing homers, isn't he?'

'Not sure that follows.'

'We let him go this evening, but I think you'll know how to find him... After all, assassins have a way of outliving their usefulness.'

'Assassins? Come on, Andi. Who do you think I am?'

'I know precisely who you are. And what you're up to. Admit it – you're a drug supplier. You've got people on your payroll who murder for you.'

'This is all just the observation of a businessman. A savvy one.'

'If Talbot's the killer, then I'm bringing him back in.'

'I wouldn't be so fast.'

'Why?'

'Do you really want people to know about us, Andi?'

'Gary. You're in the CHIS log. I've played you.'

'What's a CHIS?'

'Covert human intelligence source. You're officially a snout. We have to log the true source anonymously. It's a complex process, but you're in there, supplying key information that led to charging someone who'd confessed to paying for a murder.'

'I wish you hadn't done that, Andi. I know stuff about you.'

Elliot tried to laugh it off.

'You're an ambitious woman. You want Pringle's job.'

'Fuck off, Gary.'

'You're really going to play it that way? I know the truth about that case where you earned your nickname.'

She swallowed something down. 'Goodnight.' She killed the call. She hadn't realised how hot her skin was, burning like a day in the Lanzarote sun.

Twisting her hands around the steering wheel like it was a throat.

Hislop's throat.

She noticed another photo in the stack. She leaned down to pick it up. A family shot – mum, dad and mixed-heritage kid. She squinted. Holy shit – it was Pringle and Owusu.

So the kid was real. And Belu was the mother?

And Gary Hislop knew all about it.

Elliot got out her phone and hit dial.

'Hey, love, what's up?'

She needed to hear her husband's voice. The din of the football crowd. The kids arguing. Popcorn rattling in the microwave. She plastered a smile on her face. 'Heading home now. Just wanted to run something by you while I drive...'

CHAPTER SIXTY-NINE

Marshall stood at the pool car's open door, glaring at the back seat. It looked like a miniature tornado had torn through it, and not the usual kind. The battlefield of children's snacks remnants lay scattered across the upholstery. He couldn't bring himself to look at the smears for long. The wee sod was *filthy*.

Still, the little sod and his sister had lost their father, while their mother was being charged with crimes that'd keep her inside until they were both old enough to drive themselves.

Marshall grabbed a rubbish bag and a roll of paper towels and steeled himself. He started picking up the larger pieces of biscuit, recalling the kids' boisterous laughter, completely oblivious to the mess they were creating or the trauma that awaited them. His own fault – he'd given them the food to pacify them and now he was paying the price, scrubbing furiously at the stubborn stains, each vigorous stroke amplifying his frustration.

He was engaged in a losing battle. Every time he seemed to make progress, he'd discover another hidden mess – that sticky lollipop wedged between the seats. Where did that come from? Or the crushed crisps on the footwell that needed hoovering.

Whoever had the pool car before him... What the hell had they done in there?

A car horn beeped and pulled in. He couldn't determine make or model behind the lights. Someone got out and he steeled himself.

Elliot stood there, scowling at him in the dark night. 'What are you up to, Marshall?'

He stood up tall until his back clicked. 'I'm cleaning the pool car after the bogie incident.'

'Do I want to ask?'

'The Lorimer kids. I gave them some treats as I drove them to their gran's.'

'Schoolboy error, Marshall.' She folded her arms. 'See your text and your call, which I bounced... Do you want that word now?'

She didn't look like she was in any mood for messing about, so he gave her it straight. 'It's about Shunty. He's got a new job. Complaints in Edinburgh.'

'Seriously?' Her eyebrows disappeared behind her fringe. 'That sneaky wee bugger.'

'Must've applied when you were off and got Pringle to co-sign the application. He's been asking to speak to me for a while, but I just haven't had the time.'

'Well, good luck to him.' She looked away. 'Jim say anything about making Jolene's acting sergeant tenure permanent?'

'He didn't, but I'll push for it. She's a good cop, once you get to know her.'

'Good man.' She smiled, but it faded. 'You got another minute?'

Marshall thumbed at the car. 'This is going to take me ages.'

She pointed over at the station. 'About Talbot... Who followed up on his alibi for the murders on Wednesday night?'

'Andrea, what's going on?'

'Nothing. Did anyone?'

Marshall knew better than to argue back against her when she was like this. Something was going on – better to assemble the facts and build up a picture than to fight her. 'The alibi he gave was a sexy video call with his wife. Rakesh's team looked into it.'

'He says it was Jolene's.'

'We need to get better at working together.' Marshall got out his phone and called Jolene, then stuck it on speaker. 'Let's see what she's got to say.'

She answered immediately. 'Evening, Rob.'

'Hey, Jo. Just wondering something. Did your lot pick up with Talbot's wife?'

'Rakesh's team did, aye. Told us at the briefing about how she confirmed his story. Remember?'

'I do.' Marshall clocked Elliot's furrowed brow. 'Can you get someone to follow up on it now. Double check, please.'

'O-kay... I'm still in so I'll do it myself. Why?'

'It's important. Give me a call back. Cheers.' Marshall ended the call. 'We definitely need to sort out the— What?'

Elliot was smirking. 'Jo and Rob, eh?'

'What do you mean?'

'You two seem to be bonding.'

'Are you implying—'

'God no. It's good when people get on.'

'Unlike you and Rakesh.'

'Aye...' She laughed. 'You must be like Action Man or Ken down there.'

'Hardly.'

'Single guy like you, though. You must be getting all the action on Tinder. Or Grindr. I'm not judging.'

'I'm seeing someone.'

'Aye? That nurse? Jen, is it?'

'Andrea, I told you she's my twin sister.'

'Aye, but I thought you were both messing around. You don't look alike. That, or it's a kink.'

He couldn't hide his revulsion. 'Don't be disgusting.'

'So who is the lucky—'

Marshall's phone rang.

Jolene calling...

He answered it and stuck it on speaker again. 'Hey, you're on with DI Elliot.'

'Hey, Andi. Okay, so I just called both of her numbers and they're out of service.'

'Mobile or landline?'

'Both were mobiles.'

Marshall shut his eyes. 'Okay, thanks for that. See you tomorrow, okay?'

'Rob, what's this about?'

'I'll explain tomorrow. Have a good evening. And get home soon, okay?'

'Okay.' Click and she was gone.

Marshall pocketed his phone and looked at Elliot. 'You hear that?'

'Got the gist of it, aye. Out of service means both are burners, right?'

'I'm guessing so. Why are you asking about it? What are you thinking?'

Her breath misted in the freezing air. 'I'm thinking she's

not real, Rob. Someone Talbot paid to provide an alibi.' She fixed him with a stare. 'We've been played. We've let Talbot go, partly because of that.'

'We can just go and pick him up from the Stagehall Arms, right?'

'Called some uniform to go there.' She folded her arms. 'Room's been cleaned out.'

'What am I missing here?'

'Win some, you lose some.'

'Andrea, what do you think he was up to?'

'Paid assassin. Hitman. Whatever it was you called him. He was that.'

'Talbot?'

'Aye. They paid *him* to bump off Napier. Not Baseball. Him. Chunk. Talbot.' She slapped a hand to her forehead. 'I feel so stupid.'

'We'll find him, Andrea.'

'Sure about that?'

'No, but we'll try. Weirdly, it was a serial killer we were hunting for, just a different sort. Hard to profile a hitman, believe me. Some are stupid and only kill people by hitting them with baseball bats, but others... they vary their MO, like chucking people off wind turbines.'

'Or dropping them on their heads from a moving vehicle. Or burning said vehicle.' She sighed then patted his arm. 'I'll see you tomorrow, Rob.'

'See you too.' Marshall watched her trudge towards her car.

He looked back at the disaster zone and hadn't made any inroads. Well, maybe on the bogies. Clear them, and he could call it a night.

'Evening, you.' Arms wrapped around him from behind. Kirsten's perfume.

He twisted around to see her, face pressed hard against his.

Wine on her breath. 'Hey, you.' He kissed her and didn't care who saw. 'Thought you'd be in Edinburgh?'

'No. Just gave Sally her final warning. She's gone to an AA meeting.'

'Wow. And you smell like you haven't.'

She giggled. 'Your sister met me in the bar.'

'Well, that explains your level of obliteration. Is she about?'

'Drove home.'

'She *drove*?'

'I mean. Taxi. Left her car at your mum's.' She kissed him. 'Listen, we were going to have that chat but we never did. You probably want to break up with me because of all the drama. But I've been thinking about it all day. Talked it through with Jen. I realised I maybe need to change.'

'Maybe?'

'Definitely. I need to become a better person.'

'Come on, Kirsten, you're pretty good.'

'I need to be more trusting.'

'Don't be so hard on yourself.' Marshall smiled at her. 'Come on, let's get some food and talk this all through. And when we're done talking, maybe we can go back to that kiss earlier?'

AFTERWORD

Thank you for reading this novel – I even hope you enjoyed it!

Writing this afterword in June is a bit anachronistic, as it's a lovely sunny day outside and my dogs are frolicking on the lawn. It'll be even stranger for you to be reading it at the end of July, I guess!

I've consciously made these books unfold in real time, so I'm glad to be able to document the winters here. I've lived in the Borders for almost six years and they are that brutal, especially for someone like me who's used to coastal Scotland, where the worst you'll get is a stiff wind and freezing rain. But enough about the middle of Summer...

Down here, and living up above the snow line, when the white stuff comes, it lasts for days or weeks. I outlined this at the tail end of winter, and started writing it during the last snow of the year in late March, so it gave me a reminder of what the depths of winter were like!

As I write this, I'm about to start the draft of book four, A SHADOW ON THE DOOR, after which I'll plan out books five, six and seven, to see where the expanding cast of characters go next. This is all down to you lot reading the first two – plus FALSE START – so a huge thank you for that.

As ever, a huge thank you to James Mackay for all the work on the idea and during the early stages of the draft, then to John Rickards for the copy edit and Mary Bate for the proof. And to Angus King for narrating the audiobook.

And a final note that, TOUCH WOOD, my heart difficulties of the last few years are now a thing of the past as I had my ablation procedure last week, with a surprisingly short recovery time. My heart is fine and healthy, but the nerves near it were damaged and could send false signals. Anyway, a procedure done by the wonderful NHS staff at the Edinburgh Royal Infirmary was a success and I'm feeling great – a few more doses of my beta blockers and then I'll be on the path to becoming drug free.

Thanks again and I hope you enjoy book four when it comes.

Cheers,

Ed

MARSHALL WILL RETURN IN

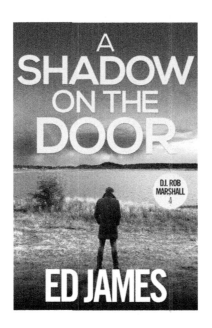

A Shadow on the Door
31st October 2023

Printed in Great Britain
by Amazon

57762204R00263